TWISTED OBSESSION

S. MASSERY

Edited by Studio ENP

Proofread by Paige Sayer Proofreading

Cover design by TRC Designs

INTRODUCTION

Hello dear reader!

Twisted Obsession is a dark romance.

Please be aware if you have triggers that are common to dark romance, this story checks quite a few of those boxes! (Including: dubious and non-consent, somnophilia, manipulation, and degradation.)

Jacob wanted me to warn you that he has one goal in mind: to keep Melody Cameron.

I recommend reading Jacob and Melody's prequel story first, which you can find here: http://bit.ly/twistedobsessionprequel

Thank you and happy reading!

xoxo,
    Sara

JACOB

I stare across the ice at one of our opposing players and pretend to scratch my nose. With my middle finger.

Knox Whiteshaw, fellow rookie and my best friend, grins back. He shakes his head and turns back to his warm-up. I follow suit, fighting the small smile on my lips.

Playing professional hockey against my friends never gets old. It would be better if he and I were on the same team, but I can't resist the opportunity to check him into the boards whenever fucking possible... and then laughing about it over drinks later.

Best friend or not, when the puck hits the ice, it's game on.

This is my second year in the NHL. I signed on with the Colorado Titans right out of college, much to my father's disappointment. But he can't stay upset forever. It's one of those things he'll just have to get over.

We're in round one of the Stanley Cup playoffs, and the energy in the building is palpable.

It's not directed at us, though. We're the visitors. The enemies. Amongst the sea of New York Guardians fans, dressed in black and gold, there are a few pops of blue and white. A good portion of fans traveled to see us in the sold-out arena.

The Guardians won two nights ago. In overtime, no less, the puck slipped into the net by Knox Whiteshaw three minutes into the fourth period.

Fucker.

Our friends are in attendance tonight. Knox scored them seats for the second game of the series, although I'm not sure where he put them. Another look in Knox's direction has him waving furiously at me, then pointing toward the glass next to the penalty boxes. I wave him off and skate in that direction, ignoring the call from my team captain.

He can piss off.

I stop short of the boards and smirk at my friends. They're on NHL teams that didn't make the playoffs— tough shit for them. It still warms my cold, dead heart that they came to watch us.

"You good?" one asks through the glass.

I nod and scan the rows of seats above them.

My gaze trips over someone, and I do a double take. I grip my stick harder, not sure if I'm seeing things right.

The woman sits there like she's never been to a fucking hockey game. She's utterly familiar and heartbreakingly different all at once. Blonde hair, unlike her normal light-brown shade I knew before. Dark-rimmed glasses. Her nails are painted black, and she uses a manicured finger to push the frames up her nose. Her lipstick is soft pink, not red like in my memories. A white sweatshirt with the Titans logo hugs her chest, the dark-blue capital T backed by mint-green waves in the center of her chest.

Melody Cameron.

An apparition right out of my dreams—and then my nightmares.

Fuck.

All at once, I know I'm going to play like shit tonight. My focus shatters, and memories come flooding back. The weeks of tortured, *twisted* obsession. The years of anger and confusion that followed.

She wasn't mine—but I wanted her in the worst way.

"Hey." Knox elbows me.

We're all staring up at her. My friends, my opponent. Me. She's oblivious, her gaze focused across the arena at some distant spot. I want to wave my arms and draw attention to myself. I want to climb over the fucking glass to get to her, to shake her and ask her where she went. And why. Even though that question has long since held any meaning. It's just the where that keeps me up at night.

I thought I had found her a year ago, but it was a dead end. In the face of that, this is a slap in the face.

"Oh, fuck," Knox mutters.

She's sitting next to a man. He's got on a Titans home jersey, mostly dark blue with stripes of the mint green and white, munching on popcorn without a care in the world. Dark hair with gray at the temples. Older than me, older than *her*.

At least they're rooting for the right team—although I'm perversely upset that she's not in my jersey.

Knox spins me around and shoves me toward my bench. "You better get your head in the game, motherfucker. You're not going to blame your team's loss on this moment."

I shake my head and allow him to push me. He practically guides me right to my team's door. I step through and turn back around, opening and closing my mouth. But I don't know what I'm going to say, because I'm a mess of emotions.

Anger.

Loathing.

Confusion.

Hurt.

And underneath it all, the worst fucking feeling in the world: *hope*.

1

MELODY

"A player is staring at you."

I jerk out of my daydream and glance at Thomas. He's been steadily working through his popcorn for the last fifteen minutes while I fidget. With my water, with my brand-new glasses. I don't like how they sit on my nose.

I follow his gesture across the rink, where a player seems to be *glaring* in our direction. Not staring, as Thomas put it. His gaze on my face is hot enough to burn. And indeed, a slow flush creeps up my neck. It's hot, and I try to battle down the urge to press my knuckles to my heated cheeks.

"Why is he looking at us?" I ask.

"I don't know," Thomas replies.

Thomas, never Tom. He's my cousin on my dad's side and ten years my senior, which puts him at forty-four years old. On his other side are two of his colleagues. He's a doctor, with doctor friends. He's got a wife at home.

I came with him to New York City because... well, he

said I used to live here. I went to school here. That, and his wife had enough on her plate without babysitting me while he ran off to a conference. He thought walking through the city, going past my old apartment and college, might help.

Except a miscommunication kept us from looking at where I used to live, and the college campus felt sterile.

"Maybe I should talk to him. After the game. He's looking right at us. Me." I pause. "Do people do that? Talk to the players?"

He shrugs, glancing at me. "I don't know, Mel. He doesn't seem particularly happy. It might not be a good idea."

I contemplate that. He's still staring. The game hasn't started yet. There are players warming up on the ice, although most are heading off. He's standing just inside the doorway that leads back to wherever they go.

"Strong emotion is good, isn't it? Maybe it'll provoke my own, uh, strong response."

The doctor on his other side snorts. "Let us know how that goes, darling."

My body flashes cold all at once, like I've been dunked in ice. My water bottle slips out of my hand, hitting the floor and rolling away.

"Mel?"

I rub my arms. They're covered in goosebumps. But Thomas is watching me like he has no idea what's wrong, and I can't really say I know any more than him. His brows are raised, his expression bewildered.

"Sorry, I, uh... I don't know."

He makes a noise in the back of his throat. Not quite believing me.

I don't believe me.

Some things make me break out into a cold sweat, and I

can't pinpoint it. I run through what my cousin's colleague said. *Let us know how that goes.* No, there's no soul-shifting terror there. *Darling.* I shudder, bile rising up my throat.

What's wrong with that word?

Who called me that to make me hate it so much?

My throat is suddenly dry and scratchy.

I try to spot my fallen water bottle, but it seems long gone. I rise, patting the front pocket of my jeans to make sure my slim wallet is still in place.

"Anyone need a refill?"

My offer is half-hearted, and the three men shake their heads. I hurry up the aisle and into the wide hallway at the top of the section. I commit the number to memory, then laugh. My memory is the least reliable thing about me these days.

What I should do is take a picture of it. I've been taking pictures of everything in an effort to burn the images into my mind. Sometimes things go like sand through a sieve. Thomas seems to be getting more concerned by the week at the things I forget. He's mentioned taking me back to the doctor, although he hasn't acted on that yet.

I get a water and lean against the wall, taking slow, deep breaths like the therapist recommended.

Three months ago, I woke up in a New York hospital with my memory wiped clean. I had seventeen stitches in my head. Fortunately, they didn't shave my hair off. There were other injuries related to the incident. But my amnesia was—and *is*—the most pressing.

The doctor said I was lucky I retained my functions. Remembering how to eat, how to walk. All okay. Even though sometimes, I trip over my words. Like my tongue is too big for my mouth. Or I just forget words entirely.

That's getting better. It's almost nonexistent anymore.

Besides my head, I had a horizontal cut across my throat. A broken forearm and dislocated shoulder. Bruises in the shape of handprints on my upper arms. Two cracked ribs. I overheard doctors speculating about my injuries. Like I was hit by a car, then someone tried to finish the job.

Someone wanted me dead... and they failed.

An investigator was brought in, but I had nothing to offer. I still have nothing to offer.

They managed to find a relative who would return their phone call. The social worker vetted him, and a month after I woke up there, I was released into Thomas's care.

What a strange thing, to go with someone I didn't recognize. But apparently, we weren't close pre-amnesia. We couldn't have been because he has little to offer about my past. Even about my parents, he's been tight-lipped.

Taking me to New York City has been the closest thing to touching something that should be familiar. Because otherwise, I've been out of my depth and waiting for my memories to come back, but so far? Nothing.

I can't go back to my seat. I drain half of my water and wipe my mouth, forgetting the lipstick. It was a gift from Thomas's wife, Natalie. The pink smears across the back of my hand. I swear under my breath and set off down the hall, searching for napkins or a bathroom.

"Melody."

I stop and turn around.

A boy stands in the hallway, wearing a white-and-blue jersey like Thomas's. His hands are stuck in his pockets, his stance relaxed. I don't know why I automatically take a step back.

"Melody Cameron," he repeats.

That's my name. I've repeated it to myself a thousand times since I woke up.

I frown. "Do I know you?"

He pauses. Considers me.

Do I know him?

My heart picks up speed. He's younger than me by at least a decade, so we wouldn't have been at school together. College, high school—none of that. Maybe through work?

"Jacob wanted me to bring you down." He clears his throat. "To, uh, talk to you."

"Is he the hockey player?"

The guy's brows furrow. "Yeah..."

I was just saying to Thomas that I wanted to talk to him. *Jacob*. If he sent this guy to find me, he clearly knows me—so what better time to find some damn answers? Maybe he can tell me more than my illustrious cousin.

"Okay." I gesture around me. "Lead the way."

He doesn't tell me his name, but I turn over Jacob's in my mind. Like a key for a puzzle I'm desperate to solve... but he doesn't fit either. I cast one look over my shoulder for the section, but it's already fluttered out of my mind. I'll have to tuck my tail between my legs and text Thomas later, asking him where we sat. To remind me of something I should've held on to.

And his opinion of me will lower, *again*.

Maybe this guy knows where I was sitting, and he'll spare me the embarrassment.

"Here." He opens a door to a stairwell.

We go down a flight, and my apprehension rises. We come out on the bottom level, now even with the rink. I'm imagining—because I can't see it from here. We're surrounded by concrete walls and equipment.

I follow him until we get to another door, and he pulls out his phone. Shoots off a text, then steps away.

"What's your name?" I pick at my nails. I insisted on painting them, but it was a mistake. I keep running my other nail under the chipped edges, flaking off more and more.

"Miles Whiteshaw."

I nod. "Nice to meet you."

He tilts his head.

"Or, uh, nice to see you again," I cover. I shove my glasses up my nose.

A door behind me bangs open. I spin around just in time to see a hulking hockey player—*the glaring one from earlier* —storming into my space. His helmet is gone, although he's still in his outfit. The jersey and pads that make him seem bigger, his skates that add inches to his height. No gloves, though. Tattoos peek out from the edges of his long sleeves at his wrists.

I backpedal, not that it matters much. He keeps coming until I'm up against the wall.

"I knew it was you," he breathes. Dark hair that's long on top and cut short on the sides, peculiar blue eyes. There's gold in the center of his irises, although it's practically eradicated as his pupils dilate. Full lips. Square jaw. Cheekbones that could cut glass.

He's handsome. Startlingly so.

I expected hockey players, from what I had read, to have missing teeth and crooked noses. While his nose is straight, I can't see his teeth. So maybe he has lost some along the way, and I'll only find out when he opens his mouth again.

"D-do I know you?" It comes out soft and low, and totally unlike whatever version of me I thought I'd been building.

He laughs in my face.

"No, really." I put my hand on his chest.

Mistake. My heart skips a beat, then keeps up that furious pounding. It might break my ribs again trying to flee my chest. I wanted to create some distance between us, but I'm not making any headway.

His strange eyes flick down to my hand, then back up to my face.

"Who are you?" I repeat. "Your friend didn't say how he knew me either."

"Jacob—" That friend steps forward. "Something's not right."

No, it's not. It hasn't been right for a while.

"Who am I, Melody?" He leans in, until we're nose to nose. "Who am I?"

I shake my head. He seems desperate with the need for me to answer, but I don't have one to give him. I was nothing. And then I was *Jane Doe* until someone gave me my name back. And I still feel like that shell of a person with a generic, dead woman's name, because—

"I don't know," I whisper.

I've never seen someone be so fucking devastated by three little words. Besides my cousin, there was no one else to break the news to about my amnesia. No one showed up at the hospital for me for the first three weeks.

It was a miracle they managed to track down Thomas.

I had no identification. No name for the first week of this new life.

Imagine that? Imagine being nameless? Until they got a hit on my prints from a background check. Then, I had a name and a face and an old, out-of-date address in Brooklyn. That apartment was long-since rented out, as Thomas and I found out this weekend.

I had moved on and not left a forwarding address, leaving more questions instead of answers.

"I was in an accident," I say carefully, straightening my sweatshirt. "I have retrograde amnesia. So, no, I don't know you. Or him. I didn't even know my name when I woke up."

Jacob jerks backward. He scans me from head to toe, frowning deeper.

"You don't remember..." He shakes his head and turns around, scrubbing his hand down his face. "*Fuck.* Who are you here with? Where—"

I step back and bump into the wall. "Do you have any answers for me?"

The door bangs open, and a shorter man storms out. "Rhodes!" he barks. "Get your *ass* in here right this minute, or you're benched."

Rhodes.

Jacob Rhodes.

I commit that to memory and hope it sticks.

"I'll take her back," his friend says quietly. He holds out a hand to me.

Jacob Rhodes is stiff. He watches me in a way that's unnerving, and my mind is too jumbled to make sense of any of it. He's practically vibrating.

I slip around him and hurry to the friend. He puts his hand on the small of my back, urging me faster. Down the series of halls, back to the stairs. Up we go, to the right section. All the way down to my row, where Thomas awaits.

"Thanks." I grasp for his name in my head, smiling when I finally latch onto it. "Miles, right?"

He nods once.

"Thank you, Miles."

The younger guy shrugs. "You might not be thanking me just yet."

Well, it's a lead. *Jacob Rhodes* is a lead.

He knew me. Clear as day.

I just need to figure out how. And why he seemed so broken up about me not remembering him.

2

JACOB

Retrograde amnesia. It's so crazy, I think I believe it. She didn't react the way the Melody I knew would've. She wasn't scared or happy or shocked. She was just curious. She went with Miles in search of answers. But I don't think she expected me.

Maybe this can work to my advantage.

We fly home right after the game. The mood is somber on the plane, and as soon as it lands, we're all climbing into our own cars and driving away. Some of them have girls to sink into when they get home, but I have silence. And beer.

I park in the garage under my high-rise condo, shouldering my bags and making my way to the elevator. I've got a perfect view of downtown Denver from my living room and bedroom. I keep the lights off, the illumination from the city enough to guide my path. I drop my bags, shower, then fall into bed.

Dead fucking tired.

We have tomorrow and the next day off, then a morning practice before game three, which we play at home. We're tied 1-1 with the New York Guardians, which means we really need to stop fucking around and dragging this round out longer than it needs to be. I've got a laundry list of things I need to do before Wednesday. The prospect of sleep doesn't stop me from pulling my phone out and searching her name for the hundredth time.

Nothing. Or, rather, too many worthless results. The real Melody Cameron is buried under articles of other women who share her name.

I shouldn't...

But I could call in a favor. Now that I know she's alive, somewhere out there, with *someone*. Maybe they can find her when I can't.

I'm dialing before I can stop myself.

"A bit late for a phone call, Jacob. Turning into a night owl?"

More like an insomniac. "I need your help."

The woman on the other end of the line chuckles. "Oh, really? Well, I hear you might have some space in your suite for the next playoff game."

"How many tickets do you need, Vicky? Say the word and they're yours."

"Ooh, someone is desperate. My husband and I, if you can spare two. Now, what is this favor? Nothing illegal? Your father taught you better than that."

I close my eyes. If only they knew how much illegal shit I've got into over the years... I'd be thrown in jail faster than I could snap my fingers.

Vicky has worked night shifts in the emergency dispatch center as long as I can remember. She was also my babysitter on the weekends and a long-time family friend. If I can't trust her to help me find Melody, I can't trust anyone. Besides my friends—they're always the exception to the rule.

"I need help finding a woman."

She hums. "So, bordering on illegal. At the very least, a little invasive. I can't just give you—"

"She has amnesia, Vicky. Please."

"Jacob."

Ugh. *Pity*.

I pull my phone away from my ear and twist my lips. I know what she's going to say, but I don't want to hear it. I never do.

"Melody Cameron," I say.

I rattle off her birthday—September 3rd—and where I last saw her. At the game. She was wearing a Titans sweatshirt, but it didn't make sense.

She doesn't even like hockey.

Did she find that out when she watched the game? Did she wince at every hit?

Vicky sighs. "There's nothing in the system. But it's not a federal database, I just have access to county records."

And she's in a precinct of lower Manhattan. A far cry from Denver, Colorado.

"Okay, thanks for checking. I'll send over those tickets in the morning."

"Thanks, honey. Sleep well." She disconnects.

I toss my phone back on the nightstand and jump out of bed. Exhaustion is still lingering, pressing down on me, but my adrenaline is pumping.

I just need to find her.

But when I replay our short conversation, something else stands out. She has questions. She was so curious for me to tell her anything at all, she followed a stranger away from the public. I've walked those halls to get down to the locker room—it's not particularly enticing or designed with female safety in mind. Anything could've happened to her.

How vulnerable is she like this?

I take the elevator down to the fitness room and hop on the treadmill. My anger is surging again, quickening my stride until I'm sprinting flat-out.

She knows how to find me.

I just have to hope she will.

3

MELODY

The Titans sweatshirt draped over the chair in the corner of the room has taunted me for two days. We flew back from NYC on Monday night. With the conference over, and all hope of my old stomping grounds triggering a memory gone, there was nothing else to do.

I have a borrowed laptop, a hand-me-down from Natalie, and a cell phone that I can never remember to charge.

But one thing I have held on to is Jacob Rhodes. I just haven't worked up the nerve to do an internet search for his name, because I'm afraid of what I might find.

My head aches, the pressure building behind my left eye. I finally open the laptop and type his name into the search bar. Quickly, before I can lose my nerve, I hit *enter*.

Dozens of search results pop up immediately.

No, hundreds.

His face is front and center, a row of pictures of him in action on the ice, his headshot, him in a suit at a press conference. I lean in and examine him closer, without fear of him staring back at me.

I wait for the slightest tingle of some familiarity.

He knows me and I don't know how. I've got that desperate fluttering in my chest dragging me forward. I *need* to know what he does.

It's why I end up clicking on the Colorado Titans schedule, my eyes going wide when today's date jumps out at me.

They have a home game tonight. But not just any home. *Denver*. It's why Thomas is a fan, I guess. Natalie grew up just outside the city. They met in a grocery store, of all places, and fell in love. I was fed that story in bite-sized pieces over dinner one night, like I might not comprehend it.

I mean, maybe I don't. The idea of love is as foreign as my name was at first. There was no settling in my bones that assured me I could recognize it if I felt it or heard it.

No, the word, the concept—it's all cold.

My whole life seems to be on ice. Did I have life goals? Did I have... ideas? Hopes and dreams? Thomas doesn't have answers.

But maybe Jacob Rhodes will.

I get changed in a hurry, slipping my feet into my shoes and heading for the door. My room is a converted office on the first floor, and I call out to Natalie and Thomas that I'm going out for a little while.

Neither stop me, although Thomas looks at me weirdly, and Natalie asks that I call her if I forget their address. Like she didn't program the house into my maps and their contact information as soon as I arrived.

I close the door gently behind me and head toward the train station.

The road to get a new driver's license has been painfully slow. We're waiting on my birth certificate to come in, and a new social security card. New York issued me a temporary state ID, since that's where my last known residence was.

The state ID apparently isn't enough to unlock my bank accounts, however.

The sooner I do that, the sooner I can start to move on. And move *out*.

Thomas and Natalie will eventually ask me to find my own apartment. I've been looking already, the weight of being a burden heavy in the back of my mind. But with an apartment, and rent, must come a job. Some sort of income.

Another mystery.

I can barely work the hand-me-down laptop Natalie gave me, and I don't know what I was doing for work pre-accident. Or, incident. Since I don't think whoever did this to me did it *accidentally*.

Once I'm on the train, I insert my earbuds and choose the next music station on my list. It's some sort of loud, semi-screaming music that hurts my eardrums no matter how low I turn the volume.

So... not a fan of whatever the hell this is.

Maybe it's just the song.

I keep it on and wince through the next six songs. I get off the train and walk up the steps near the arena, and I cross out that station from the list on my phone. Not a winner. So far, I've enjoyed the country station, the pop punk one, and some of the Top 40 music. The last one is a hit or miss.

Anyway.

I don't have a ticket to the game, and I don't plan on buying one. There's a bar along the main drag in front of the arena, and I take a seat on an open barstool to wait it out.

And lucky me, it's on multiple televisions around the room. It's filled with fans of both teams, all intensely watching the skaters onscreen. I order a wine—I seem to like some, but I'm trying to narrow that down, too—and set my phone in front of me.

Third period. From my experience at the game the other night, there are only three periods. The Titans are up by two, and there's five minutes left on the clock.

I don't know anything else, but I watch like I care. Really, I just scan the players trying to find Jacob Rhodes. He can usually be found near the goalie. He's number fifteen. There are a few people wearing his number in here, his name written across their backs.

"Need anything else?" the bartender asks.

I snap my focus to her. "Do you know where the Titans hang out after games?"

She gives me a weird look. "Here sometimes. Depends on the night, but we usually get at least a few players in."

I nod to myself and take a sip of the wine. It's a room temperature red and seems to sink claws into my tongue. I can't say I like it, and first impressions seem important. But, as with everything, I try it again.

By the time the game has ended, with the Titans pulling ahead in this series 2-1, I've managed half the glass. Another quarter is gone when some players arrive.

I spin on my stool, eyeing them. They're in street clothes, but it seems like everyone knows who they are anyway. A cheer goes up around the room, and I join in on the clapping.

Jacob comes in next, and his energy is palpable from here.

Not particularly happy, but... intense. He always seems intense. On the ice, glaring down at me... I swallow and fidget at that particular memory.

He glances around the room, and it seems like it only takes him a handful of seconds to spot me. My breath catches, but I square my shoulders instead of shrinking away. I came here for *answers*, damn it. I'm a grown-ass woman intimidated by a twenty-something-year-old.

Unacceptable.

Not for the first time, I wonder what sort of person I was before. Was shrinking something I did regularly? Is it genetics?

Never mind the nature versus nurture debate rolling through my head when I'm trying to sleep at night. If nurture plays such a vital role, we may as well acknowledge that I'm running on half a tank of gas. That is: all nature, no nurture.

Jacob Rhodes makes his way through the bar, stopping to chat with various people who catch his arm—but never his complete attention. All that intensity is burning through me, and it scares me. From this distance.

I've drained my wine by the time he steps up to the bar, taking the empty seat at my side. It wasn't empty a moment ago, but whoever sat there evacuated it. Probably for him, because of who he is.

The bartender is back over in a heartbeat.

"A margarita for my friend, no salt, and a beer for me."

His deep voice does something strange to me.

I frown at the wine I drank, but it's whisked away and replaced with a margarita in no time at all. I haven't made it to mixed drinks yet. They kind of scared me with how many options I have. Vodka, tequila, gin—and those are just the light-colored liquors. What if I was a dark-liquor person? If

I enjoyed a spiced rum or whiskey, or if my tastes ran into the more expensive scotches? What if I only liked my whiskey on ice and ruled it out because I ordered wrong? Or if the bartender made it poorly?

"Tequila, triple sec, and lime." His gaze is on the side of my face. "They make good ones here. Not so much at the place across the street, so you picked a decent bar."

That answers one of my worries.

I take a sip. The flavor bursts across my tongue, and I almost groan. It's so much freaking better than any of the wines I've tried.

"It's delicious," I murmur, setting it down and pushing it away. "Thank you."

He lifts his beer bottle to his mouth. "But you don't want it?"

"I was drinking wine."

"You don't like red."

I sit up straighter. "Oh?"

This is more information than I managed to get out of Thomas. That's what happens when you become estranged from your family... or maybe he just never cared to know me in the ways that counted.

I won't deny my gratitude toward Thomas for stepping up. But it's been a frustrating few months.

But *Jacob Rhodes* knows my drink preference.

"White wine at home, pinot grigio usually. You like the sweet stuff, and never red. Mixed drinks when you're out. Being social." His gaze roves over my face. "You're missing the red lipstick, though. That was your signature look."

"Red lipstick," I repeat, soaking up this knowledge.

I don't even realize I've swiveled to give him my full attention until his knees press on either side of my thighs. His legs bracket mine, and he props his elbow on the bar.

"Yeah. Messy hair, red lipstick. The glasses are different."

I shrug. "I didn't have them on me when I was..." *Found.* Can't quite say that out loud.

"Who were you to me?" I ask instead.

It's funny. I analyzed his photo. Zoomed in and stared until I thought I had my fill. But now that he's in front of me again, I can't stop looking. Maybe it's because he's handsome, in a roguish, dangerous kind of way. Or just that he's looking back at me with just as much... curiosity?

He's silent for a moment. He might be debating how much to tell me. I want to reach out and shake him, to demand he answer me, but I don't have that much control. My position is tenuous, at best. He could walk out the door and refuse to tell me anything else. He could disappear.

And then where would I be?

"I was just a friend," he eventually says.

He grabs my phone from the bar and swipes it open, frowning at my lack of a password. Or, well, I don't know. I guess I'm assuming that's what makes him frown. It could be my lock screen—a picture of Thomas's neighbor's dog— or the generic flowers on my home screen.

He messes with it, then hands it back.

"It's late," he says. "Are you staying out?"

I shake my head. "Thomas will probably be worried if I don't come home at a reasonable time."

"You've got my number now. Let me know if you have any more questions."

I suck my lower lip between my teeth. I have a *million* questions, and not a single one comes to the forefront of my mind.

He nods to himself and rises, tossing some money on

the bar. "Put her drinks on my bill," he calls to the bartender. "See you around, Melody."

I mull over what he's said, and I take another sip of the margarita. My last sip, otherwise I won't be sober enough to get home. Well. I don't know what sort of lightweight I am, although I kind of assume that I am one. The wine has made my head a little fuzzy, and the tequila threatens to tip me into another category.

Riding the subway at night, drunk, seems a bit too radical. Especially for me.

Margaritas are *good*. Maybe he's right about the wine and the lipstick, too.

Which begs the question even more—who was he to me?

4
JACOB

I t's been two days since I saw her. But she found my number and made the first move... which is what I had hoped for her to do after dangling the carrot of answers in front of her face.

MELODY

I was wondering if you were around for more questions?

I'm heading to practice in about an hour, but go ahead

You mentioned lipstick... what shade of red?

I groan. Is she trying to kill me?

MELODY

[IMAGE]

She's at a drugstore from the look of it, standing in front of a million shades of lipstick. I wrinkle my nose. She wouldn't wear something from a drugstore. Not that there's anything wrong with it, but of the bits and pieces of Melody's life I picked up and held close, I learned that she had expensive makeup taste. The kind that was vegan and not tested on animals and felt like silk on the skin.

> None of those.

MELODY

> There are so many choices

> Well, none of them are right.

> Thanks, Captain Helpful. I'm gonna buy a handful and see if it helps.

> With the amnesia?

Or with my hard-on? Because my dick is thickening just picturing her pouting lips in different shades of red.

MELODY

> Where did we meet?

I need to burn off this energy in a productive way. Otherwise, I'll be no better off than I was two and a half years ago. The first time we met opened up something inside me. It cracked me wide open and exposed me to a whole new level of fucked up.

Melody Cameron. I still remember the first time I saw her. And then the first time I talked to her, and the first time I fucked her. *Like it was yesterday.* The pain is there, too. It's been rotting for two years.

I toss my phone on the counter and consider my next move. Like how much information I want to give her all at once, how I can keep her coming to me. Because I like that. I like her initiating our conversations. I like her needing me.

Once upon a time, she wanted *nothing* to do with me.

There's another debate, too. I can tell her the truth or I can fuck with her. Take advantage of her weakness and bind her to me as hard as I can.

If she ever remembers the truth, by then it'll be too late.

My jaw is set, and I latch on to that.

MELODY

Please, Jacob. Give me something.

Come to the game tonight. Meet me after.

I wish I could see her face or hear her reaction. It's the response from her body that I've always craved. My attraction to her mind came next.

But now her mind is gone.

I roll my shoulders back and crack my neck. For the first time in what feels like two years of anger and confusion, I let a real smile curl my lips.

MELODY

Okay. Tell me where to go.

My energy is creeping higher—so much so that I stuff my shirt into my bag and lace my sneakers tight. I run all the way to the arena, and it doesn't put a dent in the feeling in my chest. And it doesn't distract me from replaying memories with Melody.

Now isn't the time to get distracted.

It's time to scheme.

I need to have an answer when she asks me how we met, where she knows me from. My lungs burning, I walk through the locker room doors. Our gear is all laid out in our lockers, our names printed above them. It's quieter than usual.

What I need is to come up with a plan, then clear my head and focus on the game. A win tonight will put us one step closer to winning the series and moving on to the next round.

I lace into my skates and grab my stick. The way to the rink is silent, and I step out onto the perfectly smooth ice with little fanfare. Everything is all lit up in preparation. I catch sight of people in the doorways behind the upper sections. Workers preparing for the crowd that will once again be swarming the arena.

"Hey." Knox skates toward me. He's wearing a backward cap pressing his hair down, a long-sleeve shirt and jeans. A puck floats out ahead of him. "Getting in some last-minute practice?"

I scoff and stop the puck with my skate. "We had morning practice already."

He nods. "Us, too. So... You want to talk about it?"

It. *Her.*

"Steele said Miles said she didn't remember." He braces his hands on top of his stick. "What does that even mean? That she forgot?"

I skate away from him, taking the puck toward the far goal. I pretend to swerve around oncoming opponents and aim for the top-left corner. The puck sails in with a satisfying whoosh.

"Impressive," Knox deadpans. "Focus."

"I'm focused on how you're getting your information third-hand." I raise my eyebrow. "Miles still not talking to you?"

"Not when he can help it." He shrugs. "I'm hoping a Stanley Cup ring will make him forgive me."

Forgive him for nearly killing the love of his brother's life?

I snort.

Knox rolls his eyes. "For real. What's going on?"

"She has retrograde amnesia." I collect the puck and pass it back to him. "I don't fucking know, man. But she didn't recognize me in the slightest."

He ponders that, handling the puck in front of him before taking a sudden slap shot at the wall. It rebounds with a crack of noise, coming back to him.

"Well, I guess you get a do-over. Don't fuck it up this time."

I sigh.

"That's the plan." That, and a whole lot worse.

———

Game four starts in an hour and a half.

Sometimes the playoffs seem to go by slowly. Other times, the games are a blur. Blink and you miss it.

Because we have an extra two days off before game five, Knox is sticking around for another night. It throws a slight wrench in my plan with Melody, but I've also missed my best friend. And when's the next time I'm going to get to knock his ass out of the Stanley Cup playoffs?

I stand outside the arena, my cap pulled low. It's kind of hard to go anywhere in this city without being recognized by at least one person, especially in playoff season. But I've stripped all my Titans apparel, and I stick close to the wall. I scan the crowds for Melody, my heart beating erratically.

She comes up the steps alone, the same Titans sweatshirt masking her curves. My gaze travels down her black leggings, to the black boots with a slight heel, then back up. She has a cross-body bag slung diagonally across her chest.

No lipstick.

I hide my frown and stride forward, intercepting her path.

She lets out a little gasp when I catch her arm. I lead her away from the throng of people quickly, and she doesn't protest too loudly.

I've got her up against the wall again.

She leans back to meet my gaze. "I didn't think I'd see you before the game."

I'm accruing a nasty fine for every minute I'm late, but it's fucking worth it.

I press a ticket into her hand. In reality, I could've left it for her at will-call. That's what I'd do for my family, if they didn't already have tickets for the suite.

Thinking about them and her in the same space... *No.* They like to talk, and surely one of them would bring up Crown Point. What if that triggers a memory?

Do I want that?

I hold up my other gift: my jersey. People spend a lot of money to get their hands on these, and she's getting one for free. I gesture for her to remove her bag, which she does carefully. I take it and pull one of her hands through the sleeve, then the other.

She doesn't resist until I've got her head through the last hole, managing to avoid knocking her glasses off her face. I get the hood of her sweatshirt through it, too, so it sits nicely. Her breasts are nearly irresistible. To the point where I need to physically take a step back just to control myself.

Control has never been my problem—but right now, I'm being tested.

This isn't the first time she's worn my clothes. *And it won't be the last.*

"Thank you." Her fingers brush mine. "I don't really understand it, but thank you."

"You're welcome." I jerk my chin toward the door. "Stay in your seat after the game, okay?"

"Yeah."

I turn away, but she reaches out and grabs my arm. I stare at it for a second, until her fingers slowly loosen and withdraw. Her cheeks flush, and she shoves her glasses up her nose.

"I don't know anything about hockey," she confesses. "I don't—"

"You don't have to. Just keep your eyes on me." I wink.

As soon as I'm around the corner, I press my back to the wall and close my eyes. I breathe deeply, trying to rein in the furious beat of my heart. Adrenaline is pounding through me, worse now that the game is so close. I'm going to have to rush to get ready, and even then, Coach will have my ass. But she's here. She came alone.

That has to soothe me. It has to be enough to get me through this game.

She's wearing my jersey.

And if that isn't the biggest 'fuck you' to her husband, wherever he may be, I don't know what is.

5
MELODY

I'm not sure I like hockey.

I don't understand the rules. I don't understand the violence.

Every time Jacob gets slammed into the glass, or does it to someone else, I flinch. I start watching the game with my hands hovering in front of my face, ready to snap my fingers closed when the players come racing down the rink. Jacob spits blood onto the cut-up ice, and nausea rolls through me.

A horn bellows through the arena, and I look up at the big squared-off screen hovering over the center line. The clock has run down, ending the game. 2-1 in favor of the New York Guardians.

Thank God that's over.

The people around me are quiet. A guy four rows back has been yelling jeers at the Guardians for most of the game, although even he eventually stopped as the clock ticked down. I don't know what it means, their loss. All I know is that they're in the playoffs. Thomas tried to explain it to me.

It's just another forgotten thing.

My hands are shaking. It seems worse than the other game I went to, because this time I watched Jacob act like a violent beast. Something in me doesn't like that. Doesn't want anything to do with the manic glee I saw in his eyes as he side-checked another player, or when he smiled with bloodstained teeth. There was no missing that.

I follow the crowd up the steps and down the hallway, sort of a mindless shuffle all the way to the exit. It isn't until I've made it to the end of the street that I recall Jacob telling me to stay in my seat.

This behavior seems so bold for me. For two months, I've lived with Thomas and Natalie and tried to piece my mind back together. After nothing, of course I latched on to something crazy.

But maybe Jacob Rhodes is just that—*crazy*. Maybe he's taking advantage of someone he only knew for a brief span of time, preying on my lack of memory?

I touch the scar on my throat. It's low enough to go unnoticed by most, and Thomas's wife bought me creams and ointments to rub into it in an effort to get it to fade. I do it, although I'm not ashamed of the scar. It's proof that someone wanted me dead.

> Sorry, I don't think hockey is for me.

I've come a long way since I woke up in that hospital bed. Tried a thousand new things, even if nine hundred of them didn't stick. I don't think I ever watched Jacob play hockey. Before, I mean. It doesn't feel familiar, like when I finally found the perfect combination of cream and sugar in my coffee.

JACOB

It never was.

Something deep in my chest flutters.

Then why make me go?

JACOB

Because I wanted you to.

Where are you?

I suck my lower lip between my teeth.

Heading for the subway

JACOB

You didn't wait for me?

I thought I was going to pass out.

His little typing dots emerge, then disappear. I lean against the wall of a building and touch the back of my hand to my cheek. I'm still shaky, the adrenaline overwhelming my system.

Finally, my phone chimes with his response.

JACOB

Well, you shouldn't travel alone. Let me.

I stare at the words. At his... offer?

I'm already halfway there, so...

JACOB

I'm already walking toward you. Stay where you are.

I could ignore it and push off, crossing the street.

My phone goes off again, and I glance down at the new text from my cousin's wife.

NATALIE

We're headed to bed, Mel! You have a key for the front door, right?

Yep. I'll be home soon.

Okay, great. Hope you had fun. Xoxo

A shadow crosses in front of me. Without thinking, I drop my phone and yell. It takes a minute for my eyes and mind to catch up—that it's not a mugger approaching, but Jacob Rhodes.

I swallow and bend to pick up my fallen cell. It landed unscathed, luckily.

He tilts his head. "Scared you?"

"You shouldn't sneak up on a girl like that."

He holds out his hand. "Come on. Let me drive you home."

I tilt my head, staring at the offering. If I turned his hand over, would I find his knuckles scraped and bruised?

"Does this feel familiar?"

I jerk my attention to his face, my breath catching. "Should it?"

His gaze heats my face. Like he's trying to press something into me, but it just hits a barrier in my mind and slides away. Whatever memory he's thinking of, it's lost on me.

"Melody."

"Jacob," I reply.

He smiles. "Come on. Let me drive you home."

With a little exhale, I put my hand in his. It's the first time we've touched, I think. Well, the first time I'm more conscious of it, and the first time I've initiated it. Passing me the tickets was transactional, and at the last game in New York... he thought I was someone else.

Or rather, he thought I was *me*. But now I'm someone else.

A spark travels down my spine.

I allow him to guide me back the way we came, to the parking garage I passed. He still has my hand. I trail after him through the parking garage, down one ramp, and the lights on a flashy sports car flicker at us.

"I assumed you were more of a truck guy."

I don't know why. He just doesn't seem like he has to compensate for something with a high-end, too-fast car. I envision him in a pickup truck. Not tricked out or anything, just kind of plain. Good for getting a job done.

He laughs. "Yeah?"

I shrug.

"Do you like Denver?"

His car has a million colored lights and a whole computer embedded in the dash. The engine comes on with a soft purr, unlike Thomas's behemoth that groans and growls like it's on its last limb. It's just a different level of luxury.

"It's growing on me," I answer.

"I haven't decided about it." He eyes me. "How's the memory thing going?"

"I don't know." I sink into the seat. It's a lot more comfortable than any I've been in before. "I have lists that I'm working through, doctors in New York to check in with. But it's been a lot of nothing."

"What's on the list?"

"Everything."

He nods slowly. "Where am I going, by the way?" He

taps the screen and brings up a GPS system. "Can you type it in here?"

I have to look at Thomas's contact details on my phone to get the house number right. But once that's done, the address pops up and the time to destination appears in the bottom corner of the screen. It's double the time it took me to get here.

"Post-game traffic," Jacob explains. "It's always congested downtown with everyone trying to leave."

Sure enough, we round a corner and stop behind a long line of cars.

"So, the list?" he prompts.

I twist to face him. In the glow of brake lights, his face is illuminated in shades of red. His dark hair is damp and pushed off his face. Or maybe it's sweat. He's got a scrape on his cheekbone from one of the fights.

"Did you get into more fights tonight because of me?"

He shakes his head. "Nah. The Guardians were shit-talking more than usual."

"You lost," I point out.

"We need to win two more games to move on. But so do they."

"Hockey isn't my sport," I mumble.

He smirks at me. "So you said. So, the list. What's on it?"

I shake my head and fish out my phone. "First was coffee. Figuring out if I liked it, or how." I scan my notes on the topic. What felt like a million combinations until I settled on one that felt right.

"How do you take it?"

"I like the mocha drinks if I'm out, but otherwise, cream and two sugars."

He nods along. "Have you tried hot chocolate?"

Something weird goes through me. Like a phantom finger drawing a line down my spine. Goosebumps spring up on the backs of my arms.

"What was that?"

I shake it off. "What?"

He frowns and doesn't reply.

"I haven't had hot chocolate." I rub my arm with my free hand. "Um, after coffee it was food. Obviously that list is a bit exhaustive. There are too many choices. Breakfast, lunch, dinner, snacks, *dessert*. What if I was a vegetarian? Or vegan? What if I exclusively ate something weird, like tofu and peanut butter?"

Jacob snorts. "I'd like to see you try that."

I set my phone on my thigh and cross my arms. "I already did."

"And?"

I crack a smile. "It was disgusting."

I don't know what made me think I might like it. It just popped into my head, and I wondered if it was a memory. So, with an obsessiveness that was definitely unhealthy, I made Natalie drive me to the store to get my items. Preparing it was a nightmare in and of itself, and then slathering the peanut butter on it... Well, let's just say I knew it was a mistake before I even took a bite.

Vile.

"You seem to have a lot of unanswered questions," he says carefully. "Why is that?"

I sigh. "Thomas isn't very helpful."

Jacob stiffens. "And who is Thomas?"

The right answer is on the tip of my tongue—but then I look at Jacob. I mean, I really look. At his clenched jaw and the way he's holding the steering wheel.

"Are you jealous?" Incredulity blooms in my tone.

"No."

Uh-huh.

We get out of the parking garage and head for my cousin's house. I didn't expect Jacob Rhodes to show any sign of jealousy. Actually, I wouldn't have expected him to go out of his way to get me to a game—or see me home safely afterward, either.

"I'm not telling you who he is to me until you answer some questions."

His jaw tics. "Melody."

I gesture. "You need to turn here."

"*Melody.*"

"I don't know you, Jacob Rhodes. You haven't answered any question for me except my supposed drink of choice."

He grunts.

"Why are you driving me home?"

He turns. There are mere moments left in our ride. We pass the station I use to get into the city and count the blocks we pass. One, two, three.

"I wanted to." He glances at me. "Is that a problem?"

"It is if you're jealous *and* withholding information."

He's silent. Because I'm right?

Finally, the car coasts to a stop in front of my cousin's house.

"You're right. I just don't want to overwhelm you." He hits the *unlock* button.

"I need more," I whisper.

When he doesn't answer, I fish my keys from my purse and jump out of the car. I go up the porch steps, unlock the door and lock it behind me without once looking back.

I didn't hear the car drive off, which means Jacob waited. Now, the rev of his engine as he pulls away is clear.

By all accounts, that's gentlemanly. The romance

movies say so. But he just admitted that he's keeping things from me. Things *about* me that could help trigger my memory.

My stomach flips.

In a weird way, I kind of like his jealousy. I like that he thinks of *me*, and any idea he has of me with another man sets him on edge. He's got to be younger than me by a decade, he's gorgeous, and I'm just... *me*. Plain. Too much weight on my frame. Scarred. And unable to remember my life before.

How could I ever compete with the women who throw themselves at hockey players successfully?

I guess I'll just have to wait and see if Jacob Rhodes is true to his word.

6

JACOB

She stokes my anger like no other.

I sit outside the dark house in my truck, contemplating my next move.

After I dropped her off, I went home and returned the shiny sports car. It would've drawn too much attention parked in the residential neighborhood. And like she said, *I'm a truck guy*. It's been my old faithful through college, and even a multi-million-dollar contract with the NHL hasn't changed that.

My phone has been blowing up with messages from Knox, Miles, Steele, and Greyson. My best friends, one of whom is celebrating with raucous abandon, and the others who are along for the ride.

They know Melody is here. They know my focus has been pulled. I warned them as much before the game, because I didn't want to just ghost them. Not like what Melody did to me.

Not for the first time, I try to fill in the gaps of her life. There was a before me, and there was an after me. But now that she's back, there is no before—and there will be no after. I'm not letting her go.

It's why I watched until a bedroom light flickered on and her form moved across the window before I sped home. It's why, even now, I consider ways to embed myself into her. Not just physically, but mentally. Emotionally.

I climb out of the truck and slip between houses. I cling to the shadows until I get to the back door of their garage. It takes little work to jimmy open the lock and crack the door. My phone's flashlight illuminates the space in front of me.

The door into the house is unlocked, and I walk carefully down the hall. I make note of the photos on the wall. They're mostly of a couple that doesn't consist of Melody. The man who was beside her at the game in New York and a woman I don't recognize.

I don't know what to make of it. I assumed the man with Melody was her husband. But these photos make me think differently. I file that away and continue to check the rest of the downstairs, leaving her bedroom for last. My curiosity is too high. I must know if she's sleeping beside *him*. The other woman in the photos could be a fluke.

Perhaps I'll walk in and catch them in the act, and I'll have the pleasure of cutting his balls off.

My hard grip on my phone makes the light tremble.

I switch it off and palm the knob. The door opens silently, swinging inward. I step in, closing it behind me. My eyes adjust to the darkness and the single body in the bed. She's stretched in the center of it, like she's not used to sharing.

The thought pleases me.

I'd give her the center of my bed, too.

I circle the bed until I can see her face. Her hair is fanned out around her head, and she hugs another pillow to her chest. My jersey is slung over the chair, along with the sweatshirt that she wore under it.

Did seeing her in my jersey make me play harder?

Yes.

It didn't matter in the end because my team played like absolute shit tonight. Coach Matthews warned us that we'd be practicing early tomorrow. He probably intends to run all the drills, to practice shooting instead of passing the puck around like a bunch of pussies. To make us sprint until our legs feel like they're going to fall off.

It's well deserved. None of us want to lose on home ice, and we were just embarrassed.

Melody rolls onto her back, and I go still. My attention lasers in on the swells of her breasts, free of any bra or restriction. Her nipples are pebbled under the cotton t-shirt. I step closer and kneel beside the bed.

She doesn't stir when I pull up her t-shirt. Exposing the softness of her stomach, her pale flesh almost glowing in the faint light from the window, and higher still. Until her breasts are bared to me.

My cock is hard. It strains against my pants, but I ignore it in favor of touching her. I would rather torture myself and savor this moment than rush through it.

I reach out and run my finger over her nipple. Her skin puckers, her nipple stiffening. I do it again, flicking it gently, until a low whimper slips from her throat. She made a similar noise the first time I knelt in front of her, hidden behind her desk in her office at Crown Point University, and made her come on my tongue.

Now, I lean forward and take her other nipple in my mouth. I suck and lick and bite until she's writhing in her sleep under me. Until I'm sure there will be a mark left there when she wakes.

"You're mine," I whisper in her ear. "Nothing can change that."

I leave her with her shirt up to her throat. I take a pair of panties from her hamper and tuck them in my pocket. Cotton boy shorts that aren't sexy at all, but I think on her they'd be a wet dream. I make my way back outside and into my truck, where I finally unzip my pants and free my erection.

I pull her panties out and drape them on my thigh, spitting into my hand before I stroke myself. As I do, I keep my eyes across the street, on her window. And I think of all the times before that I sat outside her house in the dark, waiting to enter. For the sight that met me all those years ago. Her naked body, the way she comes.

The way she'll look with her lips wrapped around me, her signature red lipstick smeared across my cock and her cheeks.

It takes no time at all to get to the edge. I slow my movements, drawing out the pain and pleasure. My balls are so tight, I'm going to explode any second. I imagine her reaction when she wakes up, when she sees my handiwork. I use her panties to cover the head of my cock. I groan through my teeth as I come. My dick twitches, pulse after pulse of cum filling the cotton panties.

But it doesn't satiate me.

Instead, it leaves me wanting more.

7

MELODY

I t's still dark when my fingers dip into my pussy. I'm wet and aching, the need built by a dream that slips away the closer I come to consciousness. I rub my swollen clit, my hips shifting. My other hand comes up and cups my breast, pinching my sore nipple.

Waves of heat spread through me.

Why is it sore?

I knead my breast and rub my clit harder, until pleasure washes over me.

It isn't until the trembling has passed that I realize my shirt is already up to my collarbone and my hand had easy access. I sit up and reach for the lamp. It smells a bit like sex in here, the scent of my orgasm clinging to me even as the feeling fades.

The warm light sears my eyes. A few rapid blinks later, and I examine my skin.

My breast.

There are bite marks over my nipple. Reddish marks that skirt the line of bruising.

Hickeys, my mind supplies.

I've never had one before. Not that I know of anyway. I touch my nipple, wincing at the tenderness of it.

Suddenly uneasy, I shift my gaze to the door.

Who would've done this?

I get up, yanking my shirt into place, and lock my door. I haven't felt the need to do so before. Now, it gives me another modicum of safety.

The clock reads four a.m., and my eyes feel like sandpaper. But I can't go back to sleep. I check my window and let out a breath when my fingers graze the latched lock.

Maybe I did it in my sleep. I was dreaming of a man mauling my breast, maybe I did it to myself.

Yeah, that's it.

I won't get answers on that, but I *can* get answers on Jacob Rhodes. I pull out the old laptop and plug the charging cable into it, balancing it on my thighs. The fans on it automatically whir when I crack it open and fire it up, protesting after years of abuse.

I type his name into the search bar again and wait. Eventually, the search page loads...

With millions of hits.

Most are articles about him as a rookie, various news sources covering games and when he signed on to the Titans.

Before that, he was at Crown Point University in Maine. He graduated two years ago.

I search his name and mine together, just for the hell of it, but nothing useful pops up. I've done this before, sitting next to Thomas on his faster computer, watching as he slowly typed in my name. At the time, he was unconcerned by our lack of success.

"There are a lot of Melody Camerons," he pointed out.

I saw it for myself in the results. Nothing about a

Melody Cameron in New York. The closest I get is finding a small write up about a woman found nearly dead in an alley. I assumed it was me. It wasn't comforting.

And it isn't now, when I'm trying to uncover any piece of my past.

My phone has five percent battery left. I set aside the laptop and plug my phone in, too. I lean on my side to go through my messages. I've got a conversation thread with my therapist, with my cousin. Natalie. Jacob.

That's it. It's painfully bare. My contacts are just as bad. I can count them on one hand.

No relatives.

No other friends.

A pang goes through my chest.

If I had friends, are they wondering what happened to me? I downloaded social media apps ages ago, but I couldn't get into them. I didn't have any idea what my email address would be, let alone a password.

I should just make a new profile and go from there.

I sit up straighter, practically vibrating.

There have to be people out there besides my cousin. People who aren't blood related, who *care* where I went. They've got to be out there. They've got to be worried.

Or maybe...

Maybe I'm just a shit person, and I don't have anyone except a cousin who can't tell me anything about myself.

That thought stills my hand. It's not the first time I've thought it, but I doubt it'll be the last.

Am I really so afraid of that?

I close out of the social media app and open my lists. Nearly all the way to the bottom, just above a section I don't want to think about, is *Fears*.

Spiders made the list. I added the word *darling* after the

hockey game in New York, although I still don't understand it. Snakes don't bother me, along with a plethora of other animals. The dark is iffy, not that I've put myself in that situation very much. The walking-alone-outside kind of dark, not just my room before bed.

But now I can add another one, and it rots in my chest. It hurts to breathe deeply.

Confrontation. I'm afraid of action and reaction. Of consequences.

And okay, I'm a little bit afraid of having ruined all previous life-relations.

I've been here for two months. Not a single memory has come back. My therapist in the hospital, toward the end of my stay, shifted talking from memory recovery to moving on with my life. To getting a job—in what? I don't know—and friends. Widening my circle.

I should move the fears section farther up the list, because it's definitely the most prominent right now.

I drop my phone facedown beside me and flop back.

There's no way I'm going back to sleep. I stare at the ceiling in a weird in-between state until the sun rises and my doorknob jiggles. My heart skips, and I wait for Natalie or Thomas to call out. When I remain silent, footsteps recede.

Only then do I get up. I shower, taking care to check the mostly healed scar on my head, and dress. I need to catch a ride downtown and continue to job search. I slide my glasses on, which feels a bit like a mental armor, and unlock the door.

The house is quiet except for the rustle of newspaper coming from the kitchen. I head in and pour myself a cup of coffee, adding the cream and two spoons of sugar. I join Thomas at the table and eye him.

He's not bad looking, if I was judging. Which I'm not. Maybe a little too LA—his wrinkle-free forehead gives away the Botox—but overall, a nice face. Natalie seemed to have picked a good guy.

"How was the game?" He folds the paper and sets it aside. "I was watching it here. It was a tough loss, but did you have fun?"

I force a smile. "Yeah, it was good. I've got some errands to run downtown, could you give me a ride when you head to work?"

He nods without comment. I let out a slow breath, then smile again. He rises and pats my shoulder.

My skin crawls.

I barely stop myself from flinching away from him.

Why? Because he's the only one who could've come into my room.

It only gets worse when we're in the car together. I focus on my breathing, on not panicking, and barely make it without losing it. Thomas seems lost in his own thoughts, and the low croon of his favorite radio station, one that only plays smooth jazz, fills the silence.

When he pulls to the curb, I snatch my purse and spring out of the car, calling thanks to him before closing the door and putting more distance between us.

Fuck.

He drives off with a wave, and I just... stand there on the sidewalk. I watch his car until it disappears around a corner.

Before I can move, though, another car pulls up alongside me.

A familiar one.

The passenger window rolls down. "Melody?"

I duck down to make eye contact with Jacob. "What are you doing here?"

"Practice." His blue eyes seem to go straight into me. "Are you okay?"

"Yeah. Of course. Just... had stuff to do." Have stuff to do.

Vague stuff. Stuff that was really just an excuse to get out of the house and keep myself occupied. *Errands*, applying for jobs. Distractions.

He nods slowly. "Okay. Are you staying downtown for the morning?"

"I have to start applying for jobs." I fold my arms across my stomach. "If that doesn't take forever..."

"Meet me for lunch."

I eye him. What I don't want to say is that I'm financially dependent on a loan that Thomas and Natalie gave me. That I can't really afford whatever lunch place a guy like him probably dines at.

"No thanks." I step back and smile at him. "I'll catch you around. Thanks for the interesting time last night."

With that, I spin and rush all the way to the train. And I definitely don't spare another thought for Jacob Rhodes.

8

JACOB

I leaf through the mail left on the side table by their front door, a flashlight between my teeth. Thomas and Natalie Cameron. I take a picture of their names and address and text it to my brand-new private investigator, then slip my phone back into my pocket.

Everyone is asleep.

It's been two nights since I was last here. Almost thirty-six hours since Melody blew me off on the side of the road. Never mind how it brought up old wounds, and how my first instinct was to get out of the car and show her just how persuasive I could be. And I would've done that if she knew our situation the way I do. Now, I'm doing a deeper dive while the family sleeps, and I come across a hospital bill addressed to Melody. It's amongst the stack, but it's been opened. I reopen it carefully and inspect the pages.

They're charging her for her month-long stay. Thousands of dollars for a myriad of treatment, half of which I don't understand. I fold it up and tuck it in my pocket. She's not going to pay a fucking dime of this.

I need to know what happened to her.

My phone buzzes, a new text from my investigator filling the screen when I fish it back out.

> **BILL**
>
> Thomas Cameron is her first cousin. Only relative hospital could track down at the time.

Okay. I suspected he wasn't her husband—knowing he's blood related is a huge fucking relief. But it's quickly followed by confusion, because there's a very obvious person who should have been found and notified.

Her husband.

> Then we keep looking.

Almost a year ago, "Mr. Cameron" made himself known to me in an obscure version of a pissing match. I couldn't find anything to go off of—the paper trail I used to chase Melody didn't even pan out that well, leaving me with another dead end.

It's infuriating—but Bill and I ultimately concluded last week, when I hired him, that whoever Mr. Cameron is needs to be a priority. There was one lead almost immediate: court documents filed in a district court in Manhattan with Melody's name on them. But it was another dead end. Ninety percent of the filings were redacted from the public.

The next step might be bribing a court official to release a name to us. But that could have the reverse effect and throw Mr. Cameron onto our trail. I don't know how well connected he is, and tipping him off would be detrimental. Especially since he seems to be out of the picture.

BILL

Cameron could be a fake last name.

I huff.

> Yeah, right. I knew her. She couldn't have
> gotten a job at CPU with a fake name.

The issue we've been running into is that there are a million Melody Camerons. And even more married couples with the same last name. He's been looking into getting records from Crown Point University, but they've been stonewalling him.

She doesn't know she has work history there, as far as I can tell. But I remember Professor Cameron clear as day.

BILL

A lot of things can be hedged... I'll check
into the possibility.

Fuck. I don't even know what that would look like. Fake social security card? Or fake birth certificate? Fingerprints logged under the false name, a realistic history to fool a background check.

Never in a million years would I think Melody capable of such a thing, and so I set that notion aside. Then again, I didn't think I'd be adept at breaking and entering, but here we are.

I leave the main living space and head into Melody's room. When I checked in earlier, she was snoring lightly. Now, she's splayed out on her stomach with one knee hitched up, her lips parted and her breathing deep.

I lock us in and step toward her bed. From my pocket I produce a tube of red lipstick, which I nestle in her makeup bag with the rest. The little spy camera comes next. I kneel on the counter to reach the ceiling fan in the bathroom, carefully removing the cover to slip it in. I use my phone to check the angle, then replace the plastic.

Those steps are repeated in Melody's bedroom, although I settle for the grate in the ceiling that connects to the central air. And I manage to reach it without making too much noise.

I get a perfect view of her bed, the lens fish-eyed enough to allow me to see who enters her room and the doors to her closet.

She makes a noise, and I slip my phone into my pocket.

This is what I really came for.

Her.

I wonder if she's noticed her panties are missing? If she did her laundry and wondered where her favorite pair went? They might not have been her favorite. She might not give a shit at all about clothes.

She used to dress in a way to conceal all her curves. She used to stand at the front of a classroom and command respect with her voice, but she lost half her students on her style of dress. Although, to a degree, I got it. She couldn't bare her chest to them, that would just cause her to lose the other half's respect.

And she still managed to ensnare me.

It was the lipstick. And the way her tongue flicked out before she read a passage. The black slacks that clung to her hips and ass.

The first time I propositioned her, she slapped me. And then, later, I was captivated by the sweet noises she made when my head was buried between her legs.

I shove that memory away.

None of that made her stay.

"I will figure out the mystery of you," I promise.

I stare at her until I can't take it anymore. My dick is so hard it hurts, and I undo the button and zipper on my jeans with quick movements. It springs free. I let out a sigh and palm it, sliding my hand up and over the tip before squeezing on the way down. Her ass is perfect. In the low light, I imagine I can just see the glistening wetness of her pussy. It's only shielded by a thin strip of fabric.

She decided to sleep in a t-shirt and panties.

Lucky me.

I press one knee into the mattress and lean forward. No niceties, no easing in. I slide my finger under her panties' defense and over her clit, dipping into her sweet cunt. Her muscles clench around my finger. I finger-fuck her for a moment, then draw back again.

She's not drugged. She could wake up at any moment. Not that I would mind it, but I don't want to scare her.

The Melody I knew saw me coming. She saw my obsession for what it was. She was a deer caught in headlights and unable to move, even in the face of the impending impact.

This version of her knows nothing.

I stand, and the shift of her mattress has her moving, too. She stretches and rolls onto her back, her arms over her head.

Like an offering. Her breasts are full and heavy, and I lift her shirt again. Precum coats my hand as I continue to jerk myself off, and I stare down at the fading red mark on her nipple.

How did she react when she saw it?

Who did she suspect?

I look forward to her reaction to this when she wakes.

I cup her breast, my thumb skating over her nipple. It pushes my incoming climax on faster, until my balls tighten and euphoria floods up my spine. I come on her perfect tits, the ropes of it painting a message just for her.

When my orgasm subsides, I run my finger through a line of cum and smear it across her lower lip. Gently, so not to wake her. Then I adjust her sleep shirt back into place and pull my jeans up. I'm satiated. A sense of peace settles over me that hasn't been present since college.

See you tomorrow, songbird.

9

MELODY

My shirt is stuck to my chest. It's the uncomfortable kind of stick that belies too much sweat, or a spill... None of which should happen while I'm sleeping. Fear kicks my heart rate into gear, and I slowly sit up in bed.

My door is closed, the lock on the knob engaged. It doesn't make me feel any safer in the moment.

I pull my shirt away from my skin, then shuck it off completely.

There are dried flakes of... *something* across my breasts, my stomach. I lick my lips and let out an involuntary noise at the taste. It's familiar and strange, and bile rises up my throat. I jump out of bed and barely make it to the toilet in time, hitting the floor on my knees hard.

I throw up, my abdomen spasming. My throat burns, and I cough and spit until my body relaxes. My mind keeps skating away from the details. It keeps my panic at bay, keeps me from derailing. Things I desperately need to *not* think about in order to stay sane.

After a shower hot enough to scald, I blow-dry my hair and sneak out of the house.

My door was locked. I didn't go to sleep with it that way. Unless I did, and I forgot.

A chill travels down my back.

I head to the train station, keeping my head low. I just need to not draw attention. Once I'm in my seat, I put in my earbuds and go to my next musical selection on the list.

Pop punk. It's cheating, because I already figured out that I like it, but now I'm trying to narrow down artists. So far, Green Day and Blink-182 are my favorites. 'I Miss You' seems to speak directly to my soul.

I queue it up and mouth along with the words.

Someone sits beside me, jostling my arm. I glance over and frown. A man leers at me. He wears a leather jacket, and a heavy beard obscures the lower half of his face. He leans in, and his mouth moves, but his words are too low to hear over the music.

I pull out an earbud. "Sorry?"

"I said, what's a girl like you doing all alone?"

A tendril of fear winds through me, closing my throat. I shift away from him slowly and stare straight ahead, while my mind turns to all the ways I might escape. Do I humor him and engage in conversation? Do I ignore him? Or pretend I'm deaf?

That ship already sailed.

He bumps my arm again. "A pretty lady like you... you got a boyfriend, babe?"

My skin crawls. I pause the music and fight the way my shoulders try to rise to my ears. Barely looking down, I thumb over to my conversation with Thomas...

Then pause.

And switch to Jacob.

Being harassed on the train. Idk what to do.

The man's hand lands on my thigh, and I wince.

"My ex-wife always talked too much. I like the quiet type. A girl who knows how to keep her mouth shut. Or open, depending on the situation." He adjusts his seat, spreading his leg until that, too, touches me. His voice drops. "You know, no one's around. You could put that mouth to good use. Since you're not the conversationalist."

"Please go away." I can barely force the words out.

My phone buzzes against my palm.

JACOB
What station is next?

I glance out the window at the flashing scenery.

The arena's, I think

The man knocks my phone out of my hand. It hits the floor and skids away, and his fingers tighten on my leg. He crowds me against the window.

"Stop." I push at his hand. "Don't touch me."

"Don't be a bitch," he growls.

The train is slowing. I have no idea if my text sent, but I do know I need to get off the damn train.

"This is my stop." I hoist my purse up higher on my shoulder, my grip tight to hide my shaking fingers. "Excuse me."

"Nah." He leans back, releasing my thigh and moving his arm over the back of my seat. It puts us in closer proximity—which is worse. "Not without payment."

The train comes to a stop. The doors open.

And he hasn't moved.

I think... I might've once had a snappy response. There's one on the tip of my tongue, something about a troll and a bridge, but the words are stuck in my throat.

I take a shallow breath, then another. The doors close, and the train is off again.

He sneers at me. "Guess you have the time now."

"No," I whisper. I scan for my phone, but it seems long gone. Slid away to an unknown place.

He's not even making that big of a fuss. His voice isn't loud. There are other people on the train, but none of them look twice at us. At *me*. I stare hard at them, wondering if they can feel my pleading gaze.

But then the door between cars slides open, and Jacob Rhodes pushes his way through.

A little exhale of relief slips out, although I know the danger isn't gone. I mean, it's still here, sitting next to me— but something *else* says that the bigger danger just walked in.

Jacob stops beside the man. He looms over him now, although I have no idea how either will fare when the stranger stands.

"Get up," Jacob orders.

The man turns, surprised. His gaze flicks over Jacob, top to bottom, and his upper lip curls. "Just walk away, buddy. This is between me and her."

"She's got no business with you—but I'm about to. Get. Up." Jacob is *pissed*. His voice is darker than I've ever heard it. The anger is barely concealed in his face, the tightness of his jaw. He grabs the guy's shoulder and practically rips him out of the seat, sending him sprawling to the floor.

The train rattles as we go around a corner, but Jacob doesn't so much as sway. He kneels and snatches the guy's wallet out of his pocket, flipping it to the plastic ID card. He takes a picture and tosses the wallet down beside his head.

My harasser seems to have gotten his bearings, shock giving way to anger, and he scrambles to his feet. He comes rushing at Jacob, stopping nose to nose.

Jacob doesn't. Even. Flinch.

"Holy shit," the guy says. "You're Jacob Rhodes."

There's a quiet little murmur that sweeps through the train car. It's slowing as we approach the next stop.

"And you're dead if you ever so much as look at another woman wrong," Jacob says, stepping closer and pitching his voice low. "But *especially* this one."

They both focus on me.

I can't breathe. I don't know what I'm doing, what my face is doing, but the guy actually pauses.

"I'm sorry, man. You're my favorite player. I had no idea—"

Jacob turns away from him, effectively silencing the man, and holds his hand out to me.

Déjà vu sweeps through my mind, brushing away fear. Not with him here. Not with his hand outstretched like a peace offering or safety.

Why do I feel safe around him? He's anything but safe.

I take his hand anyway, letting him help me to my feet and guiding me around the guy. He stoops and picks up my phone, which lies in the aisle. He checks the screen and tucks it in my back pocket. Quick, easy. His hand stays around my hip until we're on the platform, and I glance over my shoulder. The man is watching us, and he waves again just as the train lurches into motion.

And carries him out of sight.

It's only when the train is gone that the trembling starts.

"Hey, hey, you're okay." Jacob stops me. He runs his hands up and down my arms. "Did he hurt you?"

I turn into his chest and throw my arms around his waist. He seems to hesitate for a split second, then hugs me back. A weight comes off my shoulders at that. He hugs me *hard*, like he's not afraid to break me. His chin rests on top of my head, and his hand strokes my back. Then higher, touching the back of my head, his fingers running through my hair.

I close my eyes. "I'm sorry. I'm sorry for texting you—"

"Don't be." His hands pause, his fingers flexing on my scalp. "Ever."

After a moment, I'm able to rein in my tumbling emotions. I step out of his embrace and clear my throat. I go to swipe at the tears that have collected on my lower lashes, not really falling yet, but he beats me to it. His hands cradle my face, and his thumbs sweep under my eyes.

"Don't spare that piece of shit any of your tears, songbird."

My heart skips. *Songbird?*

"Why—"

He drops his hands and steps back. The tenderness I thought I just saw is gone.

"Where are you headed?" he asks. "Can I escort you?"

My cheeks flush. The heat blooms across my face, and I stride for the stairs. He keeps up with me, although he doesn't prod me for an answer. Not until we're streetside, and I have a decision to make.

"I need a job." I clear my throat. "I don't want to keep living with them. Thomas and Natalie. They took me in, and it's been two months... I feel like I'm a burden."

Great. Another confession I didn't mean to make.

"Come with me."

He loops his arm around my waist again, his fingers grazing my hip. I find myself mirroring him, my arm going around him. I grip his sweatshirt and lean in, not entirely mad at the intimacy of it.

It should scare me.

But... I don't know. It doesn't.

We walk for almost ten minutes, and I gaze up at the arena. The stop that Jacob got on the train at is just across the street, taunting me. He leads me into the building through a side entrance, waving at a security guard that sits just inside the door.

I follow in his footsteps through the metal detector, which doesn't make a peep even with my purse on my shoulder and my phone in my back pocket.

"You got to the train fast," I finally say, once we're in an elevator shooting upward.

"I was just pulling into the arena parking garage. It was good timing."

I swallow. "Thank you. I didn't know who—"

"You can always call me." He glances at me, then focuses back on the door. "Anytime. For anything."

Who were you to me? It's on the tip of my tongue—but the words simply don't come out.

The elevator chimes, and the doors slide open. He leads me into what looks like a corporate office reception area. He talks to the receptionist in a low voice, then motions for me to follow him.

"Good morning, Phil." Jacob raps on a glass office door, pushing it open without waiting for an answer.

An older man in a suit rises from behind his desk, trying —and failing—to hide his surprise. "Mr. Rhodes. Good morning."

"This is Melody Cameron," he introduces. He gestures

for me to come in with him. "She's in need of a job, and I heard through the grapevine that we have an opening. Thought I'd come and make a personal recommendation."

They have some sort of silent conversation while I stand there and fidget.

Finally, Phil exhales and nods. "Yes, of course. I'll have Denise set her up downstairs. We just hired on someone else. I suppose she can join their training."

Jacob beams. "Perfect, thanks."

And just like that... I have a job.

10

JACOB

P hil, the assistant to the owner of the Colorado Titans, walks Melody down to meet Denise. She's a human resources person, I think. I don't know, I try to avoid her whenever possible.

The position I negotiated with Phil—who owed me a favor—is as a social media assistant. Which usually means traveling with the team, especially in playoff season. I head to the gym, smiling to myself.

Job obtained. Independence—or, rather, dependence on *me*—solidified.

Getting her out of that house is the next step.

I watched on the screen as she freaked out this morning, her attention going to her bedroom door like Thomas was going to burst through it.

She doesn't suspect me. If she did, she wouldn't have texted me. She would've asked her cousin for help.

I go straight to the treadmill. I need to burn off this extra energy before I attempt to tackle the weights. We're headed back to New York for game five. We leave early tomorrow morning. I shoot off a text to Phil, making sure to emphasize that Melody needs to go with us.

He doesn't respond, but whatever. He'll listen.

I've just hit the five-mile mark when my phone goes off again.

> MELODY
>
> I don't know anything about social media.
>
> I'm going to get fired before I've begun.

I smile.

> You're going to be fine. Trust me.

> MELODY
>
> Denise just told me to go home and pack a bag for tomorrow…???

> Game five in New York. Wait for me, I'll drive you home.

I hit the cool-down button on the treadmill and toss my phone in the cupholder. Five minutes later, I use my shirt to blot sweat off my brow, then go out to find Melody.

She's waiting just outside the gym, fiddling with the strap of her purse.

"Hey," I call. "Ready?"

She turns to me, and her jaw drops.

I'm still holding my shirt in my hand, and I smirk at her. Her eyes move all over my chest. I wonder what she thinks of me this time around.

"You should put your shirt back on," she says, her voice faint. "Your abs could take an eye out."

My smirk widens into a fully fledged grin. "You like what you see?"

"I'm too old for you." She shakes her head. "What am I saying? I'm too wrong for you in more ways than just age. Stop flirting with me."

I roll my eyes. That, at least, hasn't changed. "You're wrong about that."

"I wouldn't have hooked up with you. Even past-me couldn't have been so bold."

"Maybe not. But me? Past, present, future. I've always been bold." I slip my shirt back on and motion for her to walk with me. "Besides, there's nothing wrong with a little age gap."

"So we were a thing?" Her eyes are wide.

"No," I lie. "We were just friends. I'm just saying, *if...*"

She visibly relaxes.

"And as friends, are you okay?"

"I'm fine. Why?"

I shrug. "You just have a look on your face."

Her lips press together for a moment, and she visibly swallows. "Well, I'm good. You got me a job, after all. I don't need anything else."

She may not think so, but *I* need her to need me. Getting her text this morning filled me with too many emotions. Joy that she'd reached out, fury that some guy thought he'd lay a finger on her and get away with it. I was smug about her not wanting to call her cousin. He wouldn't have got to her in time, I'm sure of it.

"Just a ride home," I say.

She frowns.

"You don't need anything... except a ride home."

"I left my car at the train station."

"They have parking here. Did HR tell you that?"

"Denise mentioned it, yeah. She said I'd get my pass tomorrow to get into the garage, along with my ID and stuff. But she *also* said we were going to New York City for the day—"

"For the game," I finish. "Yeah."

"Right." She's still twisting that strap of her purse with both hands. "I've only been on a plane twice, and—"

"Well, this one is a private plane. So I think you'll be okay."

She stops walking and blinks up at me. "What?"

"We take a private plane. We'll be flying home right after the game. The bag they said to pack is really just a precaution in case we end up stuck there overnight." I smirk. "It's protocol."

"Oh."

I wait for more questions, but none come. She seems to be in a daze, and it's only when we reach the parking garage that she grabs my wrist.

"Thank you." She clears her throat. "I don't think I said thank you for earlier. For coming and rescuing me."

A pretty blush rises on her cheeks. She isn't wearing any makeup. Her hair is down, a bit longer than when I last knew her. I can't get over the blonde.

"You don't have to thank me, Melody."

"You called me songbird earlier…" She tips her head. "Singing was one of the things I tried. In the car, of course, along with one of the songs I first learned. Or relearned. I was terrible."

That name. I shouldn't have called her that—not yet. But I'll admit that I was mildly intrigued about how she would react. And she *did* react. Which means there's some part of her that knows about us, even if she can't access it.

"It just slipped out."

"But *why*?"

Well, I won't tell her the truth. And I don't really have a

good enough lie queued up at the moment. Nothing that would douse her curiosity.

We stop at my truck, and she plants her hands on her hips.

Her gaze goes from me to it, no doubt remembering what she said the other night. About me being a truck guy.

"Interesting," she murmurs.

The lights flash, the vehicle unlocking, and she hoists herself up into the passenger seat without delay. Not thinking, I step forward and block the door, gripping her legs and swiveling her to face me.

Her lips part, her gaze dropping down. At my hands lightly holding the outside of her thighs. She puts her hands over mine.

"Jacob," she whispers.

Songbird, I reply in my mind.

"Why do you scare me so much?"

I frown when I want to smile. I let my hands slip from her legs and step back from her. She closes herself in, and I circle around to the driver's seat. Once in, I reach into the bag in my backseat and pull out a water bottle, handing it to her.

"Thanks." She unscrews the cap and takes a swallow. Then another. Her throat moves with every gulp, until she lowers the bottle half-empty and drops it into the cup holder.

"I think I remember the way to your house. Can you be my backup navigator?"

She nods. I didn't answer her question on why she's scared of me, but she should *know* why. She was scared of me then, too.

"You said Thomas and Natalie were the ones to take you in." I glance at her. "Who are they to you?"

I already know, but I want to hear it from her.

"Thomas is my cousin on my dad's side. Um, he was the only one they could find who would take me." She rubs her throat, almost unconsciously. "But we weren't close. Before."

"Because he doesn't know much..."

"I went to school in New York City, he said. He remembered hearing about my graduation from family. We walked through my old campus, but I didn't remember anything. We couldn't get into my old apartment." She looks saddened by that.

"Has he spoken about other family?"

She shakes her head. "No."

"Why not?"

"He said that he's not on speaking terms with my parents. Wouldn't know how to contact them, or something... He doesn't really want to, either."

Now I need to know. It should be easy enough to trace Thomas's family back and locate Melody's dad. And through him, the rest of Melody's history should reveal itself.

We ride the rest of the way in contemplative quiet. When we get to her cousin's house, I twist to face her.

"Are they at work?" I ask.

"Thomas will get back by three. Natalie won't be back 'til five or six."

It's only ten in the morning now. Seems like a whole day has been crammed into the space of a few hours.

"Thanks for the ride," she says, hopping down from my truck. "I'll see you tomorrow, then..."

"That you will."

I watch from the truck, idling on the curb, until she disappears into the house. Then I pick up the water bottle she drank from and put it back in the bag. The drugs that I carefully put into the water should go into effect within the hour.

But in case she's watching from one of the windows, I pull away from her street. Biding my time has never bothered me. In fact, it adds to the thrill of it.

An hour later, I sneak back into her house.

Melody is passed out on the couch. Her breathing is deep and even, her lips parted. Her glasses are askew, hair across her face. I gently brush it away and pull her glasses off, folding them and setting them on the side table.

I want her afraid of her cousin.

I want her running to me and only me.

And that will only happen if she thinks he's the worst sort of human.

But for her, I'll happily stoop to those levels.

I close the curtains, blocking the windows that give passersby on the street a look into the living room, then return to Melody. My adrenaline is flowing worse than right before a game. My fingers shake slightly as I pull her up into a sitting position and remove her top. Her body leans against mine, and I reach around her to unclasp her bra.

I set her back and then get to work on her lower half. Shoes, pants, panties.

In a matter of moments, she's naked on the couch in front of me.

And she is a sight to behold.

She's gorgeous. Those dusky nipples pucker under my gaze. One is still bruised. I lean forward and suck it into my mouth, giving it a new hickey. Until her breathing automatically gets heavier above me.

I run my hands down her body, over the curves of her

belly and her hips. She was trying to tell me that she's too fat to draw my attention, but it's her soft rolls that drive me crazy. It's the heaviness of her tits that make me harder than steel.

Too many people in her life have made her feel poorly about her body.

I refuse to be one of them.

She should be worshiped like a goddess.

Which is exactly what I plan on doing now.

I take my time with her body. Kissing down her sternum between her breasts, leaving little bite marks in her flesh. I want to possess her. I want to be in her mind all the time, and on her skin, and *in* her.

Parting her legs wider, I kiss down her stomach until I get to her core. I slide my finger down her center, then back up over her clit. Until she's wetter. Then I push that finger, plus a second, into her. My digits disappear inside her, her heat enveloping me, and I can only imagine how good it's going to feel when I sink my cock into her.

I ignore my hard-on. I ignore everything except the way she feels.

And then I taste her.

It's only comparable to melting dark chocolate on your tongue. I lap at her clit, nip at her lips. She's unresponsive except for the pulsing in her cunt against my fingers. The drugs do the dirty work for me, keeping her under.

Her orgasm builds and builds, until she crests. She lets out a low groan and tightens on my fingers again, the spasms wild and fast until it finally ebbs. My fingers come away slick with her arousal.

Fucking beautiful.

"You're already mine," I say in her ear, laying her down on the couch. I shove my jeans down and free my dick, then lift her knee and press into her. She's primed and ready, and I push into her with one hard thrust. "You don't know it yet, but you will."

I don't have patience to go slow. It's not like my dick has got much action in the past two years. I tried to drown my misery out in women in the last semester of college, but it didn't work. *Nothing worked*, let alone a warm body that wasn't hers. After a while, I gave up trying.

My self-inflicted abstinence mystified my friends and teammates. I still drank with them. Still sloppily made out with girls at bars and sometimes let them put their hand on my crotch over my jeans. My flaccid cock that would only react to one woman.

And she's in front of me.

I groan my pleasure in her ear, hoping to translate it into her unconscious mind. Like she'll wake up and know it was me.

Although that's foolish—and completely not the point.

No, the point is to drive her into my arms.

I'll be sweet, I'll be helpful. I'll be the knight in shining armor. Until I have her anyway. Then the need for pretense will drop. But by then, it'll be too late for her.

Once caught, she's never escaping me.

I jack my hips, sliding deeper into her cunt. Her muscles clench at me. I keep my forehead pressed to hers. She's beautifully relaxed. Something I rarely see from her when she isn't asleep. Or even when she is, lately. The slight pinch of her brow, the weight of worry resting heavy on her mind and body.

Now, the furrow is erased, any concern washed away.

We'll get back to this. Her and me.

I grip her thigh hard enough to bruise—and I hope it does leave a mark. I hope she discovers it tomorrow morning, or tonight. When she wonders why this is happening to her, and doubt threads through her at the idea of her cousin and her safety.

I palm her breast with my other hand, pinching and tugging her nipple. If she was awake, she'd be moaning. Writhing. I come without warning, slamming to a halt inside her. My cock pulses, and my lips hover over hers.

I'll kiss her when she's awake. When she knows me.

When she can explain why she left me.

I stay still and inside her for another minute. Until my heart rate has settled. Then I lean down, trailing my lips across her jaw and down the curve of her neck.

But I'm stopped by the silver scar on her throat.

I rise suddenly, brushing her hair away. There's a scar, horizontal across her throat like...

Like someone tried to cut it.

My blood runs cold, and I back off her entirely. I kneel between her spread legs on the couch and inspect the rest of her body with my hands. It isn't until I get to her head, gently moving my fingers through her hair, that I find the second scar.

It's longer and jagged, and I grit my teeth to stop myself from doing something stupid. But the rage is back as the pieces—the *how* to her amnesia—click into place.

Someone didn't just try to slit her throat. They wanted to make sure she was dead.

11

MELODY

"Hey, wake up. Natalie's going to be home soon."

It takes me a moment to register where I am and who's talking to me. Thomas perches on the coffee table in front of me, a glass of water in his hand.

I'm on the couch.

I sit up slowly, wincing, and take the glass. The condensation is cold, wetting my hand. I gulp it down.

"Are you feeling okay?" He eyes me carefully. "You've been sleeping for a while."

"Oh." I frown. "I'm sorry."

"No, it's okay. It's just unusual, so…"

I wave him off. "It was a weird day. I'm going to grab a shower before dinner."

His gaze lingers on me until I'm down the hall and safely tucked into my room, the lock on my doorknob twisted. I feel… off. Like I ran a thousand miles while I slept.

In the two months I've lived here, I've never fallen asleep during the day. And certainly not on the couch. I don't even remember falling asleep. One minute I was in the kitchen, finishing off an early lunch, and the next…

I shed my shirt, then pause at *that*, too. It's not the same shirt I dressed myself in this morning. That one is in my laundry basket, right on top. Along with my leggings. I'm in shorts that I never wear.

They're ones Thomas and Natalie got me when I first moved in. I had no clothes except the scrubs the hospital let me leave in, no possessions at all—not even my memories. They filled in gaps of the physical nature. Toiletries and makeup, clothes and underwear and shoes. At first, it was a poor fit. It's why I don't particularly like these shorts, which are stretchy yet snug. They show off too much of my curves and hug my skin too tightly.

In the bathroom, I strip completely—then stop.

Again.

I slap my palm over my mouth to cover my horrified noise. There are marks all down my chest. Little bruises and bites.

Taking stock of the rest of me, I find wetness on my thighs. My fingers run through it, collecting the opaque, thick liquid.

Without having known it before, I would bet that this is semen. On my inner thighs. And the more I explore between my legs, the sorer I realize I am.

And it's an awful conclusion to come to.

But the tears don't fall.

Maybe I'm in shock?

I don't feel anything except a sort of pressure, the need to get out of this house almost violent. I don't throw up, I don't cry. I can't meet my own gaze in the mirror, though. I can't look at myself and put together what happened.

"Melody? Are you all right?"

I jerk toward the door and Thomas's voice coming through it.

Now the trembling starts, and I fall back against the counter. I grip it with both hands, lowering myself to the floor. My knees are shaking, my throat closing.

Thomas did this.

He... he raped me?

There's no way I would've slept through that. Not unless he drugged me or...

Well, that's just it. My reasoning ends there.

"Melody?" The doorknob jiggles.

"I'm fine," I call. "Sorry to worry you!"

But it isn't fine. I take a burning-hot shower, rinsing away all evidence of what happened—except the bruises that I can't seem to rub out of my skin. Bruises don't work like that anyway. Or hickeys. But after, I stay in my room until I hear Natalie get home.

I know I should leave. That a smart, sensible person would call the cops or just walk out the door. And I would if I had anywhere else to go. I just got a job that hasn't started yet. I'm still waiting on my new social security card to come in the mail. Besides the loan Thomas and Natalie gave me, I've got *nothing*.

It's a weird feeling, being so stuck. Like I'm sinking in mud with no helping hand in sight.

Just ride it out. The little voice in my head is meant to be reassuring, but really it's just fucking depressing.

I manage to drag myself out in time for dinner. I echo that I'm okay, that I have a headache. But I do have news to share, so I tell them about my job. The social media assistant for the Colorado Titans.

Thomas blinks at me. "Does this have anything to do with the player you know?"

"No," I lie. "I just saw a job advertisement and applied

online. They called me in today, and I was hired on the spot."

"Congratulations, Mel," Natalie says. "We're so proud of you."

Like I'm a kid.

I guess I'm no better than one anyway. I smile at her praise and finish my dinner in silence, then I excuse myself and close myself away again. I need to pack for the day tomorrow, although it seems like we'll be in and out.

My phone goes off.

> **JACOB**
>
> Ready for tomorrow?

> What do I pack for two flights and no stayover? Socks? Snacks?

> **Definitely snacks.**

> Did I have social media? Before?

> **Why do you ask?**

> I just want to know if you knew me *that* well.

> **You did, but you didn't post a lot.**

I wait him out, chewing on my bottom lip.

> **JACOB**
>
> Your username was @melodyfliesaway

I frown, but I go to my computer and search the name. Sure enough, *I* come up. There are only a few photos, but my heart immediately thumps with a weird, new heaviness. This is some other woman's life, not mine.

JACOB

You still there?

Just trying to make sense of it all...

Thank you. Really.

See you tomorrow.

Tomorrow can't come soon enough.

My head aches, blurring my vision. I bookmark the social media page and close the old laptop. I double-check my door is locked, and the window, too, then go to sleep. And I pray that when I wake up, everything is more normal than tonight.

Except it's not.

I wake up naked.

I don't know what happened. There's no suspicious liquids on me, no extra hickeys or bruises to catalog, but tears immediately fill my eyes. Someone was in here, I know it in my bones. Not that it's hard to pick that type of lock, I'd bet. He stripped me. God knows what else he did while I was unconscious.

I pack more clothes—all of them, really. I just shove everything into a bag and wait until Thomas and Natalie have left, and then I leave, too. I practically run right out the door and stop dead.

Jacob's truck is idling at the curb. Waiting for me.

All those emotions I've been trying to suppress come roaring to the surface.

And I burst into tears.

12

JACOB

Melody climbs into my truck, tossing her bag in the back, and practically throws herself into my arms. I catch her, hugging her tightly to me. I can guess why she's upset.

The urge to drag her across the center seat and into my lap is burning through me, but I manage to resist. I stop myself from pressing my lips to her cheek, too. From any physical contact.

"I need to get out of that house," she says, her lips moving against my throat.

My fucking traitorous cock stiffens, like I didn't just jerk off over her sleeping form a few hours ago. And fuck her hours before that.

"Please. Can you help me?"

"What do you need?"

She hesitates and draws back. Her lashes are darkened by mascara behind her glasses, but other than that she's not wearing a lick of makeup. It doesn't matter if she wears makeup—her skin is flawless, her hazel eyes more green than brown today. My gaze drops to the scar on her throat.

I set Bill on finding out more about her hospital stay. I want a list of her injuries, what the doctors think it could've come from, if the police were involved. Questions I don't want to ask Melody, because I don't know if she'll remember it accurately. I need an outside source.

She avoids my eyes. Pink colors her cheeks. "Somewhere to stay. Maybe you know someone who's renting a room, or—"

"I have an extra room. You're welcome to it until you get on your feet."

Her breath hitches. "Jacob, I don't think—"

"Don't think, just do." I smile at her, trying to be reassuring. But honestly, this is the most precarious part of my plot. She could try to say no. She could try to disappear again.

She won't succeed, but she might consider it.

"Okay," she says on an exhale. She sits back and crosses her arms. "I wonder if past-me knew Thomas was a creep."

"What did he do?"

She shudders. "I don't want to talk about it. But... I've been kicking myself. Because I'm pretty sure I would've known. Why else does he know nothing about me? Where I worked or lived in the past decade, simple things about me like foods I like or hate. Did you know I had to get allergy testing? Because I didn't know if I was allergic to anything dangerous, so they ran a million tests."

"Are you allergic to anything?" I glance at her.

"Nope." She laughs. "After all that, I kind of wish they had found something life-threatening. Just to make it worth it."

"Better to not have to worry," I murmur.

"Yeah." Melody sighs. "Anyway. This job is a bit ridiculous, by the way. It's a job for a twenty-year-old, not me.

I'm thirty-four, technologically challenged, and surrounded by people a decade younger than me."

There's that age gap talk again. "Did you look at your social media?"

"I started to, but I was too stressed last night."

Figured as much. She opened the laptop after I texted her, but she closed it soon after and went to sleep. I'll be glad when I don't have to work as hard to get into her bed.

Step one: move her into my condo.

Step two: make sure she never leaves.

It sounds easy, but... well, maybe I'm worried.

"Denise introduced me to the other social media girl. She's literally twenty-two." She laughs. "I told her about the amnesia thing, so they totally know that this is a pity job."

"It's a real job." I glance at her. "I promise."

She exhales.

We get to the arena, and I walk her to where she needs to be. A group of women stand in their break room, cupping mugs of coffee, and some of them giggle and wave when they see me.

Melody shoots me a weird look.

I leave her with them, shaking my head. I can't control how other people react to me. Besides, they don't really give a shit about *me*. They care that I wear a Titans jersey and play well. And if I fucked them—which I wouldn't—they'd use it as bragging rights. Not because they want to date or marry me for who I am. That's why the puck bunnies who shadowed my college team with every step were the worst.

Now. To make it to New York with Melody on the plane, to play the fucking game, and get back in one piece.

And take her home.

I don't know which part of that I'm more excited about.

13

MELODY

Jacob skates off the ice after the second period. I dutifully follow Kristy, the twenty-two-year-old social media manager, around the rink to the opening the players just stepped through. She runs the Instagram, TikTok, and Facebook page, and even coordinates with player fan accounts. She has a long-lens camera hooked around her neck and her phone in her hand. Her manicured nails don't seem to impede her typing skills as she writes out a caption for an Instagram story.

I've been put on observation duty, where I fear I will stay until the playoffs are over. Then they'll find some nice way to fire me, because I know nothing.

Kristy, however, seems to know *everything*. She ran through a brief overview of the playoffs this morning on the plane. We sat in the front, just behind the coaches, while the guys lounged in the back. They listened to music and played cards while we worked. Or, she worked, and I watched.

But anyway. She told me there are four rounds of play-offs. Each round has up to seven games—it's essentially whoever gets to four wins first. So right now, the Titans are tied with the Guardians, two games to two. We're guaranteed to play two more games—tonight's game five, and number six in two days' time—and then the last if the teams split those wins.

It's enough to do my head in, but I manage to keep it straight. As long as I focus on the Titans' journey and no other.

Like the other fifteen teams playing.

We watch the Zamboni go around the ice, taking the chopped-up mess and making it glassy smooth again.

Today's been a weird experience. From rushing out to Jacob's truck, fighting the overwhelming feeling that he's safe and the Camerons aren't, to getting on a private jet and being haphazardly introduced to the hockey team and the coaches—spoiler alert: no one really cared that I was coming along—to being in New York City. For not even a full night.

We're in a different time zone. Something that probably was normal, and *feels* normal, but is completely odd. It's nine o'clock at night here, but in Denver it's seven. Thomas and Natalie are probably finishing dinner, preparing for work tomorrow.

Meanwhile, my life is just fracturing, over and over again.

For once I'd like to get a handle on it. To put my mind back together.

Being back in New York does nothing for my memory. I've been mindful of the senses of déjà vu, but even those are lacking lately. No cold foreboding, like when Thomas's colleague called me *darling*. A word that, even in my head, makes me shudder. No tingling heat, like when Jacob looks at me a certain way.

I should *not* be attracted to him. He's young. And he says we were friends, so it's not like anything would even happen anyway. But I can't figure out what sort of friends we were. He could've been a well-meaning acquaintance, for all I know. The probability that we were anything more is low. Right? Where would I have even met him?

See? I know nothing.

"Melody?"

I spin around, expecting someone on my level. In the alleyway that leads to the lockers.

"Up here!" A blonde leans over the rails above me, waving. "What are you doing here?"

I don't recognize her.

Shocker.

I'm working out how to convey that with the ten-foot gap between us, but the words aren't coming.

The woman grips the railing, her brow furrowing. "What, two years of silent treatment isn't enough?"

I open my mouth, but she's already straightening and turning away.

I memorize her outfit.

Black leather jacket over a gold Guardians shirt. Black-and-gold beanie. Jeans, boots.

"You know her?" Kristy asks.

"She knows me," I answer. "I don't know who she is."

"You should go after her." She nudges me, then points at how to get up into the stadium. "You have your lanyard, you'll be able to get back here. Go."

She's right.

I seize the opportunity and give chase, rushing and pushing until I've made it to the top of the section. I scan the crowded hallway and spot a leather jacket.

"Hey!" I catch up to her, tapping her shoulder quickly

before I lose my nerve. My stomach is suddenly in my throat.

She turns, her eyebrows hiking.

People flow around us.

"I'm sorry," I offer, because... well, I *am* sorry. For past-me's mistakes, for whatever I did willingly or unwillingly.

Her expression softens, and it's then that I know two things: I must've been good friends with her. And I really fucked up. Because she still appears hurt, even after the annoyance fades.

"I..." Fuck it. "I'm so sorry. Who are you?"

She takes a step back.

"Wait, please." I hold up my hands. "You know me, don't you? This is coming out all wrong. You said my name. You must know me."

"I do..."

"I woke up in a hospital three months ago," I blurt out. "No memories. Nothing."

"Whoa."

I press my lips together.

She extends her hand. "I'm Lucy Page."

"Melody Cameron," I say as I shake it. "You knew that. Sorry."

"Stop apologizing, my God." She doesn't release my hand and instead pulls me forward.

I crash into her chest, and she hugs me. *Hard.* Like we fit together, or hugged a thousand times before, I instinctively hug her back.

"I missed the fuck out of you," she whispers. When she finally releases me, she quickly wipes tears from her eyes. "Your hair is blonde."

I touch a lock. "Was it not always?"

Her gaze roves over my face. "No, it was light brown.

You never colored it. In the summer you'd get little high-lights from the sun, but it was all natural."

"And it's been two years since we've seen each other." I shift my weight.

Kristy will want me back, probably. Eventually. I feel the need to return pressing into my spine. Conscious of my job, of getting fired, of a precarious line I walk. If I get fired, would Jacob still let me crash in his spare room? I wouldn't be able to afford anything else, and the thought of returning to Thomas's house terrifies me.

"Yeah." She frowns. "I'll be the first to admit, I'm not the best at keeping in contact. We were so busy, me with my job and Theo's—my husband—and you with teaching—"

I hold up my hand, trying to hide my shock. "Wait, teaching?"

She tilts her head. "What *do* you know?"

Before I can answer, the horn in the arena blows.

"I need to get back," I murmur.

The hallway is clearing out.

"Worst timing ever," Lucy says. "Okay, here. Put your contact details in, and I'll call you."

I take her phone and frown at it. "We're just visiting, though. I live in Denver."

"*Melody.*"

"Okay, okay." I input my details, having been forced by Thomas and Natalie to memorize my number just in case, and hand it back. "Thank you."

She hugs me again. "I'll call you and fill in the details I can. I promise. We'll make it work."

I don't know what to say to that, so I don't. We part ways, and I head back toward the opening Kristy pointed me through. I get all the way back to her with this new hope bubbling in my chest, before it's squashed in one, foul moment.

She said I hadn't seen her in two years.

So where was I in that time?

I let out a breath and focus on work. Kristy is talking to the equipment manager when I return, and she's got that look in her eye. Like someone with a crush.

"Just in time," Kristy says, breaking away from the equipment manager and smiling at me. "We're pretty much done, so we can just watch the rest of the game from here."

The players are already on the ice, although the game hasn't started. They seem to be doing another quick lap.

Someone skids to a halt in the opening, showering ice shavings against the lip of the boards. "Having fun?"

I smile at Jacob. "It's interesting."

"I'll take that, I guess."

"Rhodes!" his coach hollers from the bench.

Jacob winks at me and skates off. Someone closes the door, sealing it off from the rink, and only a moment later, the third period starts.

Kristy and I watch the game from the glass, tucked just out of the way. There are fans right over us, and sometimes I feel their gaze. But none is as heavy as Lucy's.

Lucy Page.

I found a friend.

I pull out my list and make a note that my hair is naturally light brown. Thomas didn't say anything about it. But now that I think about it, my hair has been looking dull at the roots. Now I know, it's not dullness, it's just a different color.

I smile.

Sometimes, it's the little things. And sometimes, it's a whole lot more.

14
JACOB

"Hey." I run my knuckles down Melody's arm.

She lifts her head, blinking groggily at me.

"Did I fall asleep?"

I suppress my smile. "Just a little. Do you want me to carry you upstairs?"

We're in the parking garage under my high-rise building. She was drowsy when the plane touched down and snoring by the time we hit the highway. Her bag is in the back, and I make quick work slinging it and mine over my shoulder.

She's already got her door open, rubbing her eyes carefully under her glasses. I don't give her the chance to put her feet on the ground, instead scooping her straight out of the truck and into my arms.

Melody pitches into me, yelping and throwing her arms around my neck. It puts our faces close, just the way I like it. Although by the way she immediately cranes back, I'm thinking it's not reciprocated. *Yet.*

"This is not very friend-like," she breathes.

"On the contrary." I kick the door shut and head for the

elevator. "This is the epitome of friendly. Can you hit the up button? Fob is in my breast pocket."

"You want me to feel you up?"

I lift her higher, trying not to smirk. My cock is doing his thing again, making himself known. Last thing I need is for her to feel it and get *really* freaked out. Carrying her is one thing. Letting her know I'm lusting over her curves before she's ready is another.

"If I wanted you to feel me up, I'd be less subtle," I promise.

She hits the button to call the elevator, shifting slightly to get to where I stashed my condo key and fob. Her fingers slip against my chest, and goosebumps rise on the backs of my arms.

Seriously, what other woman could do that to me? With the slightest touch?

We step in.

"Eighteenth floor," I tell her, dipping her so she can reach.

She lets out an exasperated sigh. "You can put me down. I was sleeping, my legs aren't broken."

Well, I *could*...

"Plus you're carrying both our bags? *Jacob Rhodes.* You just played hockey, and—"

She squirms in my hold until I drop her feet.

I keep my other arm around her back, holding her exactly in place at my side. She looks up at me uncertainly, but I ignore it. And my hard-on that refuses to go away, like a freaking teenager pressed against his crush.

When the elevator arrives on my floor, I guide her to the right condo door. I free the keys from her hand and unlock it, moving her in ahead of me.

"Welcome home," I say. My gut tightens. Fuck, I like calling it that. To her. For her.

She lets out a little sigh, like maybe it feels right to her, too. And she walks in.

I follow in her wake as she silently explores the condo. The wide, open-concept kitchen and living space, the dining room tucked around the corner, the floor-to-ceiling windows that open onto a balcony overlooking the city. She runs her hands along the back of the sofa I only bought a few months ago, picked out by an expensive interior designer who crafted most of this place.

Melody goes into the hall that splits in two directions. To the left is her bedroom and the guest bathroom off the hall. To the right is my suite. She goes left.

"This is yours," I say when she steps into the room.

The designer styled it. It's a haven of creams and different shades of turquoise. The bed, with a cream-colored headboard, is in the center of the far wall. To its left is another floor-to-ceiling window. There's a small desk and chair, a rug that feels soft to bare feet, and a million pillows on the bed.

Her closet is half-full, waiting for the discovery.

Her bathroom is stocked.

To say I've been waiting for this would be an under-statement.

"Is it...?" I set her bag just inside the door, then stick my hands in my pockets.

She takes in the room, then the windows. Our reflections bounce back at us, and I easily read the uncertainty in her expression.

"It's too much," she whispers. "This is a lot, Jacob."

"It's enough." I shrug. "Don't worry, Melody. I'll start

charging you rent after your first paycheck if that would make you feel better."

Relief pours over her face. "Yeah, actually. That would make me feel like I'm not taking advantage of you."

I tilt my head. She wouldn't ever take advantage of me. Not in the way I'm taking advantage of *her*.

"Sleep," I say instead. "It's been a long night."

She nods. I step back then. It takes too much willpower to close the door, so I leave it open and return to my room.

I drop my bag on the bed and sit, my gaze going straight to the painting hanging on my wall. The turquoise bird with tar smeared across its wings. Stuck and unable to fly, even though it's desperate to do so.

Melody's painting.

My friends say I spent too much money on it. That, when provoked, I went down a rabbit hole I couldn't easily climb out of. But they couldn't have known that I was already chasing Melody. Chasing her blindly, through the dark, just waiting for her to make a noise. To draw a breath and reel me in.

I was so fucking aware of her, of course I would spot her in a crowd of thousands at one of the biggest games of my career.

Of course I found her painting and won the bid for it, even though her husband—the mysterious "Mr. Cameron" we cannot find—tried to outbid me.

And then the rest.

They're around the apartment. Five that I bought from her brother-in-law's gallery. Two from an art show she had here in Denver with some other artists.

I went there hoping to see her, but the owner informed me that the paintings were shipped in from California. He wouldn't give me any more information than that, a fact that still makes me grind my teeth.

No matter.

We lost the game tonight, which puts us down three to two. We need to win the next two games, or our time in the playoffs is over. I showered in the locker room and changed on the plane, so there's nothing left to do except kick off my shoes and flop into bed.

But it seems impossible with Melody separated by only a few walls.

I lie back and stare at the ceiling.

Thankfully, I only spend a few minutes of trying to breathe deeply or meditate before my phone buzzes.

> BILL
>
> Got something

I dial his number, and he picks up immediately.

"What did you find?" I'm aware of my voice and how it might travel.

"Melody Cameron made contact with a friend tonight," my investigator says. "Lucille Page. I was able to track her much easier than Ms. Cameron. Lucille has a robust social life, especially online. Her sister is married to Mafia in New York City."

He lets that sink in.

What the hell kind of friend does Melody have?

"Anyway, I was able to go back and find Melody in Lucille's history."

"Tell me."

"Lion's Head. It's a private school in Beacon Hill, New York. I accessed an online yearbook from when Lucille graduated, and sure enough, there she was: Melody Cameron."

"Her name? So it's her real name. Her... maiden name?"
I shake my head. "Send me that, would you?"

"It's in your email." Bill's voice is gruff. "Now that I have
her school, I can get her records, social security number, the
works. The rest should come easier."

Relief sweeps through me. "Thank you, Bill."

"Don't mention it, boss. Talk later."

The line goes dead, and I immediately open my email.
He's sent a link to the online yearbook, and I click through
the rows of seniors until I get to the C last names. *Cameron.*
Melody. There she is.

She's not wearing glasses. Her light-brown hair is in
soft curls over her shoulders, falling to the tops of her
breasts. She's wearing a red, ruffle shirt with a square neck-
line. Her eyes are more green than brown. Her face is
rounder, the baby fat still clinging to her cheeks and jaws.
But her smile is just as devastating.

I run my finger over her face, committing the younger
version of her to memory.

One day I'll show her. One day, I'll lay out the pieces of
her life like a feast for her to devour. To pick up what she
wants and leave the rest.

Maybe high school was terrible. Maybe she wore braces
for most of it and got made fun of, or bullies picked on her
for her weight. Maybe she wasn't popular.

Or maybe she loved high school.

I know I hated mine. I played hockey and used it as a
way to kiss girls, but it wasn't fulfilling the way kissing
Melody is. No matter where I'm kissing her, or if she's
asleep or awake.

I miss kissing her.

I miss the feel of her lips on mine, the way her tongue
slides against mine. The little breathy moans that a nip of

her lower lip can elicit, or the way she grabs at my biceps and tries to pull me closer even when she wants to shove me away.

I've missed it for years, but I only allow myself to feel it now. To revel in that specific, angry kind of pain.

Two years. There are two years of Melody's life missing, and I'm determined to find them.

Because I can't punish her for leaving me when she doesn't remember.

When she can't tell me why or where. When I lived out a nightmare those first few weeks of winter break my senior year of college, and she was just... *gone*.

15

MELODY

"I don't think I should work for the team."

Jacob turns away from the window, his eyebrows drawing up.

It takes a lot of effort not to stare. His white t-shirt clings to his frame, giving a hint of the abs that I know hide under the fabric. His biceps are huge. The tattoos on his arms—well, I want to know more. I want to hold his wrist and twist his arm every which way, examining every bit of ink.

An insane urge.

"Coffee?" He goes to the kitchen and ignores my statement.

But I thought about it. My social media is practically nonexistent. Even the page I was able to see, there were only fifteen posts. *Fifteen.* I need to look at them in closer detail, but it's a shockingly low amount. Not when other people have hundreds or thousands.

I don't know the first thing about TikTok or making a hockey team look good—or, really, whatever social media is about. Driving people to the games? Gaining fans?

I'm not even a fan.

"I'm going to continue my search for a different job." I trail him.

My gaze catches on a framed drawing. It's large and takes up the perfect amount of space on the wall. It's charcoal, I think. The artist captured a woman's profile, but it's like it's consumed by darkness. There's darkness all around, giving it a chaotic feel.

I don't stop until I'm right up next to it, taking in every inch. The way the artist managed to draw her hair as fluttering in her face, but not obscuring any of the other details. Not her nose, or her lips, or her dark eyes pointed skyward.

I *feel* something when I look at it.

I just don't know what.

Jacob stops beside me and holds out a mug. "Like it?"

"I do." I take the mug and wrap both hands around it. "What made you buy it?"

He seems to contemplate the question, and I'm grateful he's not going to brush it off. At least, I hope he's not pausing only to say that he got it because he likes it. Because for some reason, that would be disappointing.

"It gives me a fluttering feeling in my chest," he finally says in a low voice. "I saw it and knew I had to have it, because that girl seems lost. Maybe the artist is lost, too. Just hoping someone finds her."

Yes. Yes, that's right.

I eye Jacob. Up close, he's *tall*. Like, our height difference is drastic. And I suppose I already knew that, but it's another to acknowledge that in the quiet moments. When we're still.

"Do you want to remember?" Jacob asks me suddenly.

I blink, jerking back to face the drawing. "Of course. Why wouldn't I?"

"What if the past is bad?"

"That's a possibility..." I sidestep, putting some distance between us. I finally take a sip of my coffee, and the sweet flavor bursts on my tongue. It's so much better than what I had made before, even though I thought I had narrowed down what I liked. "What is this?"

"Hazelnut creamer." His eyes gleam. "Do you like it?"

"Too much." I take another sip. Hazelnut creamer. "I thought I found out what I liked."

"You did. But now you have another option."

"This is like a drug." I shake my head and lower the mug. I'm in the kitchen now, and I lean forward. My back cracks as I brace my forearms on the counter.

Jacob just watches me, coming to the other side and dragging out a chair.

"Make yourself at home," he says. "Mi casa es su casa."

"My house is your house?"

He laughs. "You know Spanish?"

I mirror his smile. It's kind of infectious. "No, I've heard the saying before. Natalie used to say it... when I first got there. I had to get a translation. And then an explanation."

But I take his words seriously. I go to the fridge and open it, examining the contents. It's a lot of healthy stuff, minus a few dark chocolate bars tucked off to the side. Juices and milk and veggies, packages of chicken and steak.

"Do you cook?" I ask him. "Do you like to cook?"

"I do. Do you?"

My brow furrows. "I don't know. Natalie always did the cooking. I just... I tried to stay out of the way, you know?"

"No."

I face him, letting the fridge door shut. "No?"

"No, I don't know. You tried to stay out of the way —why?"

"Because it wasn't my house."

"It was," he argues. "While you were living there, it was yours. Just as this is yours."

I laugh. "This? This isn't mine. It yours. I didn't do anything to earn it, or deserve it—"

"You deserve it," he replies, completely serious. "You deserve to not make yourself small for anyone."

His gaze hasn't left my face, and it's making me hot. A full-body blush that starts at my toes and works its way up to my hairline. He circles the island and stands in front of me, picking up my hand.

"And you deserve a home. So make this one yours. Okay?"

"Okay," I whisper. "Why are you doing this?"

He shrugs. "I don't have an answer to that besides wanting to help you. There's no deeper meaning here, Melody. We were friends once."

I found a new friend. I catch the words before they come spilling out. I don't know anything about Lucy. I don't know anything about Jacob either. But I do know that this conversation is too much, and I need to job hunt.

"Thanks," I manage. "I'm going to..." I hook my thumb in the direction of my room and make my way there, coffee in hand. I get to the hallway before he speaks again.

"One more thing," Jacob calls. "This is your key and fob to get into the building."

I glance back. He's set the key and fob on the counter, front and center.

"The elevator won't work otherwise," he says. "I'm going to hit the gym."

"Okay. Thanks."

He nods, still watching me like he expects something else.

I just don't know what.

After the world's most luxurious shower, in which I try every soap and scrub, shave every inch of my lower body, and then spend some time just standing under the pounding water, I get dressed. I swipe on mascara, then unpack my bag.

I haven't broken the news to Thomas and Natalie that I'm not returning. They think I'm gone for a few days at most, and Thomas didn't say anything to the contrary about NHL travel schedules. No matter that Jacob apparently has a home game in a few days.

The clothes I brought with me are laid out on my bed. Just a few shirts, pants, underwear. Not enough to sustain me, but I guess I've got money coming in soon. It'll last until then, and I may as well stay organized.

I open the closet and go still.

There are already clothes hanging in neat rows. Same with in the bureau on the other side of the closet, half the drawers are filled.

Did Jacob have another roommate before me?

Or worse—a girlfriend? Did he put her clothes in here and then forget about them?

My throat closes, and a wave of nausea rolls through me. I storm out of my room and into the living area, which is empty. I spin on my heel and burst into his room.

There's a chance he won't even be here. He said he was going to the gym...

But that was before my hour-long shower, doing my makeup, puttering around the bathroom.

Right as I stride in, I realize my error.

He *is* here. Fresh out of his own shower.

Naked.

His back muscles ripple, the towel up over his head as he rubs his hair dry. I follow the planes of his back down to his glorious ass. The backs of his thighs, hell, even his calves are amazing.

"Oh God." I slap my hand over my mouth, when it should be my eyes that I cover. But *fuck me*, I can't stop staring.

He turns to face me, shock flickering across his expression. But then I forget what his expression even is, because my attention goes down... and down...

His cock is swollen, jutting out from his body. The head is red, almost angry looking. It twitches and goes up more the longer I stare.

"You okay?"

"You're not covering yourself." My voice is thick.

"No," he agrees. He twists farther in my direction, until his dick is pointing at me. His muscles in his abdomen tighten.

"Why not?"

He flips the towel over his shoulder. His dark hair is going every which direction. But he doesn't answer and instead takes a step toward me.

"Sex is the last thing on my list," I blurt out.

He pauses.

"Um, it occurred to me that I don't know what I've done. Or like. Or want to do. So it's on the list, and now I guess I can cross off seeing a penis in person. It's a, uh, good one to see first. That I can remember. Obviously. You know, I was kind of afraid that the guy on the train was going to whip out his dick, and that would be an awful first one. How traumatizing."

Shut up, Mel.

"Anyway." I back toward the door. "Lovely. Fine specimen. I don't really have anything else to say, so I'm going to go—"

"Melody." His voice sends tingles straight through me.

I squeeze my eyes shut. It's the only way I can break the staring contest with his cock.

"What else is on your list? Besides seeing a dick."

I huff. "I don't know."

He's moving. I hear him, and then suddenly his hand is on my waist. It dips lower, into my back pocket, and he removes my phone. I stay where I am, barely breathing, while he finds the list and reads it in silence. Probably still naked, because he's an ass.

"Hmm."

I crack one eye open. "Don't judge me, Rhodes."

He chuckles. "Never."

My heart thumps extra-hard at that. I glance down, maybe somewhat surprised to find it still... erect.

"Why are you hard? Were you jacking off before I walked in?"

He looks up from my phone, then hands it back. "Third one down."

Give someone a hand job.

"Oh, I..."

"I'll walk you through it." He smiles. "Unless you're afraid? Or you'd rather stumble through it with a stranger..."

"We're friends," I protest.

"And friends help each other out." He eyes me. "You can walk out this door, Melody. I'm not stopping you."

I automatically glance to my right, at the door. The one I flung open when I barged in without knocking. But then... well, I guess I consider what it would feel like to touch his dick, and I can't deny the shiver of excitement that runs through me.

"This is wrong."

He shrugs. "Then go back to your room."

I...

I could.

Or, I could *not*.

"Decisions, decisions," he teases, dragging the towel down his back. He sits on the edge of the bed, spreading his legs and giving me a view I won't forget anytime soon. He leans back on his hands.

I shuffle forward until I'm right in front of him. He doesn't move. Doesn't so much as flinch. So I drop to my knees. His dick is suddenly right in my face. Up close, it's... well, it's *big*. I reach out and run my finger along it, and he sucks in a sharp breath.

"This is wrong," I say again.

"I know."

I take him in my hand, my grip light. I don't really know what to do next. I hadn't got so far as searching for answers on the internet, if such a thing even exists.

Jacob's hand encompasses mine. "Squeeze more."

He drags my hand up, over the mushroom head that's oozing a clear liquid, then back down. To the base. He does it twice more, then releases me. And I'm on my own.

All except his gaze, which is burning me up. I bite my lower lip, hesitating for a moment, then lean over his dick.

"What are you—?"

I spit on him. And on my hand. My saliva gives my hand more slide, and he releases a low groan. With my other hand, I cup his balls. Gently, because I don't know if that even feels good. His dick twitches and jumps.

"Is that okay?" I bite my lip again, daring a glance at his face.

"Yeah, keep doing that."

I do. And I shift on my knees because this is doing things to my body. I'm acutely aware of the swing of my breasts with every move of my arms, and the sensation between my legs.

"Melody," he warns. "Slow down. I'm going to come—"

"Good," I whisper, keeping my pace even. Because the faster I finish this, the sooner I can rush back to my room and take care of my own business.

"Fuck," Jacob groans. His cock pulses, and suddenly a rope of cum shoots from his cock. It lands on his chest. And then another on his stomach, across his twelve-pack of abs. Just kidding, he only has an eight-pack. I don't even think twelve is possible. But if it was, he'd have it.

His abdomen flexes, and my grip on his cock loosens. Holy shit. I just gave him a hand job. In his bedroom. While he's completely naked.

I *just* moved in, and now he's going to kick me out. I bolt to my feet and flee before the awkwardness sets in. It isn't until I get back to my room and spot the open closet that I remember why I went into his room in the first place.

16

JACOB

I lap at Melody's clit. Her legs are hooked over my shoulders, my face buried in her cunt. Just the way I like it.

She's asleep. Forced asleep. She didn't object to the after-dinner cocktail I made her, although she didn't know about the sleeping pill mixed into it to ensure that she doesn't wake up.

I finger-fuck her to the edge, until she's about to come, and stop. I stop everything. I pull back and watch her pussy, her muscles clenching and releasing like it'll help with the aching agony.

It won't.

Her hands on my cock this morning was unbearable in the best way. How do I tell her that she's done that before? That she's stroked me before, guiding my cock to her entrance. That she's looked at me with all the need in the world—and it still wasn't enough to satiate us.

A body like hers deserves to be worshiped, and I'm more than happy to say my prayers at her altar.

I lean in and resume my ministrations. Licking and

sucking until her clit is swollen and red, just like my cock head straining against my sweatpants. Backing off when it's too much. I could spend hours doing this. Tasting her body, taking her to the edge and driving her wild.

She might be dreaming of me.

She might blame her horniness, when she wakes, on the dreams.

I'll take immense pleasure in driving her mad with want. Until the look on her face from earlier, her barely concealed desire as she jerked me off, is permanently etched in her features. Until she wants to be in my bed willingly.

My songbird makes a beautiful noise, and I move away from her clit. I kiss up her pale stomach, over the stretch marks that she tries to hide when she's awake, to the swell of her tits. I flick my tongue against her stiff little nipple.

I missed her and I hate her and I'm obsessed with her.

This is torture.

Finally, when I can't take it anymore, I back off. I jerk off over her, catching my release in her panties. Then I right her clothes, pull the blanket up over her, and exit her room like it never happened.

When I finally fall asleep, I dream of the past.

"I'm going to keep you, Melody Cameron." She's buried under my skin. More than a fascination. And once I admit it out loud, it solidifies. It becomes my truth.

"I'm not keepable."

Not a word. An action.

She wants to leave after that. She gets in my car, and I drive her home, watching as she walks up the front steps and closes herself in her house.

I go home. I'm smiling, thinking to myself that this is the start of something new. An obsession that won't end badly. I love hockey, and I could love Melody Cameron, too. Because it's more than just her body. It's her personality, her banter.

But the next day, I don't hear from her.

And I never hear from her again.

My alarm startles me awake. I reach for my phone absently, hitting buttons until it stops making that god-awful noise.

The dream lingers, so much so that I hop out of bed and slip down the hall. Into her room.

There, I freeze.

She's on the cusp of waking, but her hand is down her sleep shorts. Her thighs are squeezed together, the sheets thrown off her. Her shirt has ridden up to just under her breasts. Her hips jerk.

I need to leave the room before she opens her eyes—but I can't seem to move.

It's only been two nights, but I'm tired of pretending that she's not mine.

"Want some help with that?"

She goes still. Her eyes flutter open, finding mine.

"Like you could do it better?" Her voice is husky, sleep-tinged, *perfect.*

Fuck.

I lift my shoulder. "One way to find out."

Melody withdraws her hand slowly. Her fingers are wet. "A one-time thing."

That's where you're wrong.

"To cross another thing off your list?" I smirk at her.

"I guess so."

I step forward, and I have no intention of stopping until she's coming on my fingers. Then my tongue.

She sits up and watches me approach. Even though

she's older than me, in this area, she's not wiser. And actually, her amnesia puts her at a disadvantage.

I take charge and pull her shorts and panties off in one clean move, drawing a squeak of protest from her lips. Maybe she didn't think about that. The fact that I'd want her naked.

"Shirt," I order.

"No." She frowns at me.

Fine.

I spread her legs and lean down. Her pussy smells like her arousal. "What did you dream about?"

Her thighs tense. "Why are you asking?"

I run my finger up her center, and she shudders.

"No reason." Just wondering if her dream was of me. And if I was satisfying or infuriating.

"This is just for the list," she breathes. "Nothing else. This is so far past friendship—"

"It's what friends do," I interrupt. I position myself between her legs, once again hooking them over my shoulders. Because I like an up-close-and-personal view.

Was I only in this same spot a few hours ago? Except now, her breathing is ragged, and her gaze on me is pulling another reaction from my cock. It wants to be enveloped in her heat—but for now, my tongue will have to do.

I lean down and kiss her lips.

The lower ones, that is.

"Jacob Rhodes!" she yelps.

"Hush."

Her core is slick with her arousal, and I make my way down to her slit, then up the other side. I pay attention to everything except her clit. My fingers dig into her thighs hard enough to bruise, keeping her legs open for me.

Her head falls back, her chest heaving, and it's then that

I lick her clit. I suck it into my mouth and graze it with my teeth. She tries to squirm, but I hold her down.

"How are you so good at this?" Her voice is as ragged as I feel.

I release her thigh and slide my hand up her body, until I find her hand. It's clenched in her sheets, and I make quick work of prying her fingers loose. I direct her hand to my head.

The weight of her palm sends electricity right to my groin. My hips shift, the tip of my cock brushing the mattress. I'm going to come from the taste of her alone.

Her nails scratch my scalp, and another wave of pleasure travels down my spine.

"You like that?" She's watching me again.

I lift my eyes to meet her gaze, then dive back down. My hand now free, I use two fingers to slowly thrust into her. Careful, like I've never done it to her before. Like her body doesn't already know me.

Her back arches at the invasion, and her fingers tighten in my hair. I go back to ignoring her clit until she tugs.

I smile and attack her clit.

"There," she groans. "Fuck, Jacob, don't stop."

I have no intention of stopping.

And I don't. Not until she comes, her muscles squeezing around my fingers and her fingers tugging my hair hard. Trying to lift me off her.

Not done.

I wedge myself in closer, sucking on her lips. I thrust my fingers lazily in and out of her, curling them and rubbing a spot deep inside her.

"What are you doing?" she moans. "I came. You can stop."

Can and will are not the same.

She falls back against her mattress until I drag another climax from her. This time, my tongue is buried in her slit, and my index and middle finger rub tight little circles on the sensitive nub. She tastes like temptation.

Melody goes limp, and I slowly pull back. I resist the urge to climb up her body and take this the rest of the way. I can't. Instead, I hop to my feet and adjust my sweatpants, ignoring my aching cock. Her eyes, the only thing moving on her body, go from my face to it. Her cheeks go red.

I make a show of capturing the remaining liquid around my mouth with my thumb, and I lick it off.

"Add oral to your likes." I grin. "And cross it off your list of firsts."

17

MELODY

I slip on Jacob's jersey, grumbling to myself. He made me promise to wear it, and I grudgingly obliged. I don't really *want* to go to the hockey game, but he mentioned something about being worried about me.

Have I been sulking for the past day and a half? Yes.

Did I quit the job as the social media assistant? Also, yes.

Kristy is great. Actually, half the people I met—the ones who cared to talk to me—were nice. It just wasn't the right job for me.

I'm meeting Lucy Page before the game. Game *six*.

She and I texted a bit yesterday, enough for her to convince her husband to fly to Denver and come to the playoff game. They're Guardians fans, and there's a chance their team could win and move on to the next round. Which would end Jacob's season.

JACOB

I'm sending a driver.

I roll my eyes.

Lucy is picking me up. It's fine.

JACOB

Text me when you get here.

He's been at the arena since eleven o'clock this morning. Doing what, I don't have any fucking idea. Or interest. But I swore I'd wear the jersey, and that's what I can't go back on. And that kind of locked me into going to the game, too.

Besides, I want answers that Lucy can give me.

I finally checked my social media. Of my meager posts, Lucy was in three of them. Jacob was in none—unsurprising, actually. I searched for *his* social media page and found it even more impersonal than mine. Shots of him on the ice both recently and in college, signing the Titans contract, posing on a lake with some friends. Barely any captions. But he sure is tagged in a lot. Seems like, for all the warmth he shows me, he's not friendly toward his fans.

LUCY

We're out front!

Be right down.

I found a tube of red lipstick along with the other makeup I brought from Thomas's house. It seemed unused, so I caved. It sits in my purse, waiting for me to put it on. Another thing I'm oddly afraid to do. I shove my glasses higher up my nose and flip my hair back.

The checklist of things I need runs through my head as I stride for the door. Phone. Key to the condo and the fob that'll get me in the elevator. Purse. The ticket from Jacob is on my phone.

In the elevator, it dawns on me that I haven't actually

left Jacob's building. We went down to the gym yesterday, and he showed me the pool on the tenth floor. The building is terraced, so the pool is at the top of the widest level. It's enclosed in the winter and open in the summer.

I don't know if I like swimming. Or if I know how to swim. Jacob made a comment offhandedly about pushing me in to find out, but I think the panic in my eyes stopped him. So... that's a mystery for another day.

Lucy is standing on the curb beside a large, black SUV. She's got a Guardians jersey on, one that fits her form instead of like a shroud. She waves and bounces forward, dragging me into a hug.

"Sorry," she exclaims, releasing me quickly. "Getting used to the memory loss thing."

"You and me both." I try to laugh. It's a little strained, but... whatever.

The back door of the SUV opens, and a tall man gets out. He's gorgeous. Tall, dark hair, clean-cut. He drops his hand on Lucy's shoulder, and I automatically flinch.

"This is my husband, Theo," Lucy introduces. "He went to the rival high school, and we ended up at college together."

They trade a look I can't decipher.

"Nice to meet you, Melody."

I shake his hand. Because... well, I guess that feels better than hugging? I don't want to hug him. He's kind of scary, in a rich, pretty-boy way.

"Same," I manage.

"Ready?" Lucy asks.

"Lux," Theo warns.

She sighs. "He thinks a hockey game might be a bad first date for us. Not that it's a date, but you know. Meeting."

"Oh, no, it's fine." I wave off their concern.

"Well, it's just that you don't really like violence."

I laugh. "I figured that out already, thanks. But Jacob is playing, and he asked me to be there, so..."

"Jacob Rhodes?" Theo cocks his head.

"Yeah. Why?"

He eyes me. "It's nothing, I'm sure."

Okay. I mean, maybe he's judging me. Hell, *I'm* judging me. I woke up more turned on than I've ever been, and then *Jacob* walked in. Burst in, just like I did to him. And then he went down between my legs and... well, I think I found my new religion.

Jacob Rhodes' tongue.

I clear my throat and climb into the SUV. Lucy follows. Theo takes the front seat beside a driver I hadn't realized was waiting in the car for us.

"We're fancy." Lucy laughs. "Sorry, should've warned you."

"It's okay." I pull out my phone. "I made a list of questions for you."

"Oh. Cool. Hit me with 'em."

I scan the list. I made it last night, endlessly worried that I'd get too caught up in the evening to ask everything I want to know. And yes, I'm reasonably sure Lucy isn't going to disappear on me. Part of this is a test to see how much she knows.

"Where did we meet?"

Lucy grins. "Easy. We met freshman year in high school. We weren't friends, though. You had a few friends, and we just interacted kind of at the surface level. Like, we were partners in Biology to dissect frogs, for example. We didn't get close until after. I think it was four years later, babe, right?"

"It was after you came back," Theo says.

I don't know what that means. Came back from what?

"We ran into each other in Beacon Hill, where we grew up." She goes quiet. "I think you were back for your grand-mother's funeral."

Oh. The idea of a grandmother is strange. But weirder still is the idea of her being gone.

"We grabbed a drink, realized how much we had in common, and the rest was history." She makes a face. "Well, I guess... okay, it's history to me. Hopefully it comes back for you, too."

"What do you do for work?"

"I'm a journalist. I was working for a paper in Boston, but I decided to start my own online platform. It gives me more freedom, and I work on longer investigative pieces." She smiles. "I've got a remote staff of four. Three of us work together, the other two maintain the site."

"Wow." That's really cool. "What's the site? Can I check it out?"

She nods and types it into my browser. I bookmark it and switch back to my questions.

"So, I lived in Beacon Hill, New York. When I woke up in the hospital, the investigator wasn't able to locate my parents..."

Lucy doesn't seem surprised by that. "Your parents weren't good people. They wouldn't help you even if they were around."

Something settles in my chest.

An acceptance, maybe? I think I already knew, deep down, that I didn't have a happy family.

"Where are they?"

Lucy sighs. "Your dad is in prison. Your mom..."

Here it comes.

"She died."

Oh.

"I think I already knew she was gone," I say quietly, my gaze on my knees. Still, it kind of hurts. A lump fills my throat. Did I go to her funeral? Did I mourn her?

What did my father do to end up in prison?

"Did I... where was I when she passed?"

They both hesitate.

"What?"

"We don't know where you went," Lucy says. She grips my hand harder. "You weren't at her funeral. Her sister organized the whole thing, but you were off the grid."

Where was I?

"And before that?"

"Teaching." Lucy brightens. "You were a college professor. English."

"I feel like my mind just keeps getting blown," I whisper.

"Your undergrad college hired you first. That's where you were living when you met..." Lucy stops.

"Please." Jesus, I'm practically begging.

"Henry," Theo says from the front. His voice is colder, the disdain evident. "That's where you met Henry."

The name doesn't ring a bell. I shrug, shaking my head.

Lucy groans. "This is not where I wanted the conversation to go. I wanted to talk about *us*. How much fun we would have together. Not... this."

"What *is* this?" I glance at the driver, who's studiously ignoring us. "Lucy, I know I don't know you, but you know me. Would I bury my head in the sand over this?"

Her face falls.

"Yeah, Mel. You would."

That stings more than I anticipated.

I *was* a coward.

Deep down, I knew that. I had figured it out weeks ago. But now, it's just a matter of changing my own perspective. This is a fresh start, and I can choose to be braver.

"Tell me."

"You met, and fell in love with, a man named Henry Armstrong," she starts.

She paints a pretty picture. Dazzling dates in the city—New York, that is—and a fast-paced romance. We moved in together within a few months, and he proposed after six. Whirlwind was one word to describe us, but from all accounts, we were in love.

Until the bruises started showing up.

Until I cut off my relationships with *everyone*. Lucy and my other friends, any family.

Until he took away my phone and made it impossible to call for help. My car was next.

I feel the weight of each word like a sledgehammer against my skin. I was a victim of domestic violence. I fell into a trap, thinking that this man loved me. That he loved me more than anything in the world.

"You divorced him," she finally says, and a ray of hope lights me up. "You got a restraining order against him. We repaired our friendship, Mel, but you... You were different. Softer, less secure. Not like now."

"How am I now?"

"You're alive again."

We pull up beside the arena, and the driver opens first Lucy's door, then mine. Theo meets us on the sidewalk, and he curls his arm around her shoulders.

I feel alone.

I'm *alive* again? Because I don't have the weight of abuse on my shoulders? Because I can't remember a horror-filled past? I still have what Thomas did to me, and the man on the train, and the awful realization in the hospital that someone tried to kill me. I touch the scar on my throat, probing it with my fingers, and a wave of nausea hits me.

"I'm so sorry, Mel," Lucy whispers. "I shouldn't have brought it up. I knew I was going to mess this up—"

"Lucy," I interrupt. "It's okay. I'd rather know."

Maybe I was a coward before. But his name doesn't strike fear in my chest. I've got no attachment to it, which makes me *strong*.

Henry Armstrong.

I write his name down on my list. Another thing to search when I'm feeling brave enough. And now my mother, too. An unexpected name to add. Once I have her obituary, I'll be able to unlock the rest of it. My family history, maybe, or just blow away the mystery surrounding them.

Me.

I allow Lucy to loop her arm through mine, and we head into the arena.

"Do you have more questions?" she asks, once we're through security and following Theo to the right section.

"Of course."

I scan the list again.

"Do you know my favorite drink?"

"You're partial to a margarita. Coffee can go two ways— I think you like cream and two sugars, but if they have hazelnut flavoring, you're a goner."

Jacob *does* know me.

"What else?"

"Coconut is on the Do Not Fly list." She laughs. "Write that down. You *hate* coconut."

I smile. I hadn't got to coconut yet.

"Oh, oh!" Lucy does a little skip. "Your favorite book. Which is freaking hard to narrow down, by the way, Ms. English Professor. *Circe* by Madeline Miller."

I type that into my list, too. My excitement is rising swiftly, matching Lucy's. A book. I bring up the book's details and read the description. My heart skips.

"Oh, what I would do to read my favorite book for the first time again," Lucy moans. "You're lucky in that regard."

"We like to read, then." It's not really a question—if I was an English professor.

"We love it."

What else do I love? The question is on the tip of my tongue. Before I can get it out, though, Theo is leading us down a set of steps. All the way down, down, down.

To the glass.

I swallow.

"Theo," Lucy calls. "You can explain the game to Mel, right?"

He nods once.

"Sit between us." She urges me to follow Theo into the first row.

We drop into our seats, and I let out a little huff of laughter. We're right next to the penalty box. Whose, I don't know. But across the ice are the players' benches.

Kristy is standing in the open doorway, talking to the equipment manager. For a moment, I contemplate waving to her, trying to catch her attention. An impossible task, I think. So I sit back and smile to myself, and cast a good luck thought in her direction. For if she ever gets the nerve to ask the equipment manager out.

We're just in time for the warm-up. I spot Jacob immediately, and we're on the right side. The Titans skate by us, all of them seeming focused. Well, all except one, who slows and winks at me on his way by.

"Rhodes is a talented defenseman," Theo comments, watching him pass. "He has a reputation."

I frown. "What kind of reputation?"

"For being cold."

My mind flashes to the other morning. "He's not cold with me."

"Just be careful," Lucy murmurs. "You don't have the best record when it comes to guys."

"I don't have any record," I reply. "I'm a blank slate."

Jacob shoots at the empty net. He fist-bumps a teammate and keeps going, skating around and making it look easy. Moving on the ice is natural, his body moving fluidly. His helmet obscures his dark hair, the long sleeves of his blue, mint, and white jersey hiding his tattoos.

Maybe he is a bad choice. As a friend, or whatever he is.

But I'll have to learn the consequences on my own.

18

JACOB

I skate hard for the puck, reaching with my stick. We're down by two, damn it, and the clock is ticking. Four minutes left in the third period. If we lose this, we're done. The Guardians will move on to the next round, and all our hard work will end in a disappointing playoffs run.

Not happening.

I catch the puck and guide it around with me sharply, casting a quick glance at my left. Knox is rocketing toward me, a fierce expression painted on his face. I pass the puck to my teammate, Scofield, a moment before Knox collides with me. We slam into the boards, and the feeling vibrates through me.

It doesn't hurt. There's too much adrenaline for that. I pick myself up and race after my best friend—although right now, he's my enemy. Our goalie, Joel Haverhill—nick-named Hammerhead—stops a shot from the Guardian left wing. It bounces off his pad and back into play. I slam into Knox again before he can regain control of the puck that skittered his way.

"Fucker," he manages under his breath.

I steal the puck and put on a burst of speed in the opposite direction, taking it back toward the opposite end.

Knox and I have raced countless times. He's faster. *But I'm more agile.*

I dodge around an oncoming Guardian, leaping over his stick and slipping the puck between his skates. I pass to Church, our team captain, who immediately takes a shot at the net.

It sails in.

The red lights over the goal flash, the horn blows. The crowd erupts. Relief and joy flicker through me, the screaming and cheering like a rush of wind in my ears. Our captain takes off in celebration, throwing his arms up in the air. I crash into him, slapping him on the helmet. We're immediately joined by the others. It's a mob of happiness for a brief moment, before Camden Church shakes us off.

"We need two more, boys," he yells. "Focus. Let's get it done."

There's a line change. I switch out, taking a breather, and join another of our starters.

Scofield, our left wing, grins at me. "Nice assist."

I smirk, popping my mouth guard out. I hold it while I gulp water, then refocus on the game and stick the guard back in. I keep playing with it while I watch.

The ref makes our center switch out, and all the players seem to lean in. Preparing for the puck drop.

Then it's on, and we get the puck. I glance up at the clock, my throat tight. Two minutes to go, and we're down by one. I plant my elbows on my thighs and look down the line. Soren Dawes meets my gaze and gives me a sharp nod.

Coach is suddenly motioning. The tide is turning, the puck in our possession.

Line change.

Dawes and I jump over the wall and hustle into Guardian territory. Our goalie, Haverhill, skates like hell for the bench. He steps up, leaving our net wide open, and Scofield joins us.

Last chance.

We hustle. Church is there, and I pass it to him. To Scofield. Back to me.

There are a mix of bodies in front of the goalie, blocking his line of view, so I send a wild shot up high. It sails through the air—and somehow, almost faster than I can comprehend, it flies into the net.

Goal.

My teammates surround me as the horn bellows. The screaming crowd is even more frantic. I check the score-board. At the time now frozen in place.

0:05.

Talk about a close one.

"Overtime, baby," Dawes crows in my ear. "You're on fire tonight. An assist and a goal."

I shake him off and follow Church off the ice. I cast a glance toward where Melody sits with her friend and the friend's husband. I had them vetted yesterday. Nothing unusual to report. But I will hang any credit of me being on fire on Melody's shoulders.

She's here. She's wearing my jersey.

A year ago, I wouldn't have even dreamed of that.

The possibility, I mean.

In the locker room, I grab my phone and check for messages from her. There's one letting me know that she arrived—from a few hours ago—and nothing since.

Having fun?

The typing dots appear shortly after. They disappear and come back twice before her message comes through.

MELODY

Yeah, actually. Theo's been explaining the game, and it makes more sense now. Not saying I'm going to be an expert, obviously.

And you're getting questions answered?

I used to be a college professor.

I stare at the words.

If I close my eyes, I can still picture her standing at the front of the classroom. Her handwriting at the top of my papers, failing me time and again for theories and interpretations I didn't understand. She was a light. She was the object of my obsession. There was hardly a day that passed in that semester that I didn't think about her.

So what if I forced my way into her life? It's not dissimilar to how I'm acting now. It's habit with her. She resists, and I take anyway. No matter what lessons she tries to teach me, I just don't learn when it comes to her.

What can I say?

I was always a bad student.

"Rhodes." Camden Church, team captain and right wing, drops onto the bench beside me. His helmet is off, his hair damp. "You look distracted."

I roll my eyes. "I'm fine."

"Now's not the time to lose focus."

"Fuck off, Church."

He grins and stands again. "Whatever you say, pretty boy."

I shake my head.

MELODY

You still there?

Always.

We're right next to your penalty box. We saw Dawes thrown in there earlier (Theo told me his name, and that he's a starter like you)…

Is there a question in there?

Do you ever get put in the penalty box?

Only when I'm naughty

You fight?

I got ejected from a game once. For fighting.

Because I was so fucking pissed at the world, and at *her*, that I could barely see straight. The guy said one wrong thing, and I snapped. But it worked out fine, because it led me to the art auction on the suite level, where I found the bird painting by Melody.

I wonder if she knows she's an artist. If her friend mentioned her paintings.

Would she still have the talent without the memory?

If I forgot everything, would I be able to play hockey?

What a foolish thought.

I'm stuck with the desire to get Melody an easel. Paints. Whatever her heart desires. I want to sit her in front of it and set her loose on the canvas, just to see what happens.

Maybe she can fly. Without memory of it… maybe she can forget the tar stuck to her wings and taste the wind.

19
MELODY

JACOB

> I got ejected from a game once. For fighting.

Flashes of his bloody knuckles, his face, cross my mind.

> I guess I was in an abusive relationship. Before.

There's a weird rushing noise in my ears. I can't believe I just told him that over text. Or worse, maybe he already knew. It could be one of those things that he was trying to hide from me or protect me from.

The urge to spill out more has me typing and erasing. It wars with doubt.

JACOB

> If I ever meet that bastard, I'd do unfathomable things to him.

My skin heats.

But at least I know the two haven't met.

Lucy drops down into the seat beside me, handing me a beer and popcorn. She's got a beer of her own. Theo returns a few moments later, his gaze sweeping his wife. Doing inventory? Making sure she's okay? It's kind of sweet.

> Not necessary. Apparently, I have a restraining order against him.

JACOB

> Still married?

> Name?

> We never talked about him? Before?

> No, but we're going to.

I swallow. I don't know what there is to talk about. I don't reply, and he doesn't push. The time has passed quickly, the little counter ticking down to the start of the fourth period.

I'm actually anxious for them.

The Titans, that is. There's this energy in the arena that only picked up in the last few minutes of the third period when they drew even with the Guardians' score.

Now it's tied, and my heart is in my throat.

"Do you feel this at every game?" I ask Lucy.

The roar of the crowd as the players re-emerge interrupts her answer, but she nods emphatically.

"It's addictive, isn't it?"

Is it?

I ponder that. I suppose, in a way, living for the excitement of the game, the rush of the tied score—or even better, when your team is on the verge of winning—would be indulgent. That's why people buy season tickets, right? To experience a sort of high.

Jacob comes out, his mouth guard hanging out. He finds me in the crowd and waves. It draws attention, and I instinctively sink lower in my seat. I glare at him through the glass as he passes, but his smirk just widens.

The game resumes.

I can't take the stress. It builds in my throat, and I have to cover my mouth with both hands. If I didn't have glasses, my eyes would be covered, too.

The time ticks down. After a certain point, the crowd gets on their feet and stays up. I rise, too. Lucy and Theo, on either side of me, are screaming at their team.

Jacob gets the puck. He takes it down the far side of the rink, racing toward the Guardians' goalie. It's practically one-on-one, with the other players surging to catch him. He shoots, and my heart stops.

The puck slips just under the goalie's leg pad and into the net.

They won. They're not out of this race, not out of the playoffs.

Lucy slaps my back. "On to game seven," she crows. "We better see you in NYC."

I grimace. "I don't know. We'll see."

I can't exactly afford to keep flying back and forth. Especially without the fancy, mostly fake job that Jacob got me. We return to Jacob's high-rise. The driver picks us up one block over from the arena, somehow magically avoiding all of the gridlocked traffic.

We make it there in record time.

"Do you want to come up?"

Lucy smiles. "Thanks for the offer, but I think we're going to head back. We've got an early flight tomorrow."

I cover her hand with mine. "Thank you for filling in some gaps."

"Any questions, please, don't hesitate to ask."

In the elevator, I check my phone.

JACOB

Are you waiting for me?

Oops.

I'm in the elevator at your building

JACOB

At least wait up for me?

Six innocuous words.

But from him, they sound... *more.*

I shiver and chew on my lower lip.

Guess you'll find out...

In the condo, though, I get a burst of courage. I slick on the red lipstick. I shed my pants and bra, dropping them on the other side of my bed. It leaves me in just his jersey, which barely covers my ass.

Why?

Because seeing him play hockey and not break out into a fight was oddly erotic. And if *I'm* riding on a high, I don't even know how he's feeling.

I sit on the couch—but that lasts all of three minutes.

I check my phone.

Nothing.

My feet are bare on the cold floor, and goosebumps rise on the backs of my arms. I stand in front of the window, my attention flicking between my reflection and the view. I adjust my glasses, then tap my phone again.

I drift to my bedroom and perch on the end of the bed, extending my legs and crossing them at the ankles. My breath comes out long and slow. But there's too much tension now, and I'm getting *nervous*. Second-guessing myself.

What did I expect? For him to run home?

He probably went out for a drink or something. To celebrate another win with his teammates.

I go to his bedroom and sit on the edge of *his* bed. Straight ahead is a painting, framed in the center of the huge wall. It's kind of mesmerizing. There's a row of mini lights over it, designed to illuminate—and perhaps showcase—the art. I flick the light on and take my seat again, running my fingers through my hair.

Blue bird. Unusual color.

It's caught in a black substance. I inch closer, until I'm barely a foot away. My gaze moves all over the painting, taking in the strokes, the lines. The way the artist managed to put panic in the bird's eye.

Who knew birds could panic like that?

I feel it. It's in my throat, constricting my breathing. My chest is tight. I roll my wrists, just to convince myself that I'm not shackled. Which is a weird impulse to have, isn't it?

Abusive ex-husband.

I examine the skin on my left wrist. Under the mini spotlights, I feel, I *see*, the barest hint of a raised scar.

My body goes cold. The temperature in the room may as well have plummeted.

There's the same on the other one. A ring around the outside of my wrist, just a little whiter and jagged than the rest of my skin.

"Holy shit," I whisper.

Bile rises up my throat.

I rush out of Jacob's bedroom and into my bathroom, my stomach heaving. I make it, kneeling in front of the toilet. I close my eyes as I puke, gripping the edges of the toilet tightly.

When my stomach settles, I brush my hair back. I wipe the stupid lipstick off. I slip into my room and get changed for real, pulling on the most unattractive pajamas I can find. I toss a sweatshirt on over my shirt and head into the living room.

My phone is still on the counter, but I ignore it in favor of the little wet bar Jacob has set up in the corner of the living room. All his liquor and glasses are on a rolling cart, but I gather he doesn't drink much—judging by the liquid levels anyway.

If I like margaritas, I probably like tequila.

I lift the bottle from the row and pour myself a splash.

"Here goes nothing," I mutter to myself.

Down it goes.

I grimace. It doesn't taste *great*, but it's also not the worst thing in the world. I pour myself another mouthful and swig it back. It's slightly better—and now the heat is diffusing through my abdomen.

Okay.

Yeah.

Another gulp. It goes up my nose a bit, and I end up sputtering and coughing. I take the bottle and my glass to the couch and drop onto it, my head falling back.

Damn Jacob.

"Cheers." Talking to myself.

By the time the door opens, I'm *drunk*. My eyelids are

heavy, and I can't stop tracing the scar on my wrist. Now that I know it's there, it's like a fresh wound to pick at.

"Melody?"

The couch moves.

I huff a laugh. "I was going to seduce you, you know."

Silence.

"In your jersey..." I drop my voice to a whisper. "And nothing else."

"I would've liked to see that."

"But then I discovered something." I think my eyes are closed.

"What's that?"

I lift my wrist and kind of throw it in his direction. His warm fingers close over my bare skin, and I shiver. I twist my arm. "Scars. I saw the bird in your room. It made me think of shackles. And *poof*, here's the proof." I giggle at the rhyme.

He traces the scar.

"I'm not crazy," I whisper.

He drags me into his lap. It's rough and sudden, and I flinch a little. He catches my hands and brings them down to my lap, tugging my upper body until I lean on him. My cheek touches his shoulder.

I crack my eyes open and stare at the stubble on his jaw.

"I'm not crazy," I repeat.

"You're not. You *are* drunk, though." His Adam's apple bobs as he talks. His jaw tics. "Why?"

"I thought alcohol would unlock a memory." I sigh. "It didn't."

"Okay. It's time for bed."

I shudder and shake my head. "No, no, I don't think so. I think I'm going to stay awake forever."

"Why?"

I force my eyes open wider, tilting my head back until I can see his face. His nice, flushed-cheeks, intense-eyes *face*. "I don't want to be that bird, Jacob. I can't get stuck."

He stares into my eyes for too long. Until I start to feel like he's picking me apart.

"Okay," he finally says. "But you're not going to like the alternative."

He rises, taking me with him. My stomach heaves, but it doesn't matter. He holds me close and walks easily with me in his arms. Down the hall, past the illuminated painting, and into his bathroom. He sets me on my feet and leans into the glass shower. He turns on the water...

Then pushes me in.

It's freaking *cold*.

I don't know where I lost my glasses, but they're not on my face. In an instant, my hair is soaked, my pajamas —*everything*. My teeth chatter, and I try to get out of the shower as soon as my body unlocks.

Jacob shoves me against the wall, then steps in after me. He heaves my sweatshirt over my head, tossing it behind him. It hits the floor with a wet slap. My shirt is next —although this he doesn't bother trying to remove gracefully. He grips the collar with both hands and rips it.

My mouth drops open. "W-what the fuck?"

He pulls the remaining fabric down my arms. I cover my breasts.

The water is heating. Either that, or I'm going numb and my body is adjusting. I lean against the wall, my knees threatening to give out on me, but Jacob surprises me. *Again.*

He steps right up, his shirt gone—*when did that happen?* —and presses himself to me.

Chest to chest.

He's warm. Hot, even. I shiver again at the contrasting sensations, because the water's got nothing on him. He lifts my hand and presses it against the tile next to my head.

"Scars," he murmurs. "You're covered in scars, songbird."

This is the second time he's called me songbird. I should latch on to it, I should ask him more about it, but the tequila has me acting stupid. I lift my chin. I know the worst of the scars is hidden by my hair, but the obvious one is across my throat.

He runs his finger along it.

"You didn't know me with scars?" I ask. "Or you didn't know me well enough to notice them."

Jacob growls under his breath. It seems to vibrate his chest, going straight into mine. Well, into my freaking nipples, which are already stiff from the contact.

That's not the only stiff thing.

His cock is growing between us, pressing into my belly.

"I've cataloged every mark on your body," he says, still tracing the scar on my throat. "You want the truth?"

"Yes. *Please.*" There's that familiar desperation fluttering in my chest.

He groans. "The truth, Melody, is that you *are* that bird. The one in the painting. And I thought your husband was the tar holding you down, the binding making you stick to the earth."

"Ex," I whisper. "Ex-husband."

He shakes his head. "But it's not him. It's *me.*"

I lean into him. His erection is even harder. That's how close together we stand, his hips pinning me to the wall. Which is what I need. I don't think I'd be able to stand on my own.

"Truth time of my own, Jacob Rhodes."

He raises his eyebrow.

I want him in the worst way.

It could be the tequila. It could be the tension that's been ramping up between us for days. It *could* be my past coming back to haunt me. But then the truth escapes my lips, and it hovers between us. For him to do as he pleases with it.

"I'm afraid of flying."

20

MELODY

One minute, I'm staring at him. Pleading, silently, for him to *do* something.

The next, his lips are slanted over mine.

And holy motherfucking electricity.

You can't tell me this is the first time we've kissed. It isn't. I know that in my bones, kissing Jacob Rhodes comes as naturally as breathing. I crave him. I want him. He still has my wrist pinned to the wall beside me, but I waste no more time throwing my other arm around his neck. I arch into him, reveling in the slide of his lips on mine. The way his tongue traces the seam of my mouth, then presses.

A little pressure, and I'm cracking open.

I yank my hand down, going to his sweatpants. Fuck the tequila. Fuck the impropriety. I need him *right now*. I get his cock free and my fingers around his thick length before he captures my wrist again. He pulls my hand away, twisting it behind my body. It's suddenly caught between my back and the tile, and he uses the leverage to keep me against him.

I part my lips and let his tongue into my mouth. He

kisses like a god. His teeth catch my lower lip, and the blip of pain only increases the ache between my legs.

I'm going to go mad with lust for him.

"Fuck me," I breathe. "Please fuck me."

He groans. His free hand tangles in my wet hair, yanking my head back. My arm is still around his neck. I slip my hand down to cup the side of his neck, my thumb capturing his pulse. Just to see if he's as worked up about this as I am.

His heart rate matches mine. His stare nearly burns from the intensity.

"I won't fuck you drunk," he finally says. "But I will drive you insane with need."

He shuts off the water.

I blink, suddenly swaying at his absence.

He kicks off his wet sweatpants, and I find myself mimicking him. Yanking down my shorts and panties, kicking them aside. I follow him out, to where he wraps me in a towel from behind. His arms come around me, just under my breasts, and I fight the urge to lean into him.

"Dry off and get on the bed," he tells me, his lips nearly touching my ear.

Yes, sir.

I shake that off and do as I'm told. My buzzed brain makes my motions languid, slow. It seems to take forever to drag the cloth up my legs, over my belly and curves, to my hair. I finger comb it and half-heartedly rub it dry.

He watches me, his own towel tossed over his shoulder and forgotten.

And then he follows me into his bedroom.

I stare at the bird for a moment, then crawl onto the bed on my hands and knees. I'm about to turn around when he stops me. He holds on to my hips. I crane around right as his lips touch my ass cheek.

"Fuck," I hiss.

He bites me.

He *BITES* me!

I lurch forward, but he just drags me back. His tongue laves at the spot, and then his teeth are marking me again. I groan, the pain going straight to my core. My arousal is climbing, and he doesn't seem to care. He ignores everything except my ass, complete with cellulite and extra fat, and rolls on my hips.

When he spreads my cheeks, my face flames.

I drop my head to the bed. Burying my face, metaphorically and literally.

At the first touch of his tongue, I'm a freaking goner.

I cry out. His fingers dig into my skin, keeping me open, as he tongue-fucks my asshole. Pressing in until it admits him, taking and taking until I'm a quivering mess.

"Please," I whisper.

"Good girl," he replies, and his fingers slide through my slick core.

He finds my clit, rubs it and then dips into my pussy. Then back. Over and over again, while he continues to pay special attention to my *other* hole. Two fingers thrust into me, twisting and caressing a spot that desperately wants attention.

Two becomes three.

"Tell me when you're going to come," he says suddenly, pulling back. "I want to hear you say it."

"I—"

"When you're on the edge, songbird."

I grip the covers, my arms stretched out over my bowed

head. I want to rock back into him. I want to urge him to move faster. I want him inside me.

And then it's there. Cresting like a wave.

I can barely get the words out. "Going to come."

He stops.

My pussy clenches at nothing, my clit is painfully abandoned. My body is screaming with need, and he just —*stopped*.

"Jacob?"

His knuckles brush my ass cheek. The one he didn't bite.

Even that is sensitive.

"Turn over," he orders.

I flop onto my side, then manage to roll on my back without kicking him. I eye him, his cock. It's pointing at me, oozing the clear liquid. He grips it in one hand, stroking his length. Up, down, up, down.

He's mesmerizing.

My heartbeat slows. The climax fades, but the ache lingers. Reminding me that I was *right there*.

He touches me again.

I'm not ready for it, even though I see him move. I see him come toward me, his finger running past my clit, to my slit. Where he pumps in a single finger.

In and out, in time with his hand stroking himself off.

"Your list," he says softly.

I blink, trying to focus on something other than *sensation*. "What?"

"Your list. I looked at it."

"When?"

"Before I put you on my lap." He retracts his finger and runs it across my clit.

"What about it?" My voice is breathless.

"You forgot kinks."

Oh.

"The boring, necessary stuff? We'll get there in no time." He smiles. It's positively wicked. *I'm the tar.* Hadn't he said that? "But the *interesting* stuff?"

I lick my lips. "What's interesting stuff?"

His expression is dark. I can't read him at all. I mean, I see the lust. I feel it, as every stroke of his hand brings his knuckles up against my inner thigh. Proof that he's turned on by me, by what he's saying.

Something tells me I should be afraid.

"One thing at a time," he whispers.

I can't fathom what he means.

"I'm going to enjoy ruining you for anyone else."

One finger becomes two, and I close my eyes. I fall back on the bed, my attention locked on his face. He takes my hand and puts it on my clit.

"Make yourself come before I do, or you don't come at all." He smirks.

A challenge?

I dip my fingers into my pussy, my muscles automatically contracting. I'm drenched. So fucking turned on—and by what? By how he's treating me?

Before I can puzzle it out, I put my fingers on my clit. I rub myself hard and fast, the tingling sensation building, but I'm too late.

And I think that's the point.

His cock is suddenly pressing into my slit. I yell at the sensation of being stretched—but he doesn't press inward. He's so fucking shallow, barely the tip is inside me.

That's when he comes, jerking himself off. He spills inside me, and I can only stare.

I'm not on birth control.

I didn't think...

It didn't occur to me. Unless the old Melody has an IUD and the doctors forgot to mention it, I'm screwed.

He pulls out, and immediately his fingers are there.

"You know what I'm doing, don't you?"

I close my eyes.

"I'm pushing my cum back inside you. Keeping you plugged up with my fingers until I fuck you for real." He leans over me. His weight descends, and I sink down, down, down. His fingers are inside me, completely still. Just holding, his fingertips twitching.

I move my hips.

I need *something*.

"Hush," he whispers, kissing my neck. He settles in against me. His fingers inside me, his lips at my throat.

21

JACOB

When she falls asleep, I shift my weight and slip inside her again.

I don't know what it is about her, about her *sleeping* that turns me on, but it's the worst sort of balm for the ache that threatens to destroy me on a daily basis. Just assuring myself that she's under me, that she's here, isn't enough.

Being inside her is.

I fuck her slowly, lifting her leg up to get deeper. To feel the sweet squeeze of her cunt on my length. I trace the scar on her wrist and add it to the list of things I don't know about Melody. Was it her *ex*-husband? The one she apparently has a restraining order against?

Was it her mother?

She once confessed that her mother was obsessed with her weight. She'd measure her. Count her calories. Do all sorts of traumatizing things to a child.

I like the softness of her. I like that she's my opposite. She's not tiny compared to other women, but she's a good eight inches shorter than me. She lets me pick her up, and bury my face between her legs, and—

She groans.

Softly.

I wrap my hand around her throat and catch the vibrations of her noises in my palm. Her eyes flutter.

Without thinking, I squeeze. My fingers and thumb press into her pulse points, slowing the flow of blood to her brain, until she seems to relax again. Slipping farther into unconsciousness.

I thrust into her again. I keep my hand on her throat, the pressure light. I like the feel of her fluttering pulse against the pads of my fingers. At this rate, I'm going to last an embarrassingly short amount of time. She just drives me crazy.

I can't help it.

My balls tighten, and I slam to a halt inside her. Filling her as I come again. I need this. My cum inside her is too good to resist. So I won't.

I stay there. I kiss her neck, careful not to leave any more marks. I don't want her to associate me with her cousin. I don't want her to think anything of him when she should be thinking of me. When my cock finally goes soft, I slip out of her and crawl backward down her body. I stand, watching her for a moment.

She's so fucking pretty.

When she's sober, when she chooses me for real, I'll be ready.

Right now, she doesn't know what she wants. She doesn't know herself.

After dressing, I close her in my room and head to my office. It's tucked out of the way, behind the kitchen, and is neglected ninety percent of the time. My agent said I should have an office, so I did. I had the space for the design, and the interior decorator didn't object.

I sink into the leather chair and kick my feet up on the desk, dialing a number by heart.

"A bit early for you, isn't it?"

I bite back a smile and check my watch. It's just past one o'clock. "I felt like mixing things up."

"Well, I suppose that's something." Vicky chuckles. "Thanks for the tickets, by the way. Of course it's a game that you lose."

"I can't exactly predict that," I defend. "Did you like the suite?"

"It was great."

I had to pull strings with Knox to get it, but it's worth it. Vicky, the 9-1-1 dispatcher who works in my father's district, deserves the best.

"The limo was an extra touch," she adds.

"Well, it's just for the favor I'm about to ask. Preemptively sweetening the deal, you know?"

She groans.

"I haven't even asked yet."

"Yeah, but it was a limo. I'm sure it's going to be a big ask. I'd bet money on it."

"Game seven tickets are calling your name, Vicky."

She's quiet for a beat. "In a suite. With a limo."

"Done." I snap my fingers. "Can you tell me about a TRO that was filed in New York City? Filed by Melody Cameron."

"Oh, Jacob, what the hell are you up to?"

I think of the scars. The fear on Melody's face. She needed to get drunk to face it, and it kills me that she's going through this alone. Without knowing where her ex-husband is, or what his name is, I know I need to find him.

And maybe end his miserable life once and for all.

"Give me a moment," Vicky finally says.

Giving in.

"Henry Armstrong."

I suck in a breath—then write down the name. I almost don't bother, but it gives me something to do while my mind whirls. Months ago, a man I assumed was her current husband revealed himself to me as Mr. Cameron. Clearly that was a lie to keep me at bay or to conceal his identity. Both in that he's her ex and has a different name.

But it worked. I was sent down a rabbit hole of trying to find Melody's maiden name, court documents for the change, their marriage certificate. To come up blank because Cameron *is* her maiden name.

"Last known address?"

"He put his forwarding address out of New York to California." Her voice sours. "The report is from four years ago. Jacob..."

Her tone belies how bad it is, and I grip the pen hard enough to crack it.

"Can you send it to me?"

Hesitation.

"Vicky. I just want to protect her, and I don't know how. I'm flying blind here."

"I'm not going to send it to you," she says in a low voice. "I will not be complicit in that, Jacob."

I wait for the *but*.

And then it comes.

"But... If you meet me for dinner, we'll see."

"I could kiss you, Vicky."

"Your father is going to kill me," she says on a laugh. "You're trouble. You've always been trouble. Now get off the damn phone and go to sleep. Please. You've got a big game coming up."

Yeah, we do. My chest tightens again. This anxiety is familiar. It's induced by the sport, by the need to win. I've been competitive all my life. It started before my dad put me into hockey, even. I was pushing myself to be the best at t-ball and soccer, I just wasn't very good at either.

On the ice, though, I found my feet. I found my home.

I rub my chest absently and say goodbye to Vicky. I'll have to remember to make a dinner reservation when it's a normal hour, and also figure out how I'm going to get Melody to New York again. I could put her on a plane with the other wives and girlfriends, but...

Well, Camden Church, our captain, is perennially single. Seems like clockwork. He gets a girl in the off season, woos her over the summer, and then dumps her right before our season starts. I don't think Lawson has ever had a girlfriend. No idea about Dawes, the guy clams up when I mention women. Haverhill and Scofield are the ones who fuck around with any beautiful woman who looks at them.

So maybe that's out.

Maybe I have one of my friends—

Aha.

"It's the middle of the night, you fucker," Greyson Devereux groans in my ear. "You better have a damn good reason for waking me up."

I grin. "Yeah. I need to talk to Violet."

If I was standing in front of Devereux, he'd probably try to punch me.

"Call at a normal hour."

"No." I recross my legs. "The only reason I didn't call her directly was a courtesy to you."

That, and he's insane. Over-protective. If her phone rang in the middle of the night, he'd still answer it—and then I'd be faced with a million more questions. This is just easier.

Maybe.

"I'm already awake," Violet's voice comes through. "Just give me the phone."

"I'm putting it on speaker," Greyson snaps. More at me. He'd never fucking snap at her.

Unless she's into that kind of thing?

"Hey, Violet," I greet her. "Are you guys still in Denver?"

"What, you want to meet up for middle-of-the-night drinks?" Greyson's a sarcastic asshole.

"Or did you kill someone?" Violet quips.

I groan. "Fuck off, both of you. Are you?"

"Yeah, Rhodes. Now spit out what you want or need."

"Someone's grouchy," I mutter. I examine my fingernails. "Why can't I just call to have a little conversation with my friends?"

"At one-thirty in the freaking morning? Get out of here."

"I want Melody to come to New York."

Silence.

"And you're flying commercial..."

"Oh." Violet laughs. "That's why he's happier, Grey. He wants to keep her."

"I am keeping her," I interrupt. "Jesus, I should've called Steele." Or Miles. "I just need to know if you can get her on the plane."

"Yeah, yeah. No worries."

"And be nice to her," I add. Because... fuck. I don't know. I just want her to like them. I want her to start to like *me*, and my friends are an extension of that.

"*Fine*," Greyson says.

Violet scoffs. "We'll be nice to the professor."

I bite the inside of my cheek. "But you can't tell her you know her."

"Oh my God," Greyson mutters. "It'll be fine. We're hanging up now."

22

MELODY

Teacher.
Professor.
Ex-husband.
Restraining order.
Jacob.
What the fuck am I doing?

I peel my eyes open. It takes a moment, as it seems to do these days, for me to figure out where I am. Like my mind was sleeping a little too hard, and now it's playing catch-up. It isn't until I spot the painting that my location registers.

Jacob's room.

But there's no Jacob.

I stretch out and close my eyes again. Like most mornings, I spend a few minutes just trying to remember. *Anything.*

The word 'darling' keeps echoing in my head, and I don't like it. My skin crawls, enough that I abandon pressing for more memories and hop out of bed. I slip down the hall and into my bathroom, taking a cold shower. It soothes my hot skin, and I tip my head back under the water.

Did I really try to seduce Jacob last night?

"I'm a mess," I groan, covering my face.

How much more fucked up can I get?

When I can't bear any more cold water, I jump out and get dressed. I need to leave the apartment. I need to answer the texts and calls from Thomas and Natalie. They started off with light concern, but now it seems like full-tilt worry.

I just can't tell if it's real or forced.

I brush out my hair, examining the blonde. Maybe I'd feel better going back to my natural color?

Another thing that requires money.

A laugh escapes. I'm in an impossible situation. No memory, no support. I can't lean on Jacob Rhodes forever, just as I couldn't have done that to Thomas and Natalie.

I sit on the edge of the bed and make yet another list.

Hair, job, darling. I shudder. Not to mention flying across the country with Jacob. I don't know how I'm going to begin to afford paying him back.

My phone chimes, a notification dropping down from the top of the screen. It's an alert from the bank.

The social security card I requested must've come through to Thomas's house, as well as my birth certificate. Maybe he forwarded copies of the documents, or went to the bank even though I've been ignoring his calls. A lot of them. I just can't bring myself to answer.

Either way, I've been verified. I click the login button, set up a new password and email, and suddenly... my accounts are there.

I could cry. And then I see the numbers, and I *do* cry.

I'm flat broke.

My checking account has $2.51 in it. The other, the savings, has $4.13.

Before I know it, I'm sobbing for real. I toss my phone down and fold over, wrapping my arms around my head. What the *fuck*, past-me?

"Hey! What's wrong?" Jacob's voice drifts over me.

I ignore it. No way I'm lifting my head and letting him see *this* mess. Not until he pries my arm away, then the other. He squeezes my fingers, letting me hold on to him. I sniffle.

"Don't hide," he urges.

I carefully pull my hand away and grab the phone. Needing to see his reaction, I turn my head to watch his face as I show him the abysmal amounts. "Why would I do this to myself?"

He stares down at the numbers.

He clicks, opening a drop-down of transactions. Nosy, but I didn't know it could do that. I find myself leaning into him, trying to see it better, while he still has one of my hands caught in his.

"Lump sums were withdrawn in cash," he says carefully, angling the phone so I can see it.

Fifteen thousand dollars from my checking account. And double that from my savings.

"Why?" My voice is hoarse. "Who would do that?"

"You might've," he says. "It's dated before you were in the hospital. Almost six months prior."

He's thinking something. Calculating, or counting back.

"What is it?"

Then I remember.

Lucy said I dropped off the face of the earth just over

two years ago. Subtract the three months since I woke up in the hospital... subtract six months from that? Something significant happened nine months ago.

There are three events, then.

When I disappeared.

When the money was taken out.

And when I ended up in the hospital.

I run my finger across my throat, contemplating it all. Three big events, and so far, none of them seem tied to Jacob. In that regard... I might be safe. From him, with him.

"I have an ex-husband," I say.

He nods. "I know."

"His name is Henry Armstrong."

His silence tells me he knows this, too.

Something flips in my stomach, but I continue. "I have a restraining order against him, but it might be useful to... find him."

"He's in California."

I jerk back. It's not enough distance, with the way my skin suddenly crawls. I didn't have a reaction to the name, but to this?

I go to the window. It's a good view in the daytime— almost as pretty as everything lit up at night. I can see Jacob's reflection in the glass. He's standing behind me with his hands in his pockets.

California.

"Where in California?" The word tastes foreign on my tongue. I can't imagine going there, or living there, or... I don't know. "California," I repeat, just to test.

He shakes his head. "I don't know. I'll find out when we get to New York tomorrow."

"Okay." I stop. "No, I can't go to New York tomorrow. I have things to do. I need to get on with my life, Jake."

He stops.

Hell, *I* stop. "Why did I call you that?" I force a laugh. "Sorry. *Jacob*."

"Melody." He comes up beside me and runs his knuckles up my arm.

I hate and love when he does it, because goosebumps unerringly rise in their wake.

"You can call me Jake."

He leans into my back. I press my palms to the glass, but I'm unprepared for him to slide my hair off my shoulder. His lips touch the crook of my neck, and more goosebumps rise on my back.

"Call me Jake, Melody."

"Jake," I repeat, tilting my head to give him more room.

He takes advantage, kissing a trail up my neck. He nips my earlobe, and heat flushes under my skin.

"Have you called me darling before?"

He stops.

I kind of regret asking, but the need to know outweighs it. I face him and wait.

"I haven't. Do you remember something?"

"Just that the word makes me feel... *awful*." I wince. "I know how that sounds, but—"

"It's a fair question," he interrupts. "I get it. The search for memories isn't going to be easy. If you remember anything."

Right.

"I called you songbird."

That feels... *right*. Although— "I can't sing for shit."

He laughs. The sound is startling and sudden, and as soon as my surprise fades, I find myself laughing, too. Maybe he already knows, and it's an ironic nickname.

"One day soon, I'll show you why I call you that."

He steps back.

I watch him go, and only when he's gone do I realize I'm hopelessly turned on. A far cry from the fear and hurt I was drowning in when he came in.

23

JACOB

There are a few things at play—a few mysteries to solve.

But the first and most urgent thing is figuring out who is investigating Melody's attack. I'm done calling it an incident—it was never *incidental*. It was an attack from someone trying to kill her.

But all of that is put on hold when my father calls me.

Dad doesn't call often. We're not really the social conversationalists.

"Hey, Dad," I greet him, putting the phone on speaker. "What's up?"

"Vicky mentioned that you're taking her and Richard to dinner."

I pause. "Um, yeah. We fly in tomorrow, and it's been a while since I've seen them."

"And your old man wasn't going to get an invite?"

Oh.

Well, I can't exactly get information out of Vicky with the police chief breathing down our necks, can I? And that kind of messes with bringing Melody—no doubt he'd comment on her age or ask her questions she can't answer.

Can. Of. Worms.

"Do you want to come to dinner with us tomorrow night?" Then the game the following night. There's way too much potential for family bonding.

My father grunts. "It's not me you should be asking, but your mother."

Right.

"Okay. I'll give her a call—"

"Are you not sleeping?"

He's checking points off a list. Just breezing down it so he can get off the phone faster. First up, soothing whatever hurt Mom feels at the thought of being left out. Even though I just saw her a week ago. Now the insomnia. Which means Vicky mentioned something of our conversations... and since her shift doesn't start until eleven-thirty, he's put two and two together.

Wonder what else is coming.

"I'm sleeping," I hedge.

Just... not a lot.

If I thought it was bad without Melody, it's ten times worse with her here. Now I just stay awake to watch her, to touch her.

"They have pills to help that sort of thing. Or more exercise—"

"I exercise plenty." Jesus. "It's fine, Dad. Tell Mom I'm sleeping."

"Okay. Fine. And now, Fourth of July..."

Fucking hell.

"Is there a particular question involved in that?"

"Are you coming home for it or should I tell your mother that you're going to abandon her for that, too? We were planning on going to the house in Crown Point. You're more than welcome to come."

"Maybe," I hedge. Never mind that the holiday is literally months away, I haven't told them anything about Melody. And judging from his lack of questions in that direction, neither has Vicky.

Small blessings.

"Anything else?" I wince at the sharpness of my tone.

"No. Call your mother."

"Yes, sir." I hang up and toss my phone down, groaning and dropping my head in my hands. I'd be better off smashing my forehead off my desk. After a moment of recollection, I dial my mother.

She's a general practitioner at the local hospital, which means she keeps pretty normal hours—for the most part. Seeing as how it's the middle of the day, I might get her voicemail. Hoping for it, at any rate.

It isn't that I don't want to talk to her. I do. I just… I don't want to answer questions.

"Hey, honey. I was just thinking about you."

I stifle my eye roll. "Yeah? My ears must've been burning. Are you busy? We can chat later…"

"No, I was just about to go on my lunch break."

There's chatter behind her, then a burst of laughter that quickly fades.

"Today's been a strange day. Everyone is on edge—it's a full moon tonight, and goodness knows that people are superstitious—and then I had a few new patients that asked if I was related to you! I'll never get used to that."

"Rhodes is a common last name." I sigh. "Sorry if that causes any issues."

"It doesn't. I kind of like it. My baby boy, the famous hockey player. All the ladies in the office swoon over you,

you know. Janice has a poster with your face on it in her cubicle."

"*Mom.*"

"What? It's true. She wanted me to get her tickets to the playoffs. I told her she should be nicer to my assistants, and I'd consider it." She sniffs. "Anyway, enough about her. You're coming into town tomorrow? Or is it the day after?"

"The day after. I think I'm going to stay an extra night, though. See my friends, relax before jumping onto a plane again."

And show Melody the college she attended, then taught at. She said she'd already toured the campus, but she didn't really experience it in the way she should've. I drive through Crown Point sometimes and hardly feel the same connection I had with the town when I went to school there.

It's just different.

"Oh," I add, "I invited Vicky and Richard to dinner in the city tomorrow night, and I was wondering if you'd like to come as well?"

It kind of pains me to ask. And Melody thinks she's not going to New York with me, which is just wrong. She said she wasn't going, then she called me Jake. And damn it, it evoked memories I wasn't ready to replay. Of telling her to call me Jake when we first met. Wanting *someone* to call me that, since no one else does.

"That sounds wonderful." Mom's voice is lighter. She's smiling, I'd bet money on it. She smiles a lot. It's easy to draw it out of her. Just a small kindness, some thoughtfulness, and she's happy. "Send me the details, would you? Oh, I haven't caught up with Vicky in a few months. How fun!"

"And Amy? How is she?"

Younger sister. *Very young*, younger sister. We never really clicked, as far as friendship between siblings went. By the time she turned eight, I was leaving for college. After that, I was rarely home. So she's grown up the past six years basically as an only child.

"She was asking if you'd be home for her birthday."

I suppress my sigh. "In July?"

"July third, just before the holiday. Your father and I were thinking of taking a trip up to Crown Point, stay at the house there for a little while."

She's regurgitating information I already know, but I can't exactly tell *her* that.

"Let me know if you can make it," she says softly. "We miss you. And you have summers off—"

Off is a fancy term for *work harder*.

"I'll let you know, okay?"

She sighs. "That's fine, honey. Let me know what time dinner is tomorrow, okay?"

"You got it."

"Love you! Thanks for calling. We'll chat soon."

We hang up, and I close my eyes again. I love my parents, but sometimes they're exhausting. And I wish people would let them live anonymously. But with every game, it seems like awareness of me has grown. I sometimes just watch my social media following tick higher and higher, wondering what the fuck my life is. I never post anyway. It doesn't really matter. It doesn't stop people from following me.

"You okay?"

I jerk.

It's been a while since anyone has snuck up on me, but Melody has succeeded. She stands almost behind the doorframe, half hidden by it. Just peeking into the room. Her hair is down, messy from sleep and a bit wild.

"What are we doing today?" I ask her.

She lifts one shoulder and drifts farther into the office. "We?"

"We fly tomorrow. My friends are in town, we can get lunch with them."

Better to introduce Melody to Devereux before I shove her on a plane with them.

She wraps her arms around her stomach. "You fly tomorrow," she corrects. "I don't know. Your friends? Have I met them before?"

"Actually, no."

Her relief is evident from here. "Okay. Maybe. I want to keep job searching, and..." She bites her lower lip.

I want to tell her that every time she bites it, it makes my dick twitch. I drop my feet off the corner of the desk and use it to hide my growing erection like a teenager.

"And?"

"I can't keep using your girlfriend's clothes," she blurts out. "And all that makeup—"

"Wait." Fuck hiding my hard-on. I jump to my feet and stride around the desk. "*Girlfriend?*"

Her gaze drops to my groin, her lips parting.

"Eyes up here," I demand.

She gives me that, and I reach for her. Her sharp exhale when my palm brushes her throat tells me she doesn't want soft. She doesn't want coddling.

She thinks I have a girlfriend?

I'll prove her wrong.

I push her by her throat against the wall, and her pupils fucking dilate.

"You're the only one who gets me hard," I say in a low

voice. I grind my erection into her belly. "Feel that, songbird?"

Her gaze slants away. "Doesn't mean you didn't have someone before I crashed back into orbit."

I chuckle and lean in, barely touching my lips to her ear. "You'll see."

She shivers. She's just as affected by me.

I wrap my hand around the back of her neck and lead her to the office chair. I plant her on it and lean on the desk, facing her. I grab my phone and shoot off a text.

"Do you trust me?" I watch my phone. The response comes immediately, and I set the phone facedown beside me. "At all?"

"Yes."

"Okay. Then go get dressed and come back here."

Her brows furrow, but she does it. She disappears out of sight, while I remain where I am. My dick calms down. She returns just as I get another text.

"Sit." I point to the chair.

She's wearing dark jeans with rips in the knees and a flowy white blouse. It hides a lot of her, and I make a note to urge her toward the better-fitting shirts. This one has a few buttons up the center, hiding her cleavage. It'll be like unwrapping a present later.

"I'm not going to restrain you." I run my finger over her wrist. "But I need you to promise that you're not going to move."

Her breathing hitches. Whether it's my words or touch, I don't know. Either way, I keep tracing the faint scar until she nods.

"Promise," she whispers.

I nod back and go to the door.

The woman waiting there isn't familiar. I don't

remember taking her number or talking to her. She's young, maybe my age. Model thin. Conventionally pretty. Why a girl like her is wasting her time chasing hockey assholes like me, I'll never know. Her red hair is pulled away from her face, and she's wearing arguably the skimpiest top imaginable. A strip of violet fabric across her breasts. Jeans that come up over her navel.

It's an interesting style, but I guess it makes sense for a booty call.

Which is what she thinks this is.

"This way," I say, stepping back and allowing her inside.

"You have a gorgeous place," she says to me.

I wrinkle my nose, although she misses it. It *is* gorgeous —and I paid top dollar for it to be so. Thinking I had anything to do with it except opening my wallet is stupid.

"In here." I point to the office and step up behind her, blocking her exit.

Predictably, as soon as she spots Melody, she stops short.

"No, no," I murmur. "She wanted to watch. It's her kink."

Melody's jaw drops. "I—"

"Quiet."

My tone brooks no argument. And true to form, my songbird closes her pretty little mouth. A new curiosity, tinged with distrust, enters her expression. But she stays seated, which is more than I could hope.

The girl in front of me, the one who could grace the cover of a magazine, is frowning.

Ah, well.

I crowd the girl around to the side of the desk, until she leans on the edge of it. It's what she wants, and it gives

Melody a perfect view of the two of us. I lean into the girl's body, inhaling her scent. She seems to forget that my songbird is even there. In a second, she's plastered against me. Running her hands up and down my arms, then my chest.

Her lips touch my throat.

"I need to ask you something."

She hums. Her hands skim my waist. Inching lower.

"Yeah?" She draws back to meet my eyes.

"Are you trying hard enough?" I look down pointedly.

Her cheeks redden.

"Maybe take off your shirt," I suggest. I step back. "Or get on your knees..."

To no one's surprise, she does both. Her shirt, the skimpy bit of fabric, hits the desk. She's got tiny tits. Which is good for some guys, but me? Not so much. If Melody had tiny tits, I think I'd be into it. If she was blue, I'd be into that, too.

But I refuse to think about Melody. I reach out and palm the girl's breast, and she fucking moans like she's climaxing. It's fascinating, at any rate. I drop my hand, and she goes for my pants. Unbuttoning my jeans.

I grab her wrist and make her palm my dick through the denim.

"What do you feel?" I ask in a low voice.

"You're..." She's getting redder. "Not hard."

"You should do something about that," I suggest.

Her tongue swipes across her lower lip, and she pushes my jeans and boxer briefs down. My cock is still a good size when it's flaccid, and she takes it in hand. Her other cups my balls.

Not even a fucking twitch.

She leans in and wraps her lips around the head, sucking and swirling her tongue around. She's making noises that grate on my ears; her grip isn't right. It's just all wrong.

I grab her hair, forcing her to take me deeper. Proving a point, even without looking at my songbird. Even soft, I hit the back of her throat, and she gags around me.

Nothing.

"Pathetic," I finally spit, unable to hold it in any longer. I drag her off me, practically tossing her to the floor next to the desk. "Your mouth can't get me hard? Clearly you haven't been with a real man before. One that doesn't get turned on by parlor tricks. Get out."

She stares at me from the floor, unmoving for a moment. And then she bursts into action. She scrambles to get her shirt back on and stammers something toward Melody. Or me, I don't know. I don't move until I hear the sound of the condo door slamming. Only then do I look at Melody. I take in her white-knuckled grip on the arms of the chair.

I look at her, at her thighs pressed together and the anger on her face.

"Take your shirt off."

She shakes her head. "Fuck you, Rhodes."

24

JACOB

I smile. I like a challenge. I welcome it, and I approach her without fear. She leans back in the chair, tipping back to keep her eyes on mine. I slowly take off her glasses and fold them, setting them aside. Then, with one finger, I trace the collar of her pretty white blouse.

And then I rip it open.

The buttons pop off, falling to the floor and scattering. Her breasts greet me, barely trapped in a plain, beige bra. I tug the cups down. It frees them, but the underwire keeps them lifted toward me.

A present, exactly like I first envisioned.

Her gaze drops to my stiffening cock.

"Only you do it for me, songbird. Don't you ever fucking doubt that again."

I slide my fingers into her hair and draw her forward. She comes, bowing toward me, and I don't even have to tell her to part those full lips of hers.

Her mouth on me is *heaven*.

"Fuck," I groan.

Her hands leave the chair and grip my thighs. Her nails

dig into my skin, but it's a good pain. I look down at her and force her to swallow me deeper. She gags around me, and I swear I almost combust on the spot.

"Take more of me," I urge. "Show me how *furious* you are that another girl had her lips on me."

Her teeth skim my length, and I groan through a laugh.

"Careful." I pull her off me. Her lips release me with a slight *pop*. I trail my cock head over her cheek. "No biting."

"You're an asshole," she spits.

"For proving that you're the only one who can do this?" I fist my cock and stroke myself. "I think that's quite charitable of me. Removing any fucking doubt from your mind that you're *it*."

"I hate—"

I thrust back into her mouth. Straight in, until I hit the back of her throat, and deeper still. Her throat grips me as she chokes. Her fingers twitch on my legs. I draw out just enough for her to suck in air through her nose, then I'm filling her again. Fucking her face like an insane person.

She takes it. Her eyes lift, and I stare down at her. I have to lean over and brace myself on the back of the chair. Her tongue moves, curling against the underside of my cock, and I grunt. I want to hold on, to draw this out.

But Melody Cameron is some kind of elixir I can't consume fast enough.

"Swallow."

I come, not giving her time to think about the order. I'm deep enough in her mouth that it's hardly any work to swallow—or choke. As soon as my cock stops rocketing cum down her throat, the euphoria fading, I pull out and drop to my knees. I clamp my hand over her jaw, forcing her mouth closed and her face close to mine.

"Hate me all you want, but the thought of me inside you

in more than one way..." Fuck it, my dick isn't even a little deflated. "If you're not dripping wet at what we just did, then I'll apologize."

I won't. She is turned on. I'd bet my fucking life on it.

Her chin lifts, my hand moving with it.

"Did you swallow my cum, songbird? Can you taste me lingering on your tongue?" I remove my hand, peeling my fingers away, and kiss her before she can protest.

She melts into me. Enough that she doesn't stop me from slipping my hand to the apex of her legs, under her pants and panties. My fingers curl in her sweet, *wet* heat, and I stroke her clit as my tongue strokes her mouth.

She smiles against my lips.

I taste her saliva and her essence and *me*, and I almost lose control again. I draw back and put her on her feet. I'm still kneeling in front of her, and I'm struck by déjà vu. We've been in this position before, behind a desk like this. Only then, she was wearing a skirt...

I guide her pants off her legs. She holds on to my shoulder and kicks them off.

Her cunt is as familiar to me as the back of my hand, and yet, I marvel at it. At the cushion of her thighs, the scent of her slick arousal. At her lips waiting to be kissed, her clit already swollen and waiting.

I kiss just above her pelvic bone, then over her belly. I lift myself and kiss higher, until I've reached her jaw. I grasp at her waist and turn her, setting her ass on the edge of the desk. Her legs part for me.

"I can't go slow with you," I confess.

She reaches up and grips the back of my neck. "Who said anything about slow?"

"Fucking perfect."

I run the tip of my dick through her folds, eliciting a

shiver from her. Another pass, then a third, before her nails dig into my skin.

I chuckle. "Impatient?"

"Ye—"

I thrust into her. Fully, in one go. Her cunt stretches around me, her muscles automatically tensing in a way that doesn't happen when she sleeps. I steal the word from her mouth, and then I kiss her again. She drags me into her as hard as I am her, grinding closer. Deeper.

Her breath hitches when I pull back for a moment. I roll my hips and slide back in. I do it again, demonstrating I *do* know how to go slow.

For a moment. To savor it.

But her legs loop around my hips, her heels digging into my ass, and she not-so-subtly tells me to quit tormenting her.

Message received.

I lay her back on the desk, knocking my laptop out of the way, and palm both her breasts. She reaches up and grips the edge of the desk over her head.

With every thrust, her body jiggles. Her breasts sway. I pinch her nipples, knead the sensitive flesh, and drive harder into her. I'm obsessed with the way she moves. With the flutter of her eyelids after every stroke.

First time having sex—*that she can remember*.

On a desk, no less.

How fitting. In the most ironic of ways.

I run one hand down her body and find her clit. She gasps and writhes under me at the added assault, and I increase the pressure until she comes undone.

It doesn't take long.

She shatters around me, crying out my name. *My name.*

"Jacob, *fuck me*, that feels too good," she moans, her eyes squeezing shut. "Oh my God. You've got to stop."

"Stop?" I haul her up, slamming her against the wall. I grip the bottoms of her thighs, keeping her up. "We're just getting started."

"Jake," she breathes.

"Touch yourself." I lean down and suck her nipple into my mouth.

She moans above me. I slide in and out of her, relishing the feel. The noises she's making. My fucking songbird, right where she belongs.

"Make yourself come again." My teeth graze her nipple.

"I can't," she whimpers.

That phrase isn't in my dictionary. I take over her fingers' movement, stroking her clit and dipping my fingers into her cunt alongside my dick. Stretching her more, hitting her G-spot with the pad of my index finger.

"Holy shit." She's nearly hysterical. Two orgasms and *this*?

"We need to work on your stamina." I kiss her throat, coasting my tongue over the edge of the scar. Then higher, working toward her jawline. There's a frantic energy building inside me. It's driving the need for her to come. To come *with me*.

Finally, she lets out a low moan that sounds more like pain than pleasure. Her thighs tense around my hips, her back arches. It's her sound that undoes me. My balls tighten, and I drive her to the cliff's edge at the same time that I sprint off it.

Her orgasm triggers mine. She screams, and I'm right there with her. I capture her mouth with mine, absorbing her wordless pleas. Fully fucking buried in her.

I don't know if I've ever been so completely obsessed.

After a moment, or maybe two, I pull back. I lower her legs to the floor and slip out of her. Satiated. *Tired.*

And for a moment, her expression seems to mirror mine.

Until she recalls what I did to get us here.

One minute some gorgeous young woman is sucking Jacob's flaccid cock. And the next, he's fucking *me* with his very large, very hard...

"That wasn't okay."

My voice isn't shaking, but my hands are. I ball them into fists and muster my best glare. I just ran a marathon in terms of sex—I mean, I *think* I did. I don't have much to go on except the jelly feeling in my limbs. And the way he brought not one but two orgasms crashing down on me.

"Seriously," I add, seeing his smile. "You—"

"I showed you what it means to be my only." He touches my chin. "I don't give a shit if the room was filled with naked women. I only want you. I only react to you. I'm only obsessed with *you*."

My eyes fill with tears.

"You made me suck—I had to taste *her* saliva on your dick."

His expression goes blank. And just when I think he's going to change the subject or... I don't know. Ignore it? He steps closer and rights my bra. The cups make a noise as they flip back into place, and he slowly tugs my shirt closed. The buttons are missing, but maybe he thinks it's the thought that counts?

"That wasn't my intention." He runs his thumb across my lower lip. "But it is a just punishment for doubting me."

My mouth drops open.

"And besides," he adds. "Something about that turned you on."

Oh. *Yeah.*

But I'm definitely not telling him. Instead, I inch around him and out of the office. My feelings don't have a space here. My heart doesn't either. Everything about this morning, and last night, has left me confused.

And maybe a little bit broken.

Once I'm locked in the bathroom with my phone, I thumb through my few contacts. There are more messages from Thomas and Natalie, a few from Lucy. One from an unknown number.

I click on it.

It's a voice message. One of the ones that can be sent by text. I hold my thumb over the play button, hesitating.

Get over your fear, Melody.

I play it. When no one speaks, I turn up the volume. All the way up, until there's an underlying hint of static—and breathing.

The hair on the back of my neck stands up.

The message is a minute long. I've gone through forty-five seconds of it.

So when the voice does come through, I nearly jump out of my skin.

"*I'm coming for you, darling.*"

I drop the phone and run out of the bathroom. My

earlier plight with Jacob forgotten, I all but dive into his arms.

"Whoa." He barely rocks when I crash into him, banding his arms around my back. "What happened?"

"I—" Tears flood my eyes. "I got a message—"

"Okay." He pries me back a little, searching my face. "Okay, what did it say?"

I shudder. My stomach flips, and I know that I'm about to lose it. Hysteria bubbles up my throat, and my face crumples. I can't do anything to stop the sobs from bursting out of me.

"It's okay," he murmurs, dragging me back into his chest. "Where's your phone?"

"In the bathroom," I manage.

He picks me up. I squeak, but he doesn't seem to notice. Or acknowledge it anyway. One minute my feet are on the floor, and the next I'm being carried like a freaking princess back to the bathroom.

My phone is on the bathmat. He sets me on the counter and grabs it.

"Show me?"

I take it and go to my messages. The top one is from Thomas, not the unknown number.

"Did Thomas say something to you?" He clicks on it, but it's just about wanting to know if I'm okay. Not worthy of... whatever reaction that was.

I clear my throat and dash away my tears. "It was a texted voice message from a private number. It said..."

He sets down the phone.

"*He* said he was coming for me. He called me darling." I stare at Jacob through my tears.

Jacob, who has never seemed afraid of anything.

Jacob, who looks at me like I'm his world.

Who must have some answers that he's not telling me.

"Those messages erase if you don't save them," he says softly, brushing a tear from my cheek. "If you get another one, get me before you play it."

I nod.

There's something he's not telling me.

"I'll be okay," I lie. I hop off the counter and pluck my phone from his hand. "I need to call Natalie, and I think I just want some air. Sorry I freaked out on you."

He follows me into my bedroom. I change my shirt under his watchful eye, not even bothered that he's seeing me in just a bra. Wasn't what we did so much worse than that?

I yank the sweatshirt over my head, and it's only then that I realize I forgot my glasses back in his office. I lace into my shoes, grab my purse, then retrieve my eyewear.

Stupid fucking glasses.

I shove them on my face, barely breathing in his little office. I double-check that I have my keys and practically run out of his condo.

I'm coming for you, darling.

Was it my ex? That's the only reasonable guess I have. And if it *was* him, at least it answers the question of why I hate the word darling so much. Just thinking it makes me nauseous. And... well, he blocked the number.

Does he know I forgot *everything*?

I have the restraining order against him. At least, I think I still do. I have no idea if they expire or not.

Suddenly, getting on a plane to go to New York tomorrow doesn't seem like the craziest thing in the world.

If he found my new phone number, what else has he found?

Where I'm staying?

Who I'm living with?

The life of Jacob Rhodes isn't exactly subtle.

Instead of calling Natalie, like I should, I call Lucy.

"Hey, girl! I wasn't expecting to hear from you until tomorrow." She sounds... bright. Warm and bubbly.

"Before I dropped off the face of the earth, where was I?"

"Are you okay?"

"Yeah." I rub my forehead. "Well, no. Where was I? Teaching somewhere?"

"You were teaching a class at Crown Point University. We got together the one time, it seemed like you were doing okay. Theo and I were passing through for work. The timing was good."

I fish out earbuds—courtesy of Jacob—and plug them into my phone. "Hang on, I'm looking something up."

She waits while I do a stupid search in the maps for Crown Point University. It's a little town in Maine. On a lake, no less. I switch over to a regular search, and a million articles pop up.

"Fancy shit," I mumble. They've actually got an impressive school. An array of D1 sports, and— "What the fuck?"

"What?"

I clicked on their website. And there, on the *home page*, is Jacob. In a Crown Point University... hockey jersey, I guess. And helmet. There's a little note about having a fine array of students go on to be professional athletes.

"Melody, *what*?"

"This day just keeps getting worse and worse." I've been putting off finding out more about Jacob. Looking a gift horse in the mouth type of thing. But now I think I have to do something.

Knowing who I'm living with is one thing—knowing who I'm fucking is another.

Shit.

"I'm sorry. I'll see you tomorrow, maybe."

"Maybe?"

"Hey!"

I look around. I've been pacing on the street, but now I yank one earbud out and watch the girl from before come closer. She's... still here. And pissed.

I really can't get over how some girls can get away with wearing such little clothes.

"Hey," I greet her, more out of politeness than anything else. If we weren't in public, I don't know what I'd do. I certainly wouldn't talk to her.

"You tell Jacob that he can go to fucking hell," she seethes, coming right up to me.

I raise my eyebrows. "You not being his type isn't a him problem."

Okay, technically it is, and saying it isn't might go against women everywhere... but damn. Who gets rejected, then hangs around for an hour?

"Why are you still here?" I question.

Her mouth drops. "*Excuse me?*"

"Why are you hanging around his building like a stalker?"

"Melody?" Lucy's voice is still in my ear. "Who the hell are you talking to?"

"One sec, Luce." I glower at the girl. "You're out of line."

"*I'm* out of line?"

"And a parrot, apparently."

"You fucking bitch." She comes at me.

Like a moron, I just watch her swing. I wait for her palm to collide with my cheek, for the pain to ricochet up into my eye, for my skin to redden. *Things I shouldn't know anything about.*

But it doesn't connect.

Because of Jacob.

I didn't notice him, and neither did she. Whatever her name is. Her jaw slackens when she sees who's holding her wrist, and she doesn't fight when he drags her toward him.

My body tenses, though. Because *fuck* if I want to see her touching any part of him. Even if it's just her wrist against his palm.

"If you ever want to step foot in my arena again, you'll apologize to her. Right. Now."

Her face goes white. Well, as white as it can under the layers of makeup. Her eyes roll to me, but she doesn't seem willing to actually say sorry.

"I apologize," she forces out.

Not really meaning it either.

"Let her go." I sigh. "She's just a stupid kid."

He drops her wrist. Just like I thought, she turns and rushes away. No doubt *someone* will hear about this. I'm gathering that Jacob, who had a freaking girl on speed dial to come suck his dick, is important.

Obviously important enough that the school put him on their banner.

Wait. Shit.

When did he graduate college?

Is that where we met?

"You okay, Melody?"

I cringe. Nope. Definitely not okay. I back away. "What part of needing space do you not understand? Jesus."

He scoffs.

"What?"

"Nothing," he snaps. "Go on, have your *space*."

He makes a shooing motion, and that infuriates me all the more. I'll show *him*. I'll make it on my own tonight. And maybe tomorrow, too.

Who needs to go to New York? Not me.

I have a mystery to solve and a brain to unlock.

26

MELODY

Jacob Rhodes has a freaking Wikipedia page. I skipped it the first time I searched his name, but now I skim the intro paragraph, which details who he is—a defenseman on the Colorado Titans, an NHL team— along with his age and where he was born. It confirms that he's a decade younger than me, at any rate.

It makes me feel worse about my age.

I knew he was young, but... *that young?*

With a sick feeling in the pit of my stomach, I scroll down to his schooling. He was a defenseman on the Crown Point University team, too. He graduated two years ago.

I was teaching there at the time.

Fuck. Fuck, fuck—

"Miss?"

My head snaps up. An older woman is in front of me with glasses perched on top of her silver-blonde hair. She's got a lanyard around her neck with an ID.

She works here.

"Sorry." I rub at my eyes under my glasses. "Sorry, was I talking out loud?"

"You were hitting yourself in the head..."

I drop my hands immediately, pressing them palm down to the table. "Was I? Um... it's been a weird day, and I didn't really have anywhere else to go."

Her expression is nothing but sympathy and under-standing. She gestures to the chair across from me, and I nod slowly. She takes it, folding her arms in front of her.

"Anything I can help with?"

I press my lips together. I came here because I don't really know what the fuck I'm supposed to do or where I should go—which is ninety percent of my problem. The ten percent is all Jacob Rhodes.

"You don't happen to know a cheap place to stay around here, do you? Motel, hotel..."

I have the money from the loan Thomas and Natalie gave me. Money I'll eventually have to pay back. But this qualifies as an emergency.

The woman writes down the name of a motel and slides the paper toward me. "I hope that helps."

"It does. Thank you."

She gets up and wanders away.

Around noon, she finds me way in the back of the library, by the glass-walled conference rooms. "I was checking in with the motel," she confesses. "And then four others. But with the hockey playoffs, everything is booking up. So, until that clears up, I can offer you a room in the back of the library. It's *very* temporary, but it could do for a night or two."

"Oh." I stare at her. Standing, she's quite a bit taller than me. "No, you don't have to do that."

"You look like you need help. Where else are you going to go?" She sets off.

I follow. Because I'm curious, not because I'm going to

take her offer. She unlocks a door and leads me down a rather narrow hallway, then unlocks another door. She steps aside for me to enter first.

It's a whole-ass apartment. Well, like a studio apartment. There's a kitchenette, a twin-sized bed, a two-person table. Even a television.

"This..."

"Used to be our break room," she supplies. "Until we converted it to help out one of our graduate students last year. She was here for about a month."

"I was expecting something creepier," I admit.

She tuts. "It has its own entrance, too."

We go around the corner, where there are two doors. One for a bathroom, the other a thicker door that must lead outside.

She presses the key into my hand.

"I don't have any clothes or toiletries or—"

"There are supplies stocked in the bathroom. I can't do anything about the clothes, unfortunately, but you're welcome to the laundry in the basement." She backs away. "Just for the night. It's okay."

The door swings shut behind her.

I lock it, then drag out a chair and fall into it.

Holy shit.

I got away from Jacob.

27

JACOB

I hoist myself in through Melody's window and scan the small space. She's asleep on the tiny bed, her arm thrown over her eyes. Her mouth is open, her breathing coming slow and deep. My truck idles outside, and I make quick work collecting her few belongings. The phone, the purse, her jeans that lie folded over the back of the chair.

When I pull the blanket back, I scan her for signs of trauma. Hurt.

Nothing new. Nothing physical.

I pick her up and cradle her head to my chest, careful not to wake her. Not until we're out of here anyway. We leave out the side entrance, and I set her down in the passenger seat of the truck. It's reclined a bit, so she doesn't fall forward, and I lean over her to buckle her in.

She doesn't stir until we're turning into the parking garage of my high-rise. Her breathing changes first, and then her head lifts. She looks around as I pull into the parking space next to the car I sometimes drive in the city, and her gaze lands on me.

She sucks in a breath. Like she's surprised.

I meet her stare. "Is there a problem?"

"Yeah. *You.* How—?"

"Quiet."

Her mouth closes.

"I've been thinking about what you liked about this afternoon."

I unbuckle and twist to face her, killing the engine. It fades into silence, which seems loud in my ears. Funny, that. I've always liked quiet. Before hockey games, I sit with the noise-canceling headphones on and no music. Being alone with my thoughts never scared me.

Being alone with Melody?

Well, I wouldn't say I'm afraid. But it affects me in a way not many other things do.

"I don't think you're into that form of voyeurism." I tap my chin, pretending to consider it. "Get out of the car."

"Take me back to the library."

Cute to think I follow orders the same way she does.

"Either you get out of the car, or I haul you out."

Her glare is acidic... but she moves. Grudgingly, she unbuckles and opens the door. It's only when she gets out that she seems to realize she's without pants.

I smile to myself and collect her purse and jeans from behind her seat, then hop out. She's tugging on her shirt, trying to get it to cover more skin.

"Hey," she gasps. She goes for the jeans.

"No." I keep them out of reach.

Her glare is adorable. I put my hand on the small of her back, forcefully leading her to the elevator bay. We call an elevator down, and it chimes almost immediately.

She steps in, and I follow. I position myself right behind her, my front touching her back. As soon as the elevator doors close, I drop the purse and jeans and grab her.

She struggles. Her head flies back, narrowly missing my face. I bite the shell of her ear, digging my teeth in and holding on while one hand keeps her against me. My arm is just below the swell of her breasts. My other hand dips into her panties.

"Stop."

"This is a test," I say through my teeth.

I slide one finger into her cunt. She's only a little turned on. I release her ear and press my lips to it instead.

"You're a pathetic little whore," I whisper. "So desperate for attention you'd do anything."

Wetness hits my finger, and she lets out a shaky breath.

I unwrap my arm around her torso to shove her shirt up, exposing her breasts.

"You want to look like a little slut, don't you? You want someone to make you feel worthless."

"No," she groans.

"Your cunt is giving you away," I laugh. My dick is stiff, and I shift my hips forward. Showing her exactly what *she's* doing to me. "It's gripping at my finger like a vise. And you know we're still on the garage level, don't you? The doors could open at any moment and expose you."

I pull out of her and step back. She's left trying to balance, her knees shaking.

I drop the fob that'll make the elevator move.

She falls to her knees after it, scrambling for the tiny chunk of plastic. She presses it to the sensor and hits the button for our floor, and she sags to the side as soon as we start to move.

"Your breasts are out," I comment, trying to keep a straight face.

She gasps again, yanking her shirt down. I can see the dampness on the strip of her panties between her legs, and my cock twitches again.

The doors open.

Melody starts to climb to her feet, but I push her back down. I crouch in the opening of the elevator, her things back in my arms. The fob tucked in my pocket.

I toss her my phone, which is locked with a passcode.

"Stay." I step into the hall.

The elevator doors slide closed between us.

28

MELODY

I scramble for the doors as soon as they close, but I'm too fucking late. My fingers hit the button to open the doors again.

They don't budge.

I wait. This is just a practical joke. One of Jacob's... I don't know. Quirks? Kinks?

The elevator moves with a jolt, and I gasp again. It drops a few floors, and it chimes as the doors slide open.

A couple step onto the elevator.

I stand in the corner, and my eyes close for a moment. Shame burns through me, so hot I might as well be breathing fire. They turn away from me, their expressions accusing or pitying, I have no idea which. Probably judging. I have no idea what I look like right now, but it's probably not any good.

We take the elevator to the first floor. Not the garage, where Jacob's truck is. They stroll out, and I shrink against the wall again. Hiding from sight in case anyone's in the lobby.

The doors close, but the elevator doesn't move.

Jacob's phone, on the floor by my feet, rings. It's my name on the caller ID. I grab it fast, swiping to answer. It's a video call, and I only belatedly realize that as his face fills the screen. He's on the couch, it seems. Relaxing while he torments me from afar.

"You're a bastard," I choke out.

"Show me your pussy."

I jerk back. "Excuse me?"

He smiles. "Put one of those pretty feet on the wall, pull your panties to the side, and show. Me. Your. Pussy."

"You're vulgar."

"I know. Just think how good it's going to feel when I finally fuck you. Instead of aching for something, *anything*, to touch you. Like you're feeling right now."

"I rode the elevator with a couple," I hiss.

I'm shifting my weight. Not really considering this, right? I'm not going to cave to his demands... *right?* Not unless I want to.

"There's nothing wrong with playing my game," he says softly. He leans forward, his gaze intense. "There's nothing wrong with the kind of kinks you and I like to divulge in. Do you understand me?"

My body is trembling.

And slowly, I pick my leg up and pull my panties to the side, and I drop the phone down so he can see.

"Good girl," he breathes.

I can't describe the weird sort of bliss that fills my chest.

The call ends. And a moment later, the elevator lifts. I watch the numbers tick higher, stopping at eighteen. The doors slide open, the hallway empty. I step out quickly, not wanting to be caught in the elevator again, and hurry to Jacob's condo door. That, too, has been left open.

It's dark inside. A stark contrast to how it was just lit in the video call.

I lock the door behind me.

"Melody." Jacob's voice hits me like a whip. "On your knees, songbird."

It takes me a moment to adjust to the darkness. But by that time, my body has already fallen to his command. He's by the couch, standing at the back of it. The city lights coming through the windows behind him cast him in shadow, so much so that I can't see his expression.

"You took my cock so well. Like a practiced whore. Isn't that right?"

I suck in a breath. Each word is a strike between my legs, and I let out a low moan. He's not even touching me.

"Whores crawl for their dessert."

I'm moving. One hand, one knee, then the opposite. All the way across the apartment, and I have the luxury of feeling *everything*. The sway of my belly and breasts, the rub of my thighs together. The arousal that's driving me insane.

I'm stopped by his foot on my shoulder.

His foot.

He lowers it and circles me carefully. I stay where I am. My heart is pounding, the rush of blood in my ears nearly drowning out all other sounds. Until I feel him lower to the floor behind me.

There's a pressure on my hips. Fabric straining, and then it gives way. The material rips and flutters to the floor.

Jacob runs his cock up from my clit, notching at my entrance. There's no formality, no waiting. In one movement, he's slammed to the hilt inside me.

We both groan.

He leans forward, his chest brushing my back. Forcing me lower. My chest hits the floor first, then my stomach.

My hands slip out from under me, and he quickly wrenches my wrists behind my back.

"Jacob," I manage. "What—"

He pulls out and thrusts back into me. My back bows, my eyes shut on their own.

"You're soaked," he grunts. "Because you secretly like to be humiliated, don't you? You wear the shame so well. You're beautiful like this."

I press my forehead to the floor.

"But you ran away from me." His voice is suddenly cold. "Which means, as much as you're enjoying this, you *won't* get to enjoy it to the fullest."

"I—"

"Unless you're about to tell me why you suddenly decided to *move out*, I don't want you to open that pretty mouth of yours."

He continues to fuck me. His grip on my wrists is iron-clad. There's nothing I can do to evade him, but that only serves to turn me on more. He hits the deep spot inside me, but he's hitting the mental spot, too. The one that makes me hunger for more. That reacts to his words with a vehemence I don't understand.

And with it comes the truth pouring from my lips.

"You were my student," I cry. "You've been messing with me. Playing with me—"

"*Yes*," he groans. His weight presses me down.

Down, down, down.

"Yes, I was your student. You fucked me from a position of power, Professor, but guess what? *You had no power with me.*"

I cry out.

The orgasm rips through me, and he swears. His hand wraps around my throat. Not tight, not squeezing or strangling, but he catches every noise I make. As I scream and thrash against him, as his tempo increases until he's fucking driving me into the floor with every thrust.

My hips will be bruised. My shoulders ache from the strain.

And still, we don't stop.

I beg for more.

More, more, more.

He gives it to me. His teeth in my shoulder, holding me still as he pummels me. I'm fully possessed, and I don't know how I'm going to be able to breathe on my own again. Not when his fingers move up from my throat to my jaw, then my lips. He presses down on my tongue, keeping my mouth open wide.

The sounds that come out of me are unhinged.

Another orgasm creeps up out of nowhere. He hasn't touched my clit, but my body is burning with desperate desire. I shudder. I clench at his cock, and it isn't until he pulls out and flips me over that I realize my orgasm was only starting—and now it's fading before it's even begun. He turns around. He's straddling my head, facing my body. They call it a sixty-nine, I think.

"The first was an accident," he murmurs. His cock is at my lips, and he pushes it into my mouth. From this angle, he slides right past my defenses and into my throat. His balls are on my face, blocking my sight. "You don't come again until I say."

I taste him and me both on his dick, and I have to squeeze my thighs together. My hand creeps lower, toward my clit.

Smack.

The pain on my breast echoes through me, and I gag around him. Another thrust, and he's blocked my airway.

Instead of withdrawing, he lingers.

When the room tilts, he pulls back.

I suck in a breath through my nose. It smells like him. Musk and sweat and *him*. And then he's stealing my air again. His pace doesn't stall out this time. He moves the same way he does when he fucks—but this time, he's taking what he needs from my throat.

His fingers knead at my breasts. He pinches my nipples, tugging them up. I go for my clit again and am met with another smack on my breast. My back arches.

"Naughty," he tsks above me.

Something shifts. He slides down my body, and then something wet and hot envelops my clit.

He continues to fuck my mouth as he plays with my clit. Licking it, kissing it.

It's not enough.

I make a noise of frustration, and I grip his hips. To pull him closer or push him off, I don't know. But I dig my nails into his ass, and I sure fucking hope I draw blood.

"Oh, baby," he chuckles. "I want to feel you scream around my cock."

His teeth scrape my clit, and I buck. I shiver. He's still somehow face-fucking me, even with his mind on whatever insane goal he has planned.

I'm going out of my mind.

He bites.

And I do scream. It comes out muffled around his cock, and my teeth skim his shaft before I realize.

Doesn't matter.

Or maybe the pain gets him off, because his balls tighten, and he's sucking and licking at my clit as he spills down my throat. It triggers my orgasm. Him, or the pain— maybe both. I cry out again, my body tensing. Pleasure detonates through me, and only when it releases me do I sag to the floor.

He carefully pulls out and climbs off me.

I suck in huge gulps of air through my nose, blowing out through my mouth. Like my freaking therapist taught me. She probably didn't mean for it to be used post-sex. I lick my lips. I taste blood and cum.

"That's it." Jacob scoops me up.

I barely register that I'm in the air, being carried, until we're in the shower. The warm water rains down on us, plastering my hair to my skin and washing away all of it.

"I—"

He kisses me.

It's not too hard or too fast or too demanding. Although one could argue his whole personality is demanding, this kiss is anything but. It's asking a question.

"You're perfect," he says against my lips.

"What?"

He sets me on the little bench in his shower and picks up a bottle of shampoo. I don't recognize it until I catch its scent.

I grab the bottle and inspect the label.

It's nothing I've used before... that I know of. But the smell tickles something in the back of my brain. Something just out of reach.

He lathers it in his palms and runs it through my hair. He scratches my scalp, and I automatically close my eyes. I relax against him, my shoulder on his chest, and let out a sigh. It's funny—I don't even know what time it is. All I know is that I called Lucy after getting settled at the library apartment. I used the last of my dollars on a sandwich from the gas station on the corner.

There were no plans beyond that.

"How did you find me?"

He snickers.

I look up at him, frowning. He's too fucking handsome. His dark hair is slicked back, and his blue eyes beat into mine with the steadfast intensity. His brows raise. Telling me that maybe I should already know how he found me.

"I never left you," he says.

My heart skips.

"I don't know you." Something I've been repeating for a while.

"Yes, you do." He tips my head back and rinses the soap away. "You know me, Melody Cameron. You just have to remember."

You just have to remember. Dread is a lead ball in the pit of my stomach.

"And if I don't?"

He shrugs. Kisses my cheek. "Doesn't matter. I'll make you fall in love with me all over again."

29

JACOB

"You ready?" I lean in toward Melody. I hook my arm around her shoulders and draw her closer.

"To meet your family? Yeah, sure. No biggie." Melody runs her hands down her blouse. "Way to spring this on a girl."

I roll my eyes. "You'll be fine."

"Did you tell them that I have amnesia?"

"No."

"Did you tell them I used to be your professor?"

I smile. "No."

She hasn't let that one go. Unsurprisingly. She didn't quite let it go when she *was* my professor either. Some things don't change.

"I think there's time to explore a new kink tonight," I add.

She narrows her eyes at me. "What does that mean?"

I shrug. I mean, I know exactly what I have planned, but she doesn't. She won't until it's too late. We put our names in at the hostess stand, and the woman tells us we're the last to arrive.

Fantastic.

Melody pats my hand. "Ready?" she parrots.

We're led to the table. My mother jumps to her feet and practically launches herself at me. I release Melody long enough to hug my mother back and ease the withering glare of my father. I introduce Melody to the group and circle around to greet Vicky and her husband, Richard.

I don't know what Melody makes of it, and I ignore the rogue looks Vicky shoots my way. I end up sitting between her and Melody, across from my parents and Richard. After a brief pause, conversation kicks back up. Richard and my father are discussing the latest reform bills, talk of defunding the police, and some odd political move by Senator Devereux.

"He's aligning himself with the Wests," Richard spits at one point. "And the governor is just as bad. There are whispers she has ties to the Mafia."

My eyebrows rise. "The New York governor? Sandra White?"

"She's as corrupt as they come," Dad mutters. "The DeSantises had her in their pocket until the war that broke out between the Wests and DeSantises a few years ago. Although just the other week, she had someone arrested for rescuing her daughter."

"She's just trying to do her best," Vicky says. "And I heard it was kidnapping, not rescuing."

Mom frowns. "A truce with the Mafia would go a long way."

Melody's eyes are wide, bouncing back and forth between them. Organized crime has always been an interesting subject of debate for my father. Of course Richard would latch on to that, and it seems like Vicky is just as eager to discuss.

"You must get a lot of calls from... victims of those sorts of crime," Melody offers across to Vicky.

The latter makes a face. "Most of the victims are cowards. They think snitching will get them further harmed. More often than not, the calls come from concerned citizens, third parties who witnessed something, things like that."

"Are you familiar with the city, Melody?" my mother asks.

For not knowing I was bringing someone to dinner, they're taking it surprisingly well. Vicky knew, maybe, or at least suspected.

Melody answers about going to school in the city smoothly, lying through her teeth.

My fascination with her deepens.

"Excuse me," she murmurs after dinner, pushing back her chair.

She heads in the direction of the restroom, and I swear, as soon as she's out of sight, the table's focus comes crashing at me.

"So, who is she?"

"Where did you meet her?"

"It's serious enough to bring her from Denver?"

I turn to Vicky, waiting for a question from her. But she just smiles.

Mom rolls her eyes. "Of course Victoria is in on it."

"Well, she's my late-night conversation buddy." I clear my throat. "Her name is Melody. She's... Well. Let me put it this way: I'm going to marry her."

Everyone starts talking at once.

"I'll be right back."

I follow Melody's path to the restrooms. There are just two single toilet rooms, one locked and the other open.

Instead of using the open one, I lean against the wall and wait. When the door opens, I surge forward and catch her with a palm to her chest, immediately pushing her back in.

She starts, and I take advantage of her parted lips. We hit the far wall, and I undo the button of her pants.

"Jacob," she whispers against my mouth. "What are you—?"

"Quiet." I kiss down her neck, lowering myself to get her pants and panties off one leg. I hitch it over my shoulder and press a new kiss to her *other* lips.

She moans above me. Her fingers slide through my hair. I love the taste of her. I know she's rather new to this, and that her brain is still playing catch up. That my emotions are a hundred miles ahead of her.

Because I've had to deal with them for *years*, and she hasn't known me for more than a few weeks. But her body knows me. I lap at her clit and thrust two fingers into her, hard enough to make her gasp over me. Her head hits the wall, and I fight my smile.

"This is indecent."

I smirk. "You want me to stop?"

"Not at this moment," she murmurs.

I work my fingers and tongue until she comes.

As soon as she does, I'm hoisting her up and sliding into her. She's slick and tight, her muscles still clenching and pulsing in the wake of her orgasm. My cock's intrusion only makes her groan more. The sweetest noise I've ever heard.

"We are at dinner with your *parents*," she groans in my ear. "You really are insane."

"Only for you, songbird."

And it's true. I'd do anything for her.

"You drive me crazy." Her nails bite into my neck, and

then her lips are on my jaw. She's leaving smears of lipstick across my skin, no doubt. I welcome it.

I don't want to ruin it for her and tell her that none of this is accidental. The greatest play I'll ever make won't be on the ice—it'll be getting Melody to fall in love with me.

I fuck her fast. Bathrooms aren't for savoring sex, or her body, although I can't help it. Her weight in my hands, her breasts pressed to my chest. She deserves to be savored like dessert.

Later.

My balls tighten, and I make a noise in the back of my throat as my orgasm takes me by surprise. I fill her completely and come that way, my eyes nearly rolling back.

Perfection.

After a few moments, my senses come back to me. I pull out of her and lower her feet to the floor, leaving her leaning against the wall in a daze. She slowly tugs her jeans and panties back into place.

"Melody."

Her eyes come to me.

"Be a good little slut and clean my cock."

She levels me with a glare, and my dick twitches. I wait, somewhat curious to see what she'll do. If she'll drop to her knees or go for the paper towels. I know which option I want—and it isn't her rubbing cheap paper towels across my dick.

When she doesn't move, I come forward and push her to her knees. The tip of my dick runs across the seam of her lips.

"I don't—"

I seize the opportunity of her talking and thrust into her mouth, smearing our arousal and cum everywhere. I slide in hard and dig my fingers into her hair, twisting the strands. It'll mess up the curls she put into it, but I'm past the point of caring. I drag her closer and shift my hips, fucking her mouth slowly. She shoves against my thighs, which I ignore.

When I draw back, saliva clings to her lip and the tip of my cock, which is fucking hard again.

"Tuck me back in my pants." My order comes out hoarse.

She reaches for me. Her fingers on me, on my balls. I bite the inside of my cheek hard enough to draw blood.

Then my pants are zipped back up, my cock somehow pressed up toward the waistband of my slacks. She pats the fabric, smoothing it, but all it does is make my dick twitch more. I push her hands away and help her up.

Her brow is furrowed.

"Come on." I hold out my hand. "My father is going to piss himself—"

"No."

"Melody."

"Jacob." She glares at me again. "I'm not going back to the table like this."

I sigh.

"And you're not going out looking like that." She points at me.

I stare at her finger. She painted her nails again. She had a manicure when I first saw her, or at the very least, paint on them. Black, if I remember correctly, or some dark color. Now it's dark blue. The rest of her nails are different. White. Mint green.

Colorado Titans colors.

For some reason, that makes me feel shitty.

She moves to the sink and scrubs her hands, then tries to get the smeared lipstick off her skin. She ties her hair up in a bun on top of her head. I catch a glance of myself over her head. There's pink on my jaw, my neck. Remnants of her rogue kisses. My hair is messed up, too, but not in a bad way. In a sex way, sure. Not that I really give a fuck about that.

"Wait here so it doesn't look like we did what we did." She slips out of the bathroom without a word.

I sigh and grab a paper towel, wetting it and rubbing at the lipstick. Although I'd love to leave it there, she's right. We're walking a delicate line here.

Except when a few minutes have passed, and I return to the table...

Her chair is empty.

30
MELODY

I don't know where I'm going.

I should. The city *should* be as familiar to me as breathing, since I lived here for so long. Apparently. Yet, as I walk, I just feel sad.

Where did my life go?

I just let a guy ten years younger than me, my former student, do... unspeakable things. Unsavory things. And while my body seems to crave his touch and his demeaning words, my mind doesn't. I hate that he has such a hold on me. That he can look at me and my skin heats.

That he can tell me to clean his dick and push me to the floor of that dirty bathroom and I open my mouth for him. That I crawl to him.

Jesus.

Was I religious? Thomas certainly couldn't answer that. Natalie, neither. They were the only family the investigator with the hospital could locate, and they don't know me.

I take a deep breath. The city is foreign, yes, but it also has this weird appeal. So I walk and walk, my pace unhurried, until I reach the campus that Thomas once took me to.

Now, I look at it through a new lens. One that says I didn't just go to school here, but I taught a class, as well.

Where did I live?

Who were my friends?

What did young Melody want to be when she grew up?

Tears prick my eyes, and I focus on the sky. That's one thing different about New York City—here, the stars are hidden under a layer of cloud cover. The clouds aren't even pretty or dark. They bounce back the yellow-tinted lights from the city, creating a brownish color. Maybe out by the water would be prettier.

I stop in front of the school's library.

After Jacob stole me out of the library apartment, I didn't go back. There wasn't really time, but I had liked it there. It was peaceful, safe. Until he proved otherwise.

So many questions. They do my head in.

I sit on the steps and bury my face in my hands, letting tears spill out finally. My shoulders heave with the force that comes over me. *Sobs.* It's mourning for my lost memories, grief for knowing some things will never come back.

I just want *something*.

Anything.

And then... well, I guess maybe my past doesn't want to stay buried. Because my phone rings, and I fish it out expecting to see Jacob's number. But instead, it's a prison. An automated voice tells me it's a collect call from a New York prison, and it tells me who's calling.

"Jack Cameron."

Holy shit.

I accept the call.

"Mel?" His voice is gruff. Foreign.

"I... yeah." I grip the phone tighter. There's only one person I know in prison that shares my last name. "Dad?"

"Been a long time."

Do I tell him I lost my memories? Does he already know?

"How did you get this number?" I ask instead.

He chuckles. *That's* more familiar, and I find myself closing my eyes to savor the sound.

"I've got connections, baby girl. You weren't at your momma's funeral, so I started asking around." He makes a noise. "Of course, I expected to see you there. It was a shock to discover you were completely off the grid."

A raindrop hits my face.

"You didn't know where I was?"

"No. Care to enlighten me?"

"No." I laugh. "Because I don't know."

Silence.

"I woke up in a hospital with amnesia a few months ago."

The rain is picking up. I tuck my arms around myself, but I don't move. I don't know if I like the rain, or if I want to get drenched. But something about it seems to mirror the turmoil I'm feeling on the inside, and that's why I don't get up and stand under the covering by the library door.

"They said you were in the hospital," he mutters. "Wouldn't tell me what happened."

"What happened between you and me?" I ask. "And my mother—"

"Come visit," he interrupts. "I've got maybe thirty seconds left of this call, baby girl, and there are no answers I can give in that time to satisfy your curiosity. Visit me."

"I don't know..." The rain is soaking my skin, my hair. I tip my head back and let it wash over me. It's melodramatic, but I don't care in the slightest.

He laughs again. "Think it over. You're on my accepted visitor's list."

I suck my lower lip between my teeth for a moment, then release it. "Have I visited you before?"

Pause. Then, "No."

Why?

"I gotta go. Stone Ridge State Prison, that's where I am. Think it over."

I don't answer. I don't know if I love him or if I'll visit him. And after another moment, the line goes dead.

My head hurts.

"Hey."

I lift my head. Jacob's jacket is on, his collar popped to protect his neck against the battering rain. He's so fucking handsome like that, clean-shaven and gruff, his hair no longer messy but pushed straight back and slicked with water, his blue eyes meeting mine with confidence.

And maybe a little bit of an apology.

With sudden longing, I realize I miss my mother.

In my mind, she'd know what to do. She'd know what to *say*. Guidance to steer me right when it comes to Jacob Rhodes, and life, and everything else. In my imagination, we were close. And her death was fueled by a broken heart at my disappearance.

"True or false." I squint up at him. "We've done that before. In public."

He lifts one shoulder. "I went down on you in your office at Crown Point University. Behind your desk, while you sat in your chair wearing a sweet little skirt that I practically ripped shoving it up your thighs."

I frown.

"I made you grade my paper while I did," he adds with a smirk. "Is that *public* enough for you?"

"Just because you did it to me once doesn't mean I'm going to enjoy it again." I rise and push my wet hair out of my face. There's a ripple of lightning above us. "Tell me the truth. I just need to know it, Jake. Did I—were we—" *Together? Happy?*

"Yes." He cups my cheek. "*Yes.*"

That has to be enough for now.

31
MELODY

He takes me back to the hotel room and directs me to the shower. He makes a call, and I turn on the water. I set my glasses on the counter, but he's back before it's warm enough to get in.

"Do you know where Stone Ridge is?"

He nods and pulls at my wet clothes. Shedding first my sweater, then the thin shirt under it. Then my bra. He's methodical about it, as I stand there bare to him.

"It's just outside the city," he murmurs.

Tomorrow is the game. He's got press before it—he already warned that he would be leaving the hotel early, and I'd be on my own for the day. Maybe I can sneak over there with the limited funds I have from Thomas and Natalie.

That opens a whole different can of worms.

His fingers are quick to undo the button of my black jeans, carefully pushing the material down my legs. It clings to my thighs, and I grip the counter at the back to maintain my balance until it's down around my ankles. I kick them away, and he repeats the motion.

"What are you doing?" I step out of those, too.

I'm painfully aware that he's still dressed, even still wearing his jacket.

"Something I should've done before." He rises and spreads his arms. "Can you...?"

I swallow and nod slowly. I unzip his jacket, revealing the navy button-down shirt he wore to dinner. The heavy leather makes a wet *thump* when it hits the floor behind him. I go to the buttons of his shirt next, trying to be quick about it.

His hand covers mine. "Take your time."

Oh.

I look up at him. The square jaw and pink lips that I *know* feel good on my body. His tanned skin, the slight stubble starting to emerge on his cheeks. I graze his chest as my fingers move to the next button, and his throat bobs with his swallow.

The bathroom is filling with steam, covering the mirror and obscuring our images.

Good.

I finish the buttons and touch his chest. The moment my palms collide with his skin, goosebumps rise on the backs of my arms. I slide his shirt off his shoulders. Down his arms, until it lands on top of the jacket.

He doesn't say a word when I run my hands down his front. He's got tattoos on his arms and one on his ribcage that I hadn't paid much attention to. But the closer I look, the more I realize it's the same bird as the one painted in his room. It's in black and white, but it looks the same. The only difference is that it doesn't have tar on its wings—it has a delicate little chain around its leg. And the chain, a few links down, is snapped.

I trace it without thinking.

He sucks in a breath, but he doesn't stop me from touching it.

Whoever the artist was did a great job in recreating the original artist's intentions.

My fingers trail lower, and I bite my lip again when I get to the waistband of his slacks. I undo them and drag them down, waiting for him to kick out of them. I ignore the hard-on when I go down on one knee and pull his briefs off, too. It's pointing at me, red and swollen and waiting.

I rise before he can force it on me.

Now fully naked, he gives me a toe-curling smirk. He goes to the shower and adjusts the temperature, then gestures to me.

I'm still wary. I know that, he knows it. But his expression seems to be open for once, even though we aren't saying anything.

Maybe words will ruin it.

So I stay silent, too, and step past him into the shower.

As soon as he closes the glass door, steam fills the area. The shower head is huge, and I take a deep breath. His hands land on my shoulders behind me.

I stiffen until I realize what he's doing.

A massage?

His fingers work at my tense muscles until I relax, and he continues kneading and working his way down my back. I brace my arm on the wall and audibly sigh. He gets to my hips, and I think he might reverse course. But he keeps going, squeezing my ass, then the tops of my thighs. His hands come back up on the inside, and then he's pushing one finger into me.

I hold back my groan and stay silent.

One finger isn't enough.

He keeps going until I'm wriggling my hips to meet him, then he withdraws. I let out a noise of frustration.

He flips my wet hair over one shoulder and kisses the other. His hands snake around me, cupping my breasts. He pinches my nipples and tugs, and it doesn't take much movement for me to push my hips back and feel his erection slip between my ass cheeks.

We inch under the water. He grabs soap and squirts it into his palm, washing my front slowly. I lean back against him, and he brings the suds up over my chest, paying special attention to my breasts, then back down. Over my stomach and down between my legs, where his fingers slide through my arousal.

I let out a sharp breath.

He keeps kissing my shoulder as he strokes me, his finger on my clit quickly turning me on more. He bands his other arm just under my breasts, keeping me against him.

I close my eyes.

When I come, I cry out softly. He holds me up when my legs go weak and shaky, but he doesn't pull his hand away. He thrusts two fingers inside me. In and out. I'm sensitive, and the slowness creates a delicious friction that's almost too much to bear.

His teeth scour my neck.

I cry out again. The heel of his palm grinds on my clit, giving me a bit of relief every time he thrusts his fingers into me. Over and over again.

I can't come again.

But then I do.

I sag, completely spent, and he shuts off the water. It's rinsed away the soap he washed me with. Before I can move, he wraps me in a fluffy robe and captures my hair up in a towel. He brings me to the bedroom, barely sparing a moment to shuck the water from his skin and hair, and pushes me onto the bed.

I scoot back, watching him warily.

No talking. I have no urge to break this weird silence between us.

He peels the robe apart and spreads my legs, giving me another look before sinking down. His mouth finds my clit.

I don't know if I've ever met someone who likes going down on a woman so much. I'm tempted to say something, to bring that to his attention, but I can't. There's a new lump in my throat, and fresh tears burn the backs of my eyes.

Why does that make me feel special?

He licks and nips at me. He's making rogue noises now, and I can't help but fall a bit in love with it. He *devours* me.

I need to read a romance book and find out if this is a universal experience for heroines, *stat*. Because this definitely doesn't feel like real life.

Before I can come, he crawls up my body and slides into me like he's always meant to be there. He leans to the side and pumps in and out, and my breath leaves me in quick, short spurts. He's hitting a spot inside me that makes me crazy.

I bring my legs up around him, lifting my hips. His movements are getting rougher, his careful control loosening.

His hand on my throat has my eyes opening. I didn't even realize I had closed them, but his fingers dig into my jaw. His grip tightens slightly, and my heart skips. I open and close my mouth and stare into his eyes.

This connection is... it's strange and beautiful and toxic. Isn't it?

I reach up and mirror him. I hold his jaw, his stubble

caressing the pads of my fingers instead of the other way around. I spread my hand wider, until I catch his pulse hammering against my pinkie.

So he's as into this as me.

"Was I always this self-destructive?" My voice is hoarse from disuse.

He pushes deeper into me, and my eyelids flutter.

His lips brush my ear, and he whispers, "Worse."

I let out a moan. My nipples are stiff and sensitive, brushing his chest with every motion. My clit is sore. Not that he gives a fuck about that. He shifts and puts his hand on me again, stroking me with a renewed frenzy.

Worse.

It rings in my ears.

I wrap my legs around him and beg him with my eyes to take me faster. I'm holding him away from my face, but suddenly I feel this need to have him touch me *everywhere*. I drag him down by his jaw until his lips collide with mine, and only then do I let my hand slip down his throat to his chest.

He kisses me like he's been dying to do it for ages. I give everything I have into it. The pleasure in my body is rising, threatening to drown me.

And for once, I'd happily go.

He growls. The sound vibrates through his chest and into mine. Two more thrusts, and he slams to a halt inside me. He brings me right up to the edge of the cliff and shoves me over without wasting a moment, and he hisses as my muscles clench around him.

I arch my back and cry out, although I don't think the noise actually makes it past my lips. He's swallowing my sound, licking at my mouth with the same fervor he licks at my pussy.

When both of us are spent, he relaxes on top of me. His weight comes down, and I hug him tighter. I expect him to get up, but he keeps kissing me. It's languid. Easy. I kiss him and feel him in me and I don't know what else I'm supposed to do to be happy.

Because this seems pretty close.

A knock on the door interrupts us. He pulls back and closes my robe again, drawing up the tie and knotting it at my waist. He grabs sweatpants from his suitcase and drags them up his hips. I drag myself into a sitting position just as he opens the door around the corner.

"I'll take it in. Thanks."

I raise my eyebrow at the sudden rattling. Jacob appears with a rolling cart. He's ordered... something. There are a few platters covered by silver domes, and he stops it at the foot of the bed.

"First time getting room service," I murmur, crawling toward him. "What did you get?"

"Dessert." He smiles and unveils what he got. There are five bowls with different flavored ice creams, another few bowls filled with toppings. A can of whipped cream. He removes the other with flourish and reveals a thermos and two mugs.

Without an explanation, he pours the liquid from the thermos into the mugs and stirs it. He squirts whipped cream on top and uses a spoon to speckle it in rainbow sprinkles. He sits beside me and hands me a mug.

"Hot chocolate with all the fixings," he says, his gaze glued to my face.

I hum. "Interesting choice."

"It's raining. You need warming up."

"The shower did just that, didn't it? And... the other stuff."

He shrugs. He's still watching me like he's waiting for something, and I have no idea what. It's unsettling, although I try to brush it off. Maybe we've been in this position before? Maybe I'm supposed to be experiencing déjà vu?

I stare at the whipped cream. The mug is warm against my fingers. I take a sip, hoping it won't scald my tongue, and am instead greeted with the most delicious wash of chocolate at the perfect temperature. I take another sip. The cool whipped cream creates a dichotomy in my mouth I wasn't expecting. The sprinkles add the slightest crunch.

Unexpectedly, it reminds me of my parents.

"What are you thinking?"

I lift my gaze and lower the mug back to the tray. I force myself to keep eye contact with him. "Earlier today, I was missing my mom."

He winces.

"And now I'm thinking about my parents again."

"In what way?"

"I just..." Okay, eye contact is a little too hard when I'm trying to be honest. I fiddle with the hem of the robe. "My dad is in prison. Mom died while I was... wherever I was."

He takes my hand. "And..."

"I hope I had a good childhood, but I have a feeling I didn't."

Gut instinct.

And by the way his hand tightens on mine, I think I'm right.

"Close your eyes."

I watch him for a moment, but then I do. He gets up, and there's rustling, and then a cold breeze sweeps into the room. I shiver, goosebumps appearing on the backs of my arms, and I fight to keep from hugging myself.

"Open," he says softly, right in front of me. "Think of a snowstorm. Of me."

I part my lips, and the rim of the mug touches my mouth. He has me drink just a sip, barely a taste, and I try to think of that. I imagine a blizzard, the aching coldness of snow. Jacob smirking at me. There's the squirt of the whipped cream can. It bursts across my tongue, my lips, getting flecks everywhere.

He's kissing me before I can process it. Licking away the whipped cream.

"What else is there about you, songbird?" he asks in a throaty whisper.

Something cracks.

"Why do you call me that?"

I know I've asked. I open my eyes and stare at him. Before he can say anything, I'm answering myself.

"'Your voice is a wet dream personified.'" I cover my mouth. That didn't come from me. I didn't make that up.

He smiles. "In your lectures, it made me want to stab every other guy in the room in the ears."

I hear him say it now, but I hear him say it then, too. Sitting in his house. *Cold*. A mug of hot chocolate in my hands, cradled close as I... as I what? Contemplated doing something with my student?

"Songbird," Jacob says softly, moving to kneel in front of me. His hands rub my knees, up the outside of my thighs. "Talk to me."

It was wrong of me then, and it feels wrong of me now.

The situation is so different, so abstract, I can't wrap my brain around it. But I have to face what past-me has done so I can move on. Because I—

"Did I groom you?"

He scowls. "I was twenty-one, Melody. I pursued you."

I laugh. "Yeah, right. There's still the power imbalance."

"The first time we spoke alone, I asked if you'd get on your knees. And you slapped me."

My face heats, but I'm nodding. I can understand that. The shock, the disrespect of his words, maybe paired with a cocky smile.

"But let me be clear, Melody: you were never in charge."

I suck in a breath.

And he smiles.

32

JACOB

We take turns sampling the different flavors of ice cream. She likes chocolate, unsurprisingly, and the peppermint. She makes a face at the banana flavor and gags when she tries the chocolate-straw-berry-vanilla.

Staring at the offensive ice creams, she sighs. "How can I like fruit but *hate* fruit-flavored ice cream?"

I shrug. "I don't know."

She glances at me. I've claimed the plain vanilla for my own, stirring in hot fudge and chocolate chips and topping it with nuts and sprinkles. We sit on the floor, our backs against the bed, with a perfect view of the city. The lights are off. In a way, it's romantic.

That's what she deserves.

To be wooed and cherished. And sometimes, she deserves to be called a dirty little whore and fucked like an animal.

I don't make the rules.

"My dad called." She glances at me, then away, and sticks a spoonful of ice cream in her mouth.

Her dad.

The one in prison.

"How'd he get your new number?"

She shrugs. "I don't know. Figured I should talk to him, though."

I put together the pieces. "That's why you asked about Stone Ridge?"

"Yeah."

"I should go with you." I want to look this fucker in the eye and make sure he didn't hurt her. Because she can't tell me. But if she sees him, it might trigger something. A memory or a feeling. And I want to be there to catch them. I want to be there to collect all her memories and safekeep them for her.

"I was going to go tomorrow." Her eyes are on the window.

I study the slope of her nose. Her eyelashes as she blinks. Her high cheekbones. Her glasses are forgotten in the bathroom. She didn't make a fuss about them when she was blowing me at the restaurant, although I should've pulled them off. Now, it makes me wonder how good the view is if everything is blurry.

I hop up and retrieve them. She takes them without a word, sliding them on her face, then sighs.

"Any clarity?" I ask.

Melody rolls her eyes. "No."

"We can visit him before our flight. Not tomorrow, but the next day." I take her hand and press my thumb into the heel of her palm. My mom sometimes massages my dad's hands like this. They don't always see eye to eye, but they still love each other.

"Maybe."

The night seems young, even though it's well past

midnight. I don't have to be anywhere until noon. We have brunch plans with Knox, Greyson, Miles, and Steele. They're all here for the final game. And the girls. Knox is the only one flying solo nowadays, although he hasn't said a word about it.

Doesn't seem to care either. He's with a new girl every weekend. He gets his kicks however he can get them, and he doesn't want a relationship. The idea repulses him.

Fine by us. We're content to let him be managed by his agent, a big dude who used to rep some football asshole who has since retired, and steer him away from media scandals.

He'll probably grow up someday.

Melody sets aside the bowl and rolls onto her knees. She flips aside the pieces of the robe around her legs enough to swing her leg over mine. And just like that, she's settled on my lap.

"Hi," I murmur. I rest my hands on her hips.

"Degradation," she says.

I blink.

"I'm into that, apparently."

"Oh. Yes."

"Are you?"

I frown. "Do I like degrading you?"

Her lower lip is caught between her teeth again as she nods. I memorize this vulnerable, uncomfortable expression. I don't often see Melody with her guard completely down. She wants to understand herself, and she needs my help to do it. Because so far, I've unlocked way more than she has on her own.

But to understand this, she needs to understand the rest of it.

And she can't understand the hell that I went through

after she left. That I'm still angry at past-her, even if it's looking more and more like it wasn't her fault. That degrading her gives me a satisfaction that only eases when she finds release in it, too.

It just won't go farther than that. Past-her and present-her are the same person, after all.

"What else do you like?" I ask.

She shakes her head. "No, you tell me."

"Maybe you like to be fucked while you sleep." I raise my eyebrow. "*Maybe* you like to wake up on the cusp of an orgasm, left hanging, and then wonder why your skin is sticky. Why your cunt is leaking more than just arousal."

Her eyes go wide.

My cock is ready for another round. I pull her down, showing her exactly how aroused *I* am by this talk.

"How?" she whispers.

I catch her wrists and pull them behind her back. The robe hides her beautiful tits from me. Switching her wrists to one hand, I use the other to yank the robe open. I lean down and kiss the swell of her breast, nibbling my way down until I suck her nipple into my mouth.

"Jake," she breathes, leaning back slightly. "*How?*"

"Do you mean, how would you stay asleep? Or how could I break into your house and fuck you without you knowing? Hypothetically."

"That's not—"

I bring my mouth up to her ear. "I'd be happy to show you."

She squirms. "Because you've done it before."

"Do you *really* think your cousin was the one to leave your cunt full of cum?"

She jerks back, just as I expect. Her eyes are wide, her nostrils flaring. I've surprised her, and I relish it. Along with the spark of fear that seems to be turning into a wildfire inside her.

"You didn't."

"I did," I say.

I shove my sweatpants down, freeing my cock. She's bare under her robe, and I fist myself. I stroke once, twice, grimacing at the feel. Finally, I hold it up.

"Ride me," I order.

"Fuck you."

"That's what I want, songbird. *Fuck me.* And I'll tell you the rest."

Her eyes light up. Caught on wanting to know more, she inches forward and lifts herself. I guide the tip of my cock to her entrance and release my grip on it. She slides down slowly, and I let out a breath at the vise grip her cunt has on me. When her thighs touch mine, we both exhale again.

"You made me think Thomas was doing that to me?" She yanks her wrists out of my grasp and flips her hair off her shoulders. "What should I do to get answers from you?"

I shove the robe off her, baring her naked body to me. "I want you to show me how much you *hate* the idea of me doing this to your sleeping body. Ride me, songbird."

She moves slowly. It takes her a few tries to get the pace right, and her balance. I hold her waist and let her do the hard work, and my gaze drops. Every inch of me she takes is another victory. Her hand skims the bird tattoo I got for her. Of her. And she doesn't even know it.

As she fucks me, I start talking.

I tell her to imagine waking up so turned on, she has no choice but to touch herself. To recall waking up in my guest bedroom with the insatiable urge to get herself off. Or in the guest bedroom of her cousin's house. The pleasure wrapped up in coming so swiftly, after being taken to the edge again and again without even knowing it...

Her breathing is fast, and so is her pace. She's racing toward the finish line without even realizing it, her gaze trapped in mine. I have no idea what she's thinking.

She's fucking beautiful.

I tangle my fist in her hair and yank her head back, throwing off her balance. It stops her movement, but I only need another second before my balls are emptying my cum inside her.

She makes a noise. Something caught between a mewl of frustration and anger.

I lean in and bite her breast again, keeping her plugged full of my seed.

She should get pregnant at this rate. At the amount of times we fuck, it's almost impossible for her not to be. She's not on birth control, not that I'm aware of. So why not put a baby in her belly and tie her to me in more ways than one?

With a slight smile, I lift her off me.

"Jacob."

I tsk. "We're experimenting."

"By..."

"Don't worry, baby. Soon." I hoist her to her feet and smack her ass.

She lets out a yelp, but I jump up, too. I leave her standing there and head to the bathroom. How long might she hold out before she touches herself?

And do I want to restrain her if she does?

Decisions, decisions.

I'm too aware of the scars on her wrists. Of the trauma that she's holding, even if she doesn't remember it. Paired with what we just discussed, I don't think I should.

After I've cleaned up and prepared a drink for her, I

return. She's standing by the window, her arms crossed under her breasts.

"So fucking beautiful." I hold out the glass. "Thirsty?"

She nods and takes it. Our fingers brush, and she frowns at me as she swallows the water.

"You wanted to know how?" I ask, taking the glass from her and setting it on the cart.

"How you would keep me asleep?"

I nod.

"Yeah, I do."

"Simple. I drug you."

33
MELODY

My fingers are between my legs before I'm fully awake. My core is pulsing, on *fire* with need, and I shift my hips trying to get more friction. More sensation.

But then my hand is dragged away, over my head, and caught.

I crack my eyes open. We left the blackout shades open last night, and the early morning light is illuminating the room. The sun probably hasn't risen yet, but soon it'll be too bright to go back to sleep. Not that I want that.

Jacob leans over me, his gaze analyzing my expression. My hungry expression.

"Touch me," I beg.

He's holding my other hand to the mattress, his fingers laced with mine and his arm stretched across my body. The arm closest to him is up over my head. I don't know how long he's been holding it, but he doesn't release me when I tug.

"Jacob, please."

He smiles.

It's too brilliant for however early it is.

I follow his gaze up my arm, to where he's tied my wrist to the headboard.

It should panic me, but it doesn't. I don't care about it when there's a more pressing need between my legs.

"Remember our conversation last night?" he asks.

It's hard to remember anything right now. But when he doesn't move, doesn't do anything but *wait*, I nod. We talked about him fucking me in my sleep, and I... I didn't want to believe it. There's a part of me that doesn't think he can.

I mean, come on. I'd wake up.

And when would he have had the chance to drug me, like he claimed? It's just ridiculous. Impossible.

"We talked about you waking up with a cunt full of cum," he says in my ear. His lips brush it as he talks.

A shiver shoots down my spine.

"We talked about you waking up desperate to get off."

Like right now.

Abruptly, he releases my hand. My left hand, that I'm clumsier to bring myself to orgasm with, shoots down to my bare pussy. I run my fingers through the slick arousal, but it's more than that. And my heart picks up speed at the realization. Dipping inside me, I feel it. It comes out on my finger, thicker and more opaque than my arousal.

Familiar. I've done this before, panicked about this before.

My mouth is dry. "You did that while I slept?"

"Yes." He kisses my cheek.

"Why?"

"Because I'm obsessed with you."

My skin heats. My face is flushing, I know it. My cheeks will redden first, and then it'll spread to the rest of my face and down my neck until I resemble a tomato. I still don't quite believe it. It's not... it's unusual, right?

He reaches down and nudges my fingers away, running his nail lightly over my clit.

I let out an involuntary moan.

"Because your voice is a wet dream personified," he says. They're the same the words he spoke years ago that now bounce around my head. "Because you're mine in all your forms. Awake, sleeping, with your memory or without it."

He pinches my clit. The pain and pleasure is shocking, and I cry out. Giving him the noises he craves. He takes my other hand and attaches it to the headboard next to my other one. I let him, watching his face.

When I don't struggle or panic, he looks pleased.

His cock lies on my thigh. He ignores it, although it's oozing precum. He's so close to me, his whole body lines up from his chest to our knees. Him on his side, me flat on my back. He manipulates my clit until I'm struggling to keep myself composed.

"Break," he orders, his voice rasping in my ear. "Break for me, songbird."

Two fingers dip inside me, the heel of his palm on my clit, and it's the combination that undoes me. My back arches, and I lose myself to the swift orgasm. It's strong—stronger than I've felt before.

But following it is confusion. Because he may like fucking me while I sleep, and I might like that he gets off on it, but I can't help but feel like he's deprived me of something.

He flips me over.

I squeal, and his hand strikes my ass.

Hard.

And then he's kneading the flesh, separating my ass cheeks. He pushes into me without hesitation, and I think it's supposed to be painful. But there's lube, or *something*, and my world cracks apart again.

"I came inside your ass," he confesses, leaning over me. "Just the tip. Just enough to fill that hole, too."

He slides in deeper, and my mouth drops open. I thought he was in, but it seems like it's just the beginning. He takes more and more and more, until his hips meet my ass. It hurts but it doesn't. The deep ache is just a precursor to pleasure, and it's right there for me to indulge.

"But this is the first time I'm taking it."

He pulls out and thrusts back in. Hard, quick.

I make a noise, and his fingers are suddenly in my hair, forcing my head into the pillow. I bite down hard on it and scream through my teeth.

He alternates between spanking me and fucking my ass, and I get lost. *Again.* Wound tighter and tighter. A breeze on my clit would make me come. I hump the mattress in time with him, yanking at the restraints.

I just want to come.

I think I'm crying.

His movements get faster. I have to press my hands to the headboard to keep from sliding into it. He grips my thighs and spreads my legs wider, and something cool drips down my ass.

He spit on me.

And fuck if I don't tense around him, weirdly turned on by it. But I need more. I buck and roll and catch him by surprise so much that he falls off the bed.

He pops back up and stares at me for a moment. His cock is throbbing, and I stare at it with wide eyes.

I pull myself up, my arms trapped behind me, and slowly spread my legs. My ass cheeks burn, but I ignore it.

"Look at you."

His voice does something to me.

"Your cunt is drooling for me. Do you see?"

From this angle, not fucking really. I glare at him, and he smirks.

"No? It's okay. I can see it, and I'll tell you that your asshole is gaping at me. It'll never be the same. Not after I'm done with you."

"Pretty words," I manage. My fingers work at the ties. In this position, I can reach. And I undo one just as he lunges. I roll to the side and grab at the other tie—he used his actual ties—and work at the slip knot. I get it off and jump up.

We collide, and he flattens me chest-first into the window. He kicks my legs open wider and thrusts back into me, taking my ass with renewed vigor. His hands are everywhere, and his grip is so bruising. It's all I can do to hold myself up, my chest and face smashed to the glass, my palms pressing on it with no success. He touches my breasts, my belly, my thighs. His grip on my hips is killer.

"Everyone looking up can see what a slut you are."

He skims my back and fists my hair, forcing me to crank my head back. His lips crash into mine from the side. The kiss is sloppy and wet, and I groan into his mouth. Our tongues fight, teeth clicking together. He bites my lower lip and draws blood, and I bite him right back.

"Fuck." His other hand leaves my hip and touches my clit.

Finally.

I let out a huff through my nose, and he smiles. He sucks my tongue into his mouth and thrums my clit. He moves faster, taking longer, harder strokes, until he stops.

Until my orgasm hits me like a sucker punch, and I scream for the whole hotel to hear.

Until he comes inside me like that.

I sag forward, resting my forehead on the cool glass. "So much for waking up to sweet morning sex."

He chuckles. "Sometimes the animal way is better." He kisses my neck. "Especially before a game."

I straighten when he pulls out of me, and it takes a minute for my legs to remember how to work. Every muscle in my body aches.

"And after the game?"

He shrugs, but there's a glint to his gaze. "We'll see."

Damn.

Okay.

34
JACOB

We show up to brunch a little late.

Melody is blushing by the time we find my friends seated at a round table. We agreed in our group chat that we wouldn't wear any team colors or logos this morning, and I find that everyone actually agreed to it.

I introduce Melody around, although they all know who she is. It's more for her benefit. Steele and Aspen, Miles and Willow, Greyson and Violet. Knox.

She nods and smiles, then takes a seat between me and Aspen. I think of all of them, Aspen and her definitely never met. So the weirdness level is down a few notches.

"Ready?" I ask Knox.

He grins. "Obviously."

"You need to be at the top of your game."

"I am. Are you?" His gaze bounces between me and Melody. "You're not too distracted?"

I scoff. "Wishful thinking, dude. She wakes me up."

Melody's hand touches my thigh, and I lace my fingers with hers automatically. She's in discussion with Aspen about something. Music, I think.

We order. Steele and Greyson are arguing about their teams' chances. There's a rumor that Steele's coach is stepping down, although no formal announcement has been made.

"It's too bad we can't all play on the same team," Miles says after we place our drinks order. "That would solve everything."

Knox nods. "It would."

"You guys could always get traded. Aim for the Titans." I flash them a smile. "Or not. I mean, we're going to kick the Guardians' asses in a few hours..."

"I've already bet on you," Steele says with a smile. He elbows Knox. "You don't mind throwing the game so I can win a few grand, do you?"

Melody's eyes boggle.

Knox socks him back just as fast. "Get fucked, buddy."

"Now, now," Miles calls. "There's no need for that."

Knox flips him off.

Their banter continues, and I lean in toward Melody. We were late because we had to shower, and being naked together in a confined space led to more fucking. Which led to more washing and drying. She wanted to put makeup on and pick an outfit that wouldn't relay *old*. Whatever the fuck that means.

"You okay?" I kiss her cheek.

I aim for it anyway, but she turns her head and catches my lips with hers at the last second. It's short and sweet—emphasis on *sweet*—and it knocks me off guard for a moment. I stare into her hazel eyes, noting that they're more brown than green today.

"I'm good," she finally answers, smiling a little.

"Okay."

"So, Melody," Violet calls across the table. She and

Greyson got her to New York without a hitch. "Were you able to check out the college you went to?"

Melody shakes her head. "Not yet."

"We could head there after this," she offers. "Grey knows someone who works there."

Beside me, Melody stiffens. "Oh, um…"

I squeeze her hand. "It could be useful."

And doing that will keep her from visiting her father in prison.

She eyes me like she can read my mind, and I force a smile.

"Okay. Yeah," she agrees. "Thanks."

Greyson gives me a look. I'm ninety percent sure it conveys that they're not going to let her out of their sight. Which is good, because I'm pretty sure I'd go on a murdering spree if they do and something happens to her.

Or even if nothing happens to her.

The waitress comes back by for food orders, and Melody orders waffles with fruit and syrup and whipped cream. It kind of reminds me of last night, although I'm pretty sure she doesn't like soggy waffles.

I order something I think she'd like along with my own meal, brushing it off like I'm extra hungry. And when the food comes, she takes a few bites of her waffles and starts picking at the edges.

"Here." I nudge that plate toward the center and replacing it with an omelet and bacon.

"What? That's yours."

I gesture to the biscuits and gravy and my own side of bacon. "This is mine."

She narrows her eyes. "Did you know I wasn't going to like the waffles?"

The table is watching us, but I ignore them. "Yeah, you don't like soggy sweet stuff."

"Why didn't you tell me?"

I shrug. "You've got to experience it. But I *can* make sure you don't go hungry. I tap her phone, face down on the table beside her knife. "Put it on your list."

She huffs. It's kind of cute. It's why I keep watching her type, until she stops and stares at the screen. It slips out of her hand and hits the edge of the table with a *crack*, falling to her lap.

I snag it before it hits the floor.

There's another text from the blocked number.

Another texted voice message. I wave at my friends to stop talking, and they focus in on me. I hit *play*.

Melody makes a noise of protest. "Don't—"

"Hey, darling. How's New York treating you? Tell your pops I say hello." It goes quiet, but there's still thirty seconds left. After ten, the jackass I can only assume is her ex-husband continues, *"I've been thinking a lot about our reunion. I found you last time. It's only a matter of time before I find you again."*

I hit the 'keep' button before it can disappear, and I drop the phone facedown. I'm tempted to play it again and again, just to cement it in my memory, but I fear it's already there.

"He knows I'm in New York?" Melody whispers through her fingers. "How can he know? How does he know my father?"

"This is getting ridiculous," I snap. At no one in particular, but my girl flinches all the same.

Fuck.

I jerk back from the table, taking her phone with me. I dial Bill's number and step out onto the sidewalk, heading toward the corner of the building. There's a line to get into this place, and I'm drawing a few looks. I'm half a block away by the time he answers.

"Did you get the file I sent you?" I ask.

Vicky managed to get me the details of the restraining order. Since legal jargon is far outside of my expertise, I sent them by private courier to Bill. And even though he lives in Denver, they arrived at his doorstep early this morning.

"I was just finishing going through them."

"He's threatening her," I seethe. "He's fucking sending her messages. That's got to be against the terms, doesn't it?"

"It would be," he agrees. "He's not allowed to contact her..."

"But?"

He grunts. "*But*, guess who has kept the lowest profile for the past two and a half years?"

"You think—" I laugh. "How the fuck did he keep her hidden for... for two years?"

He's silent.

He's fucking *serious*.

"Bill." My voice has changed. The humor gone. I feel it all drain out of me, down my legs and out my shoes. "He didn't find her in Crown Point, did he? Is that what this is referring to?"

"I'm looking into it."

"Text me Armstrong's address."

Bill hesitates. "Tell me you aren't planning on doing anything stupid."

"I'm not going to do anything stupid," I parrot.

I'm going to do something insane.

But *stupid*?

Never.

35
MELODY

"You look like the conspiring type," I whisper to Willow.

She brightens. "I do?"

"Yeah." I glance over her shoulder. The guys are off to the side, arguing about something. A player on another team, I think. I catch the name *Stone Foster*, although it doesn't mean anything to me. "I need to ditch you guys."

Her face falls.

"I'm sorry."

We walked through campus. The guy Greyson knows didn't recognize me, so that was a bit of a bust. He didn't even know my name.

"I got a call from my dad, and he's in Stone Ridge prison. He wants me to visit him, and Jake doesn't think it's a great idea."

Willow smiles. "You call him Jake?"

Ugh.

"No, don't get me wrong. He snapped at a girl once for calling him that."

I don't necessarily like *that* either, but... it does feel a little more special.

"You've known him a long time?" I ask to change the subject.

"Yeah. You, too, you know. You taught one of my classes at Crown Point."

"Oh God." I look away, trying to hide my wince. "I..."

She grabs my hand. "You were a good professor. Passionate about what you were teaching. It was a nice change, especially because you got us to understand it. Like some stuff I would never have gotten through, but you had the magic touch."

"That's... nice." I force a smile. "Too bad I've forgotten everything."

"Yeah." She goes quiet. But only for a moment. Then she's motioning for Violet and Aspen to come in close. "Okay, here's the plan. Violet and Aspen will run interference with the guys, and then you and I are gonna catch a car."

Aspen makes a face. "Only one of us doesn't have a permanent tracker."

They both look at Violet.

She groans. "Yep. Here." She hands her phone off to Aspen.

Willow pulls out a chunk of cash and stuffs it in my hand. "Text us when you're on your way back. You have my number?"

"I've got it memorized," Violet murmurs. "Okay. Go."

Aspen and Willow break off, drifting back toward the guys who are still caught up in the argument. Or discussion. Whatever it is.

Violet grabs my hand and drags me into a building. The door opens under her hands, luckily, and we dart down a hallway. Then another, until we find another exit onto a different street.

We call a car when we're two blocks away.

"What did they mean about the trackers?"

She smiles. She actually doesn't look that put off by it, which is an odd experience in and of itself. "Greyson tracks my phone. It didn't work one time when I was abducted, so the other guys resorted to stronger methods."

"Of... tracking them."

"Yeah." She tucks her blonde hair behind her ears. "Okay, it sounds insane. And it wasn't entirely consensual at the time..."

Huh.

But that has me wondering if Jacob's ever considered putting a tracker on or in *me*. He fucks me when I sleep, what's to stop him from doing something else? Something less... erotic. And if he hasn't, even with the opportunity, why not?

I laugh.

Violet raises her eyebrow, and I shake my head.

"I found myself being a little upset that Jake hasn't gone to such extraordinary lengths," I explain. "Which is ridiculous."

"Yeah, well, love has a weird way of getting under our skin like that."

My smile drops. "I'm not in love."

"Oh. Okay."

No, really.

There's a phantom voice in my ear. It yells as I cower back against a wall. For a split second, I'm ice-cold.

And then it's gone.

"Are you okay?"

I rub my arms and ignore Violet's concerned expression. "Totally fine. That's our car."

We get in, and it takes off for Stone Ridge. We ride in comfortable quiet. It's a forty-five-minute trek out of the city, and the driver chats quietly to someone through a Bluetooth earpiece in another language.

Violet's beautiful. We talk about her ballet career and the company she's currently dancing with as a soloist. She briefly touches on the abduction, and the way Greyson came for her. She speaks about him with love in her gaze. But not just that. It's like she glows with it, and that's what I don't understand.

Finally, the driver pulls into the prison's driveway. He stops in front of it, and he shoots away as soon as the doors close behind us. We stare at his taillights quickly disappearing, and I shrug.

"They might not let me in," she says.

"They will." I just need to channel Jacob's authority. He makes things happen, and so can I. So when I walk in and give my name to the guard, and tell him we'll be seeing my father, it checks out. Dad said I was on his approved visitor's list, and here we are. Approved.

We slide our IDs over, and Violet has to fill out extra paperwork. Once that's done, we're shuffled in with the others waiting to visit. A guard opens one of the doors and calls out loud instructions. No phones. No contact after an initial hug. All visitors are subject to inspection upon leaving the area.

I exchange a glance with Violet and follow the surge of people through the doors. We leave our phones in little lockers outside the visiting room.

"I don't know what he looks like," I whisper to her.

My belly erupts with butterflies. Not the good kind that

I experience with Jacob. Fear-inducing butterflies that make me want to throw up.

"He knows you," she whispers.

Right.

We walk in and take seats on one side of a round table. The stools are attached to the center of the table, and everything is bolted to the floor. We wait, everyone waits, for the far doors to open.

A buzzer precedes the inmates. A guard comes through first, stepping aside and watching the room. Then a beige-jumpsuit-clad inmate strolls through. He's got tattoos on his neck and face. But he spots whoever is here to see him, and the scary expression is replaced with a smile.

Okay.

It's okay.

He's not the next one through, or the next. Young, old, *really* old, *really young*. I can't believe the variety.

Then I see him.

And a memory comes back.

36
MELODY

MEMORY — SEVENTEEN YEARS OLD

D ad left the front door open again.

I creep down the stairs and peer around the corner, trying to both listen for movement and be quick. The little heat we can afford is being swept out into the cold night air. In the other room, my parents are arguing. They're in the kitchen, maybe, judging from the way their voices carry.

This isn't the house I grew up in.

I shouldn't be here at all.

But Mom asked if I would come home for the weekend to celebrate her birthday. I've been in college for six weeks. I turn eighteen in another two—not soon enough—and I couldn't find it in me to say no to her. She paid for my train ticket home from the city, but she failed to mention that she had taken my father back.

And now here he is, in her new house, drunk and causing a scene.

I make it to the front door and close it, flipping the deadbolt lock.

"What're you doing here?"

I whirl around.

Dad strides toward me. Or, more like stumbles. He's gotten older and grayer in the past few years. His skin is weathered and wrinkled, his eyes bloodshot. He's drunk or drinking more times than not.

"I came back for Mom's birthday."

"Oh, the high and mighty Melody is gracing us with her presence." He sweeps his arm out and bows, teetering to the side. "The big-shot college girl. You're trying to make something of your life?"

Hurt radiates through me.

"Stealing my money," he continues. "You're supposed to join the work force, darling. Support your family."

He reaches out and pats my cheek. I do my best not to cringe away, even when his pats feel more like slaps. But my anger is climbing, and eventually, I shove his hand away.

"Enough," I hiss. "It's Mom's birthday."

"It's her *birthday*. I fucking know that."

He reacts fast. And maybe it's because I don't expect it that I can't get myself to move out of the way in time. But he grabs me by the hair and spins me around, slamming me face-first into the door.

Pain explodes from my cheekbone across my face.

"You're worthless," he says in my ear. "Nothing more than a parasite we've fed for too long."

"Jack," my mom cries. "What are you doing?"

She yanks on his arm, but he doesn't get off me. And my breathing is stuttered, my muscles frozen. I couldn't fight back if I wanted to. I just stay still and hope he stops.

He finally jerks free. "You're a goddamn coddler," he screams at my mother on the way past. "She's grown."

"She's just here for the weekend—"

He picks up a framed picture from the side table and chucks it at me.

I duck, and the thing shatters over my head. Bits of frame and glass rain down on me, and something inside me fractures. I unlock the door and slip out.

I run to the neighbor's house.

Whatever they see has them calling the police. They show up in no time. The neighbor talks about how my parents are always yelling. The police ask me how I was injured.

"My dad," I whisper.

And then he's in handcuffs, struggling as they drag him to one of the cruisers. They put my mother and I in another, driving us to the station. She doesn't look at me until we're in the station—and she sees them lead her husband away.

Then she comes at *me*. She blames *me*.

They haul her off and shepherd me toward the social worker's office.

The sad part is that I already know her. I'd met her a few times over the years, although nothing ever stuck. But now, I sit on her couch and tears come pouring out of my eyes, and I can't stop. My mother's voice is still digging into me from another room, another *world* away.

You fat slut, you ruin everything. How dare you call the cops on your father? He's just trying to help you! How could you do this to us?

"Here." The social worker sits beside me with a mug in her hand.

I take it. And take a sip.

Hot chocolate coats my taste buds.

I haven't had hot chocolate in years.

It's then that she breaks the news that he's going to jail for assaulting a minor. That there's enough proof, enough documentation, for the prosecutor to get him locked away for at least ten years.

And in two weeks, I'll be eighteen. It doesn't matter if my mother disowns me. I'm at college. I have a place to stay, loans and grants to pay for school, and friends. *Friends*, for the first time in my life.

Dad going to jail feels right.

Justified.

My mother hating me... Well, maybe we'll be able to repair it.

So I sip my hot chocolate and try to stop the guilt from eating me up inside.

37
JACOB

I pace outside the arena.

Of all the things I *should* be doing, this is not one of them. I'm in a weird state between worry and calm. Like, I know where she probably went. And Violet should be with her, according to the call from Greyson. But Violet gave Willow her phone, and she's the only one not tracked by other means. You'd think he would've lived and learned, but he was already taking her feelings into consideration.

Not Melody, though. I didn't clone her phone or put a tracker under her skin. I've been painfully ignorant when it comes to such things, because I thought...

She's a bird with clipped wings.

Where could she go?

Turns out, she could go anywhere she damn well pleases. And as long as I'm trapped by obligation to my team, there are some times where I simply cannot follow her.

So I've been dealing with the weird floating sensation that comes with instability and mild panic, and I keep pacing. Even when Camden Church steps out to check on me, or when Dawes offers me a hit of weed to get my "anxiety" under control.

There's one thing that will control it, and that's me. When I finally see her.

My songbird appears around the corner with Violet, and the ground comes back under my feet. I hurry forward, taking in everything about her.

She's wearing the same clothes. Her purse is on her shoulder. Her glasses are missing, I don't know where.

Her eyes are puffy, her lower lip indented with teeth marks.

I open my arms, and she collapses into them. I'm not entirely surprised when she starts crying. She feels small like this. Her shoulders shake, her head stays tucked into my chest. My shirt soaks up her tears.

"We went to see her father," Violet says. "And it triggered..."

"Did you know about the hot chocolate?" Melody's voice is ragged. She curls her fingers into my shirt, but she doesn't lift her head. "Is that what you were trying to get me to remember after I said I missed my mom?"

I shake my head. "You didn't say that to me."

She's quiet. Then, "I thought it. I thought, *I miss her.* And I hoped she was a good person. Why did it only take seeing my dad's face to remember that she really wasn't?"

I don't have an answer for that.

"Did you talk to your dad?"

She shudders.

"He tried to apologize. But I told him that I remembered him slamming my face into the wall—"

"That's what got him arrested," Violet adds quietly. "Although not what kept him in prison, apparently."

I narrow my eyes. He had an ulterior motive, to see his

daughter, then? I hug her tighter, resting my chin on top of her head.

"Melody didn't talk to him." Violet frowns. "She left as soon as he said sorry. I asked him what his deal was, but he just laughed and shook his head. He said he wanted to see his daughter without the contempt in her gaze."

I hate him.

I stroke Melody's hair. "He manipulated you. It was a power play for him."

She draws back long enough to meet my eyes. Hers are tearstained, and I brush my thumb across her cheek. Collecting the wetness.

"Isn't that what you're doing?"

I sweep my thumb along her cheek again, for no other reason than I want to.

"Yes," I agree. "But I do it because I love you. Not because I hate you or want to get back at you. I gave you the hot chocolate because I wanted you to remember the time *I* gave you hot chocolate. And then, you told me about what your mother did to you. Not your dad, your mom. Who used psychological warfare to make you hate your body.

"While I love your body. And your voice. You and I had consensual sex. I told you I wanted to keep you—"

"I'm not keepable."

My heart stops.

"That's not a word, Professor," I whisper in her ear.

She turns her head and kisses me, and I can't tell if it's because she's starting to remember these moments like phantom sensations or if she just wants to kiss me. Because there's nostalgia here that unexpectedly soothes my frustration and my need for answers.

In another life, we've talked about what we want to do with our lives, and our parents, and a million things between. I've stared at her red lips far too much. Gotten hard in some uncomfortable places. Fell in love between lines of her lectures.

It's only right that we repeat ourselves, like history, until we fall again.

Well. Until *she* falls again.

I'm already there.

"Okay," I whisper against her lips. I taste her tears. "You have to get to your seat. I have a game to win."

She nods and steps back, pulling her glasses from a case in her purse. She slides them back on and forces a smile, then rejoins Violet. At the corner, I spot Greyson waiting for them.

Back inside, I nearly crash into Knox. He's pacing the hallway, staring at his phone like it's going to bite him.

"You good?"

He jerks, then nods. "Yeah, obviously."

"What's going on with...?" I gesture to his phone. "The dead body isn't coming back to bite you, is it?"

The dead body he handled in some sort of effort to get his brother to forgive him.

"What?" He scoffs. "No, of course not. It's... personal."

I glare at him. "So personal you're not going to tell me about it?"

He growls under his breath. "I'll tell you later."

"It better not affect your game tonight." I shove his shoulder.

He pushes me back, finally cracking a smile. The worry melts off his face like it was never there. "No fucking way. We're going to crush you and go all the way. I'm not stopping 'til I can kiss the cup."

I smile. "In your dreams."

38

KNOX

Fuck. My. Life.

As soon as Rhodes is out of sight, I pull out my phone and reread the voicemail transcription. I could hit *play* and listen to it, but once was enough.

It came from a private number, and as such it went straight to voicemail. I didn't even have a chance to answer it—not that I would've. A few years ago, someone signed me up for a bunch of subscriptions. I get a million messages and calls about finding my perfect mail-order bride, or a pill to make my dick grow a few extra inches, or hair loss supplements.

I'm not losing my hair.

My dick is perfectly huge, thank you very much.

And I sure as fuck don't need a mail-order bride.

It doesn't help that there's been talk about my replacement on the Guardians. My contract is up at the end of the season, pending renewal. If they don't want to keep me, I'll become a free agent.

Something my team is trying to negotiate, although I don't think it's working out so well.

I've been avoiding their calls, too.

"Game seven, baby," one of my teammates calls. He drapes his arm over my shoulders and pulls me into him.

"Get off," I snap, elbowing him in the ribs.

I retreat to the corner and read the transcript.

Again.

I delete it.

If the number wasn't private, I'd block it, too.

Instead, I call my mother.

"Hey, honey." Her warm voice helps ease the knots in my chest. "We're just getting into the arena now. Is everything okay?"

I clear my throat. "You've got the suite?"

"Yep. I see Miles waiting for us with Willow." She sounds happy. "I'm proud of you, you know. All you've accomplished."

"Thanks," I mutter. The question I want to ask gets stuck in my throat.

"Knox?"

"Yeah?"

She hesitates. Then, "You know I'll always help you if I can."

A lump forms in my throat. It's been a while since I've asked her for anything, and a dark memory overtakes me. One where I sat in her room, on the bed, begging and pleading for *help*. And she gave it to me.

I clear my throat and leave the locker room, striding down the hall. "I know that. And you know I'm grateful for everything you've done for me."

There's a girl with a clipboard. She's wearing a Guardians jacket.

She's cute, and that's what I focus on when she glances

my way. I smile at her, holding eye contact, and she smiles back.

"Gotta go," I say to my mother, already distracted. "See you after the game."

"Love you," she replies.

"Ditto." I hang up and slide my phone back in my pocket. I make a beeline for the girl and stop within touching distance. "Hi."

"Hey."

"Have we met before?" Sometimes a guy's gotta ask.

She shakes her head slowly. "Nope."

"Knox Whiteshaw." I hold out my hand. "Do you wanna go somewhere more private with me?"

She watches my hand for a moment. Maybe she's not used to my level of forward. But if she takes it, she'll get to know me pretty quick.

When she slips her hand into mine, I smile wider.

And a few minutes later, we're in a storage closet. She's choking on my dick like she needs it to breathe and doing a damn fine job.

I'm actually impressed.

She cups my balls, and I groan. Her hair is in a ponytail, and I use it to force her head closer. Her throat contracts around the tip, and that does the fucking trick. That and her warm hands tugging lightly on my balls.

"Incoming," I warn. I thrust my hips forward and hold her head still, spilling down her throat. I pull out slightly, finishing on her tongue. After a moment of post-orgasm haze, I step away from her.

Her hands drop, and she carefully wipes her mouth. She stands, unbuttoning her jeans.

"What are you doing?" I watch her carefully.

The girl's cheeks redden. She said her name, but fuck if I know it.

"Thanks for the blow," I add, tucking my cock away and rolling my shoulders back. "If I get a hat trick tonight, I'll credit the girl from the storage room."

I wink and head out, leaving her staring at me with a mixture of lust and annoyance.

Oh well.

What did she expect? Roses?

Outside the locker room, a man in a rough-looking polo shirt and khakis waits. He glances at me, then at the locker.

"You looking for someone?" I ask.

"Yeah. Knox Whiteshaw."

"Oh." My brows furrow. "That's me. What can I do for you?"

He holds out a big manila envelope.

Without really thinking it through, I take it.

"You've been served," he says.

My stomach drops.

Well, *fuck*.

39
MELODY

I meet the Whiteshaw family, along with Jacob's parents, and Vicky and Richard. Plus Jacob and Knox's friends. Instead of being close to the ice, we're up in a suite. It's prime-time fancy, which Violet made sure to prepare me for before we showed our faces. Sometime between us leaving to go for the prison and our return, Willow and Aspen bought me a dress.

Now I sit in it, marveling at the soft fabric. It's a deep red, and it perfectly matches the lipstick I found in the guest bathroom of Jacob's condo not too long ago. Surprise, surprise—I still had it tucked in my purse.

Violet did the rest of my makeup while Willow fiddled with my hair.

They're each wearing nice clothes, too. As is everyone else in the suite. I feel a little guilty not wearing a Rhodes jersey, but this seems good, too. The dress hides my belly, a source of insecurity, and amplifies my cleavage. It's a magic dress.

Maybe made even more perfect by the fact that I didn't have to try on eight hundred to find the perfect one.

That sounds like a hassle, especially in this body.

When the game starts, I'm joined by Miles. I glance at him, a little surprised. He, of all of them, has kept his distance. But I think I know why.

"You were my student," I guess.

He nods. He's wearing a navy suit jacket and matching tie. The color matches Willow's dress, and he seems to keep one eye on her even as he's talking with me and watching the ref drop the puck.

"Sorry," I murmur.

"Willow said she talked to you about teaching." He smiles. "I liked your class, too. You taught one of the harder English lit classes. Although Jacob thought he was going to get a different professor who would've gone a lot easier on him."

I smile. "I guess I didn't. He said I slapped him."

Miles chuckles. "I don't doubt that. Especially if he said something rude."

"Something about sucking his cock." My cheeks heat. "So you don't judge me for..."

"No."

He's tracking the players on the ice. The black-and-gold jersey players, the New York Guardians, have the puck on the Titan side of the rink. One of them takes a shot, and Miles mutters under his breath.

The goalie sends the puck out to a Titan, and I spot his number—*fifteen*—and name. Rhodes. I brighten, leaning forward, as he takes the puck up the far edge of the rink. He passes it to a teammate a split second before a Guardian player slams into him.

I wince.

"Part of the game," Miles comments. "Some of them like that shit."

"Well, I don't."

"I can tell." He's quiet for a minute. Then, "How was the trip to the prison?"

I sigh. "I'm sorry we ditched you like that."

"You could've tried to ask us to go with you." He shrugs. "We would've done it. Gone with you. We probably would've had to wait outside, but still. Moral support and all."

I push my glasses up my nose. One of these days, I should try contacts. Or get that surgery to fix my eyes. Because glasses *suck*. They're always in the way of things or getting smudged. Or worse, I take them off and then forget them somewhere. And how am I supposed to find my glasses when I can't *see*?

"Thanks," I offer. "It wasn't great. Seeing him brought up a memory, but of course it wasn't a good one. So I just... walked out without talking to him."

"What happened?"

"I put him in prison," I admit. "I mean, the rational part of my brain knows that he put himself in prison when he came at me. But I pressed charges. He assaulted a minor, and he already had a history of violence with the cops. Assault that he pled out and did community service for earlier in his life, bar fights. Stuff like that."

"And he's still in prison for that?"

I shake my head slowly. "No... he killed someone in prison a few months before he was supposed to get out. Ended up with twenty-five years added to his sentence."

Miles' jaw tics. "Did he hurt you badly?"

"Yeah." I can still taste the fear as he slammed me into the door. The pain of my cheekbone fracturing. It swelled the next day and took almost two months to go back to normal. For the black eye to fade. And even after it was gone, I was reminded of that night every time the cops came to interview me, or when they went to trial and I was called to testify.

Mom was nowhere to be seen. Not that it mattered. I was eighteen, a legal adult, and totally free.

"Kids who are involved in trauma often find themselves in abusive relationships later in life." Miles is watching the game, but his focus is so intensely *not* on me, I don't believe for a second that he's not paying attention to my body language. "Henry is his name, right?"

I let out a laugh. It's more nerves than anything, and I wrap my arms around my stomach. That's my defensive maneuver, always.

Did I really leave my parents' house and run right into the arms of a guy who reminded me of my father?

I nod slowly. "For a professor, I wasn't very smart."

He glances at me sharply. "That's not your fault, Melody."

"Isn't it?"

"No." He shakes his head. "No, it's not. If anyone, blame your mother for not getting you out of there before it got to physical violence."

"I have a feeling she was worse on my psyche than my dad," I murmur. "But that doesn't matter. She's dead. I have the restraining order against Henry—"

"He's leaving you threatening voice messages."

I wave him off. "We don't *know* that's him. We think it's him."

Jacob has the puck again. I've been tracking him as he got on the ice and off it, and now he's back and skating for his life. He hops a player's outstretched stick and drives for the goal.

I jump to my feet. Miles joins me, and suddenly the

suite is screaming. Cheering. It doesn't matter that Miles and Knox's parents are here. They're yelling, too.

He scores. I miss the puck slipping past the goalie's defenses, but Miles is yelling a split second before everyone else. Then the red siren flashes behind the goal, and the Titans fans in the crowd, few and far between, go crazy.

First goal of the game.

Violet, Aspen, and Willow take Miles' place around me. I stare at the ice, trying to keep track of Jacob and Knox, although my attention strays more often than not to Jacob. How could it not? Sitting on the bench, in perfect view of me—although his features are almost indistinguishable, just on the cusp of my vision—he blows me a kiss. And *that's* clear enough to see from a mile away.

"Oh, you're onscreen!" Willow yells. "Wave, Melody!"

I glance up, shocked to find *me* on the screen. Red dress, red lipstick. I give a little wave, and the camera pans back around to Jacob.

Wait.

I step back from the glass, my hands shaking.

"Was that broadcast?"

Aspen nods. She spots my concern and gestures for me to join her at the back of the suite. Far from cameras... hopefully. "Are you okay?"

"Yeah. I just wasn't expecting to have my face... everywhere." I grimace. "I don't like attention."

"Maybe someone who knows you will reach out?" She hums. "I'm sure you have other friends out there who just don't know that you're..."

"A shell of who I used to be?"

"Well, that's not very nice."

It's true, though. Dad said it, too. Not in so many words. But even as he was trying to manipulate me into thinking he was some wrongly accused angel—and never coming out to say that I was the one who put him in prison—he was judging me.

And sure enough, my phone rings a moment later.

I glance at the private number and consider letting it go to voicemail. I haven't set up the answering page, so an automated voice just reads off the number and tells callers to leave a message.

In fact, I haven't responded at all.

Which is why maybe I don't feel too bad about hitting the green button instead of the red one.

"What do you want?" I ask, meeting Aspen's gaze.

She offers me a small nod of encouragement and steps back. Giving me privacy. She goes back to her seat, leaving me to face this alone.

I get it. If I was her, I wouldn't want to intrude.

"Hey, darling." My ex's smokey voice fills my ear.

I can't prove it's him, but I know it nonetheless. It's a weird feeling. His voice is familiar and different. It's hard and rough, but if he changed his tone... I don't think it was all my fault that I fell for him when we first met.

"You're at a Guardians game," he continues. "In a suite. My, how the tides have turned for you."

My throat closes.

"I warned you that I would expose your relationship with your student. You went back to him when I told you not to."

He did?

"Why?"

He chuckles. "Why? Because I don't fucking share, Melody. You knew that when you agreed to marry me."

"We got a divorce. You have no hold over me."

"That's what you said when I found you in Crown

Point. You went right back to your student. Did you forget about the cameras he had planted in your house? The way he *watched* you without you knowing?"

My blood goes cold.

I knew there was something else. Something Jacob wasn't telling me.

"You ran to your stalker. The stalker who fucked you while you slept. I still have that video. Want the reminder?"

My phone vibrates in my hand, but I can't make myself lower it to check the screen.

I don't want to know.

"Why are you doing this?"

He chuckles. "Meet me when you're back in Denver, darling. I'll give you the whole story. And you might be surprised at how you ended up in the hospital, nearly dead..."

I can't breathe. White spots flicker in my vision, and it's only a miracle that I remain standing. I grip the edge of the bar and take as deep a breath as I can manage, although it feels too much like hyperventilating.

"One more thing," he adds.

I wait.

"You should look into Wild Oak Art. They're in Manhattan."

The line goes dead. It's only then, without his voice in my ear, do I open the message and click the video he sent.

Past-me is asleep on an unfamiliar bed, in a room I don't recognize. I'm still—the only passing of time is the little clock in the corner of the screen. Finally, a shadow moves across the camera. It's Jacob, clear as day. A few years younger. He moves around and strips me, lifting my body off the bed to undo my bra and drags my panties off my legs.

I don't wake up.

And then he climbs over me and thrusts into me. My body moves with the force of it, but... no, I'm still asleep. I sleep through his orgasm, through him pulling the shirt off his back and slipping it over my head.

It has his name on the back.

He let me wake up like that? Fucked without my knowledge, in *his* shirt—

The video goes dark and ends.

Stalker, he said. Even as my ex-husband was stalking me, so was Jacob.

Unfathomable.

Was that before or after he talked to me for the first time?

Jacob admitted to drugging me, and I fucking brushed it off. I thought he was exaggerating, or just.. *I don't know*. But now I have the video proof, and I watch it again just to be sure. That it's him and me in the room, in the dark.

My hands are cold. My body is clammy, and I can't control the sudden trembling that makes it hard to even hold my phone.

What the fuck, Jacob?

What else did Henry say?

Wild Oak Art.

I steady my hand on the bar and type it into the maps, not entirely sure why. I just know that I'd rather solve some mysteries than stew in the ones I won't get answers to.

It hosts art exhibits. From the online images, it looks pretty fancy. I peek into my purse and eye the handful of cash I still have from Willow. I tried to give it back to her, but she wasn't having any of it.

And now I have a means of escape.

Jacob has a habit of finding me wherever I go. Except for

when he's playing hockey. Right now, he's on the ice. This game means so much. He either wins and moves on, or he loses and his team is out of the playoffs. I get it. But also, it's the greatest distraction I could hope for, and I'd be foolish not to seize the opportunity.

Never mind that Henry wants me to meet with him in Denver. Never mind that he's setting me up to hate Jacob or drive a wedge between us. Never mind that he's just insinuated that he *isn't* the reason I woke up after almost dying.

I glance back at the girls. They're absorbed in the game. The guys are chatting with Jacob's parents and the other couple we met at dinner last night. Knox's parents must've stepped out, because I don't see them.

No one's paying attention to me, so I make a run for it.

40

MELODY

I don't know what I was expecting, but the small glass storefront of Wild Oak Art isn't lining up with my imagination. I pay the cab driver and cross the side-walk. There's an *open* sign hanging on the door, so I just... go in.

There are a bunch of white walls with mounted artwork. When I don't immediately see anyone, I head down one of the aisles slowly. I can't stop staring at the art. Some are mixed media, some just one type of paint.

It's... interesting.

Footsteps precede someone, and then a woman rounds the corner. "Sorry, I was in the back. Can I help—Melody?" She stops short and gapes. "What are you doing here?"

I shrug to hide my apprehension. "I came to visit."

"You're okay...?"

"Yeah." Do I tell her I have no idea who she is? Fuck it. "Sorry, what's your name?"

"Shelby Armstrong."

Armstrong.

I automatically take a step back.

"We've only met once. Most of the correspondence for your art has been through our husbands. Mine is Henry's brother, Frank."

Frank Armstrong. Henry's brother.

No wonder he sent me here.

I clear my throat. "Of course. It's nice to see you again. I'm sorry I'm a bit hazy on the details, but I just wanted to get a handle on things while Henry's away," I lie. "Could you fill me in?"

"Of course." She gestures for me to follow her to the back, behind a tall standing desk with a slim tablet beside a medium-sized monitor. She clicks on the tablet and brings up a few pieces of art.

Seven in total, in tiny thumbnail-sized images.

"These were the pieces Henry had given us to sell," she explains. "You can click on each one and it'll give you the details. Where or to whom it was sold, how much it sold for, when we paid, and the commission details."

"You get a commission off of... my price?"

"Yes, of course. We're doing the leg work of marketing your art."

My art.

I squint at the tablet screen. "May I?"

She hands it over.

I wander away from her and click on the first one. It was sold a year and a half ago. It's a side portrait of a young girl and labeled as mixed media. What that might be, I have no idea. Perhaps the sellers got more information. It sold for over a thousand dollars to someone in Florida.

I swipe to the next, and it says, *Sold in a group* under it. No more details. So I keep going, counting five total.

Then the name beneath it: *Jacob Rhodes*. His Denver, Colorado address.

My throat closes.

I swipe again, and I might actually pass out.

It's the teal bird. The one stuck in the tar. The one Jacob has featured in his bedroom.

Have I seen the others? The more I think about it, the more I realize, *yes*, I've been admiring the art in his condo. Praising, silently, his good taste. And all the while it's been my art I've been looking at.

Under the bird it says: *Sold at New Jersey Stars charity auction.*

There's a list of bids under it.

Mark Zimmer - $800

Jacob Rhodes - $10,000

Henry Armstrong - $15,000

Jacob Rhodes - $50,000 - winning bid.

I don't think I can take many more surprises. He has not one, or two, or even three pieces of *my* art. He has six pieces. I count in my head, noting that there are actually two more that aren't here. One's hung right by the door.

Where did he find that one?

"Where is the payment submitted?" I ask my supposed sister-in-law.

"To the banking details on the next screen." She comes over and coos at the image on the screen. The bird painting. "Oh, I love that one."

"Thanks," I manage.

She reaches for the tablet and switches to a new tab, and I scan the details. I fish out my phone and snap a picture of the account number.

If my ex-husband was the one who took me against my will, if he forced me to paint to sell—or worse, gave me an escape from reality and then snatched them away—then I'm owed that money.

Minus the fifty thousand, which apparently went to charity.

That's a shit ton of money. Did Jacob grapple with the situation? Did he consider that I might not want him to own a painting of mine?

"When's the last time you received art from Henry?"

Shelby sighs. "Those were the last. He said we might be hearing from you soon, so I hope this is you informing us that you have more artwork? They're really striking, Melody. I don't know where you find the inspiration, but I hope it never leaves you."

I smile to keep from screaming.

Whether or not I knew about it, I can't imagine I would let *him* sell my art.

"Thank you. I've got an appointment to get to, but it was lovely meeting you."

"Of course. I'll let Frank know you stopped by."

I don't tell her not to. I have no doubt advising her to keep it a secret would only backfire on me.

But it does confirm one thing.

Jacob *is* a stalker. He's hunted down multiple pieces of my artwork in the last two years.

A chill skates down my spine as I leave the building.

What if Jacob was the one to hurt me?

What if he found me after I left Crown Point and decided to teach me a lesson?

After all, don't some stalkers have the mentality of, *if I can't have her, no one will?*

He hasn't physically hurt me—but he's done plenty of other things that should've raised a million red flags. And now they're all waving in my face, and I can't believe I missed them.

I can't go back.

I scroll through my phone, desperate for someone. Anyone.

And then I spot Lucy's name.

Before I know it, I've got her address and am on my way to her condo. She meets me out front and takes a minute to take in my dress, then hugs me tightly.

"Theo and his friends are having a little watch party," she warns me in the elevator. "Just so you aren't freaked out by four loud guys in the living room."

I smile. "No, it's okay. I appreciate—"

"None of that," she interrupts. "You'd do it for me. I'd do it for you."

Okay.

Lucy leads me into their condo, and I'm shocked at how large it is. It's two stories, a spiral staircase tucked in the corner as well as another elevator. By *living room* she must've meant *game room*, because we go down a hall and into a room with a pool table and other games, plus a couch and the largest television I've ever seen.

"Holy shit, Lucy," I murmur.

There are three guys, including Lucy's husband, and two other women. They're engrossed in the game on the screen, and I admit that I'm drawn in, too. Jacob is there. His friends and family. His best friend, playing for the other team.

"This is Melody," Lucy calls. She drags me up to the couch and points to an empty spot. "Sit, I'll make proper introductions at the next commercial."

I nod and turn my attention to the screen. It's easy—*too easy*—to spot Jacob. My heart jumps into my throat when he takes a nasty hit. Him and the other player fall to the ice, but he shoves off and chases after the puck immediately.

The violence doesn't even faze him.

And I still can't stomach it.

Finally, it cuts to a commercial break. Lucy appears with a mixed drink for me, and she draws the attention of the rest of the group.

"This is Melody," she repeats. "Mel, you met Theo. That's Caleb, Margo, Liam, and Skylar."

I nod my hellos, losing track of their names immediately. They all smile and greet me warmly, though, which is more than I can ask for.

"What brings you by, Melody?" Theo asks. "We weren't sure if you were going to make it back to New York." He glances at his friends and adds, "Lux and Melody went to Lion's Head together."

Margo grins. "Sorry, Melody, you're in an Emery-Rose Elite crowd tonight."

I smile. "Yeah, well, I don't remember any of it. So I'm willing to drop any high school rivalry."

The couple on the end, I think it was Liam and Skylar, exchange a glance. And then Skylar is shifting seats, dropping down next to me.

"I had a trauma-based amnesia surrounding my childhood," she says quietly. "It had to do with my C-PTSD."

She's around my age, I think. Pretty as hell. Her blonde hair is braided back and threaded with gold and black. They're all wearing Guardians colors, and I can't help but be a little jealous of this comradery.

I don't know if they're local, or if they support this hockey team for real, but Theo and Lucy do. So their friends show up.

Maybe I'm romanticizing it.

"Does it get easier?" I ask. "Or... did the memories come back?"

She bites her lip. "Some, yeah. Not everything. But it was traumatic, so...."

"I wonder about that." I pick at a hangnail. "If my life was so traumatizing before, maybe I'm better off not knowing. Dad's in jail, my mom is dead. I seemed to have moved in with my stalker, who's also playing in this game right now..."

One of the guys, Liam, I think, looks over. "Who?"

"Jacob Rhodes."

He whistles under his breath. "Tell us more. You okay? Did you just find out he was stalking you?"

"I... it's complicated."

I shift. I don't know them. I don't want to admit all my secrets. And maybe that's apparent on my face, because Theo elbows his friend.

"Were you at the game?" Margo asks. "The one playing now?"

"I was there until I got a call from my ex-husband. He sent me to an art gallery, and I found out that he was selling my artwork through them and not giving me a cut. And that Jacob's been buying everything. I've been in his condo, looking at this beautiful art, and had no idea *I* painted them."

Silence.

"Yeah," I say on a laugh. "Stupid. I probably need to file some sort of legal something. I don't know if my ex has more of my art to sell. Oh, and I think I was with him before my incident, even though I have a restraining order against him."

More silence.

I clear my throat. "So, um... thanks for letting me hang out."

41

JACOB

I'm skating for my life. It's like all the pressure has formed into a spear being driven through my chest. Every breath hurts. I'm sweating, bleeding, definitely bruised. And the score climbed to 2-2 in the second period, and it's sat there ever since.

Our goalie, Joel Haverhill, is on fire. He's blocked shot after shot. The Guardians wingers are slipping past us easily and putting more pressure on Haverhill, but he's risen to the challenge. It's infuriating to *know* you're playing like shit and be unable to stop it.

Something's up with Knox. He's not playing like himself. He's not really playing like he even gives a shit. The whistle blows, and I almost collide with him. I grab his arm and shake him a little.

"What the fuck is going on?"

He focuses on me and frowns. "What?"

"Get your head in the game," I snap at him. "This is not the time to screw around."

Knox glowers at me. "I'm fine."

Yeah, right. I step through the doorway and take a seat

beside Church. He glances at me and pops his mouthguard out.

"What was that?"

I shrug. "He's my friend."

"You shouldn't give pep talks to the enemy." He's got a scrape under his eye from an earlier tussle. "You want to win, don't you?"

I laugh. "Yeah, of course. I just don't want him to come back and say he was distracted or some shit."

He eyes me, then leans forward and looks down toward the home bench, where Knox sits. "No excuses."

"Exactly."

The game resumes. Dawes, our center, lines up against Knox. His mouth is moving, which really isn't surprising. He loves to yap. But something he says to Knox has my friend adjusting his grip.

The puck drops, and the Guardians get possession. But my attention stays glued on Knox, who bursts forward and slams his stick into Dawes' chest. The whistle blows as Dawes reacts to the hit, grabbing Knox's stick and tossing it.

Their gloves come off, and then they're fighting.

Church barely manages to keep me from the ice.

Their helmets go flying and blows are traded. The other players circle around, watching. The crowd around us is amped up, louder still when Knox gets Dawes on his back.

"Fuck," Church mutters.

I can barely hear him.

The refs tear Knox away, breaking up the fight. There's blood coming out of his nose, staining his teeth, and he spits onto the ice.

Knox goes straight to the penalty box. His teammates tag after him, returning his stick, helmet, gloves. He leans forward in the smaller box, the attendant closing the door, and shakes out his hair.

Fucking idiot.

The refs come back with a five-minute penalty for both players. Except there's only three minutes left on the clock. The door opens, and Knox and Dawes leave the rink. They head to the locker rooms to do whatever the fuck they want until the game is over.

I let out a breath. "That sucked."

The game restarts. At one minute remaining, I tag back in with Church and Scofield. I ignore the muscle fatigue, the ache in my jaw, the way I'd love nothing more than to flop on the ice, and do my damn job.

With twenty-four seconds left, Church scores.

I can barely believe it.

We're ahead by one, and the celebration comes hard and fast. We restart and somehow hold off the Guardians. They pull their goalie, and we work double time with the extra offensive player.

Until Joel gets the puck and sends it flying back toward their net.

The horn blows right as it bounces off the post, only inches away from a freaking goalie goal.

But then the realization hits me.

We did it.

We're moving on to the next round.

———

"Mom." I kiss her cheek. "Thanks for coming."

"Congratulations, honey." She cups my face. "We're so proud of you."

I shake Dad's hand. Knox is nowhere to be found,

although his parents are chatting with Miles and Willow off to the side. I greet Vicky and Richard, accepting their congratulations, and move on to my friends.

"Where's Melody?" I ask Greyson.

Violet shifts beside him, biting her lip.

I narrow my eyes.

He glances at Aspen, under Steele's arm.

I round on her, even when Steele gives me a warning look.

"Aspen?" I question. "Where is Melody?"

She hesitates, then, "Um, she got a phone call, and then she... I don't know, I didn't see her actually leave. I think it was a call from that private number."

For fuck's sake.

I ball my hands into fists, willing myself not to overreact. It would be *so easy* to overreact, but with my father watching? No way. Then I'd have to deal with his questions, which always turns into an interrogation. Hazard of the job. He's interviewed far worse than me, I suspect.

"Guys," I say in a low voice. "What the *fuck*?"

"Does she have any friends in the city?" Miles asks.

I blow out a breath. "Yeah. Lucy Page."

Violet pulls out her phone. Willow peeks over her shoulder, and soon Violet is smiling.

"Got her," she announces. "According to her social media, she lives in a high-rise condo only a few blocks away."

"How can you tell?" I demand, stepping forward.

Greyson shoves me back. "Go easy, dude."

I'm trying not to lose my shit, and they want me to *go easy*? I cast a glance back at my parents. They're talking with the Whiteshaws. Meanwhile, fans are beginning to notice me. There are pops of light as their camera flashes go off, documenting my misery.

And then I get an idea.

"Hey, man," one guy in a Titans jersey calls out. "Great game. Congrats."

"Thanks," I murmur. I eye the phone in his hand, and then the ones around me. There's a younger girl, a teenager, and I zero in on her. "You on social media?"

She stares at me. "Obviously."

"And you know who I am?"

"I run a fan account for you."

Oh. That's... weird.

"Thanks," I manage. "Can you record me and post it immediately?"

She nods and lifts her phone.

I clear my throat. "Hey, Titan fans. I'm trying to find someone. We're playing a game of hide and seek in New York City... but I'm at a disadvantage. While I was playing game seven, she snuck off." I pull up a photo of her on my phone and hold it up. "First one to find her will get two tickets to our next playoff game."

The girl's eyes light up. "Can we have any hints on where she might be?"

I nod slowly. "Her friends live in a high-rise a few blocks from here. She's wearing a red dress. Her name is Melody."

"Melody," the girl repeats. "Where should hunters send proof?"

A chill skates down my back. The thought of them hunting her down for me... well, it's fucking brilliant. The thought of *me* hunting her down and stripping her naked is an even better idea.

Back burner.

"Tag me in your social media posts." I motion for her to end the video.

"Thanks," I tell the girl.

"Can you sign my boobs?"

I tilt my head. "How old are you?"

"Twenty-one."

She doesn't look twenty-one.

"How about your arm?" I take the marker she's holding and scrawl my name across her forearm before she can say no—or worse, drag her shirt up and expose her tits. Wouldn't be the first time that happened, but I don't really want to get into it with a minor.

"Can you get that posted?"

She does, adding a caption and then flashing me the video. I look... well, bruised and exhausted. But not too bad either.

I don't think of myself as having a fan base, personally. It's more of the team, and I just get swept up in it. Not like Knox, who's made himself the poster child of the NHL. Star rookie, on billboards and advertisements. The media doesn't leave him alone. Probably because he's skilled, he's young, and he's objectively handsome.

"Thanks again." I jog back to my friends and family, and I spit out some lie to my parents about a meeting. I hug my mother, kiss her cheek, and I don't feel *too* bad leaving them.

Greyson, Miles, Steele, and their girls join me. Or follow me.

I hand Willow my phone. "Can you keep track of notifications?"

Already, the little red flag above my Instagram icon is shooting up. It was at ten, but now it's more like 200.

"They work fast," she murmurs. "People are sharing the video."

"What do you want us to do?" Miles asks.

"I need to know why she ran." I take my phone back and dial her number. Something I should've done in the first place. But I know her.

This cannot be a repeat of the past.

It goes to voicemail, and I almost chuck my phone against the wall. Someone plucks it out of my hand.

I let them and repeat to myself that she left of her own free will. She isn't in danger. She may be running—but that's fixable.

It's so unlike last time, when I was helpless to stop it from happening.

When I found her house abandoned and had to deal with the fallout...

42

MELODY

MEMORY — THIRTY-TWO YEARS OLD

I'm holding on by a thread. Today's just been a lot. I got an email from my ex-husband, a veiled threat about telling my father where I am. My *father*. He's in prison, and I can't say I've ever worried about him figuring out that I've moved once again.

The fact that my father gained more prison time makes me feel a little better. But my ex knowing where I am is another issue all together. *He's* the one I have the restraining order against. The one I'm hiding from in Crown Point.

On top of that, a student is failing my class.

There's nothing that makes me feel quite so much like a failure as having to fail *them*. So instead of giving him the F he deserves, I wrote, *see me after class*. Like that's going to help. Like giving him a second chance means he's going to take it.

He probably won't, because I know his type.

Hockey player. Cocky. He's going to grow up to be an

arrogant jerk, maybe, or simply expect doors to open for him because he's an athlete.

My gaze flicks to him, then away. Like I don't care.

Because I don't.

I know why he chose my class. Some of his hockey buddies probably told him it would be easy—and it would've been, two or three semesters ago. After a somewhat stern talking-to by the administration, I upped my requirements to pass. But holding the students expecting an easy A accountable has been tricky.

So when I got his dismal paper... I wanted to do something about it. Help him, rather than fail him.

But he'll need to help me help him, or else he'll fail. And failing will result in his coach shouting at me, most likely, or dragging this issue to the administration. All of it is a pain in the ass, but it's not like I can ban student athletes who don't give a shit.

Let's be honest. He doesn't care about Chaucer or Homer. He doesn't care about analyzing texts and pulling out pieces to examine against modern standards.

I wet my finger to get traction on the paper, turning the page and continuing to lead the discussion. Besides *him*, there are quite a few good students who contribute. I guide their perspective, playing devil's advocate when possible, and smile at their arguments.

Running my hand over my stomach, I pluck at my sweater. My hair is longer than it's ever been, and I resist the urge to flip it over my shoulder. A move reserved for the younger crowd, I think. A giggling schoolgirl, I am not.

I push my glasses up my nose and eye Jacob Rhodes. He's slouched in his chair, his gaze on me. Always on me, even though I'm ninety-nine percent sure he hears *nothing*.

I look away.

See me after class. Maybe not my best decision.

Students have questions, and I take my time answering them until our time runs out. There's a flurry of activity as they all rise and head out the door, and I busy myself shuffling papers until it's only Jacob Rhodes and I left in the massive room.

I climb the stairs and stop a row short of his chair.

"Jacob," I call.

His gaze comes to me, and he leans forward. He's moved the table that covered his lap, putting his elbows on his thighs. "You can call me Jake."

He fucking flexes.

"What's this 'see me after class' bullshit about?"

I suck in a breath.

So brash. So *angry*. At me.

"I can't flunk this class."

"Well, that's why I didn't grade it." There's a week left until the final exam, and I don't want to say it out loud, but he *is* flunking my class. Albeit, it's close. "Read my notes. Edit it, and I'll give you a passing grade. Even if you half-ass the final exam, you'd still pass."

He stands.

It's kind of intimidating how explosive he seems to be. In his movements. So much energy, I suppose I could see how it would translate into sport.

Stop it.

He comes down a step in the aisle, and fuck if I don't have to tilt my head back to keep my eyes on his face. Perfect timing, as his gaze ticks down to my chest. And lingers.

My face heats.

"How about we figure something else out?"

I step back and cross my arms. My stomach twists, and there's something else in his gaze. A challenge, maybe?

"I don't like what you're implying." I keep my voice even.

"So you're saying you don't see yourself getting on your knees and worshiping my cock?"

I choke. What the fuck?

What is *wrong* with him?

"Absolutely not," I snap. My face is even hotter.

Am I imagining this? What kind of student just... just says those things?

"You're right." He sneers. "If you're doing me a favor, I should do you one. My face between your pretty thighs..."

My hand is moving before I can stop it. I slap him across the face, *hard*. My palm immediately stings from the impact, and his head whips to the side. His eyes open wide, his lips parting.

I just hit a student.

I stumble away from him and shake my head. The scenario plays out in front of me, on and on and on. Him reporting me. Him getting me fired. His smiling face as I do a walk of shame out of Crown Point University.

"I'm going to get fired," I mumble, more to myself than him. I hurry down the row to the other aisle, just trying to get away from him. I mean, he *deserved* to be slapped. What kind of monster says something like that to his professor?

I bolt out of the room and burst into tears in my office. But it isn't until I get home that I realize I forgot all my stuff.

No matter. I'll get it later. After Jacob has moved on to another class, or hockey practice, or *something*.

Yet hours later, after I've made it home and managed to regain my breath, I still haven't worked up the nerve to return. He was just... crude. He looked at me like he wanted to devour me, and I didn't like it.

Didn't I?

My doorbell rings.

I clear my throat and tuck my hair behind my ears, hurrying to the door. I take a second to smooth my t-shirt, check my face in the mirror in my foyer. No sign of the tears now, although my eyes are a little bloodshot. I push my glasses up the bridge of my nose and take a deep breath.

I open the door and jerk back.

Jacob Rhodes.

He's got my bag slung over his shoulder, his expression decidedly cocky. The fact that he's standing on my doorstep right now gives me butterflies. When I realize that he's here for *all* of the wrong reasons, I force those butterflies to chill the fuck out.

He wants to pass my class. That's clearly his motivation, and I'd be a liar if I said I didn't have a certain thrill holding that over his head. Especially now. When I clearly haven't been reported—*yet*.

"Melody." He braces his forearm on the doorjamb, leaning in. "Are you going to let me in or just stare at me?"

"It's professor," I automatically correct.

His smirk widens. "Professor Cameron, will you let me in?"

Before I can answer, he strides past me. Inside. He sets my bag down and keeps going. I check outside, finding the street empty, and close us in.

Jacob makes some noise in the back of his throat. Part of me wants to grab him and haul him out. The other side wants to see what he's planning.

How far he'll take this.

Temptation has never been your strong point, Mel. And neither has curiosity.

"Do you have a boyfriend?"

I squint at Jacob, who approaches with quick, sure steps. I back up, but he doesn't care. He keeps going, herding me in the direction he wants, until my shoulder blades touch the wall. Even then, he doesn't stop. He leans down and cages me in, his forearms braced on either side of my head.

"This is inappropriate," I breathe.

"This is the least inappropriate thing we'll be doing." His gaze goes down to my chest, then back up. "Now... Do. You. Have. A. Boyfriend?"

I lift my chin, claiming a bravado I don't possess. "I do if it makes you go away."

He chuckles. "It won't. It'll just change the terms slightly. But no matter—I'll find out eventually."

My body is on fire, and he's not even touching me. I don't want him to find out anything about me.

Danger, danger, my mind screams.

I clear my throat. "Terms?"

"Every game has rules, songbird." He nudges the side of my face with his nose, inhaling sharply. "Fuck, you smell perfect."

He called me songbird.

43
MELODY

I wake up in a cold sweat. I burst upright and come face-to-face with a shadowed form. Like a classic horror movie. But even though I open my mouth to scream, the shadow is faster. A rough hand covers my mouth, the other holding the back of my neck to keep me from jerking away.

It takes a long few seconds to register *Jacob*.

He shoves me back down and nudges my legs open wide. I barely have time to react before he's thrusting into me.

I gasp against his palm and try to shake him off, but he's too strong. A faint light catches my eye, and I spot my phone propped up on the nightstand. The video my ex texted to me is playing. The one where Jacob snuck in and fucked me while I slept, and—

"Shh," he says in my ear. "You just take this."

I whimper.

He moves in and out of me slowly, letting me feel every inch of him, while my gaze bounces around the dark room.

My location hasn't changed. I'm still in Lucy's guest room.

I snuck off to bed shortly after the Titans won, leaving them to their celebrations. But somehow, that translates to him being *here*.

And what's worse is that I remember our first interaction. In the classroom. It was just a little snippet of interaction, flashes of Jacob smirking at me, his bold proposition. My palm itches with the feel of my slap.

He followed me home then, too.

That was the first time he called me songbird.

"I've been so patient," he says in my ear, turning my head to the side. "Look at us."

The video loops. The quiet, stillness of the bedroom, past-me's sleeping form.

Chills break out across my back when Jacob in the video enters. When he climbs on top of me and—

"Just." *Thrust.* "Like." *Thrust.* "This."

I shouldn't see stars.

But there's something so toxic about this, it makes me want to indulge. Even though fear is present—it seems to heighten everything.

"Oh, songbird," he whispers. His fingers tighten on my cheeks, his palm still covering my mouth. Good thing, because a groan is barely trapped behind my teeth. "You've woken up my monster."

I let out a huff.

He shoves my sleep shirt up and palms my breast. His fingers pinch my nipple, and I squeak. He continues to fuck me so slowly; every slide has my muscles trembling. I hover on the edge of pleasure while he takes what he wants from my body.

Eventually, his pace quickens. He slams to a halt inside

me, groaning through his gritted teeth as he comes.

"Now." He peels his fingers from my face. "Do you want to come?"

I lick my lips. My head is still turned, watching that stupid video, even as I nod.

"Say it, songbird."

I wince.

"Beg for my mercy, for me to be nice and play with your clit until you scream my name."

For the whole house to hear? No.

"I won't be screaming," I promise.

His face is covered in shadow, but I stare up into his eyes. There's a good chance his eyes are more adjusted than mine, and that he can see my cutting glare.

"Get off of me."

He flexes his hips, and his dick moves inside me. It's annoying how good it feels, an itch being scratched that I didn't know existed.

"Here's the thing." He shifts to the side and trails his hand down my chest. Over my belly and down between my legs. He strokes my clit softly, and my hips automatically jerk at the sensation. "Something I didn't make clear before."

"Jacob…"

"Be quiet."

I stop talking. More out of surprise than anything.

"You're mine. *This* should demonstrate that no matter where you go, or where you hide…" He pinches my clit.

I barely stop my surprised, pained scream. I arch off the bed, trying to twist away from him, but there's nowhere to go. He eases the pressure and resumes stroking between my legs. Building me back up again, slowly, *slowly*.

Something occurs to me.

"I did hide from you."

He stills.

I flatten my hand on his chest. He's still wearing his shirt. He didn't strip completely for me, sitting naked in the dark and waiting for me to wake up.

Or maybe he didn't want you to wake up at all.

"Somehow, I hid. That's why you were so surprised to see me at the game."

He doesn't reply.

Instead, he shifts lower. When his mouth closes over my core, I drop back flat to the bed. I stare at the dark ceiling and try not to react, to scream, as he brings me to a shuddering orgasm. My limbs are jelly, the equivalent to the aftermath of tough exercise.

He stops the video on my phone and slips his shoes back on. He leans down and cups my jaw, and I'm surprised when his lips touch mine.

Because it isn't just a simple kiss.

It's a ravishment. His tongue invades my mouth, tasting me and giving me back my own flavor. His teeth nip at my lips. He may as well suck my soul out of my body. And when he pulls back, all I can do is stare at him with a weird expression.

Whatever he sees is enough to make him kiss me again. Slower. Lazier, in a way.

Another way to kiss. Like time is on our side.

He breaks away and smooths my hair back. He finishes getting dressed and slips out of the room, and I'm left contemplating the hows and whys.

How did he get up here? Lucy had to come retrieve me at street level.

Why does he keep coming for me?

And why do I suddenly want him to do it again?

44
MELODY

I wondered *how*, and the answer smacks me in the face the next morning: a video posted on a fan account that quickly went viral. In it, he holds up a photo of me on his phone. He promises tickets to whoever can find me.

So someone saw me come in, I guess.

Lucy and Skylar are in the kitchen when I enter. They both smile when they spot me, and Skylar grabs me a mug for coffee.

"Thanks," I murmur. I fix it up in the new way, with the hazelnut creamer, and close my eyes when the flavor coats my tongue.

"What's the plan?" Skylar asks. "Are you going to stay in New York or go back to Denver?"

I shrug.

Caleb comes in. He's in a suit at eight o'clock in the freaking morning. He smiles at us and pours himself a mug of coffee, then disappears back the way he came. When he returns a few minutes later, he's empty-handed.

"Thanks for the party, Lucy," he says. His gaze ticks to me. "Can I talk to you for a moment?"

Me?

I follow him around the corner. Down the hall, back toward the game room. Caleb steps inside after me and closes the door.

"You mentioned a restraining order against your ex-husband." He pauses.

"Yes." I clear my throat. "That's what Lucy said, and I think Jacob mentioned he found it..."

"Was it filed in New York?"

"I don't know. Probably."

He nods. He's handsome. If I didn't have Jacob, I'd think he was attractive. His dark hair looks perfectly tousled, a messy style on purpose. His suit is pristine. His dark eyes meet mine, and I can't help but *miss* Jacob. Even knowing what he did to me last night, and two years ago, and... well, since I re-met him, he's been fucking with me.

"They're not forever. You probably knew that before your amnesia. But they only last a few years, and then there's another hearing for renewal."

Oh.

Oh no.

The panic that rises in me is swift and sudden. It constricts my throat, and I turn sharply away from Caleb. He's a lawyer. He knows these things.

Did I?

At one point, did I know all of this?

"I'm sorry," I manage, touching my neck and trying to get rid of the tightness. "I don't—"

"With your permission, I'll check into it and see when we need to renew."

My heart skips. "We?"

He nods. "Yeah."

"Lucy put you up to it?" I mean, it would make sense.

"Nah." He grins. "Liam did. He owns a clinic. Not the medical kind, but the therapy kind. It focuses on trauma healing."

I make a face.

"He asked me to talk to you." Caleb shrugs. "I'm a named partner of a law firm practicing in New England and New York, so I'm able to handle this."

He's just trying to help.

Right?

I mean, I guess it comes down to if I trust Lucy. I trusted Jacob, and look what happened. I thought my father would be a good lead, and *that* didn't end well either.

"Did you know me in high school?"

He doesn't seem put off by the abrupt change of subject, and he shakes his head. "No. Why?"

"So we weren't friends."

"Not even a little."

I narrow my eyes. "Then why—?"

"Theo is my best friend," he interrupts. "Theo loves Lucy, so much so that she's an extension of him. Same with Liam and Skylar. Because you're *Lucy's* friend, you're all of our friend."

Huh.

"Okay," I allow. "If you could look into that for me... I'd appreciate it."

He opens the door, our confidential conversation clearly over, and I hurry past him.

"Bye," he calls to the girls in the kitchen.

The front door closes, and I rejoin Lucy and Skylar. The latter is dressed for the day, although in clearly casual clothes. Her blonde hair is up. Leggings, a dark-blue sweat-shirt, white sneakers.

"Are you leaving, too?"

"Once Liam finishes getting ready," she says with a smile. "We've got to get back to Boston."

I take a seat at the breakfast bar. Theo emerges and goes straight for the fridge, pulling out food. My stomach growls, and my face goes hot. I need to figure out how to get home. Before I can check out flights back to Denver, my phone screen illuminates with an incoming call.

"You good with eggs, Melody?"

"Sure," I murmur, distracted by the name.

Jacob Rhodes.

Of course.

I answer it at the last second. "You're calling me?"

"I want to meet your friends," he says.

His voice is honey. And I press my thighs together automatically. I don't need the reminder that he was able to sneak into—or rather, *break into*—this place without permission. And when I woke up this morning, with his cum smeared on my inner thighs, it made me ache all the more.

"I don't know about that," I reply. "You're not very nice."

"I'm perfectly nice." He scoffs. "I'm the nicest. I made my girl come on my tongue last night, even though she was decidedly naughty."

"Maybe I like it that way."

"Which, my tongue or being bad?"

"Both," I whisper.

"Let me up."

I bite the inside of my cheek. "I told them that you stalk me."

He laughs.

I glance over at Skylar and Lucy and Theo. Liam's here now, too, and he glances my way. I let my attention skip away from them and sip my coffee while Jacob laughs in my ear.

"Let me up," he repeats. "Our flight home isn't until tomorrow. We have all day... and all night."

"Wild Oak Art," I say suddenly.

He goes quiet.

"Your snooping through my phone didn't tell you I went *there*, did it?" I close my eyes. "You bought my paintings. A *lot* of them, Jacob. You can't—"

"They didn't belong anywhere else."

"If I was doing it to be famous, then—"

"Is that what you want?"

I don't know. I don't know what past-Melody wanted. What her goals were when she painted those things or what she was thinking. Or dreaming. There are so many *things* I just don't know about myself. And now I have this memory of teaching, of talking about old, classic works of literature, and having eyes on me. And having Jacob's eyes on me.

When it was forbidden, it felt... dangerous. *Good.*

That scares me, too.

What kind of person was I, to be attracted to my student? To allow him to come into my house and push me up against a wall, to intimidate and proposition me and not immediately report him?

"You still there, songbird?"

I pull the phone from my ear.

The sudden clarity of not being a *good* person—it hurts.

So I hang up on him.

45
JACOB

Knox drags the chair out across from me and drops into it.

He looks like absolute shit. Bruises on his cheekbone and around his eye, a split lip. His dark-blond hair is mostly hidden by a backward black ball cap.

The waitress brings over a mug and fills it with coffee for him, but I wave her off before she can say anything. She already clocked exactly who he is the moment he walked in. Half the waitstaff did.

Doesn't mean they need to say it to his face when he's like *this*.

"You're not going to ask?"

I roll my eyes. "Nope."

"You don't want to know?"

"Of course I want to know," I counter. "But I'm not going to ask because you're going to tell me either way."

He pouts.

"You're acting like someone kicked your puppy," I point out.

"We're out of the playoffs. Of course I'm acting like that."

"Well..."

"Yeah." He slurps the coffee. "Why did you pick this joint? A little out of the way from your hotel."

I gesture to the building across the street. "She's up with her friends."

"And you can't get in?" His brows draw together. "Since when has a doorman ever stopped you?"

I lean back in my chair. I ordered waffles and bacon for both of us, and the waitress is heading our way. Once she's dropped it off and wandered away again, I answer him.

"I bribed the guy last night to get me up. Picking their condo lock wasn't terribly challenging. A simple deadbolt and knob lock. But Mel apparently told them I'm a stalker, so..."

"Showing up on their doorstep would be bad form." He hunches over his food, gaze contemplative across the street. His attention snags on someone exiting. "I know him."

I follow his line of sight to the dark-haired man heading for a matte-black car someone just brought around.

"Caleb Asher. Defense attorney." Knox smiles. "He helped Willow out."

"Has she forgiven you, by the way?"

He snickers. "Let's put it this way: she was *definitely* rooting for your team last night."

Well, he kind of deserves it.

"So what's your excuse?"

He stares at me.

I wave my hand. "What's your excuse for playing like shit last night?"

"Oh." He chooses that moment to stuff waffle and

bacon—*together*—in his mouth. Asshole. He chews slowly and finally fucking swallows. "That."

"That," I repeat.

He goes for another bite, and I snatch his fork.

"Knox."

He straightens in his seat. "Never come between a man and his food, Jakey."

Oh, fuck that. I grab his plate of waffles and bacon and set them on my side of the table. He lunges forward, and I palm his forehead and shove him back. There's a clatter of silverware, and he glowers at me.

"Speak, and you'll get your waffles back."

"You're such a buzzkill."

"I want to know what you're going to blame this on whenever you're done moping," I snap back. "Please don't say you ate a bad burrito or you couldn't find a girl to service you before the game—"

"I got my dick sucked just fine." Knox cracks a smile. "But *jeez*, you insufferable baby. I'll tell you." He shifts in his seat. "Maybe later."

I take a bite of his waffles, and he groans.

"Okay, okay. I got served."

Served...

"With legal documents?"

He nods.

That's not really what I was expecting, but it wouldn't exactly be unusual. Dad works closely with the state's attorney. They have people who go out specifically to serve subpoenas, and sometimes they must pick places they know you're going to be. Like game seven of the cup playoffs.

Apprehension prickles up my back. "Is this about your brother?"

His expression changes to confusion. "What?"

"About—" I shake my head. "Never mind. What did you get served with?"

He shifts again. "Papers."

"You're so fucking forthcoming." I reach for the bacon on his plate.

"Stop," Knox hisses. He shoots up. "You know what? I'm not talking about this."

He's serious.

That has me more worried than anything. When has Knox Whiteshaw *ever* been serious? He steps out of the booth and manages to take one step before I'm calling out after him.

"I'm sorry," I mutter when he returns to his seat. I slide the plate back to him, along with the coffee. "I won't ask."

"But you will pry, huh?"

"Yeah, I'm gonna call up my dad's secretary and see what you've got yourself involved in. I'll let her fill me in on the trouble you're causing."

To my shock, he actually relaxes. "You go ahead and do that."

I watch him as we both return to our breakfasts. He doesn't mind me going there—which means it probably isn't something that a police station in New York would have access to. If it was even legal to search for that kind of thing.

"So, what's up with Melody?"

I shrug. "Nothing."

"She just... left to go hang out with her friends in a high-rise you can't get into?" His tone is skeptical.

Which, honestly, *fair*.

"Her ex-husband is being a nuisance."

"So take care of it."

"I'm not your brother."

He scoffs. "I'm not suggesting murder. I'm just saying... maybe he needs to get the fucking message. That you're in her life and he's out of it."

That could work... if I had time to go to California and hunt him down.

"You forget." I point my fork at him. "My team didn't just lose. I've got three hockey games next week alone."

"So make him come to you." Knox grins. "Hang some bait out for him."

A flash of color catches my eye. Melody and another dark-haired girl are exiting the building. She's wearing the same red dress as last night, although when I found her in the guest bedroom, she had stripped and kept only her sleep shirt and underwear on.

"Gotta go." I drain my coffee and leave Knox at the table.

"Hey!" Knox yells after me. "Did you pay?"

"Loser pays," I call back over my shoulder, barely hiding my smirk.

He swears—but then it doesn't matter, because I'm out on the sidewalk and catching Melody's attention from across the street.

And she smiles.

E asel. Paint. Canvas. Subject.

I don't know why I'm *scared*.

Jacob went all out, sometime between me finding out about the paintings and arriving back to Denver. When we walked into his condo this afternoon, there it all was. The supplies were spread across his kitchen island, displayed in a way that made me think he was proud of his ingenuity.

Now he's in the gym, supposedly he's going to be cooking us dinner later, and my only job is to try and put paint on the canvas.

I adjust my smock and pick up one of the charcoal pencils. I touch the sharpened tip to it first, dragging it in a half circle.

The red apple is taunting me.

Because it's not really just red, is it? It's red and yellow and orange, with speckled flecks and parts that smoothly blend from one shade to the next. There are shadows and highlights, and a bit of reflection from the light behind me.

The fear still grips me, and I have to ask myself *why*. Why am I so afraid of this?

It's not like I can get it wrong. It's art. There's no right or wrong—

But there is good. Better. *Worse*.

What if I paint an apple, and I compare it to the bird hanging in Jacob's bedroom, and it's *worse*? If it's sloppy? Or off-putting? Or if I get some crucial detail completely wrong?

"Just start," I say. Because if I don't say it, I won't do it.

I take down the canvas and put it on my lap, and I suck my lower lip between my teeth as I draw the apple. Over and over again, the lines getting slightly more refined. Shaping it until I'm satisfied.

Then I set the canvas back up and stare at the dark blob on the white canvas.

Now what?

I grab my phone and put on music, then dip one of the fine-edged brushes into the red paint.

"It's okay if it looks like a twelve-year-old did it."

I jerk around.

Jacob stands behind me, his gaze soft. He's been *softer* this afternoon. Something eased in him as soon as we touched back down in Denver. And now he's a sweaty, shirtless mess.

I set the palette and brush aside, swiveling to face him fully. I spot the bird tattoo on his ribcage.

"You got that for me."

Songbird. The bird I painted. It makes sense.

He smiles. "Guilty."

Reality crashes back down around me. "Don't smile at me like that."

"Like what?"

"Like you like me."

He scoffs. "I don't like you. I'm in love with you."

No.

"I don't believe you." I untie my smock. "I don't believe that you can fall in love with someone when you barely know them. I don't believe that you loved me after a semester—less than that. I do *not* believe that you held this flame for me—"

"I GAVE UP."

I stop.

His chest heaves. "I gave *up* on you, Melody. On ever seeing you again. I was so fucking close to putting you out of my head completely when I saw the painting. The bird. Do you know how crazy you make me? I thought you left—"

"You don't know I didn't!" I jump to my feet. "You don't *know* what happened, Jacob. You weren't there. I was."

"And you suddenly remember?" He steps closer. "I went to your house the next day. I was *happy*. You and I—" He shakes his head. "I thought you found the cameras. They were scattered everywhere in your kitchen. I hadn't even checked them because I was happy."

I throw my hands up. "Maybe I did!"

"Maybe you weren't smart enough for that," he counters. "You trusted me."

"I wouldn't trust you if it was my last option," I snap.

Enough.

I brush past him, grabbing my purse from the side table near the door. I make it all the way to the elevator before he catches up to me.

"What are you doing?"

I tap my chin and pretend to consider. "I could go back

to Thomas and Natalie, since they're *safe*. Although they're probably pissed that I ghosted them—"

"No."

"No?"

He leans down and grips my waist, and the next thing I know, I'm draped over his shoulder. He pins my thighs to his chest, and his free hand smacks my ass.

I yelp. "What the hell are you doing?"

"You're not leaving," he growls.

He marches me back inside. My stomach is knotting, and it's all I can do to keep my glasses on my face upside down. He kicks the condo door shut behind him and heads for the bedrooms.

But instead of his, he goes to mine.

"Jacob—"

"*Quiet.*"

He throws me on the bed and disappears.

I stare at the door and am *just* about to move when he comes back with something in his hands. He looks from the object to me, his expression turning slightly guilty. But before I can do anything, he latches a metal cuff around my wrist.

"Where did you get handcuffs?"

I yank at my arm, but his grip is solid. He threads the other part through the headboard and goes for my other arm. I roll away and curse him out, while adrenaline and fear kick up my heart rate.

This suddenly doesn't feel like a game.

"Stop," I try.

I struggle even as he flattens his body across mine to get to my wrist. He wrenches it up and clicks the cuff around it with impressive strength, and I go still.

He's not done, though.

He drags me down by my hips, until my arms are straight up over my head.

A weird sort of shiver goes through me. Not the good kind—the nausea-inducing kind.

"You don't want to do this," I murmur. "Jacob—"

"You're okay." He brushes my hair off my forehead. It's damp with sweat. "I'm not hurting you, Mel."

He just stopped me from leaving. I went from free to... *to this*. In an instant.

"You are, though," I whisper. "How does this make you any better than my ex-husband?"

His head dips, and the guilt returns.

"Because this is for you."

I swallow. "And how do you know he didn't used to tell me the exact same thing?"

That does it. His expression closes, and he pushes up off the bed. He strides out like nothing's wrong, although my insides are churning. I'm going to lose my shit, cry, or throw up—I can't figure out what would be worse.

He doesn't even close the door.

Because why would a captive have privacy?

47
JACOB

I fucking tied her up.

How does this make you any better than my ex-husband?

The next time I go into her room, I take a picture. She's in short shorts, her pale legs curled up into her side, and a baggy white t-shirt. Her hair is braided back away from her face, so there's no mistaking the vitriol painted in her eyes.

I sit on the couch just out of sight and watch her on the cameras from my phone. She's just lying there, staring at the wall. The camera optics aren't clear enough to see the details of her face. Whether she's sad or angry or something else. Not until she uses her upper arm to wipe at her face do I realize she's crying.

Fuck.

Before hesitation can get the better of me, I send the picture to the unknown number that sent her the video of me.

It all became clear once I found that on her phone.

Yes, she left me in New York—but only because she doesn't have an accurate picture of the events.

No one should have that video. And, actually, he didn't have *my* video...

He had his own.

The only culprit could've been her ex-husband. He was the only one she was afraid of, so much so that she needed a restraining order against him.

Her phone chimes.

Henry: Who is this?

Me: Do you want her back?

There's another problem.

If he was the one who took her from Crown Point, then he must've kept her off the grid. Bill already revealed that Henry was operating as such for six months prior. It wouldn't be a stretch to assume he was doing so to prepare for Melody.

A phone call to *Shelby* at Wild Oak revealed some interesting information. Henry manufactured all of the deals between Wild Oak and Melody's art. It was his bank account that collected the sums.

That pisses me off more than I can say.

But at least the payment for the bird went to a charity.

Nine months ago—almost ten, at this point—Melody or Henry withdrew most of the money from her accounts. I'm operating on the assumption that she got away from him.

But why didn't she come to me?

For a myriad of reasons, I suppose. It could've even been this video dangling over her head like a guillotine. Because if she *did* leave him, as I suspect she did, then he would've been outraged. He may have even tried to kill her, and he definitely would've threatened to ruin us. Me and her.

Henry: Yes.

I nod to myself. Of course he wants her back.

Me: You know where we'll be.

Round two of the playoffs starts in Los Angeles. I have no doubt Henry Armstrong is just selfish enough to follow Melody's movements through social media, and therefore knows she's connected to me.

It isn't the first time he's heard my name. It's pasted on the back of the shirt I put on her in the video, after all.

Henry: I know where you'll be. But will she still be waiting when you get off the ice?

Henry: You can't protect her around the clock.

I toss her phone on the coffee table and stand. When I go back to Melody's room, she's asleep. I wrap her wrists in fabric to save her skin from the bite of the metal. But that's all.

There will be more to come in the morning.

48

MELODY

"Have I mentioned how much I hate you?" My voice is hoarse with thirst. It feels like I've screamed for an eternity, although I know I didn't let any noise out during the night. Not when Jacob slipped in and put something around my wrists. Not when my nightmares reared out of nowhere and sank their claws into me.

He unlocks one of the cuffs, then the other. They stay wrapped around the post of the headboard and slide down, out of sight. I sit up carefully and pull the ties off. I drop them beside me and stand.

My legs wobble.

He's right there, catching my elbow to steady me.

"Don't."

He kisses my temple.

I lock myself in the bathroom and take the world's longest shower. My wrists aren't even red, although my muscles ache from the tension I held through the night.

A tear slides down my cheek.

When I finally compose myself and turn off the water, I find the clothes I left on the counter gone. The only towel hanging on the rack is a small hand one.

And the door is unlocked.

I dry myself off and brush out my hair, squeezing the excess water.

"What torture have you decided to inflict on me today?" I call, cracking the door and stepping out.

My bedroom door is shut.

And, upon further discovery, *locked*.

"Bastard," I blow out on an exhale.

Naked, I go straight for his room. If I can't have my clothes, I'll wear his—

But his bedroom door is locked, too.

Finally, I walk out into the open.

He sits on the couch fully dressed, a drink in his hand. His gaze rakes over me as I do the same to him.

Dark slacks, a white dress shirt tucked in with the top few buttons undone, a dark-blue tie draped around his neck. The color is familiar. Is that what he wrapped around my wrist last night?

He keeps his legs spread, his arms on the back of the couch. He slowly sips his drink, then returns to the sprawled position.

"Going somewhere?" I finally ask.

"I am, yes."

"Where?"

"A press conference." His eyes gleam. "I didn't want to keep you chained, songbird. So I'm allowing your freedom."

"Without clothes."

He shrugs. "Whether or not you choose to leave naked is up to you."

That sounds like a challenge.

And yet, I already know it's one I can't meet.

"What if there's a fire?"

"Then the street will see your pussy," he allows. "Better pray for no fire."

I grind my teeth. "So, what, you want me to wander around your condo naked? It's so... unsanitary."

He smiles. "What's the difference between this and fucking you on every surface available?"

I stop.

"See?" His gaze drops to the apex of my legs. "Does that idea turn you on?"

"Not anymore," I lie.

"You're right." He nods to himself. "You shouldn't sit on any of the furniture in this state."

My mouth opens and closes. "What?"

"You heard me. No chairs, no couch. You're *right*. You should be happy, I'm agreeing with you. You sit on something, you're just going to leak your arousal all over it."

My face flames. "I'm not aroused."

He finishes his drink and rises, going to pour himself another. When he returns, he doesn't sit again. He comes right up to me and cups my pussy.

But there's something in his hand, and I gasp too late. He has an ice cube in his fingers, sliding it along my hot clit. He slides it down further, pushing it into me.

I don't react.

I can't.

Cool water drips down my thighs as he keeps the ice inside me. The intrusion shouldn't feel good, but the bite of pain and the pleasure of being filled makes my head spin.

"I can't fuck you *on* the ice, so I may as well fuck you *with* ice."

I glare at him.

"Drink." He lifts the glass to my mouth.

I part my lips and let him pour the amber liquid down my throat.

"Will you hate me if I continue to love you the way you need to be loved?" He brushes my lip with the back of his thumb's knuckle. Catching the spilled liquid before it can drip off my chin.

"Yes."

He smiles. "But not forever."

Okay, well, I don't know *that*. Especially when he moves his fingers, hitting a spot inside me that makes my knees go weak.

"Hold my shoulders, songbird, let me make you feel good and bad."

I do what he says. *Fuck*, I just do what he says.

"Why do you want to make me feel bad?"

He sips the remainder of his drink, then leans in and presses his lips to mine. The smokey liquid pours into my mouth, a bit warmer from *him*, and I swallow it. He chases it with his tongue, deepening the kiss.

The ice hurts.

He tosses the glass. It hits the carpet with a dull *thud*, clattering as it rolls onto the hard floor, but we ignore it. He wraps his arm around my back and leans me back in place, kissing and finger-fucking me.

I'm naked.

He's fully dressed.

The disparity should kill me.

The ice is nearly gone. Water drips out of me, down his hand. It rolls down my thighs and pools at my feet. I'm so fucking close to coming. He's moving faster, stroking me on the inside and the outside, kissing me without reprieve. But as soon as the last little shard melts, he pulls out. He stops kissing me. He licks his fingers clean and releases me entirely.

I stumble into the wall, and it's the only thing that keeps me upright.

"Why did you do that?" My voice trembles.

"So you crave my touch." He watches me. "Do you?"

"Do I..."

"Do you want me to touch you, songbird? As hated as I am? As repulsive as my actions?"

"No." I don't know if it's a lie or the best truth I've ever spoken. My mind is a mess. I'm turned on, I'm disgusted. I run my finger over the scar on my throat.

None of this fazes him. He leans in and kisses my cheek.

"Okay. I've got to go." He makes it to the door before something else occurs to him. "Oh, Melody..."

I gulp. "Yeah?"

"Be a good girl and take the pill I left next to the sink. I expect you to be asleep before I get back. But remember, not on the furniture."

He leaves.

I stand in silence for a long moment, trying to get my head on right.

The only conclusion I come to is this: I don't like him.

Pretty sure I hate him.

But I avoid the couch on my way to collect the dropped glass, and I don't sit at the breakfast bar either. I set the glass in the sink and eye the pill left out next to another cup of water. It's white, small. It doesn't have a label on it, no markings to give me any clues.

Not that I even know where my phone is.

There are two options: I ignore him and curl up on the

couch, binge-watch television until he gets home. Or... I take the pill.

I get a thrill from that. A little chase of it up my spine.

Because it's a drug?

Because I don't know what it might do to me?

He could've lied and just *told* me that it would put me to sleep. Or maybe it's a stimulant, meant to purposefully make me unable to follow his rules.

Nothing I've read about has spoken about sexuality like *this*.

Natalie, quite embarrassingly, had a sex talk with me the first week I lived with them. Because apparently I wouldn't know about condoms, or where to stick a penis, or pregnancy. I don't think amnesia works like that, because it seemed like common sense.

I check around for my phone and come up empty-handed.

His office door is locked up tight. The television is on mute, showing some news report, but even the remote has gone missing.

Bastard.

I grit my teeth and peruse the kitchen. I drag out the broom and sweep the floor, then pour myself a glass of wine from the fridge. I drink it probably faster than I should, and droplets of white wine escape from the corners of my lips and run down my face.

What does it matter?

I'm naked anyway. It's not like I'm making any more of a mess of myself.

I fiddle and putter for over an hour. Until I spot Jacob—blurry, of course, because my glasses are still in my room—on the TV screen. I get closer to see better.

His blue tie is done up in a perfect knot at his throat, his hair combed into something presentable. The tie makes his eyes seem more two-toned, pulling the gold color out from the starburst around his pupils.

His lips move, and I frown at the lack of sound.

There aren't any buttons on the TV to get the words out —not that I can reach anyway.

I laugh.

He probably did that on purpose.

And now I'm frustrated all over again. His fingers drum on the podium. He's miles and miles away, and those fingers do something to me. To my heart, or... I don't know.

I turn away sharply. It's easier to ignore him when I can't hear. I go to the bathroom and shower again, if only to *do* something.

When I return, there's another player talking.

Something flips in my gut, and my gaze is drawn back to the little pill. It's so innocent, sitting there on the counter and minding its own business. I find myself being pulled in its direction.

Am I no better than a drug addict chasing a high?

I tell myself it's different as I pick up the pill and place it on my tongue.

Instead of swallowing it right away, gulping it down with water, I let it start to dissolve. The bitterness feels more right than anything else. When I can't take it anymore, I swallow it down with the wine. I focus back on Jacob and silently cheers him.

He'll get what he wanted, in whatever form that comes.

It doesn't take long for my eyelids to grow heavy. I'm blinking slower. Still standing—or more braced, really, with my forearms on the counter—but caving. I slide to the

floor and crawl, on my hands and knees, to the rug in front
of the couch.

I'm alone, and my nakedness has never felt so loud.

But that doesn't stop me from falling asleep anyway.

49
JACOB

Knox waits for me outside. I raise my eyebrows on my way by, and he joins me.

"You holding a grudge?" I ask.

He laughs. "Me? Nah."

"What's up?"

And by that I mean, *What are you doing in Denver?* He doesn't live here. And analyzing his outfit, he kind of looks like he slept on the sidewalk. He's wearing gray sweatpants and that black cap pulled low over his face. A black, logo-less hoodie. He's got nothing with him, or on him. So maybe he got a hotel, or he just flew here to talk to me.

"Want to get a drink?" he asks.

I shake my head. "I can't tonight. We're flying to LA tomorrow afternoon."

That's just an excuse. I'm *dying* to get home. My brief peek at the cameras revealed Melody leaning on the kitchen counter, watching the muted television. Naked. So, fair to say my dick immediately responded to that. And it's been threatening to burst the zipper of my slacks ever since.

"Do you think Melody will regain her memory enough

to teach again?" Knox asks. "Has she shown that she's remembering anything?"

That's out of left field. "She's remembered some things. Will it all come back? I have no idea."

He grunts.

"Why?" I question.

"Can I talk to her?"

I stop.

He continues for another few steps, until he's realized he left me behind. He whirls around and meets my quizzical expression. He tilts his head. "I just want her opinion on something."

"Uh-huh."

"Yeah." He nods to himself. "Yeah, I just, you know. She's an English professor. She knows her shit."

He's acting fucking weird.

I tell him so, then add, "She *was* an English professor, asshole. You want to bring up that she's not anymore?"

"It's still in there."

I sigh. "She tried to paint this afternoon. It, uh... it didn't go well."

He grunts.

"Whatever. Tomorrow morning, yeah? We'll meet you for breakfast."

Knox brightens. "Yeah. Thanks."

"Okay..."

"This is my street," he says, hooking his thumb to the left. "See you tomorrow! Text me."

So fucking strange.

I stand on the corner and watch him jog away. There's a hotel halfway down the block, and he turns into it when he reaches it.

I continue on to my car in the parking garage and zip

back to my condo. My anticipation notches up with every mile I cover. The elevator can't move fast enough. Then I drop my fucking keys in front of the door.

When I open it, the only light on is the flickering television, now showing some commentators discussing hockey highlights. They've got my team on the screen behind them.

But what I focus on is Melody, asleep on the rug.

I unbutton my slacks and free my suddenly raging erection, letting out a breath. Instead of going to her, though, I head to my room. I unlock the door and shed my fancy clothes, then return for her. I pull her up and into my arms, taking her to my bed.

Where I part her legs and slide into her like I was always meant to be there.

I fuck her with barely restrained anger, gripping her wrists and pinning her lax arms up over her head. Her scars create this fury in me that's unmatched.

"Your husband will come for you," I whisper in her ear. "And then I'll show you that he doesn't need to stalk your nightmares anymore."

50

MELODY

Knox Whiteshaw sits across from me in the small diner's worn booth. It's not exactly where I thought I'd be today, especially since yesterday was so... *eventful*. I woke up tired. In Jacob's bed, with his cum inside me, with the man himself wrapped around me.

I closed my eyes, and it seemed like only a split second later his alarm was going off.

When he said where we were heading, however... well, I guess I just didn't really believe it. Not until we got here, and Knox sat opposite me.

Jacob is beside me. I try not to think about it in terms of him *keeping* me here, cutting off my escape route. But a lump formed in my throat when I noticed it.

"I brought you something," Knox says.

My brow furrows.

He pulls a paperback from his jacket pocket and slides it across the table to me.

"Oh. Thanks."

It's got an interesting cover. Dark, with a skull and a

gold snake on it. I don't recognize the author's name, not that *that* means anything.

I meet Knox's blue eyes. "Can I ask... why?"

"I just want to know what you think of it." He shrugs. "You know, if it's good or not."

I glance at Jacob. He lifts his shoulder, too. I guess neither of us can find Knox's motivation for giving me this book. I mean, it looks like a dark romance. Which isn't really *his* speed.

"Why?" I repeat. "You could read it and decide for yourself."

He makes a face. "I don't have time for that. I just want to know if it's doing well. Which... I mean, books that are good sell well, don't they?"

I snort. "Can I see your phone?"

Knox slides that toward me. I open the internet browser and search the author's name. She's got a website. She publishes on her own. Or rather, she owns a publishing company for her works.

I click on one of the sales pages and scan the reviews— there are over ten thousand of them—and the sales rank.

Both are impressive.

"Where'd you buy this?"

"The bookstore down the street."

"Well, there you go."

He shakes his head.

"Bookstores don't just stock indie books, Knox. Like, self-published books. One, those authors don't have a team at a publishing house getting those books on shelves." I hold up a finger. "And two," I add another, "they don't do a thousand-book print run, it's all print-on-demand these days."

"So..."

"It's popular enough that the employee in charge of inventory heard of the book and got approval for them to get it in stock."

"How do you know that?" Jacob asks.

I frown. "I... I did my undergrad thesis on the changing environment of publishing."

He smiles.

"What?"

"What do you mean, what? You just remembered all that."

Oh. It's startling, but I find myself smiling back. "But it wasn't like a memory. It was just there when I started talking about it."

"That's okay." Jacob leans in. "What did I do when you got in my truck for the first time?"

I wrinkle my nose. "You stuck your face in my lap."

Knox bursts out laughing.

I cringe, but Jacob is grinning ear to ear. "You *remember*."

"Maybe," I mumble.

But the thing is, I don't feel different.

I thought remembering—or at least remembering some of the big stuff—would mean my old personality would come back, too. But even though I remember getting to my classroom only to realize there was a snow day, and Jacob finding me and goading me into joining him, it doesn't mean I'm the same woman who followed him to the parking garage and let him twist me toward him.

But at the same time, who am I if not her?

Who am I if not *me*?

"Melody." Jacob holds my cheeks. "Breathe, songbird."

I blink rapidly, focusing on his face. On the whistling, exaggerated breaths for me to mimic. I match his speed, trying not to let myself go out of control again, until my pulse slows.

"Sorry." I cough. "Sorry."

"You don't have to apologize." He gives me a look and slowly drops his hands. "What's up?"

"You liked the old me." I eye him. I will not say *love*, even though he oh-so delicately announced it to me. "But if I remember and I'm still the new me... what then?"

"I love both," he says firmly.

"This is so cute, I might barf," Knox comments.

Jacob flips him off.

His best friend slides out of the booth, patting the table. "See ya on the flip side, Jakey."

I look over and sigh.

He's left the damn book.

"Are you going to read it?"

I shrug. "I've got to start somewhere, right? I loved reading. And... I kind of want to reread my old favorites, just to see if they're the same as how I remember them now."

Even as I say it, I know they'll be the same. Maybe shifted a little by my different experiences. But they're just... *there*.

"Songbird."

I drag my attention back to Jacob.

"Do you remember the night you... left?"

I think back. To the snowstorm, the hot chocolate. Being so pleased that he thought of it, with whipped cream and sprinkles and everything. There's not much more after that. A haze of him kneeling between my legs behind my desk and discussing... something.

"It's fuzzy," I confess. "I—"

"You'll get it." He squeezes my hands. "This is encouraging."

Yeah. Except then how do I explain the sudden sick feeling in the pit of my stomach?

Whatever's coming—it isn't good.

51

JACOB

She's remembering.

It's weird, though. The more she tells me, the more upset I feel. Off my game, in a way.

For so long, things have been status quo. Melody coming back with no memories didn't even change things for me. I brought her to games, I had my way with her sexually and mentally.

But now she's remembering.

I have a feeling she's going to call me on more of my bullshit. She was already doing that a little—like the dinner with my family. She went along with my plan, let me fuck up her makeup and hair by choking her on my dick, but then she left.

Which is more of a turn-on than not.

Hmm...

Have I been taming her too much?

"You're staring," she says softly across the table.

"You're so far away," I reply.

She lifts one shoulder. She opted for a dark-blue dress that was packed for her by the team stylist. Her eyes nearly bugged out when she saw it sitting in a suitcase she didn't recognize.

She flew with the team this time, sitting up front with the social media manager. No one said a word, which was fine by me.

Game one against Los Angeles starts in just a few hours.

We're at an early dinner at the restaurant across the street from the arena. The team has the whole back room reserved, although everyone seems to be caught up in their own little bubbles.

"You sat across from me," she points out.

I run my fingers over the heavy white tablecloth. "You could get closer by crawling under the table."

Her heeled foot touches the inside of my ankle and runs up my leg. "Or you could."

I hum.

"It is time for dessert," she adds.

"You don't have to tell me twice, beautiful."

Her eyebrow goes up.

"You are beautiful," I tell her. And I'm going to tell her cunt that, too. I duck under the table, flipping the table-cloth out to hide my legs. In truth, I might be slightly too big to fit. My back grazes the underside of it.

I spread her legs, running my hands up her bare legs and pushing the silky blue fabric with it. I grip her knees and drag her forward a bit, her ass reaching the edge of her chair, and I *live* for her gasp above me.

Her thighs twitch as I trace her skin with my nails, finally moving her panties aside. She's wet for me, and she shudders when I blow on her heated skin.

My first taste has her gasping again.

All of a sudden, her thighs try to close around my head.

"Can I interest you in dessert or coffee, miss?"

The waiter.

I lap at her clit and wait for her answer.

She clears her throat. "Coffee, please."

"And your partner...?"

"No, he's had his fill."

Not yet, but I will. I thrust two fingers into her, and her upper body hitches forward in surprise.

"Jacob," she hisses.

I ignore her.

I bring her higher and higher, judging from the way she's fidgeting above me. I avoid her clit, even though she's on the edge. Not until her hand snakes under the table and fists my hair, redirecting my mouth to the small bud.

"Fuck," she whispers, moaning under her breath.

She can scream for me another time, but I take this. And the contracting muscles around my fingers. I take until she sags backward, spent, and then I slowly withdraw.

I climb out and make a show of licking my fingers clean, then dab at my mouth with my napkin. "You didn't order me dessert?"

Her face is flushed, her eyes wide. "I can't believe you just did that."

I smirk.

"Jacob." Camden Church stops at our table. "Hello, Melody."

"Camden," she replies. "Excited to face off against your brother?"

He smiles. "Rhodes mentioned that?"

I smirk. I mean, I mentioned it in passing. Didn't think she'd remember, much less bring it up.

"It's our form of pillow talk." She rests her chin on her knuckles and smiles sweetly at him.

I roll my eyes. "Okay, okay. What's up, Church?"

"We're heading over in ten." He moves off without another word.

I look to Melody.

"I'll be fine," she says. "Kristy got me a pass. It'll be like the good old days."

The one game she worked. I snort a laugh and nod at her, rising from my seat and kissing her fast before following our goalie, Haverhill, out the door.

Knox, Miles, Steele, and Greyson are in the front part of the restaurant. At the bar. They're not eating—or drinking, for that matter.

"Hey," I greet them. "Haverhill, you know my friends?"

"Pleasure, guys." He eyes Miles. "Good goaltending. Sorry your season ended sooner than it should've."

They shake hands, and I grin.

"You here to support Rhodes?" he asks. "Must be nice— my high school didn't produce shit for hockey players. That's why I skipped college and played in the AHL."

"We're here on a covert mission," Knox says.

"Which is not covert if you tell everyone," Steele adds under his breath.

Knox glares at him. "I haven't told everyone."

"The flight attendant," Greyson says.

"The cab driver." Steele.

"The bartender," Miles adds.

I hide my smile.

Haverhill's gaze bounces between us. "I'll give you time to chat about this covert mission in private, then."

He ambles for the door, and I elbow Knox.

"Ow," Knox complains, rubbing his arm. "What was that for?"

"Having a big mouth."

He seems in better spirits, though.

"You've got a game to win," Greyson says. "Let us keep track of Melody."

And Henry. After all, I expect him to make a sudden and devastating appearance. A snatch-and-grab sort of thing.

"Everything bad to ever happen, does during a game," Steele mumbles. "It's bad luck."

I wave my hand. It's not like I can back out. This is my career, my livelihood—and I trust my friends to keep Melody safe.

They have to, or I'm going to fucking kill them all.

52

STEELE

I feel like I'm in the CIA. Or running an undercover sting operation for the FBI. All we're missing are those invisible earbuds to chat with each other.

As it is, we have cell phones. And constant texts.

The group chat is blowing up, but it's mostly Knox. He's with Melody, having apparently had breakfast with her this morning. Which is one of the stranger things to have happened.

Weirder than Knox carrying on a bet for almost a year.

Weirder than snow in July.

Weirder than—

"O'Brien." Greyson stops beside me. "You had a look on your face."

I shrug. We don't have anything to go on, really. We don't know what Henry looks like, and neither does Melody. She sits in the section below us, near the glass, in a dark-blue dress. It goes well with the Colorado Titans colors, although I'm sure the stylist had no idea when she picked it out.

Sarcasm.

Knox texts that he and Melody are going to check out the upper levels, and I frown at my phone. He shouldn't be moving her in general.

Greyson frowns, too. "What's he up to?"

I shake my head. We move out of sight as Melody and Knox come up the aisle and head toward the stairs to the second level. Then we follow.

Miles raises his hands in a, *what the fuck?* expression.

Can't say I blame him.

Knox and Melody go past where we're standing, and the crowd erupts into cheers. Greyson and I both look toward the ice as the LA players break out in celebration.

Goal scored.

Greyson sighs. "Just gives them something to fight for, right?"

"Yeah."

Miles finally catches up to us. People are flooding out of their rows and into the hallway, the break after a goal almost always a good time to rush to get a drink or have a piss.

"Well?"

"They're only a few minutes ahead of us," Greyson murmurs. "Let's go."

Except this place is a little bigger than we thought, and it takes us another five minutes to find the way to get to the second level. It's all well and good until we enter the stairwell and find Knox's broken phone on the stairs. And no sign of our chatty friend or the woman we're supposed to be protecting.

"Well, fuck," I breathe. I exchange a look with Greyson and Miles. "Jacob is actually going to murder us."

53

MELODY

"The suites!" Knox crows, shoving open the stairwell door. "You were up in the New York ones, right? Well, my friend told me the LA arena suites are a hundred times posher."

"Posh?"

"You know. Fancy."

I shake my head. The only reason I'm somewhat okay with going with Knox is because he said he could talk us into one of the suites and get us free wine. That, and the players keep fighting. Peacocking, Knox called it. He also called them some other choice names, so I figured a walk was in both of our best interests.

"Hey, Mel."

I turn.

A familiar man comes up the stairwell, stopping on the landing just below Knox and me.

"Thomas? What are you doing here?"

Knox's gaze bounces from me to him. "Um..."

"Thomas is my middle name, darling."

He smiles while my blood goes cold. *Darling*. His voice. His words. It all comes together in a cyclone in my mind, scattering everything else.

"I kept waiting for you to put it together," he continues. "Kept waiting for you to wake up and say, 'Oh, you're not my cousin. You're my *husband*.'"

"Ex-husband," I automatically correct.

"That's fucked up," Knox breathes.

Thomas—*no, shoot, Henry*—scowls. "Fucked up? You think what *I* did was fucked up?"

"Did you try to kill me?" My voice comes out squeaky.

Knox subtly steps in front of me.

"I don't want you dead." Henry's gaze hardens. "I just want you back with me."

"You—" I press my fingers into the bridge of my nose. My glasses rise, but I close my eyes anyway. "Did you know I was in the hospital?"

"I didn't until I got a phone call telling me so. I came when they explained the memory loss. And it was with great joy that I watched your lack of reaction. I thought, what a *wonderful* way to torment my wife." He pulls out a gun and aims it at Knox. "Step away from her."

"Fuck off."

"I'd be happy to shoot you in the face."

Knox glances back at me, then faces my ex-husband. Who keeps calling himself my husband.

Because he's delusional.

"What about Natalie?" I blurt out. "You're married to her."

"Natalie is my legal wife," he allows. "That much is true. She thinks I go by Thomas, as well. Funny, that. Once I started building that separate identity, I met her and things just... went so nicely. She was scarred by the world, a bit like you."

No. That's not right.

"I wasn't scarred by the world," I hiss. "I was scarred by *you*."

He laughs and comes forward. Knox flinches when Henry-slash-Thomas jerks the gun, but it doesn't go off. And Knox doesn't move. He reaches back and squeezes my wrist, easing me up another step. He follows.

He stays in front of me, but I'm sick with worry. For me, for him.

We have to run, right? Up is our only option. I glance over my shoulder as subtly as I can.

The gun goes off.

Knox and I both flinch, nearly falling backward, and Henry lunges forward. He shoves Knox against the wall with one hand and tangles his other fist in my hair, dragging me against him. The pain makes me go with him, even as bile rises up my throat.

How fast the tide turns.

"Take out your phone," Henry orders Knox.

The more he talks, the more I disassociate it with the cousin who helped me and connect it to the rough voice on the phone. The voice memos. Why is my memory of him warped?

Why didn't I realize it was *him*? I talked to him on the phone as Henry, and didn't put it together that he was Thomas.

Knox complies with Henry's demand slowly, lifting his cell out of his back pocket.

Fear flashes across his face for once, and my expression must mirror his.

Henry tightens his grip on my hair. I cry out at the burn in my scalp.

"Drop and stomp," Henry orders.

Knox does it.

"Good." He drags me backward, leaving a gap for Knox to go downstairs. "Now, move."

He goes, and I'm pushed ahead of my ex-husband.

What did I see in him?

"Natalie," I remind him. "What about Natalie?"

He seems to consider that. "You disappeared on me. You took out a restraining order on me. I couldn't just let you go. We're soulmates."

"We're not," I whisper.

"I created Thomas. Stole the last name Cameron from some random dead schmuck, which made me feel a bit closer to you. I wanted to share your last name, since you refused to take mine. Funny how that works." He chuckles as we go down another flight. We're in the parking garage levels under the arena. "It's never the man who has to change his last name. But I liked it. Quite a bit."

He's revolting.

"You're supposed to be in California—"

"Henry Armstrong *is* in California." He chuckles. "I sold that identity eight months ago. Told him it came with a little restraining order against a stranger, but he was fine with that. Up until then, I lived the double life. Henry in California, with you. Thomas the doctor in Denver."

I shudder.

"This level," Henry barks.

Knox goes through the door. We head for the back corner of the parking garage, to a dark SUV. The windows are tinted almost completely black. At a beep, the trunk door lifts. He shoves me toward Knox.

"Tape his wrists."

I spot the roll of duct tape sitting in the back of the SUV, then glance up at Knox.

"You need to run," I whisper to him. "I'll block his shot—"

"No."

"Tape his wrists, Melody," Henry calls. "Or I fucking shoot you in the knee. You don't need it for where we're going anyway."

I look up at Knox. I don't know what's going on inside me. I'm so numb. All the fear, all the anger, is just gone. I need him to run, though. Because if he doesn't, Henry will use him against me.

I know that with certainty.

"*Run*," I mouth.

He finally nods once.

I spin and rush at Henry at the same time that Knox bolts across the garage aisle. I crash into my ex-husband, and the gun goes off right next to my head. The sound is worse than a thunderclap directly overhead. It stabs into my ears, and I let out a shriek that *feels* solid but sounds like nothing.

There's just a piercing ringing.

I'm shoved to the concrete. It bites into my forearms and knees, bits of stone and dirt clinging to my skin. I crawl, flinching when another shot goes off.

A weight presses on my spine, flattening me to the ground and stopping my desperate movement. Hands touch me. I can't tell if I'm hallucinating or if this is actually happening.

I should scream.

But all I can do is suffer flashbacks of pain, and it freezes me from the inside out. Even as I'm hoisted up and maneuvered toward the open trunk.

He's going to take me and I'm going to disappear.

"Hey!"

A door crashes against a wall in the distance.

"Get away from her!"

Henry huffs.

We're so close to the trunk.

My fight kicks in. And suddenly I'm scratching and swinging with everything I have. I put my feet on the bumper of the car and propel us backward, and he drops me flat on my back. Pain echoes through my body, knocking the wind from my lungs.

His laugh haunts me. "Until next time, darling."

And then he's gone.

I lie panting on the ground, unable to move. Not until someone grabs my arm and helps me into a sitting position.

Willow.

"Breathe," she says, rubbing my back. "He's gone. Take a deep breath for me, Mel."

Miles is right behind her, his phone to his ear.

"The police are coming," he says to us.

My chest finally loosens, and I inhale.

The other two guys, Greyson and Steele, are helping Knox out between two cars—and Knox is bleeding. He cradles his arm against his stomach.

"Oh, no," I gasp, climbing to my feet and shooting forward. I stop short of touching his arm. "Was that from his gun?"

"I think it's just a graze," Knox says with a wince. "Hurts like a bitch, but I'll be okay."

And Jacob is still playing.

The police come. Jacob appears only a few minutes after them, bursting out in his full kit—minus the skates, which have been replaced with slides. His gaze burns into me as he approaches, and I try not to fall apart.

Henry tried to make a play for me—and I just don't understand it.

How it could've gone so wrong on his end.

Isn't he more calculated than this?

I tell the police about the restraining order and the false identity. They have someone collecting shells and taking photos, and they mention needing me to come down to the station to give a formal statement in the next few days.

They're going to search for Henry, but I already have a feeling they're not going to find him.

"What happened with the game?" I ask Jacob as soon as they're gone.

His gaze is scouring mine, and he cups my cheek.

Fuck.

Suddenly, the reality of what almost happened comes crashing down on me. Tears burn the backs of my eyes, but it doesn't take long for them to spill out.

"Shh." He reels me into him. "He won't get you."

"You're the reason he's here, aren't you?"

He goes still.

My brow furrows, and I add, "Because he knows I'm with you."

"Oh. Yeah."

He's lying.

I don't draw back, though. I don't even call him out on it. I just let him comfort me, and we go up to the main level. There's more security here, and Greyson raises his eyebrows at them.

"Rent-a-cops?"

Jacob shrugs.

"Let's get back to the hotel. Game's shot anyway." He makes a face. "Sorry, dude."

"What's the score?" I ask.

"LA is up by six."

I wince.

Jacob touches my chin. It's tender, and I think I might've hit it on the concrete when I went down. My scalp burns, too. There's a phantom sensation of his fingers twisting and pulling.

"It's okay," he says in my ear. "We're going back to the hotel. He can't get to you there."

Greyson and Miles take Knox to the hospital to get stitched up, and Steele accompanies us to the hotel. I'm shivering.

I can't stop shivering.

"He was going to take me and do something terrible to Knox," I whisper.

They trade a glance.

"What was that?"

Jacob focuses on me, brushing my hair back. "What?"

"That look. You know something?"

He grimaces. "Well, I may have... goaded him."

My stomach swoops. "You *goaded* my crazy ex-husband?"

He shrugs and straightens. "That's why I had the guys watching you. We're here for another day—and I'll bet anything that he'll come for you during the next game. Which gives us some time to prepare."

I scoff. "Prepare?"

Steele chuckles. "Told you she'd take it well."

"We had a little team meeting, songbird. Not the Titans, but *us*. My friends. We knew... all of us knew that there was risk, but we wanted to draw him out."

We make it up to our floor in silence before something *else* occurs to me. I grab his arm, stopping both Jacob and Steele.

"He took me to *your* game."

They both go still. More still anyway. Their attention brings back some of the warmth to my cheeks that I had lost, but I ignore the weight of it.

"Thomas. *Henry*. He took me to New York. He said he was in a doctor's conference, but I don't know if that's real. What *is* real is that he chose to take me to a game."

Jacob rubs his jaw. "Bastard knew my connection to you. Bet he delighted in you not recognizing me."

"That's messed up," Steele comments.

"Is that why he lived in Denver?" I whisper.

They don't have an answer to that... but I have a feeling it's true. Every decision he made was based around me. Including living in Colorado, going to New York, being a hockey fan. It was all a lie. A dirty experiment to see when I'd remember something.

And I never did.

In the room, I sit on the edge of the bed. Jacob and Steele move around, checking under it, in the closet, behind the shower curtain. They're more paranoid than me. Although I'd be doing the same if I was here alone.

Jacob opens his bag and quickly changes, seeming not to care that Steele is in the room. He removes his jersey, the protective padding under it, then the compression pants. Until he's just down to his briefs. He grins at me and unbuckles the cup, tossing it on top of the rest of the stuff, and my face flames.

Finally, he's back to fully dressed. Dark jeans, black t-shirt, and a dark-gray sweatshirt over it. He reaches into the bag one more time and withdraws a handgun. He checks it, then slides it in the waistband of his pants.

I can't seem to comprehend what just happened.

And because Steele's not reacting, all I can do is furrow my brows.

Because what the fuck?

"Hungry?"

"We just ate," I point out. It *was* hours ago, but still.

"We went through a traumatic event," he says. "And I played two and a half periods. I'm ready for some ice cream."

I shake my head. "You have a gun."

He glances at Steele. "Give us a minute."

His friend grunts and leaves. The door clicks shut softly behind him.

"Yes, I have a gun."

"Why?"

"Because I don't trust that Henry Armstrong will leave his gun behind next time." He takes my hands, pulling me to my feet. "How would you feel if I shot that motherfucker in the face?"

I think about that. The violence is coming back. Not just, you know, *hockey*. But what I know about Henry. And Jacob, too. He wouldn't hesitate—I know that. So when I think about the fear that lives in my chest at the thought of my ex-husband, it's easy to think that a restraining order won't stop him.

Restraining orders stop law-abiding citizens.

Not mad men like him.

If he was dead, would my fear lessen? Would it go away entirely?

Jacob waits for my answer. His blue eyes are dark, the gold almost entirely erased by the dilation of his pupils.

He's holding my hands, but some part of me thinks he might be preparing to try his case in a court where I'm his judge, jury, and executioner.

"I don't like the thought of murder," I say gently, removing my hand from his and pressing it to his chest. "But if anyone should meet the Devil sooner than planned, it's him."

54
JACOB

No sign of Henry Armstrong.

Now that I know he's also Thomas Cameron, I spend a good thirty minutes mentally kicking myself.

I was in his home. I looked at photos of him on the wall with his wife. But a family truly must be the best undercover story, because I didn't suspect him.

Knox showed up with a stitched and bandaged arm at almost midnight, apologizing to Melody for his impromptu desire to go see the suites. I almost hit him in the arm for even *thinking* leaving their section was a good idea, but Melody smiled at him.

Whatever they went through seemed to have solidified him as a good guy in her mind. Strange, considering Willow and Miles have the opposite opinion.

Well, that's not quite fair. It's been a few years, and they're working through it. They're amicable. I guess.

But Melody waves him into our hotel room, even though she's in her PJs, and motions for him to sit on the couch beside the bed. She sits next to him and waves the book he gave her.

"You brought it?"

"I read it."

He nods carefully. "And?"

"It's a dark romance." She shrugs. "Kind of exactly what it's advertising. There's an arranged marriage, a kidnapping, a lot of sex."

"Sex?" I blurt out. "You've been reading a sex book?"

She bites her lip and bats her eyelashes at me. "Only when you're otherwise engaged."

"Out." I march forward and grab Knox's good arm, towing him up and practically dragging him out of the room. "See you tomorrow. *Bye*."

As soon as the door is closed behind him, I wheel around and stalk back to Melody.

"Now... tell me more about this sex book."

She laughs.

———

"I don't feel like an adult."

I glance at Melody. She's in a fitted version of my jersey, black leggings, and boots that end just below her knees. They encase her calves deliciously, and the slight heel makes her ass biteable. We're both getting ready in the hotel bathroom. She's curling her hair, I'm shaving my face.

"What's more adult than this?" I gesture with the razor between her and me.

"Living on my own, figuring out who I am..."

"You know who you are."

She frowns. "No I don't, Jake. That's the problem."

"Some memories came back, right?"

"A good portion," she allows.

"Do you remember living alone? In Crown Point?"

"Some of it." She shifts her weight. "Why do *you* think he picked Denver?"

I tilt my head. "What do you mean?"

She sets down the curling iron and faces me. I mirror her, although I've got shaving cream on half my face still.

"Henry said he was building the second identity, Thomas Cameron, in Denver. Eight months ago. The money came out of my account nine months ago, right? So... why Denver? If I was from New York. If I was *found* in New York. It wasn't like I already had amnesia and he was setting up this life to torture me."

Our first assumption was that he picked Denver to fuck with her.

"The hospital was in Beacon Hill, New York. Then Thomas came to get me, and we flew to Denver. That's where I met Natalie..." She shakes her head. "There are three important places, right? I mean, besides Crown Point. I went to high school in Beacon Hill, New York. I grew up in that county, so that's one. I moved to the city for college, so that's two. And Henry had me in California."

She doesn't seem upset by that. She's talking so matter-of-factly, I don't think she's registering it at all. And that's okay for now. Sometimes sticking to the facts makes things easier.

Once Henry is gone, we can process it together.

"Did he have you in California?"

She frowns.

"Or did he have you in... Denver?"

Melody's already shaking her head. "No. I think... I

remember palm trees. And being locked in a room I've never seen before. He kept me in a house outfitted for a captive. Every door had a lock only he had keys to, even the front door. The windows were sealed. He let me paint..."

"You're remembering."

"I don't *want* to remember that," she whispers. "I don't want to relive the year he had me."

"Because he took you from Crown Point."

She meets my gaze and nods. "He did. He threatened you."

She *remembers.*

But her expression shutters, and she's right back to business. "New York City. Beacon Hill. Somewhere in California. And, let's say Crown Point. Because it was safe, but he still found me there."

"Okay. So..."

"So why Denver? Before I even escaped him, he was building this second identity." She raises her eyebrow at me.

I connect the dots. "You think it's me."

She lifts one shoulder. "I don't know. It would make sense, wouldn't it? He knew your last name from... from that video. So maybe he wanted to be close. Just in case."

She quirks her lips, like she's trying to hide a smile. A *smile* at a time like this. Fuck, I knew she was as deranged as me.

"If I took a bunch of cash and ran away, and you knew I had previously been seeing some hot young hockey player... Where would you assume I'd go?"

"To me." Damn. I can't help but feel a bit of an ego boost. "Young and hot, huh?"

She laughs. "You *were*. Now you're in danger of having your teeth knocked out on a nightly basis."

I grab her waist and reel her in. "How do you know I haven't lost some teeth already?"

She smirks and takes my jaw, pushing my lip up to reveal my teeth. "Unless you paid a lot of money..."

"I would," I comment, moving against her finger. "My pride wouldn't allow for anything less."

She taps her nail against a tooth. It feels weird, but her smile is worth it.

"That one feels real," she murmurs.

"You're an expert on... *teeth*."

"We don't know what I'm an expert on."

I drag her leggings down, then hoist her onto the counter. I'm careful of the hot iron, and she moves it to the other side of the sink. When I lean in to kiss her, she leans away.

"You have shaving cream on your face."

Oh, for fuck's sake. I'm tempted to kiss her anyway.

"And I just spent forty-five minutes doing my makeup."

I growl and wipe it off with the damp cloth, tossing it behind me. "Undo my pants."

"Hmm." Her fingers trace my skin just over the waist-band. "Do you have time to finish what you're about to start? Because I don't want to be left disappointed."

"Seize every orgasm like it's your last," I say solemnly.

She nods just as seriously.

I like this side of her. It wasn't there without the memories. The teasing. There's a bit more confidence coming through, too, although I can't say if that's because of *her* or *us*. Or the gun I plan on putting in her purse for the game.

I cover her hand and undo my button and zipper. My cock is already hard for her—of course—and I lean in to claim her lips at the same time that I pull her thong to the side. When I saw her choose the dark-blue thong from her bag, I almost lost my shit.

How am I supposed to play when I'm thinking about that?

About *her*.

The little band of fabric that's been rubbing her pussy for the last hour is damp, and I smile to myself. She's turned on by me. And maybe it's our daring sexy talk or just my good looks and charm. Either way.

"You're so stuck with me," I murmur.

"I figured." She loops her arm around my neck and pulls me in. "Kiss me."

Bossy.

"Yes, Professor." I press my lips to hers. She hasn't put on lipstick yet. Half my face is covered in stubble. But it doesn't matter.

I push my finger inside her, curling and playing with her until I can't help it. Our mouths war, licking and biting and sliding together. I'm dripping precum on the counter between her legs, and it feels like heaven when I remove my finger and notch at her entrance.

She makes a noise in the back of her throat.

I move in a fraction. Spreading her open, allowing her cunt to squeeze at the tip of my cock. But I don't give her any more.

"Beg," I say against her lips. "Like a perfect little whore."

"Fuck me, please," she gasps. "I need to feel you inside me. Right now. I need to come apart around your dick."

It twitches.

I *like* it when she says things like that.

I give her more of me, and her mouth tears away from

mine. She drops her head back, exposing her neck. I kiss and bite my way down it, making sure to leave marks that'll be hard to hide. Marks she won't have time to magic away with makeup, or bruises that will slowly come to the surface as the night continues.

"Fuck me *harder*, Jake." Her fingers are in my hair, tugging and yanking.

I push in slowly until I'm buried all the way inside her wet heat.

My control doesn't last. I give in to her pleading, pulling almost all the way out and slamming back into her. I don't give her a moment to recover before I'm repeating the same thing, pummeling into her like I'm drilling for oil.

She moans. Her lips find my jaw, my neck. Her teeth leave their own marks as I fuck her.

"Touch yourself," I say in her ear. "Use your fingers to make yourself come."

Melody reacts immediately. She slips her hand between us, her fingers sliding on her arousal. I lean back just enough to see our connection, while she keeps one hand on the back of my neck. Her nails dig in.

I relish the little snaps of pain.

"Are you close?"

She nods frantically.

"Good," I growl. My balls are tightening, lifting, and a tingling pressure builds at the base of my spine. It drives me faster. I brace my hand on the mirror over her shoulder, curving into her. I lick her neck.

She cries out. Her muscles spasm around me, clenching in pulses. It tips me over the edge easily, and we fall into oblivion together.

For a long moment, we're still.

Then I press a kiss to her forehead and slowly withdraw.

My gaze drops to her stomach and back up. "When's the last time you had your period?"

She sucks in a breath.

"Songbird?"

"A few weeks ago," she murmurs. "Before I moved into your condo."

"Hmm." I pick up a new cloth, wet it, and clean between her legs. My cum is oozing out of her, and it's erotic enough to make my dick go half-mast again. I ignore it, cleaning myself before doing up my slacks again.

She stays on the counter, leaning back on her hands, as I reapply shaving cream to my face and resume my task.

"I'm not pregnant," she says.

She seems a little cross about it.

"I'm not," she repeats. "You're the one fucking me without a condom."

I straighten and meet her hazel eyes. It takes me a second to realize she's *angry*. Or upset. Or some combination of the two.

"Let's get one thing straight," I say carefully. "If you're pregnant, I'd be thrilled."

She narrows her eyes.

"I want my baby in your belly. I want you pregnant. I want—"

"What do you want?" Her voice is raspy.

I grin. "I want little yous and mes running around. We'd get a bigger house, of course. Outside of the city, where we can have a yard. Fresh air. A space for a family. A dog."

"A dog."

"Yeah, songbird, I want a dog."

"That doesn't sound so bad." She shifts. "And if I don't... if I can't get pregnant?"

Well... I don't know what to say to that.

She hops off the counter and hikes her leggings back up. She picks up the curling iron and resumes doing her hair, leaving me to squint at her in confusion.

55

MELODY

hy Denver?

And for that matter—why New York?

It's a question I hadn't asked myself before.
It didn't really seem relevant, especially when Thomas
—*Henry*—mentioned I went to school in the city. But why
Beacon Hill Hospital? Why was I so far outside of the city,
unless I was feeling nostalgic?

Did I return home?

But my mother is dead and gone, and I don't know of
any other family I'd be willing to visit. I can't think of any.
My father in prison... well, he'd be the closest one. Stone
Ridge State Prison is only a town over from it. But when he
said I hadn't visited him before, I believed him.

A wonder. It seems like some of my memory has
returned, and the little details like geography seem to be
surfacing for my use easily. Like how Lion's Head, my high
school, was in Beacon Hill.

So... familiar territory, in a way.

I doubt I'd be visiting my father.

And the time between Crown Point and the hospital is

still too murky to decipher. It's not really there at all. Just flashes of fear and adrenaline. Being caught like a bug in Henry's web, pointlessly struggling. It's enough to make me scared of remembering more.

Meanwhile, Henry went to Denver. To stake out *Jacob*. Because he's the last person I fucked? Because... because he's a threat to Henry? Because he hoped to catch me there?

A chill sweeps down my back.

If Henry was in Denver, if he thought I was going to show up there, then he probably didn't find me in New York.

The other night is proof, even. He denied hurting me, said he only found out when his Thomas identity was contacted. He was going to shoot me in the leg, if at all. He tried to kidnap me. And sure, torture is probably on the list of activities he enjoys.

Not murder.

I touch my throat again. The white scar that's more proof that someone *did* want me dead. But if not Henry, then who?

Caleb: Restraining order is valid for another year. You had a video hearing with a judge who granted it four years ago. I let the LA police know.

I got that text before we headed to the game. I updated him about the situation, and the run-in, yesterday. While he offered to fly out, I didn't even want to think about how much that bill would be.

Because lawyers rarely do things for free. Even lawyers who are best friends with my best friend's husband.

Now, I sit with Violet, Aspen, and Willow. The guys are hovering on the edges. Knox keeps glancing at me like he wants to say something, but he's so far kept his distance. He's favoring his injured arm, keeping it close to his body.

Besides the bandage under his sweatshirt, there's no outward signs of damage. To either of us.

We have very clear instructions: *stay put*. Our seats are at the glass. Jacob, skating past, winks at me, and my heart skips.

I'm safe here.

With his friends, with the security alerted to a potential problem. The police gave them a bulletin. Something about Henry with his new face. Not that he was ever arrested. No mugshot on file. The news came right from Caleb, and he confirmed to me that the police presence would be noticeable.

Seeing a photo of him now—even though I just saw him in person, it's not the same—compared to my memory of him from when we first dated was shocking.

He changed his nose and hairline. His *hairline*.

It's strange. He had surgery on his face to fool everyone. To become Thomas. But it also served to not trigger my memory, which worries me.

What kind of psychopath goes through all of that just to mess with someone?

A horn blows, and I glance up at the scoreboard. The Titans are up by two. A stark contrast to game one, when they got steamrolled by the LA team. The Titans are rushing around celebrating, and the row of us leap to our feet. I join them in cheering and clapping, and Jacob comes skating over.

He presses his hand to the glass, and I quickly mirror it.

My smile's brightness is unmatched.

By the end of the second period, Jacob's scored twice.

"He's on fire," Knox crows. He hops to his feet along with seemingly half the people in the arena. "I'm going to get beer. Willow?"

Miles scowls at him. "Get fucked, man."

Knox rolls his eyes. "It was a joke."

"A bad fucking joke."

I wince.

Willow sighs as Knox disappears up the aisle. "He tries. He was actually on a good streak for a while. But he's just been getting worse the last week or so."

Huh.

"I don't suppose my wardens will let me go pee?" I ask her.

She cracks a smile. "Aspen and I will go guard the stall door for you."

We let Greyson, Steele, and Miles know where we're going. Violet joins us, and soon we're heading back down. On the ice, there are little tiny players skating around. They're fully kitted out in hockey gear, and they move in a pack around the ice.

It's kind of cute.

But my heart aches at the sight.

Because I'm seventy percent sure I took the permanent solution when it comes guarding against pregnancy. Either that, or I went to a clinic for an entirely different reason. All I remember is walking in the door and feeling the pinch of pain *inside*.

Did I do that to keep myself from having Henry's babies? Or *any* babies?

I don't know. But telling Jacob what I suspect might just cost me his obsession.

56

JACOB

I've got a missed call from my private investigator. He's kind of worn out his usefulness, as he got the Henry Armstrong thing so completely wrong. Well, the Thomas-Henry thing. He missed that. Missed that Thomas was a made-up person or a stolen identity.

I consider not calling him back. Last we left it, he was going through the restraining order. Melody told me we now have the bigshot defense attorney, Caleb Asher, on the case. He happens to know Mel's friend, Lucille Page. And, surprisingly, my friends. He helped Willow out of a jam before. Smoothed over some legal shit for us involving a dead body...

Anyway.

"Rhodes."

Heads turn my way in the locker room. I toss my phone in my bag and follow the general manager—the guy who usually doesn't step foot down here on game day—out into the hall.

"What do you know about Knox Whiteshaw?" he asks me in a low voice.

I frown. "What do you want to know, sir?"

He makes a vague motion.

"He's an excellent center. We played together in Crown Point." I pause. "Is Dawes out?"

The GM scowls. "That's above your paygrade."

Okay, fine. "Well, if I may be so bold... Knox would make an excellent addition to the team. His personality would mesh well with Church. And the rest of the guys tend to fall in line with him."

He gives me an appraising look. "Okay. Thanks, Rhodes. Keep playing the way you are, yeah?"

"Yes, sir."

I go back in the locker room and smile to myself. If Knox joins the Colorado Titans, then my year will be fucking *made*.

Church is sitting next to my cubby when I get back. He raises his eyebrows, but I shake my head. He stands and gathers us around, giving a hyped-up speech that has all of us refocused. We head out of the locker room as a group, and I'm the third one on the ice after Church and Lawson, the other d-man. Haverhill, our goalie, follows close behind.

Melody sits between Willow and Aspen. Violet's on the other side of Aspen. The guys frame them in. Well, except for Knox. He's sitting behind Melody, leaning down and talking in her ear. Her gaze is on the ice, but she nods along with whatever he's saying.

Of the four women, Melody isn't exactly who I thought Knox would befriend.

He sort of burned a bridge with Willow, and therefore Violet. He never thought twice about getting to know Aspen.

It's just weird.

Melody smiles when I stop in front of them.

"Next goal is for you," I tell her.

Her smile widens into a full-blown grin.

And that's what I do. I don't know if it's the feeling of my girl cheering for me or the adrenaline of what we went through after the last game. *After.* I'd left mid-game when I'd noticed them all gone.

I had to pay a hefty fine to the team, but they didn't suspend me once they found out what had happened. So all's well that ends well.

An LA player checks me into the glass. The hit is hard enough to rattle my skull in my helmet, but he's gone before I can shove him away.

It's a big fat sign to keep my head in the game, *not* on solving Melody's mysteries.

Of which she has quite a few.

I glance over just in time to see her, Violet, and Greyson heading up the aisle.

"Rhodes!" Coach screams.

The puck goes sailing past me.

For fuck's sake.

I chase after it, barely managing to gain control before an LA player tries to crash into me. I hop over his flailing stick and pass it fast to Church. Church gives it to Lawson in the center, and I coast down toward the LA goalie.

It comes to me. It's perfectly placed, somehow gliding between an LA player's legs, and I shoot before the puck has time to stop. It sails right over the goalie's shoulder and into the net.

Hat trick.

Church, Lawson, and the rest of my teammates skate around me as I go off celebrating. They pat my helmet, tap their sticks against my legs. I grin, victorious, and go to the bench.

My gaze goes right back to where Melody is.

Should be.

She missed it.

Steele shrugs. Miles and Willow turn around, looking back up the aisle to the opening at the top of the section. There are people, but I can't see if they spot her.

Damn.

The goal was for her, regardless of whether or not she saw it, but... shitty time to go get a beer.

My vague annoyance, however, bleeds into worry the longer she's gone.

And when Knox and Steele hurry up the steps, my stomach knots. I glance at the timer and lean forward, bracing my elbows on my thighs. My lungs are tight, my muscles burning. It's the good sort of pain that comes with a hard workout. I'm conditioned for it. But I'm *not* conditioned for this sort of worry over Melody.

I glance at the bench. Then at the clock.

Two minutes remaining.

Two minutes for my friends to return Melody to her seat.

Two minutes to last so I don't get fired in the middle of the playoffs.

57
MELODY

"I'm fine," I say over my shoulder to Violet.

I mean, I'm not. I've got another text from Henry, but this one...

He's in my hotel room. On the bed where Jacob and I had sex a few hours ago. The photo is of his legs extending out on the bed, like he's sitting back against the headboard. My bag and Jacob's are both visible in the frame.

"Well, I'm following you either way," Violet says. "This is always when it happens."

I shake my head. "When what happens?"

"The bad shit."

"I just need a minute." I duck into the restroom.

Greyson groans, but Violet keeps following. Aspen, too. I go for a stall, but Aspen grabs my arm and steers me into the handicap one. The restroom is deserted. No one in their right mind would come in here *now*. There were only a few minutes left on the clock.

"Spill," Aspen demands.

I shift my weight. "I don't want to drag you into this."

"We're in it," Violet counters. "Jacob is Grey and Steele's best friend. We're *in* it, so just... trust us."

Ugh.

I take my glasses off and touch my index finger to the inner corner of my eye. My head aches. I don't know if it's from stress or remembering.

How can I trust them? They're practically babies.

Same as Jacob, you idiot.

They're out of college. I'm not their professor.

"My ex-husband is in my hotel room."

They stop. Aspen's mouth drops open, and Violet just shakes her head slowly.

"How do you know?" Aspen asks.

I pull up the photo and hand them my phone.

"He didn't say anything else?"

"No." I take it back and shut it down. I'd rather not look at it any more than I must. "No demands, no threats. Just the picture, which I guess in and of itself is a threat."

"Maybe he couldn't get into the arena," Aspen suggests. "The police know what he looks like, maybe he spotted extra security and freaked out."

"Breaking into your hotel room would be the next best thing," Violet agrees. "He's messing with you."

It's obvious that he's messing with me. It's obvious that he wants to torment me as long as he can.

What's not obvious is how to stop him.

"I got away from him not once, but *twice*. That's got to count for something. That's got to piss him off—"

"He found you twice, though, didn't he?" Aspen frowns. "Or was it three times?"

I touch the scar on my neck again. It's the one I often go back to. "No... I don't think he tried to kill me. Not like that. He's smart."

"Then who did?"

That's just it. "I have no idea."

We all go quiet.

"Vi?" Greyson's voice drifts into the restroom.

"We're okay," she calls back. To me, she says, "You should tell the police."

I agree.

We stay up in the hallway until an officer meets us at our location. I show him the picture, explain that he's texting me even with a restraining order—honestly, all of it. He has officers dispatched to the hotel.

Knox and Steele join us in the hall before the end of the game. Knox steps up next to me and shows me a video of Jacob scoring.

"He was looking for you," Knox says.

I shrug. "There's not much I can do about that."

I show him the picture *I* got, and his face pales.

"Well, shit."

"My sentiments exactly," I reply.

I text Jacob, although I don't expect him to see it until he's back in the locker room. Something along the lines of, we're safe, it's fine. Knox relays the same thing to Miles and Willow, who are still at our seats.

"Ma'am?" The officer returns, his expression decidedly blank. "We checked your room, as well as the rest of the hotel. There was no sign of your ex-husband."

A sick feeling creeps up my throat.

"Thanks," I manage.

He nods apologetically. "Stop by the front desk and get a new key."

"Did they say how he even got in?"

He frowns. "No. Besides the photo, there's no evidence

that he *did* get into the room. We're still checking into that."

"Thanks."

Greyson and Steele move in front of me.

"Thanks, Officer," one of them says quietly.

And then we're shuffled away.

It isn't until Jacob appears, the game over and the crowd mostly gone, that I lose control of my calm facade. I fall into his chest, and the torrent of fear, of *tears*, lets loose.

"I can't do this anymore," I cry, gripping his shirt. "I don't want to live in fear."

He kisses the top of my head. "I know. That's why we're going to end it."

"How?"

I don't say the rest of what I'm thinking. That if Jacob goes up against Henry, he might not win. That's just fear.

A new expression crosses Jacob's face. One of determination. And I find myself mirroring it. Drawing on his strength. Because I definitely need some of it.

"We'll figure it out. But not here. We need to be on home turf. Somewhere that will put him off balance."

I raise my eyebrows. "Denver?"

"Nope." He glances at his friends. "We're going back to Crown Point."

58

JACOB

I t just feels better in Crown Point. I can't explain it.

I wrap my arm around Melody, tucking her close into my side, as we walk toward the CPU arena. We took a red-eye and landed early this morning, and now we're just killing time. Hoping to get spotted so Henry chases us.

Which means going a little more public than Melody might want.

"Are you sure about this?" she asks for the hundredth time. "Once we go public..."

"I'm sure." I tighten my grip on her shoulder. "I'm so fucking sure, Melody."

Our *first* stop is the arena, where Coach Roake is holding an open practice. They're not in the playoffs this year, but he opens the rink through until the end of the NHL season to encourage fitness. He works on whatever skills his players need to improve upon.

I open the door for her, and we head inside. Greyson, Miles, Steele, and Knox are all meeting us there. Although it appears we're the first ones.

"Coach," I call.

He stands on the players' bench, looking at a clipboard, but his head comes up. He spots me, and a smile cracks his lips.

"Well, if it isn't Jacob Rhodes." His voice booms out, drawing attention.

I step up into the bench area and shake his hand.

"What brings you to Crown Point? You're in the middle of the playoffs." He narrows his eyes at me. "They didn't suspend you for a game, did they?"

"Not this time." I smile. "No, we just needed a little break. Our next game is in two days in Denver."

Most games happen every other day, but sometimes scheduling for television puts an extra day in between. And this time it's worked out in our favor.

He nods seriously. "Well, I'm glad to see you."

We turn our attention to the players on the ice. "Anyone promising?"

He points. One, two, three players.

"Hmm," I murmur.

"You bring your skates?"

I grin. "Of course. And I brought some friends..."

Greyson, Steele, Miles, and Knox come around the corner.

"Holy shit," one of the players on the ice says.

Coach greets all of them, slapping their backs. He pats Knox on the cheek. "You boys are welcome back any time."

Melody joins the other girls in the arena seats. I wink at her, then drop the bag with my skates. We lace up fast, all of us eager to get on the ice. I didn't bring a stick, but Coach orders one of the players to get us some from the equipment manager.

I step onto the ice, smiling over my shoulder at my friends.

It's been a while since we've all been on the ice together. Playing for the same side anyway.

That would be the goal.

"Jacob Rhodes." One of the players that Coach pointed out skids to a halt in front of me. "I took your place as right d-man."

I raise my eyebrows. "Well, pretty sure Tony Rodrigues took my place. You probably took his."

He shrugs and holds out his hand. "West. Griffin."

Well, fuck. Now I don't know if his first or last name is Griffin. I guess I'll just have to catch a glimpse of the back of his jersey as he skates away. Kind of pathetic, but whatever. He's got a cocky face that makes me want to punch him. But Greyson gave me the same vibe when I met him, and look how he turned out.

I shake it. "You any good?"

He nods, smiling. "I'm just here for two years. Per my contract with LA."

The very team that we're facing in the playoffs.

I appraise him with a new eye. He's already been drafted, then. I'm not *too* surprised, if he chose to come here. Coach Roake has a good reputation. I mean, he produced *us*. So...

"Congratulations," I say.

He smirks.

Greyson skates over, stopping sharply and sending a shower of ice over Griffin's legs. He hands me a stick. "Ready?"

I nod and glance at Griffin. "Well? You better bring your A game."

After a spontaneous scrimmage, in which we decimate

the CPU team, we follow Roake back into his office. He invites us back any time, to which we heartily agree, and we borrow his locker room showers before we return to the girls.

Melody tucks her hair behind her ear. Her hazel eyes sparkle behind her glasses.

She's wearing a dark-blue sweatshirt that has *book slut* embroidered on the breast. I don't have any idea where she pulled that out from, but she seems unperturbed about it. I keep looking at it—and therefore, her left tit—thinking that I'm misreading it.

Which wouldn't be the first time.

"Where to now?"

"Campus."

Greyson saw some of the players taking photos of us, their phones tilted in our direction when they broke for water. And sure enough, my social media notifications pick up right as we get onto CPU's property.

I ignore them in favor of dragging Melody away from our group and into the administration building. I'm entirely positive no one's going to remember Melody or give a shit that she's here. It's been two years. Sure, maybe a sophomore who's now a senior might recognize her... but whatever.

Her being recognized now would only help us wave the flags over our heads.

"My parents want us to come back here for fourth of July," I mention.

"To the house you took me for the snow day?"

I pause and let her words wash over me.

It's one thing to have her say she remembers—but it's another entirely for her to confirm it. Which means it's a good thing we're almost to our destination.

"That's the one," I confirm.

I stop in front of an open door. The office is clearly in use, which makes my mission even more daring. I pull her in and shut the door, then grab one of the chairs and fit it under the door handle. Finally, I yank the shade down.

Her gaze travels around the small room. It's not any different, minus some decorations that Melody never got around to putting up.

"This was my office."

"Sit down," I murmur, my hand on the small of her back, guiding her to the office chair behind the desk. Once she's seated, I grab a random paper.

She smiles. "I remember this." She runs her foot up the inside of my calf. "And what came next."

"You're going to come next," I reply.

She lifts her chin. "Better hurry, Jake. You might not mind getting caught..."

"We won't," I promise.

She lets me drag her pants down her legs and kneel between them. Her soft gasp when I drag her ass to the edge of the chair is delicious. Although the last time we were here, she wore a skirt that accentuated her hips. Now, I move aside the thong.

My dick twitches, standing straight up to attention.

"Your thongs will kill me."

She runs her fingers through my hair. "I wear them because of the expression on your face right now."

I groan and lean down. I run my nose along her pelvic bone, kissing just above the area she most wants me to touch. She's practically panting, tugging my hair, by the time I give in and suck her clit into my mouth.

"Oh my God," she moans. "Why is this hotter?"

"Because you're remembering the last time... although *this* time, I'm going to make you come."

She shifts her hips, needing more.

I give it to her. I fill her pussy with my fingers, thrusting them slowly in and out as I nibble and suck at her clit. I flick my tongue across it, graze it with my teeth. She unravels above me, arching and gasping.

And finally, she comes. Her nails rake across my scalp, and her cunt clenches on my wet fingers. I can't help but fall a bit more in love with her for her unabashed display.

When it releases her, she straightens her shirt and tries to catch her breath. But before she can, I stand and undo my pants. My cock springs out, ready and waiting for her mouth. I grab her head and pull her forward. The tip slides across her lips, then her tongue. Tracing lazily as she opens for me.

"You're perfect," I tell her.

I thrust into her mouth. She sucks and licks until I go too deep for that. She gags around my length. I take my pleasure from the tears suddenly rolling down her cheeks, and the tight squeeze of her throat, and the choking noises she makes.

She doesn't push me away. Her hands come up and grip my ass, holding me tighter against her.

More. Harder. She'd say those words if she could speak.

My cum shoots out, hitting the back of her throat. She swallows reflexively around me, and I linger in her mouth before I pull out the rest of the way.

She sags back in the chair.

"Good girl," I say, tucking her hair back.

She takes her glasses off and cleans the lenses without comment. She hoists her pants back into place as I wipe my dick clean and tuck it away.

Not a moment too soon, the doorknob jiggles. It hits the chair, stopping it from opening, and Melody gapes at me.

I shrug. We wait in silence for a minute, then two. So long that I think I imagine I hear her heartbeat. She grabs my hand, lacing her fingers with mine. After another minute of nothing, I remove the chair and crack the door.

The hallway is empty.

We leave it open and hurry away, and it isn't until we reach the stairwell that we both burst into laughter.

59
MELODY

NHL superstar quintet returns to their roots.

Rhodes & friends join Crown Point U's practice—here's what you need to know about the hottest rookies in hockey.

Whiteshaw, rinse, repeat. Knox Whiteshaw's rumored trade to the Colorado Titans seems confirmed as he's seen skating with Jacob Rhodes.

"People come up with the weirdest headlines," I murmur.

I wrap my arms around Jake from behind, resting my chin on top of his head, and he hums his agreement. He's sitting on the couch in the house that feels so strangely familiar. It's like a dream, in a way. Not so much a memory as a figment of my imagination.

If we didn't have a house full of his friends, I'd be

tempted to sit on his lap and kiss him until we both combusted.

"Is Knox joining the Titans?" I ask in his ear.

"I don't know. The Titans' GM asked me about him. He knows our history. But I can't really say..."

"This should get the message to Henry, though. I mean, *Rolling Stone* covered it."

He glances up at me. "We're a big deal, songbird."

There's another *familiar* painting in this house. Actually, more than one. They're lighter, for sure. Not as heavy. And I kind of remember sitting at an easel in the guest room of the house I rented, painting one, then the next.

"I went to see you," he says.

It's in my line of sight, framed on the wall between the television and window, but I force myself to look back at Jacob.

"I went to see you and found the cameras laid out on the table, and no sign of you. Your toothbrush was gone, some clothes, but all your paintings were still in the other room. When you didn't come back..." He frowns. "I just wanted you. But I thought you found them and freaked out."

I don't know what to say to that.

"Cameras on the table..." I shut my eyes tight.

"You slut," Henry seethed. "You think I'd let you move to a new city, new job, and not keep an eye on you?" He shook his head. "And then to watch this fucker break into your house and plant these cameras, listening devices—"

They were both spying on me?

Just when I was starting to forgive Jacob...

"And then I learned he's a student," he continued.

He pressed a kiss to my lips, but I couldn't fucking move. I didn't react. I let him linger against my mouth until he was satisfied.

"You're in some deep shit, Mel."

I glared at him. "And you're not? Or did you forget the restraining order?"

He chuckled. "Don't worry about it. Where we're going, no one will give a fuck about a restraining order. Now..." He looked me up and down. "I don't think I need to remind you what I can share with the world if you don't comply. I'm sure your employers—previous and current—would be interested to know how a professor seduced her student."

The walls were closing in on me.

Why didn't I let Jacob walk me in?

Why didn't I stay at his house?

"They're going to notice I'm gone."

Jacob noticed.

But he didn't think I was taken. Henry was too smart for that. Maybe it was because I left without a struggle. There was a broken lightbulb that should've been a clue—but it would've been the only clue.

"I am not going to disappear on you on purpose," I tell him now.

He comes to stand in front of me, and his hand goes to the back of my neck.

"I know that," he says.

"If I disappear, it's because he—"

"I want to be able to find you wherever you go." He eyes me, his grip tightening ever so slightly. "I want to be able to track you down..."

Willow and Aspen both mentioned their guys tracking them, with or without phones.

My heart skips.

"Okay," I whisper.

His eyes light.

"Do it."

He kisses me. The force of it takes my breath away, and he's gone before I fully register—or react. He leaves me swaying in the middle of the room and pulls out something from a drawer. His expression might seem a little guilty, but I brush that off.

He would probably do this with or without my consent.

But I *do* consent, so we don't need to find out.

"Where?" I ask.

He traces a spot on my upper arm, on the inside. Like where a birth control implant would go. "Here."

"Okay."

We sit, and he carefully preps the area. I can't deny the shiver of anticipation that rushes through me. I'm expecting pain, sure, but also... I don't know. It's a weird form of security, isn't it?

"Wait." I grab his wrist and stop him from picking up the tool.

"What is it?"

"I just..." I have a sense of déjà vu. "You haven't done this before? To me?"

"No."

I stare at the tool, and I can imagine—no, I *know*—there's a pinch as it slides under the skin. But it doesn't hurt, not really.

Not comparatively.

How do I know that?

"Melody?"

"I..." I touch the back of my neck.

He immediately moves behind me, shifting my hair over one shoulder. His fingers on my skin raise goose-bumps, but I hold still as he probes.

"There's a little scar here."

A lump forms in my throat. "He put it there."

Jacob is silent.

"Henry put a tracker in me, Jake." I whirl around and grab the front of his shirt.

Thank *God* the others aren't in the room to witness my hysterics. Even though I have an excellent reason for them.

"You need to get it out."

He captures my wrists. "I will. But you need to breathe."

"He could've found me in New York—"

"It looks like a more recent scar," he says gently. "Like from the last few months."

Like...

I'm going to be sick. I jerk away from Jacob and practically sprint to the bathroom, dropping to my knees in front of the toilet. He follows me, collecting my hair as I throw up. It's pathetic and of weak constitution, but I can't help the turmoil churning me up on the inside.

When my stomach stops heaving, I rock back on my heels and wipe my mouth with the back of my hand. He pours me a cup of water and holds it to my lips, letting me sip it.

"You're okay," he murmurs.

"He could already be in Crown Point."

"*Good.* No one messes with us here."

I shudder and lean into him.

I'm pretty sure I'm in love with Jacob Rhodes. But the words stick, and after a minute he picks us up off the floor. He sits me down at the table, ordering me to stay, and disappears to find everyone else.

"He's here," Jacob announces once they're seated around me at the table. "He has a tracker in Melody."

Steele makes a noise in the back of his throat. "You're kidding."

They both glance at the insertion tool. It's a bit ironic, I think. I *wanted* Jacob to put one in me, only for that to trigger a phantom sensation.

But what I don't understand is how I could've forgotten if it was so new. If I can see the tool and feel it going into my skin, but not see him do it.

At first, I thought it was because he drugged me. I was asleep or something. Exactly what Jacob *wanted* me to think about my cousin. But that's not right, because then I wouldn't remember it at all.

So... when? How?

And what kind of sadistic mastermind is my ex-husband?

60

MELODY

Unknown: Meet me at your old house, and I won't kill your boy toy.

———

The back of my rented house comes into view. The yard is fenced, and I slip around to the gate. Then in. Jacob used to come in the back, I think. The lock was broken—and sure enough, it still is. Or perhaps Henry is inside, and he left it open for me.

I step into the dark house.

My heart is in my throat, but I ignore it and keep pressing forward. My skin is buzzing with adrenaline.

The house is familiar in the worst way.

There is where the lightbulb burst, alerting me to Henry's presence.

There is where Jacob pressed me against the wall after I slapped him in my classroom.

All the furniture is gone. The glass shards from the floor,

the little cameras, even the table where he presented his evidence of Jacob's deceit. All removed.

The house sits empty and silent, and I spin in a slow circle in the living room.

A creak sounds above me. My gaze is drawn to the ceiling, and I spend only a second wondering if he's up there.

Of course he is.

Haunting my bedroom.

I leave my purse on the kitchen counter and take the gun with me. There's a safety on the side. And it's loaded. Jacob gave me a tiny little crash course before he left it with me. And he made some mention of the bullets being small enough to not make *that* much of an impact.

Which right now is not really reassuring.

Can I pull the trigger not once, but twice? Or again and again until the chamber is empty?

I make it to the top of the stairs and turn into my old bedroom.

Henry stands in the center of the empty room. It makes me want to run in the other direction. But I'm here. I can't just run away again.

I clear my throat and step farther in, getting his attention.

"Ah, Melody. Beautiful, as always." His gaze sweeps my figure, and his attention lands on the gun in my hand. "Do you plan on using that?"

"Yes." I square my shoulders. "You continuously threaten me. You tried to kill me."

He scoffs. "Did I? When?"

I grit my teeth. If he takes one step toward me, I'm going to do it. I'm going to pull the trigger and end this madness. Never mind that it makes me sick to think about.

I hit the light switch. The overhead light comes on, and I lift my chin. I point to the scar.

"You're going to make me believe you didn't try to slit my throat?"

His jaw works.

"Come on, Henry. You can be honest for a second, I won't hold it against you." I laugh. It's cold and harsh, a mirror of how I feel when I look at him. "I woke up with enough head trauma to give me retrograde amnesia. My throat was stitched back together by a plastic surgeon. I looked like I had gone through a meat grinder—and you think I'm going to believe it wasn't *you*?"

"It wasn't." He squints at me. "You were in Beacon Hill."

"Where I grew up."

His expression morphs into sympathy. I saw it so many times when I thought he was my cousin. It explains why he was being so obtuse with the details. I'd bet it was a combination of him not wanting me to remember and also having no idea about the small stuff.

"You sucked as a cousin," I tell him. "But you were a monstrous husband."

He smiles. "Don't come crying to me when you figure out the real monster in your life, darling."

I lift the gun.

I just want it to be over.

"Tell me."

He steps forward.

My pulse skyrockets. *I can't let him touch me*. I don't know how to aim. I don't know if I'd hit him if I fired from this distance. Ten feet away, if that.

"Stop," I order.

He laughs. "You and I both know you're not going to pull the trigger."

He gets closer and closer, and I'm frozen. He's right—I can't. I can't do it.

What's wrong with me?

"You're not a murderer, Mel. You don't have that killer instinct." He snatches the gun out of my hand.

One minute I'm holding the weapon that gave *me* power, the next, I'm defenseless. And I hate it. I hate myself and I hate him for taking that from me. Stripping me down to nothing but fear.

The fear is familiar. It's cold, and it locks its hands around my throat. The room tilts. I remind myself to keep breathing, but there's another part of me that just wants to disappear. To slip away and avoid what comes next.

"Here's what's going to happen," he says in a soft voice. "You're going to come away with me, and we're never going to talk about Jacob *fucking* Rhodes ever again."

"No." I back away.

I'm afraid. And I may be weak, defenseless, but... I can't be as terrified as I used to be. The fear is there, but it hasn't tightened its grip.

"No, Henry. If you make me go with you, I'm going to talk about Jacob *fucking* Rhodes every day until I'm blue in the face."

He glowers at me.

"I love him," I say. "You don't have a hold on me. I love *him*."

"Melody..."

"No. Enough. Did you even like Natalie? Did you care about her at all?"

He makes a face—but I think he *did*.

"I remember," I whisper. "I remember falling in love with you. I remember that it wasn't all bad."

There are those earlier flashes. The ones where he held

doors, kissed my knuckles, gazed at me like I was the moon. It was a fantasy. A disastrous one. But I refuse to believe that he was acting the entire time. Which means he can love someone else the right way.

"Don't hurt them."

"I won't." He's looking right through me. "I won't hurt them, Mel, because they're not you. And you're the only one for me."

He points for me to go downstairs.

My feet move on their own. Slowly. Crawling along step by step until we reach the kitchen. The door is open, just the screen shut, and my heart skips.

"Hey, Henry," Jacob says. He comes out of the shadows like a phantom. "Melody might not've pulled the trigger— but I have no such qualms."

There's a noise like a gunshot, but muted. A spray of warm wetness across the back of my head and neck.

It takes my brain a second to catch up. To turn and register the weight of my ex-husband crashing into the wall and sliding down it. To register that Jacob just shot him.

There's blood coming out of Henry's temple.

Jacob didn't just shoot him—he aimed for his *head*.

I cover my mouth with my hand.

"What the fuck?" I whisper.

He pats me down. Checking for—I don't know. Wounds?

"He didn't touch me." I bat away his hands. "Stop. I'm fine."

I mean, okay, I'm not *fine*. I just watched him kill someone.

Jacob nods and directs me to stand in the corner. "Don't move. Don't touch anything."

I nod and fold my arms under my breasts. It's then that

I notice the gloves, and I have to remind myself that this confrontation was planned. That Jacob and his friends knew I was walking over here, that they were following.

That I wouldn't leave that house with Henry.

He opens the door and admits Greyson, Steele, Miles, and Knox. They're all wearing blue latex gloves, too.

"Someone get her booties," Jacob murmurs.

Huh?

Knox disappears back outside and returns with these blue... *things*. He bends down and puts one around my left foot, covering the sole of my shoe, and then the other. He doesn't even mind when I grab his shoulder for balance.

But once he's done, my attention goes back to Henry.

Dead Henry.

"I'm not sad about it," I say. "Does that mean I'm screwed up?"

That draws all their focus to me, and I focus on Jacob. He's already shaking his head, and he comes closer with a small smile.

"No, songbird. It means you're free."

61

JACOB

Melody stands still while we clean all traces of us from the house. We remove the cameras Greyson and Steele planted earlier today, before they met us at the arena.

At the end of the day, Henry Armstrong is a predictable asshole.

He was always going to try and lure Melody away.

He was always going to stage some sort of event at her old house.

In a way, it was almost too poetic for him to resist. But after we wipe down every surface Melody touched, retracing her path through the house, and all that's left to do is leave, Melody doesn't move.

She doesn't have a big reaction. Her eyes aren't filled with tears, her lips aren't tipped down. If anything, she seems confused about what we're doing.

I take her hand, and we leave that house behind.

There's still the matter of the tracker. We need to get it out, although Armstrong isn't a threat to her anymore. I don't like the thought of it under her skin.

"We're staying at the hockey house," Greyson says. "The girls are already there. Figured you two might want some privacy."

Melody blushes.

I grin.

"Thanks, man."

I didn't want to tell her, but there's blood in her hair. Instead of mentioning it, I simply guide her into my home and lock the door behind us.

"About time," a woman says.

Melody freezes.

I do, too, for a split second. Then I locate the woman in the center of my living room and quickly tuck Melody behind me.

She's older. Light-brown hair threaded through with silver and gray, fine wrinkles in the corners of her eyes. She might be in her sixties. She's slender, petite. Her clothes are perfectly fitted, and she just seems expensive. I've been around enough *almost-rich* people to know when they're trying too hard. And she's on the cusp.

She's got a cell phone in one hand and a gun in the other, but I have no idea who she is.

Judging from Melody's sudden rapid breathing, I have a feeling I should.

Why didn't I study Melody's family history with photos?

"Mom," she says on an exhale.

Wait. "She's dead," I say under my breath. "Remember?"

"Well, clearly not," Melody whispers back.

"I can hear you," the woman says. She points to the couch. "You should sit."

Melody steps out from behind me. I follow closely,

unwilling to give up any space. We perch on the couch, and her mother takes the armchair closest to me.

"Jessica Cameron," her mother introduces.

"Jacob Rhodes."

My attention is split between the gun resting on her thigh and her face.

"The famous hockey player," she supplies. It doesn't sound exactly nice coming out of her mouth. More like condemnation.

I shrug. I don't really think it applies in this context. In my home. With my woman. Facing her mother, who seems to have faked her death—or just lied about it—and has a gun.

"You're a ghost, Mrs. Cameron," I comment. "How did that happen?"

She waves her free hand. "A convenient lie. Melody, I've been searching for you."

"Why's that?" Melody's palm lands on my knee.

All the bad things Melody once told me about her mother come flooding back. The body shaming, the hatred. The way Melody sent her father to prison.

A cold feeling trickles down my spine.

"You were in such a bad state." Her mother tuts. "Your father wanted to make sure I followed up. He said you seemed frightened when you went to visit him."

Melody shrugs. "I went because he called me, and I thought it would help me remember."

"Memory is funny, isn't it?"

Mel glances at me, frowning slightly. She looks scared. More than she did before. And I can't help but wonder if her mother triggered a new memory.

"I think we need alcohol for this situation," I murmur. "Jessica?"

She narrows her eyes. "If you try anything, I shoot."

I hop up and go into the kitchen. I don't really want to leave them alone, but I manage to type out an SOS to Knox before I return with two glasses and a bottle of whiskey.

"How did you find me?" Melody asks her.

I pour the whiskey into the glasses. It gives me a good excuse to stand between them. To block Melody from her mother. *Just in case.*

"Your father and I wanted to keep tabs on you," Jessica replies. "After you left Henry. It just wasn't right."

I pause. "What?"

Her mother lets out a sigh, leaning back. She's *bored.* Exasperated.

However she thought this night would go, it wasn't quite like this.

"Your father approved of Henry. He came to the prison and asked for your father's blessing before he proposed to you, you know." She sniffs. "And then you divorced him and just disappeared? We advised Henry to fight for you, and we were so pleased when he sent word that he had found you again."

My blood runs cold.

Melody seems to be feeling the same, because her expression is stricken.

"That whole time, you knew Henry was holding me?"

"*Holding* you?" Jessica laughs. "He was loving you." The *duh* is implied.

"He was abusive." Melody jumps to her feet. "You don't see that? He did the same thing to me that Dad did to you—"

Jessica leaps to her feet, too, and the gun waves dangerously. "Don't talk about your father like that!"

I hold out my hands. "Okay, okay."

"You wanted to keep tabs on me," Melody repeats. "When?"

She waves her hand. "After you left him. With *nothing*, mind you. You drained your accounts and disappeared."

I laugh.

Really.

We were so focused on Henry being the bad guy, I guess we forgot to account for her insane parents. Of course, up until five minutes ago we thought her mom was dead.

"Why'd you fake your death?"

She sniffs. "It was your father's idea. You were with Henry, but you refused to speak on your father's behalf. He had a parole hearing coming up, and they passed him by because I was the only one who gave a shit."

Understanding dawns on Melody's face. "You wanted me to tell them to release him? After what he did to me?"

"He should've been out already," Jessica snaps. "And then he was framed with the prison riot murder and—"

"You can't be serious." I shake my head.

"And you were living the high and mighty life in California while I struggled to even get private visits—"

Jesus, she means conjugal visits, doesn't she?

Tears fill Melody's eyes. "I was not living the *high and mighty life*, Mom."

Jessica suddenly raises the gun. "Don't you call me that. I am *not* your mother. I haven't been for a long time."

Fuck.

This is derailing, and I scramble for something else to say. To distract her from her anger. And I land on... "You've been tracking Melody? You were the one, not Henry."

Jessica glowers at her daughter, but she addresses me when she says, "She found me."

Melody stills.

"Can you explain that?" I don't know the best course of action, so I pick up the glass of whiskey and hold it out to her.

She ignores it.

"I was in Beacon Hill, and Melody was..." She waves her hand in another vague motion. "I don't know. She saw me. She knew I was supposed to be dead. Henry had broken that news. We didn't have a funeral, although I assume he told her we did. It would've been a lovely service."

Melody sits suddenly, grabbing her glass and downing the liquor in one mouthful. If I didn't want to stay alert, I'd copy her.

"I saw you," Melody says. She closes her eyes and leans into me. "I saw her. I was..."

"Hysterical," Jessica supplies. "Causing a scene in the middle of downtown."

"I—"

"You are no daughter of mine," Jessica repeats. "We've made that perfectly clear since you put Jack in prison for a mistake. A mistake he's spent the last *seventeen years* paying for."

Melody laughs. "A mistake. He killed someone in prison, *Mother*."

"He was framed," she shouts.

I feel sick. "You tried to kill your own daughter?"

"Well, I didn't actually do it."

Melody's got a tight grip on my arm. "When did you put a tracker in me?"

"In the hospital," Jessica says. "You were out of it, and you didn't recognize me."

"I'm going to be sick," Melody says.

"You're going to *sit and stay*," her mother barks.

It shocks Melody into stillness.

The storytelling has come to an end—and clearly Jessica Cameron came here to fulfil something. Something made her buy a gun and drive up from Beacon Hill to Crown Point to confront her daughter.

"So, what's it going to be, Mrs. Cameron?"

Her eyes narrow.

"You clearly want something from us. Or you want to kill Melody.... Which isn't going to happen."

"My *husband* wants Melody out of the picture." She eyes her daughter. "And I'm inclined to agree. He has another parole board hearing coming up. It would look favorably if his only daughter, who was going to testify for his release, was brutally murdered."

Bile rises up my throat. "You'd hurt her to free your husband?"

"Yes. I *love* him. And she's the reason we've been apart for seventeen years." She's back to spitting hatred.

Melody's eyes are brimmed with tears.

But then... *sirens*.

Jessica's head whips around, listening.

"You kill us, you get caught," I assure her. "Whatever plan you had is done, or else you'll never see your husband from a prison three states away."

She lets out a hissing breath and jumps to her feet. I follow, dragging Melody behind me. We watch Jessica skirt the room and make a beeline for the front door.

"We're just going to let her go?" Melody whispers, so quietly I barely hear it.

I mean... *yeah*. Absolutely.

"I've had enough of you being held at gunpoint tonight," I answer.

There's a muffled *thud* from the front porch. Then the

door creaks open again, and Knox appears. Walking backward, dragging Melody's mother in with him.

"Knocked her out," he grunts. "Where do you want her?"

"Just there." I point to a spot on the floor.

Melody stares at us.

Putting my gloves back on, I carefully remove the gun I used to shoot Henry and put it in her mom's hand. I take her gun and tuck it in the waistband of her jeans.

"Okay, now what?" Knox asks.

I practically shove Melody into his arms. "Now you both get out of here."

He takes her. She doesn't protest. I think she might be in shock. Either way, it's safer for her to go. The police can't find her with Henry's blood in her hair. And I don't want to put her through an interrogation.

So, off she'll go.

"Jessica." I kneel in front of her and shake her arm.

Her eyes crack open. "What...?"

"Leave Melody out of your story telling."

"Or what?" Her fingers tighten around my gun.

"Or I'll make sure your husband is dead before his next parole hearing." Now gloveless, I remove the gun from her hand. I'm careful about where my fingers wrap around the barrel. Got to leave my prints where it's believable, after all.

I set it on the coffee table and move to the door.

The sound of sirens is getting louder, and I smile to myself.

She's going to rot in prison if it's the last thing I do.

62

MELODY

"He's fine," Knox reassures me.

I pace the hockey house. It's weird to be here. College kids live here. Well, maybe not at the moment. Except for Jacob's friends, who are either sleeping or zoned out on the couches in the living room. It's set up to host a lot of people and *feels* like a college house.

I'm at least ten years older than all of them.

"Can you sit?" Knox grabs my arm and leads me into the kitchen. He points at the small table, smiling when I go without a fight.

Jacob literally forced me out of the house. Knox sped away into the night. We turned the corner onto another street only a moment before police cars screeched onto Jacob's road from the other end.

Now we're waiting for them to be done questioning him.

Greyson and Steele are playing a video game. Miles and Willow haven't come downstairs. And I don't know where Violet and Aspen are. Sleeping, hopefully. It's the middle of the night.

I think I'm traumatized from everything that's happened. All the coping mechanisms in the world can't help me right the jumbled mess of emotions in my head.

Knox sets down a cup of coffee in front of me. He's got one for himself, too, and he drags out the chair opposite mine.

The next best thing, besides sinking into a dissociative state and staying there forever, is a distraction. And lucky for me, Knox looks like he's got a lot on his mind. Which is all I need.

"So..." I raise my eyebrow.

"What?"

"Are you going to tell me what's going on with you?" I just get the feeling like we're friends. Whether or not he'll admit it is another thing entirely. "You've been weird."

He scoffs. "No, I haven't."

"I'm pretty sure you have," I counter. "You asked me to read a book for you. And even before that..." I motion to him. "Squirrely."

"I'm not *squirrely*."

I laugh. "Whatever you say."

He presses his lips together. He has the decency to look a little guilty, and after a minute, he blows out a breath. "I got served."

My stare is probably blank. Because I don't know what the fuck that means.

"With... papers."

"Legal papers?"

He nods. He opens his phone and goes into his voice-mails. Then to the deleted ones, which apparently don't go away even after you delete them.

He hits play.

"*Hey, Knox. It's Aurora. It's been a while... I need you to call me back. There's some things we need to discuss. It's kind of urgent.*"

I tilt my head. "That was vague."

Then it dawns on me. "Aurora as in—*Aurora McGovern*?" The author. "What the fuck, Knox?"

He rubs his hand down his face. "Yeah."

"Legal papers—what, did you plagiarize her book or something?"

Knox bursts out laughing. "You think I'd do that?"

"No." I narrow my eyes. "But if it's not that, then..."

He lifts one shoulder. He seems *tired*. And a little beat up. Which might explain the defeat in his voice when he says, "Well. There's a little issue of us being married."

I choke.

"And her wanting to *not* be married anymore."

Holy.

Shit.

"You—how—?"

He waves his hand. "That doesn't matter. The thing that matters is that she served me with fucking divorce papers and expects me to just roll over and sign them."

I stare at him. "You can't just..."

"Not sign them," he finishes. "That's exactly what I'm going to do. In fact, I already did it. I sent back the documents with my reply, which is all that was required. A big, fat, *no thank you*."

He sits back and glowers at his coffee mug.

And me? I don't know *what* to do. Because bits and pieces of the fight to get Henry to sign my divorce papers come back to me—and it wasn't pretty. It was an all-out brawl via our lawyers. Because of the restraining order, I didn't have to step foot in the same room as him.

"Knox—"

"Can we just drop it, Melody? Please." He looks at me with what I can only describe as fucking puppy-dog eyes. Batting his lashes at me.

Ugh.

"Fine," I snap. "But I reserve the right to bring it up again."

He raises his hands in surrender. "And I reserve the right to ignore it."

I snort.

The front door creaks open, and I shoot to my feet. I don't spare Knox another glance as I hurry to Jacob. He barely gets the door closed before I fling myself at him.

"Hey." He catches me easily. "Hey, we're okay. We're good."

Doubtful.

"Your mom was arrested for killing Henry," he says in my ear. "You've been here all night. Okay?"

He framed her. He shot my ex-husband and framed my mother for it. It wasn't planned—it was an opportunity that he seized, and in doing so he eliminated the threats from our lives. My life.

There's just my dad sitting in prison. And maybe one of them can still access the tracker Mom put my neck. It draws my attention as soon as I think of it. It could be a figment of my imagination, a way my brain wants to work me up, but it does the trick. Panic rises swift and sure in my chest, until I can barely breathe.

"You need to get the tracker out of me," I say. "I can—I can *feel* it. Jacob. She put it there when I was doped up in the hospital. What kind of sick joke—"

"We'll take it out," he assures me. "A doctor will do it. Okay?"

"Not good enough. It needs to come out now."

Knox frowns at us from the kitchen doorway. "Who knows how to stitch wounds?"

I shake my head. I don't know, I don't *care*.

"Get it out," I demand.

Jacob catches my hands. "Okay. Okay, songbird, we'll get it out. Just breathe for me."

Breathing is hard. I go back to the table and gulp down mouthfuls of the coffee Knox made, ignoring that it tastes *awful*. His cup sits untouched, and it's no wonder. I get grounds in my teeth, coating my tongue.

Yuck.

"Got anything stronger?"

Jacob cracks a smile. Knox goes to the freezer and unearths a chilled bottle of vodka. I grimace but accept it, taking a swig. It burns on the way down, and the smell fills my nose. I take another sip.

"I'll get the first-aid kit," Knox murmurs. He slips past us, leaving me and Jacob alone.

We stare at each other for a long moment.

"You framed her," I finally say.

He smirks.

Knox and Miles return together with the first-aid kit. The latter pulls a knife out of his shorts pocket and flips it open. Knox takes it and disinfects it with rubbing alcohol over the sink.

Jacob comes up and slips his hand around the back of my neck, through my hair. He tips my head back and kisses me softly.

"Sit down," he says, barely pulling back enough for space between our lips.

My knees bend, and I guess I'm lucky the chair is there to catch me.

He takes a moment to lay out supplies. A thread and

needle in a plastic sleeve for sutures—in case of emergency, maybe, but definitely not the average first-aid kit item— plus gauze and bandages.

I swallow. Then lift the bottle back to my lips and close my eyes as I drink one gulp, then two. I'm getting warmer, which is a good sign.

Suddenly Jacob is behind me, raking his fingers through my hair. His nails on my scalp feel too good, and I lean back into him. I hum.

"I'm putting your hair up," he says, ducking to kiss just behind my ear. "To keep it out of the way."

I offer a hair tie from my pocket.

He loops my hair through it, doing an okay job at a messy bun. Then something wet touches the back of my neck.

"Just cleaning the area," he says. "Keep drinking."

Is it me, or is he anxious?

Knox comes over and sits in front of me. He raises his eyebrows and offers his hand.

"You want a drink, too?" I'm on the fast track to getting blasted.

"I want you to take one more sip," he says.

I shrug and do it, and he reaches out and touches the bottom of the bottle. Lifting it just a bit higher, until I'm almost choking on the vodka pouring into my mouth. He whisks the bottle away and takes my hand.

Jacob makes some noise behind me.

"Easy, dude," Knox snaps. "Don't be a dick."

I giggle.

"Now, Melody," Jacob says. His voice floats over my head. "I need you to stay very still."

"Maybe you should put your head down," Knox suggests.

He pulls my arm up and folds it on the table, then guilds me forward so my forehead rests on the bend. I breathe in slowly as fear takes over.

Is this a mistake?

But then Jacob's hand is on my shoulder, his fingers digging in and loosening the muscles. "It's going to hurt, songbird."

"I know." I shut my eyes.

"Squeeze my hand." Knox's fingers slip into my hand. "Try to break it, I dare you."

Well, fine. I grip it, making some noise under my breath. This is fine. Everything is f—

Ouch.

I bite my tongue. It's an involuntary thing. Habit from when I was a teenager and Dad was in one of his rages. Back then, most of his violence was all manipulative, emotional damage. It wasn't until he struck me when I was seventeen that I realized I should do something about it.

And now the metallic taste of blood fills my mouth, and I'm reminded of every horrible thing my mother ever said to defend him. How she fed off his bad mood—especially if it was taken out on her—and amplified it in my direction.

Picking at my clothes.

My weight.

Forcing me on a scale or wrapping a measuring tape around my waist.

Withholding food, even.

The endless battle of a mother against her fat child.

Something warm trickles down my neck and onto my arm. It matches the tears that fall from my eyes to the table, dripping off my eyelashes. The pain in my neck spikes. I taste blood on my lips, and I grip Knox's hand so hard it does feel like I might break it.

And then the pain eases.

Still there, still aching. Something clacks against the table beside my arm.

Hot new pain replaces the old. A stab, a dragging sensation.

"Almost done," Jacob says. "You're doing so good."

It would be worse if I was sober.

But the stitching grows, and the vodka welcomes me into the darkness. My hold on Knox's hand loosens.

And off I go.

63

JACOB

I look down at the chip I pulled from Melody's neck. It wasn't too deeply planted, and not too hard to get out. For someone who has no idea what they're doing, I don't think I did it *that* poorly. I got it out fast, stopped the bleeding. Didn't cause too big of a wound.

Besides, she's got mine in her now. In the same place. She passed out as I was stitching it closed, and now it's protected by a layer of antiseptic ointment and bandages.

My phone goes off, and I leave Melody where she is on the couch in the basement. I sneak back upstairs and dial the number the text provided.

"This is Anthony Strouse."

"Warden," I greet him. "Jacob Rhodes."

The sun is just rising. I step out onto the front porch and take a seat on the steps. It's so peaceful in Crown Point. It makes me want to come back, forget about my high-profile career, and just raise a bunch of babies with Melody.

Although she made some comment about maybe not being able to have kids, so...

I don't know.

"What can I do for you, Mr. Rhodes?"

"It's come to my attention that one of your inmates has been complicit in... other crimes."

He's silent.

"Namely, conspiracy to murder not one but two people."

"I'm listening."

"The police are already looking into this. But privileges for this inmate should be closer examined. After all, it's your monitoring system that failed us. One dead, another ended up in the hospital because of their actions."

"Whose actions?"

I smile. "Jack Cameron. And his wife, Jessica. Newly back from the dead herself, might I add."

He clears his throat.

"You knew a woman had been visiting him. And you also knew that she didn't have a valid ID. Yet you let her in anyway. Isn't that right?"

"I don't control my guards' decisions—"

"But you're the captain of the ship, Warden. And if we can't trust you, who can we trust?"

He scoffs.

"Here's what's going to happen. You're going to put Jack Cameron in solitary confinement until these new charges are brought against him."

"You do not have the authority to make such orders, boy."

I pull my phone back slightly and hit *send* on the images Bill sent me. Of Anthony Strouse naked with a woman who certainly isn't his very devoted, loving wife. Who certainly isn't the mother of his four children.

Bill still has his uses.

"Where—"

"The press in Stone Ridge might find these interesting."

"You dare to threaten—"

"I do," I interrupt. "Test me. Solitary confinement by noon today, or the photos will be blasted across every *fucking* platform I can find."

I hit the *end* button.

Today, Caleb Asher will get started on filing an order to prevent contact between Melody's parents and herself. A prosecutor will examine the claims we've made. And an investigator will rule Henry's death an open-and-shut case.

Sometimes cops aren't lazy—but they're always predictable. And an obvious suspect is the right one more often than not.

Our job is to make sure they don't look elsewhere.

Like at Melody.

But now her father is taken care of, and so is her mother. In a roundabout way. It would've been tidier to finish both of them off and be done with them all together... I'm just not sure Melody would stomach that.

Her memories are coming back. She doesn't always say it, but I like to think of it like a window inching open. She might not notice the cool breeze until she goes looking for the source. Little triggers—good and bad.

I head back downstairs and sit on the floor in front of the couch, leaning against it. She's so damn peaceful. A little bit drunk, in her sleep, but I appreciate the way her brows aren't furrowed. There aren't little stress lines around the edges of her mouth.

Her hand is hanging over the edge, and I take it in mine, careful not to wake her. I tip my head back, resting it on the couch cushion in front of her stomach.

Tomorrow we go back to the real world.

Denver for game three against LA.

Speaking of.

Me: Do we have practice tomorrow?

Church: …

Me: What?

Church: It's the middle of the night, Rhodes. Wtf?

Me: It's seven a.m. on the East Coast. Pretty sure you're the only one who thinks five a.m. is middle of the night.

Church: Should I even ask why the fuck you're not in CO?

Me: No

Church: Morning practice at 10.

Me: You could've said that initially

My phone rings.

I answer it, scowling at the floor. "What?"

"What do you mean, *what*? Why are you on the East Coast?" Church doesn't sound the least bit groggy, after all his talk about it being the middle of the night.

"Holy shit," I murmur. "Are you just getting in?"

"No." *Defensive.*

"Yes, you are. Who'd you fuck?"

"None of your goddamn business," he growls. "I'm the team captain. How am I supposed to explain—"

"You won't. We're flying back today."

"Where are you?"

"Crown Point. In Maine—"

"I know where Crown Point is, you dipshit. I went to Shadow Valley."

The rival fucking school.

I groan. "How did I not know that about you?"

He chuckles, quiet for a moment. Then, "Your girl okay?"

I glance back at Melody. She doesn't seem bothered by

my soft talking, but I hop to my feet and head into the kitchen anyway. I'm too amped up to sleep. I'd love to, but...

Steele and Greyson are already there.

"Hey," I greet them. I put my call on speaker phone. "Did you know Camden Church went to Shadow Valley?"

Greyson shakes his head. "When did he graduate? Like ten years ago?"

Church groans. "Four years ago, asshole."

"Oh. I thought you actually had a reason for playing like a grandfather."

I burst out laughing. "Grandpas don't have random hookups."

"I didn't," Church snaps. "I'm hanging up on you now. And just know if you're not back in Denver by practice tomorrow, I'm going to have your head."

"Yeah, yeah."

The line goes dead. I toss my phone on the counter and rub my eyes.

"Where's Miles?"

"He went out for a run," Steele answers. "Knox finally passed out upstairs. Girls are getting ready, except for Willow. No idea what she's doing."

I stop for a moment.

It's nice to have people. To be surrounded again. I missed out on this portion in school, happier to live in my parents' empty house than be bothered by the whims of five other guys. But now that I'm on my own...

Maybe I should've done that.

"You're grinning like a sap," Steele comments.

I wipe the smile off my face and scowl at him instead.

Greyson shakes his head. "Coffee?"

"Definitely." Because I've had a total of zero hours of

sleep and I'm running on fumes. My adrenaline has long since abandoned me.

"I chartered us a flight," Greyson adds. He slides me a mug. "For noon. It'll put us in Denver around three."

A five-hour flight, minus the two-hour time change— but then his words register.

"Wait. You *chartered* a flight?"

He makes a face. "Dad's got a private jet. His crew knows it's available for my use when he's not using it. And since he's in New York to woo Governor White for the time being, it's free."

Well. That's unexpectedly nice.

I finish my coffee and head back downstairs. I shift Melody's legs into my lap and get comfortable, and soon enough, I'm asleep.

Until Melody starts crying anyway.

"Shh." I cup her cheek.

She blinks rapidly in the low light. She lets out a noise, somewhere between a whimper and sigh, and I move over her. I tug her shorts down. She hugs me to her, and I nudge her panties aside.

My cock is rock-hard and ready, and I easily slide into her.

It feels right like that. A weird sort of comfort I can't explain—for both of us, I think. Because she relaxes, her fingers drifting up into my hair.

"You had a nightmare," I say, kissing the corner of my mouth.

"Sorry." She turns her head and kisses me better. Direct contact. She nips at my lower lip, bringing her legs up and locking her ankles around my back.

I love that she wants this as much as I do.

Still. "Don't apologize."

"I'm not."

I smirk. "You just said sorry."

She shrugs, meeting my eyes. "Well, now that this is happening, I'm not sorry. Now please fuck me like you mean it."

She lifts her hips a bit, and I bite back my own groan of appreciation.

"What if I want to make love?"

She makes a face. Something cross.

"Songbird," I say on a laugh.

"I love you, but I really need you to move faster."

My heart stops. "You love me?"

"I dreamed about moving to Crown Point for the first time," she whispers. "I spotted a man I'd later find out was *Jacob Rhodes* sitting in my class and staring at me with pure awe on his face. I'd never seen anything quite like it. Even Henry never looked at me like that at the height of his... courtship. Maybe even then, I knew we'd do something crazy special together."

"So..."

"Yeah, I do," she says. "But not only that, I'm in love with you, Jacob Rhodes."

64
MELODY

Ask anyone, and they'll easily tell you that I don't like hockey very much. Not the violence of it anyway. I like the speed. I like the way Jacob looks in his gear, decked out in blue and mint green and white.

Which is why I'm currently painting him.

Game six—and maybe the last game—against LA. The Titans have won three, LA two. Apparently, if Jacob's team wins tonight, that means they move on to round three. If they lose, we're heading back to LA for game seven.

The logistics and rules of the game make sense, too.

Jacob's friends are in the suite with me, along with Lucy, Theo, Caleb, and Margo. Caleb said they came along so he could personally deliver the news that my parents will not be contacting me anymore. After a video conference hearing, a judge approved our case.

So that's that.

Mom was arrested for killing Henry—although I have no idea if that will stick or not—and Dad was thrown in solitary confinement awaiting an arraignment on new charges. Seemed a bit conspicuous, but they both knew that Mom tried to kill me. Not once, but twice.

That fucks me up when I think about it too hard.

Jacob surprised me in the suite earlier today with an easel and paints.

Now I've got the spread of the players on the ice below me, but all I can see is one. I sketched fast, threw down layers of paint to capture the shadows and highlights of the arena. Then I place him on it.

I barely pay attention to the score. There's a spot for the glowing red numbers at the top of the painting, plus the team abbreviations.

"Melody!" Knox comes and drops onto the chair next to me. "Can you paint me next? I'll pose for it."

I glance at him, cracking a smile. "Only if you balance on one skate the whole time."

"Done," he says instantly. "I'll send it to Aurora so she knows what she's missing."

I snort.

Still can't believe he has a wife. A wife who wants a divorce...

That's not going to end well.

Instead of asking him about it, though, I just keep painting.

"Do you think I'm nuts?"

I sigh and set down the paintbrush. I face him, frowning at the concern etched in his expression. "Do you care if I do?"

"Yeah. We're friends. Right?"

"Oh. Um, yeah."

"I tell you shit, you tell me shit. We're close. Like, best friends."

Oh boy. "Knox."

"Yeah?"

"We're—"

"Well, you can't say no. Because Jacob's my best friend, obviously, and Miles is my brother. And I love Greyson and Steele. But you're the one who listens."

He's giving me a freaking puppy-dog look again. Big eyes that he bats at me in some attempt to manipulate the situation. But I don't even know what he wants. And what if he wants something I can't give him?

"Go away." I swat at him and focus on my painting again. I like this. Painting in a high-energy place, surrounded by people. I think the adrenaline is helping— and it's such a contrast to the sharp twist of loneliness that accompanied my other paintings.

I remember them now. The bird, the portraits. More that Henry sold overseas, without my consent. I didn't even know he shipped them until I realized they were missing.

"Melody."

Knox pauses.

"Mel."

Pause.

I don't even glance at him.

"Song—"

"If you finish that word, you're going to get a black eye," I warn.

He grins. "Just admit that you're my best friend."

I roll my eyes. "No."

"I'm her best friend," Lucy says. She comes over and stops in front of Miles, her hands planted on her hips. "You can't kick me out."

"I'll be the reserve. Backup." Knox kicks his legs out and winks at her. "You're all the way in New York, after all. And I just bought a condo in the same building as Jacob and Melody."

I whip around. That warrants a response. "Excuse me?"

He spreads his arms wide. "Meet the new center for the Colorado Titans, baby. This is why we're best friends. Because your soon-to-be-husband and me are teammates once more."

Lucy groans. "Knox."

I'm stuck on the soon-to-be-husband part.

"Miles, Knox ruined the surprise."

Knox's younger brother hurries over and rips Knox out of his seat. He shoves him out of the suite, following close behind.

Lucy smiles. It's so fake. "You didn't hear that."

I don't think I'm breathing.

"Mel?"

Is Jacob proposing? "When? Why? Where?"

She grabs my hands. "Take a deep breath."

I cannot.

"Melody Cameron."

"I'm fine." I'm so not fine. I'm hyperventilating.

I turn back to the painting, trying to slow my exhales. My chest hurts, my throat is tight. Jacob proposing. He was just going to spring it on me?

I have trust issues. All caps. Bolded. Underlined. Italicized.

TRUST ISSUES.

And he's just going to spring a proposal on me?

After the way my last marriage went?

Yeah, focusing on the painting isn't enough. I stand and go to the wall of glass, so close my nose almost touches it. The Titans are ahead by two. Jacob's skating his best, according to his friends. They're on the edges of their seats, too.

The clock ticks down.

I glance back at the painting, the urge to run bubbling up inside me. My muscles twitch with the need to give in to the instinct.

Run and never come back.

Then I remember the first time I saw Jacob. That dream I had, which is really more of a memory than anything else. Seeing him for the first time. Feeling... something.

Something potentially good but also addicting.

So I guess I could run. I'd run, and I'd miss him, and I'd try to piece together a life outside of him. The same way I tried to build a life without my ex-husband.

But I really don't want to.

The horn blares.

It's like the end of the game for me, too. When I realize I won everything, and all I have to do is accept it.

I smile down at Jacob. He's pointing at me, grinning his head off as his teammates crash into him and Camden Church. If he scored the winning goal, if he had some key moment in the final play—I missed it. Because I don't really give a shit that he plays hockey.

I just care about *him*.

And that's enough.

MELODY

SIX MONTHS LATER.

The ring is in his sock drawer.

AKA the most obvious hiding spot ever.

But it wasn't like I was snooping. I was just... rearranging his socks. And looking for some of my own. The thick woolen ones that he likes to steal for under his skates, like a heathen, but they're all that keep my toes warm on cold days like today.

I open the little black box just to make sure it's a ring.

Ever since Knox said Jacob was my soon-to-be-husband, I've been waiting for the proposal... and it didn't come. Each time he took me out to a fancy restaurant, or examined my perfectly manicured nails, or suggested we take a trip, I expected it.

So he's been fucking with me.

Another mind game that he delights in, I'm sure. I'd bet Knox told Jacob about his slip-up, and now he's waiting for me to lower my guard.

Well, I'm in my PJs. My hair is in a pile on top of my

head. I've got paint under my nails, on my shirt, my fore-arms, even my thigh. *Glamorous* is definitely not how I'd describe myself today.

The ring is gorgeous, though. My breath catches the longer I stare, until I pluck it out of its silk nest and slip it on my finger.

Just to see.

First, it fits perfectly. It's kind of a huge teardrop diamond set in other tiny stones that frame it and go down the tapered band.

Second, it seems like something I'd pick out myself. Something I wouldn't have known eight months ago, waking up in the hospital with no memories. My sense of style—or lack thereof, Jacob likes to joke—came back about five months ago. He vetoed the need for oversized sweaters that, in his words, hide my body.

It's usually followed up by him doing everything to make me not hide.

Including one brazen chase down the hallway outside his condo. Naked.

I clear my throat, forcing that memory away before my body can react. I admire the ring for another second, then slip it off.

"You don't have to take it off."

I almost jump a foot. I whirl around, clutching the ring to my chest.

Jacob leans on the doorframe, his arms crossed. I love it when he stands like that, because his biceps always bulge enough to drive me crazy. His hair is pushed back, and sweat dots his brow.

He was in the gym.

But now he's here. Watching me... sneaking a peek at the ring.

When I don't move, he comes in and takes my left hand. He gently pulls the ring from the grip of my other hand and slides it on my fourth finger.

"Marry me," he says quietly. "I'll give you a big show if you want, Mel, but I'd happily just have you and me and a witness tomorrow at the courthouse."

"Today," I blurt out.

He meets my gaze, and I smile like I've never smiled before.

He gives that to me. Each draft of happiness lifting me higher feels like a gift.

"I'm so in love with you, Jacob Rhodes. The parts of you that the rest of the world doesn't get to see. The shadows." I touch his jaw. His eye contact is intense, but I want him to know I mean this. "I thought I'd never marry after Henry signed the divorce papers. But then... You changed my mind. And you knew that I knew you want to marry me, so you've been teasing me ever since."

He smirks. "It's called edging, songbird. I thought you liked that kind of thing."

I shake my head at him.

"Today." He leans down and claims my lips. Hungrily. With all the lust and desire in the world. But there's something sweeter, too. A type of cherishment I've felt coming off him in waves, but now seems to triple. "Get ready."

I open my mouth when he steps back. The ring is still on my finger.

In the closet, there's a white dress I haven't seen before.

So maybe he has been teasing me for all these months, but this was planned. I roll my eyes and shower quickly, trying and failing to remove all the oil paint from my skin. At least it's not in my hair.

We've had quite the exciting last six months.

We spent time with his parents and sister in Crown Point. Sharing the house lasted one night, until his mother made some offhand comment about creaking bedsprings. We rented a house down the street for the remainder of the week, and we had sex on every surface.

Because we could.

I studied up on literature. Reread the classics over the holidays, enjoying a lazy and hot summer while Jacob kept in shape. And when he went off to a summer intensive, I applied for an adjunct position at a community college in Denver.

No one was more surprised than me when they offered me the job. So now I teach two classes, easing myself into it with entry-level courses, and I get to talk about characters and theory I love.

I reread my favorite book. I knew most of it, but some of it still managed to surprise me.

Go figure.

At some point, maybe Jacob and I will return to Crown Point.

Maybe he'll take over coaching hockey when Coach Roake retires—or maybe he'll do as he first mentioned when we got together years ago and coach high school lacrosse.

Either way, he'll do us proud.

As a hockey player, as a man... and as a dad.

I'm thirty-four. I'm about seven weeks pregnant, if we're counting from when I got my last period. I didn't think I could get pregnant. I thought... I thought I had done something irrevocable to my body to prevent it. Down to my bones, I was terrified of having a baby with Henry.

But miracles do happen.

Either that, or fate bent to Jacob Rhodes' will.

And we're finally in a place that it's okay.

I'll have to come up with a fun way of incorporating that into my vows. If we even exchange them. But demanding Jacob to say nice, impromptu, flowery things about me in front of witnesses seems like a great idea.

So I hide my smile and finish getting ready to marry the love of my life.

THE END

Fierce Obsession, Knox's story, is coming February 16, 2024!

ACKNOWLEDGMENTS

Thank you so much for reading!

Jacob and Melody's story has been a long time coming, and I'm thrilled they got their happy ever after.

First, a big heartfelt thank you to my team: My editors, Emmy and Paige. My early readers, Rebecca and Ari, Erica, Stephanie, and Thalia. My cover designer, Najla, and photographer, Michelle. I'm so grateful for each and every one of you.

Second, thank *you*, reader, for your enthusiasm for this series. It really has changed my life, and I'll be eternally thankful for it.

ALSO BY S. MASSERY

#4 QUEEN

More at http://smassery.com/ebooks

ABOUT THE AUTHOR

S. Massery is a dark romance author who loves injecting a good dose of suspense into her stories. She lives in Western Massachusetts with her dog, Alice.

Before adventuring into the world of writing, she went to college in Boston and held a wide variety of jobs—including working on a dude ranch in Wyoming (a personal highlight). She has a love affair with coffee and chocolate. When S. Massery isn't writing, she can be found devouring books, playing outside with her dog, or trying to make people smile.

Join her newsletter to stay up to date on new releases: http://smassery.com/newsletter